IT'S MURDER
IN
DOWNTOWN
BURBANK

Edward Arno

Victory Rose Press
Burbank, California

Edward Arno Victory Rose Press
4206 W Victory Blvd
Burbank, CA 91505
www.edwardarno.com

Book Layout ©2013 BookDesignTemplates.com
Cover graffiti by kcigam
Edited by Bertha Garcia

Ordering Information:
Quantity sales. Special discounts are available on quantity purchases by corporations, associations, and others. For details, contact the "Special Sales Department" at the address above.

It's Murder in Downtown Burbank/ Edward Arno. -- 1st ed.
ISBN 978-0-9996465-2-6
Library of Congress © TXu 2-183-548

Dedication to
Emma Dewhirst and James Dewhirst

CHAPTER ONE

In the Beginning

The streetlights flickered as the power was restored from the rolling blackout to the downtown area of Burbank. Store lights came on even though they were closed. It was four forty-five in the morning. The street was empty on this late summer morning. A gust of warm air blew up San Fernando Boulevard, a relief from the night's humid atmosphere. The sidewalk trees rustled as the wind passed them by. Only one business on this stretch of shops remained in darkness, Ricardo's Hair and Beauty Salon.

Ricardo's wife who was known to the customers as Fluffy McRae. Sat slumped in the barber's chair Ricardo used daily to tease and perm the local old ladies' hair. Wrapped around her neck was the cord of a hairdryer, her head completely shaved. It was a professional scalping as no little cuts or nicks were on the pinky-white bumpy cranium. The remains of her strawberry blonde hair were scattered on the floor beneath the chair. The salon's automatic electrical timer switched on and the lights of the salon illuminated the place. The hairdryer, which was dangling near the floor attached to the cable wrapped around Fluffy's neck bust into life. Blowing her hair across the floor.

The five feet eight inches tall, light brown hair and hunched shouldered Malachy R. Moss sauntered passed Ricardo's hair salon. He looked in at the window and seeing a life-like mannequin with its shaved head. Thinking it was a little risqué for the normally conservative Burbank. He gave a little twitch at the corner of his mouth, unable to smile because of the impending depression threatening to creep over him. He turned the street corner to see his bus waiting, not for him. The drivers knew on penalty of suspension they must not be ahead of the schedule so they waited. For the passenger on the bus it was annoying but those who wanted to catch the bus it was a relief to find it waiting. It was the first of three buses he would take to get to work. The car he had loved and pandered too since college had died. The car mechanic had pronounced the death with a smile on his face. Then tried to sell Malachy a used only one-owner sedan. Although he trusted the mechanic to fix cars, he didn't trust the man to sell him one. He was secretly grateful the car had died his fear of driving had grown over the years. Since that fateful day, he had taken the bus to work.

Arriving at Santa Monica Boulevard for his third bus his mood had deepened by the journey so far. The bus arrived and the doors opened, Bill the driver's smiling face greeted the self-pitying Malachy.

"Good morning" said Bill.

Malachy climbed the metal steps each one seemed steeper than the one before. He gave Bill a weak smile and mouthed 'morning' while flashing his monthly bus pass. Bill closed the doors and began to pull away from the curb. Malachy slumped into a seat at the front of the bus, next to an over zealot catholic woman called Norma. She was saying her Rosary and gave him a disapproving glare as he tried to get comfortable on the hard-brown plastic seat.

Malachy's malady had begun a few days earlier when he was diagnosed with an incurable rare disease.

There was no treatment, but at least it was not fatal, he would end his life in a wheelchair depending on others. It was this thought that was depressing him. He had become used to the constant dull aching pain. The doctor had said in a matter of fact way you have 'Chronic Inflammatory Demyelinating Polyneuropathy and there is nothing I can do to help you. Just live with it.'

He was trying to but couldn't come to terms with how his life would be. He was despondent and saw no reason to be in any other mood.

The bus suddenly stopped and dragged Malachy out of the quagmire he was in. Betty an obese black woman of undetermined age ascended into the bus. She squeezed herself into the seat by the door after asking in a very loud voice "Can I have a seat I'm disabled." The young man who rose to give up the seat mumbled a disgruntled non-coherent comment as he went to the back of the bus.

Betty's carpetbag was full of every type of emergency product anyone may need. It took her a few minutes to settle it on her lap in front of her ample bosom. To hold the bag in place she put her four-footed metal walking stick between her feet and knees. Once she composed herself, she looked at Bill and smiled "Hello sweetie, how you doing?" she asked him not expecting a reply.

Malachy contemplated was she disabled because of her obesity or does she have some disease, which had affected her legs. Her whole body was fat, from her ankles to the mass of black hair on her head. The gray cotton training pants stretch across her legs, the seams aching to break. The tiny white blouse lifted high on her stomach due to her oversized breasts and the bulge of her extended stomach exposing her belly button. Betty repositioned herself several times before looking around the bus to see who was there. She spotted someone she knew who was towards the back of the bus and gave a wave hitting the little old Latino man sitting next to her. She continued to scan the passengers finally seeing a woman opposite her whom she knew.

"Hello baby girl, I didn't see you sitting there," she said.

The woman giggled. Betty gave her full-bodied laugh making her breast bounce up and down, crushing her carpetbag.

Malachy glared at Betty how could she be in such a happy mood; her jovial disposition irritated him. She was disabled, why wasn't she depressed like he was, you couldn't be happy if you had some form of disability.

Betty laughed loudly and then animatedly told a story about herself when she was a little girl. Her speech was distorted and in a slang dialect which the other woman understood because at the end of the story they both laughed. Malachy hated her. She had no right to be happy, their lives, as disabled was one of misery and depression.

The bus stopped suddenly and an old man on crutches climbed aboard. Betty screamed, "How are ya, baby?" The old man smiled and mumbled "Okay."

"That's good baby, you just keep going, don't let it get you down."

A young man stood up and allowed the old man to sit. Standing in front of Malachy, it blocked his view of Betty.

"That was nice," said Betty to the young man.

The young man became embarrassed and moved towards the back of the bus. Malachy tried to bury himself in the hard metal seat, is the world going crazy was everyone becoming handicapped. He wasn't, not yet. He re-examined his depressed mood he wasn't disabled so why was he being so down on himself. He would fight this disease and discover a cure and win the Noble prize for medicine. As they passed the Good Shepherd Catholic Church, several of the passengers crossed themselves, revealing their religious beliefs. Some made big gestures while others tried to be discrete about it.

Malachy sighed and spoke out loud to no one "Oh God why me?"

Norma who had been engrossed in her saying of the Rosary looked at him and in a Spanish accent said "Why not."

Malachy looked at her, unable to think of a reply. More passengers had boarded the bus and it was now standing room only. He turned to speak to Norma about her response but she had returned to saying her Rosary.

Betty was talking to the driver when a gray-haired Russian lady stepped on her foot as she exited the bus.

"Watch it!" screamed Betty

"You have big feet and you are fat," shouted the Russian woman back as the doors closed.

"No, I don't, you're just clumsy."

Malachy sank back into his seat and looked at the other passengers. He had been traveling with them every workday morning for the last year. He knew most of them by sight and some of them he had found out their names, by listening to the conversations they had. The tall, in his late fifties, mustached, white man whose occupation was obviously as a photographer gleaned from the many professional photo equipment magazines he carried. Looked at the non-American passengers on either side of him, he glared at them in contempt. To him, all non-white people must be illegal immigrants. Malachy had seen him on several occasions spread his legs so much that it made it almost impossible for someone to sit down next to him. Today he was staring ahead lost in some picturesque dream.

Standing in front of Malachy was Charlie an older man with a very bad auburn wig. He spoke in a soft effeminate voice, like an old gossipy woman. His clothes were old and fraying after years of being washed in cheap smelling detergent. Malachy caught a flash of white paper in his peripheral vision. It was Marge carefully folding her newspaper so she could read it without interfering with anyone's space. She too was old, one of the old school type of ladies who wear a dress code. It went back to before the Second World War. Her flat black soft-shoes positioned neatly in front of her, the black pantyhose. They would have been black silk stocking before the advent of the pantyhose, cover her thin legs. Her navy-blue skirt and white no-frill blouse complete the uniform. She always dismounted the bus at the Beverly Hills Town Hall. Malachy had assumed she worked there. She had that air of a civil servant has when they have been in a position for a very long time.

He had seen these people so often they had become part of his life. Although it was very unlikely, he would ever speak to them he felt responsible for them. He knew which bus stop they alighted. A Latino man of undeterminable age who had been grateful to Malachy several days earlier for waking him before he missed his stop. The man sat a few seats to the right of Malachy. He always wore a jacket with a hood, which covered his head and most of his face. Today he peered out looking where he was, seeing Malachy he gave a slight acknowledgment with a nod of the head. Malachy nodded back. The Latino man pulled his head back into the hood as though he was a tortoise. For the first time that morning Malachy smiled, the action of the man amused him. He supposed the man was scared to been seen in case someone from Immigration authority was around.

The amusement didn't last and his depression began to return. He began to wonder if the others could see he had an illness, a rare disease. This contention they care about him in the same way he cared about them was soon dispelled. As he looked around the bus the other passengers continued what they were doing ignoring him completely. They didn't know nor could they see any change in him and they wouldn't for some time. He had sensory CIDP unlike most others with the disease who had difficulty walking. Some of the people he had talked with about it could hardly walk. He at least didn't have their problems he just suffered from severe pain in his legs, feet, and hands. It wasn't that bad he could learn to live with the pain. The doctor had said he could have an intravenous infusion of new antibodies, which would help stabilize the problem.

"No, it's not all that bad," he said out loud.

"What!" said Norma.

"Nothing I was talking to myself."

"Crazy man."

"Maybe."

He looked out of the window, two more stops and he would be at his destination. He didn't mind getting up so early he just wished he worked closer to his home. Not driving had become a problem. An inner fear like the people who suffered from the fear of flying had beset him for years. He was aware his friends and office colleagues sniggered behind his back. Not willing to understand the fear, which processed him when he sat behind the wheel of a vehicle.

The bus stopped and a group of Hispanic construction workers entered. They spoke loudly to each other as they pushed passed the other passengers. The driver pulled the bus away from the curb, only to slam on the brakes as a car cut in front of him. Several of the passengers fell to the floor; Bill the driver left his seat to check to see if everyone was okay.

"I'm sorry about that, someone wanted to get to work before you did."

Malachy took the opportunity to leave his seat and prepare himself to get off the bus. With so many people on the bus, it was sometimes difficult to exit it at a stop. A corpulent man had also stood and blocked Malachy's progress to the back of the bus. He decided to wait patiently before moving to the door. His mood had changed, he now felt he could cope with his problem. It was up to him to make life as enjoyable as he could for himself.

An irate woman tried to push past him breaking his thought as he reached his stop. He ran off the bus, to turn and shout "Thanks, Bill." The driver waved and the bus continued its way.

The avenue in front of him was in darkness, only a few lights shone from the office building lining the roadway. The traffic light changed and Malachy began to walk up the hill. Today it felt like a mountain, his mind was playing games with him, every step was very difficult. The dawn light had not yet appeared, the black buildings seemed to bend over and look down on him. The few illuminated windows peered like eyes watching his slow progress. His depressing mood began to return the gloom and doom of life washed itself over him.

"No, go away," he shouted.

"What?" said the man running past him.

"Nothing."

The man continued looking back at Malachy as he ran. At the top of the slight hill, Malachy stood looking at the tall pink granite tower. It had featured in a blockbuster film several years earlier. This was Los Angeles film capital of the world. Property owners were just trying to make a little extra for themselves. It didn't matter if this street or that street was closed while filming took place. As long as the money from the film company kept flowing in.

As he opened the glass door to the office building, he was aware of the security guard hovering a few steps inside. She pounced on him.

"Good morning ID?"

Malachy showed her the plastic card bearing a picture of the building plus his name.

"Thank you, have a nice day."

He swung around and was about to challenge her. What right she had to tell him what kind of day he should have. He changed his mind. He was just passing his bad mood on to some low paid security guard who was trying to brighten their boring day.

Inside the elevator, he pressed the plastic card against the black rubber pad and pressed the button for the twenty-seventh floor. The doors began to close as an arm suddenly shot between them and they opened again. A gray haired, forty-five-year-old man dressed in business causal entered. He placed his card against the rubber pad and pressed the nineteenth-floor button. He took one look at Malachy before turning to face the door. Malachy was slightly perturbed by the way the man had looked at him. He looked at the man's back; he was defiantly a few pounds overweight. The suit was stretched tight across his back. The heel of his shoes was scuffed and unpolished, the trouser heavy creased. This was a man who was on the way down in his career or had lost his self-worth and pride.

At the nineteenth floor, the man exited the elevator. As the doors closed, he stood looking at Malachy, the stare of a man possessed. It was as though the man was trying to remember what Malachy looked like for some future reason.

On the twenty-seventh floor, the door opened the soft night-lights illuminated the elevator area. The floor was strewn with the Wall Street Journal's waiting for the owners to arrive and pick them up. He trod carefully remembering the day he had slipped on the papers and hits his face on the hard floor.

At the door to the trading floor of Weinstocks and Boller Investments, he searched his pockets for the companies ID. The door opened forcefully Bradley Cotton, III entered the corridor.

"Morning Malachy, bright and early."

"Always," replied Malachy entering the open-plan office.

Most of the employees were already at their desks, calling New York or London. Malachy sat down at his desk and opened his computer. The screen went black and he saw his reflection in it, he looked a mess, he needed a haircut. A shudder ran down his back.

A haircut, what was wrong with that he thought. Ricardo's was a good hairdresser and that wasn't a mannequin, he had seen this morning. It was Ricardo's wife and she looked dead.

The computer whirled into life. The email program loaded the four hundred new emails since yesterday. He waited for the other programs to load. Weren't computers supposed to be fast? His impatience had started to grow and it was only the beginning of the day. Like everyone else in the office, the art of patience had gone, everything had to be instant. It was another factor in the high-stress level his job was becoming. He opened the Internet and logged into a local news channel online. The TV station web site wasn't carrying anything about a murdered woman in Burbank. He typed in the local radio stations web page address. Using his telephone head set connected to the computer he listens to see if anything was mentioned. Nothing. It must have been a mannequin. Someone would have found the body by now. Los Angeles was world-renowned for its ability to report news instantaneously. If something had been found it would be on the news channel before the relatives would even be told.

He settled down to his work, as an administrative assistant to the regional manager he felt the pressure of his manager's job. Second-hand stress overflowed. He had become the whipping boy for the many mistakes and hic-cups that daily happened. He was behind on a client event and knew that if he didn't correct the problem it would only get worse. He needed coffee before he could unravel the mess. It was created by having too many chiefs, each one of them vying for control of the event. The hours slipped by before he was able to solve the problems. Exhausted he made himself some more coffee. He walked back from the kitchen. Everyone seemed engrossed in what they were doing. He was invisible to them. The dark mood of the bus ride returned. Glancing at the large wide screen TV monitor fixed into the wall. The local news was being read. Turning the small speaker on his desk up so he could hear what was being said.

"The body of the owners' wife was found in a barber's chair police say they have no suspects at this time. Now for the weather...."

Malachy turned off the speaker his mouth still open from when it dropped. He had seen the body and thought it was a mannequin, a clever advertisement. The phone rang and made him jump. Looking at it he slowly pressed the button before speaking on the headset.

"Weinstocks and Boller Malachy Moss, how can I help you?"

"Malachy, its Elizabeth can you come to my office."

"Now?"

"Yes as soon as possible."

"On my way."

Elizabeth Dellman was the office administrator, called by some of the sales staff 'the iron lady from hell'. She was newly divorced and found fault in everything the men of the office did. Although when challenged she always denied any connection between her marital problems and her attitude towards men.

Malachy walked around the corner to her office one of the few on the floor. She sat behind her desk eating a bagel piled high with cream cheese. Two donuts had been neatly placed on a paper plate next to a very large ceramic cup of black coffee. She was a very thin woman in her later forties. Her hair had been dyed a red-brown color. She wore clothes, which were intended for a much younger woman, but no one dared to tell her.

"I'm sorry to ask you this, but would you run across the road to Sandra Cartwright's apartment. She needs these papers as soon as possible for a meeting she has to be at in twenty minutes."

"Sure, I know her place."

"Thank you, Malachy, I knew I could rely on your help, Sandra seems to have her mind on other things these days."

"She did win that big account two weeks ago and it must be a lot of work getting it set up correctly."

"She had a lot of help from Mark Thompson."

"Depends on who you talk to."

"True she is not one for giving credit where it is due."

"Malachy are you okay? You look a little peaky, nothing wrong I hope?"

"I'm fine just a little tired."

"I've told you about staying up all night."

"I wasn't," he said defensively "Didn't sleep very
well that's all things on my mind."
"Well, that's okay then, now off you go."
He pressed the button for the elevator. The elevators
doors opened. To Malachy's surprise, the man who
had traveled up with him earlier was standing looking
straight at him. The door to the trading floor open and
the voice of Rosemary Smith bellowed down the corridor. "Malachy hold the elevator."
Before the man could press the close door button, Malachy had stuck his arm across the doors. Waiting for
Rosemary to arrive. She entered the elevator a with
smile on her face.
"Thanks, I need something to eat. I don't know
what's wrong with me but I'm so hungry."
Rosemary Smith was a client analyst who had been
with the firm for seventeen years. She had until recently been very overweight but by some miracle
known only to her had lost over a hundred pounds.
"You could be pregnant."
"At my age don't be silly, I'm nearly fifty. No, it's
the change."
"The change, are you becoming a man?"
"No! The change in the weather, not that, oh Malachy sometimes I think you just like to tease me."
The doors to the elevator opened as they arrived at the
lobby, Rosemary went to the café on the first floor.
Malachy walked to the street door. The reflection of
the man who was in the elevator was close behind him
in the glass door. He had seen the man staring at him
as they had ascended. Malachy opened the glass door
expecting the man to exit. He had stopped and was
pretending to look at the names of the tenants in the
building. Malachy let the door go and ran across the

street. His legs began to hurt reminding him of his health problem. He fell into a shallow depression, which lifted as he entered Sandra Cartwright's apartment complex. He turned before he entered and looked back at the office building. The elevator man was standing at the glass door looking at him. Now he was becoming paranoid, why would the man be looking at him? Maybe he was the disease police and had been sent to keep an eye on him. Malachy laughed at the thought. At least it had lifted his depression. Sandra lived on the second floor with her husband. She was one of the newer investment bankers in the firm. She was aggressive and determined to succeed in a man's world. He climbed the stairs rather than wait for the elevator. Deciding to use his legs as much as he could. The corridors were well maintained. At five thousand dollars a month he would expect them to be. The door to her apartment was open and voices could be heard from inside.

"It's okay, he doesn't know, but from now on we must be careful," said, Sandra

"Right," said a muffled man's voice.

"He will kill me if he found out and what about your wife Mark, would you leave her for me if I asked you to?"

There was no reply.

"Mark Thompson as usual nothing to say, no you wouldn't leave your precious family, would you?"

"Sandra, it's not that...."

Malachy heard footsteps behind and turned to see a tall man with black greased down hair walking towards him. The man was dressed in an expensive suit. Malachy spoke very loudly hoping the people in the apartment would hear him.

"I'm looking for the apartment of Sandra Cartwright
I'm from her office and I have some papers for her."
Before the man could say anything, Mark Thompson
opened the door wide.

"Malachy!"

Malachy jumped and swung around to face Mark his
boss a forty-two-year-old trying to look thirty. Sandra
Cartwright was standing behind Mark. She was a five
foot seven with a thin figure. Her most striking feature
was her hair shoulder-length, black, thick hair. The
straightness and straw-like quality always directed
people to gaze at it.

"The papers Sandra wanted, Elizabeth asked me to
bring them, across," he said handing Mark the envelope.

"Thanks, hello Bob," said Mark pushing past Malachy and shaking the man's hand.

"Hi," replied Bob the man Malachy had seen walking
down the corridor.

"Hi, honey," said Sandra going up to him and giving
in a peck on the cheek.

"We were just leaving for our meeting can I get anything for you before we leave."

"No, I just forgot my bag, got to the office and remembered."

"I'll get back to the office," said Malachy

"Yes, good idea, I'll walk down with you and warm
up the car," said, Mark

As they walked away, Bob pushed Sandra into the
apartment.

"Thanks for bringing over the documents."

"No problem."

"Were you at the door a very long time, waiting?"

"No, I had just arrived when Mr. Cartwright appeared."

"Oh okay, well you'd better get back to the office and I'll see you later."

Malachy left Mark at the front of the building taking a small side path to a side gate. Once outside he watches as Sandra left the building and joined Mark in the car. Her husband was standing on the balcony of the apartment watching them drive away. He opened a cell phone and began to speak to someone as he enters the apartment. Malachy returned to the office. He was bubbling with news but knew he could never share it with anyone. He had grown not to trust anyone, this from bitter experience after a few months on the job. The rest of the morning was uneventful. Lunch started around ten-thirty and the smells of some of the food made him feel hungry. He normally brought his food with him, after a visit to the café he sat at his desk eating a baked potato full of cheese and bacon bits. The phone rang; he quickly emptied his mouth to answer it.

"Malachy Moss."

"Mr. Moss I'd be very careful what you say," said a deep slight muffled voice.

"Who's speaking?"

"A friend."

"What are you talking about?"

"Mr. Moss I think you know."

"One moment please." Malachy put the caller on hold. He stood up and looked around the floor. On the far side, he could see two financial analysts listening to a phone call trying not to laugh.

Malachy pushed the on-hold button.

"Sorry about that I had to check who was around, are you talking about the drugs and sex Martin Farland and Tony Elliot have been doing?"

"What!" said Martin in his normal voice.

"Oh yes, didn't you know, they run a drug and sex ring every night, from Martin's apartment. Any kind of drugs and very kinky sex, but I thought you knew."

The phone went dead. Malachy peered between the monitors and watched as Martin and Tony left the floor in a hurry very agitated.

Malachy smiled to himself. Life wasn't that bad if he could have his little bit of fun with the likes of Farland and Elliot. He could learn to live with his disease and work out some of the problems he could expect from it.

He continued to work, answering sporadic phone calls. He smiled as Farland and Elliot approached him.

"Hey, Malachy what's up?"

"I don't know, you tell me, you both look worried."

"No, we aren't worried."

"Oh, I thought you'd had a phone call which upset you."

"Who said that?" said an agitated Elliot.

"Not sure, one of the girls."

"Look we called you."

"Did you?"

"It was just a joke, really nothing but a game."

"Was that you who told me to be careful?"

"Sort of…Yes."

"That's a relief and I was thinking my life was in danger."

"Malachy can we just forget it, please."

"Forget what? As I have said a thousand times, I know nothing."

"Thanks, we owe you."

"Just remember I'd be very careful what games you play. And be careful what you say about others Martin Farland and Tony Elliot." Malachy raised his voice so others heard his last few words. Soon there would be rumors around the office about Farland and Elliot. If he was correct it wouldn't be what they were saying about others but what was being said about them.

"Right."

"And stop holding hands in public it gives the game away."

They gave Malachy a displeasing look as they walked away. Malachy smiled to himself. Today had not been that bad after all. He closed his computer and gathered his things to leave. Looking at the TV monitor he quickly turned up the sound on the speaker. The news item had begun. 'Police are questioning several people in connection with the murder of Fluffy McRae. She was found murdered this morning by her husband Ricardo in their hair and beauty salon.

"That's near you isn't it Malachy?" asked Bradley Cotton who sat behind Malachy.

"Yes, he is my hairdresser."

"I'd be very careful next time I need a haircut."

"I'm off Bradley see you tomorrow."

"Night Malachy."

Malachy left the office and began walking down the hill to the bus stop. He became aware of someone behind him. Turning slowly and saw the man from the elevator behind him. Malachy quickens his pace. The man didn't follow stopping to watch him continue down the street. Malachy felt foolish was he becoming paranoid, or was this man following and watching him. He decided it was because of what Martin and Tony had said. A joke is one thing he would take extra care just for tonight.

Malachy joined the other pedestrians at the cross street waiting for the traffic lights to change. He moved in front of a metal lamppost so a woman in her late thirties could step into the gutter. Her impatience grew; she was desperate to cross the street. Malachy didn't hear the inline skater approaching. The sound created by the wooden baseball bat hitting the metal lamppost made everyone on the corner jump. The bat splintered and flew off in different directions; Malachy ducked just in time to miss being hit by a piece.

The skater pushed passed the woman in the gutter and raced across the street. The woman had stepped forward just as a car was turning right. The driver swerved to miss the skater but hit the woman. She took flight into the air, her shirt bellowing out exposing her pink lace Victoria Secrets panties. The contents of her handbag poured out as the bag twisted and turned in the air. They splattered onto the car like heavy raindrops.

The woman came crashing to the ground, like a sack of potatoes. Another driver turning right violently turned his wheel and plowed into the center divider. His car destroyed endless hours of gardening by the city parks department.

The skater stopped on the other side of the street. Looking back at the carnage he had created then ran away. Malachy was transfixed. He was normally the one in the gutter always wanting to be first across the street. Turning and looked up the street to see the man

from the elevator turn and walkway. It was as though
he was in a silent movie and everything was going in
slow motion.

The screaming of the woman brought him back to reality. Several people had rushed to her aid. The man on
the center divider climbed out of his car unable to believe what had happened. Malachy crossed the street
and stood by the bus stop he didn't want to be involved. For some reason he felt it had happened because of him. He was the intended victim. Had the
woman not been so impatient, he would have been
standing in the gutter. He could see the bus two blocks
away as it pulled into the side of the road for the para-
medic and several police cars to pass. As the bus arrived, he glanced back at the scene to see the
paramedics helping the woman on to a gurney.

The bus was full of the workers he had seen that morning sleeping and they were sleeping again now. At the
back of the bus he sat between two Hispanic women
who were talking, they continued their conversation
even though he had sat down. The one-woman used
her hands to talk with and hit Malachy on the chest
several times. She didn't acknowledge what she was
doing and continued to wave her hands in the air as
she spoke.

He sat as far back as he could in the seat. Had the
world gone mad, was this some terrible dream and he
would wake up in his bed. The woman hit him again,
it wasn't a dream and the world had gone mad. First,
he had a crippling disease, then Fluffy getting murdered and now the accident. He stared out of the window as the bus stopped to pick up more passengers.
He saw the skater getting into a car, he wasn't sure if it
was him. He rose a little in his seat to get a better

look, only to be hit several times in the genitals by the gesticulating woman. He sank back into the seat, was that an accident or had he been the intended victim. Then there was the man from the elevator, what had he to do with the madness. He had questions and no answers. The woman's hand brushed Malachy's face. She didn't stop her conversation or apologize to him. She became even more animated so he had to move his head back several times to avoid being hit.

The bus had filled with people and an old woman stood in front of him, this allowed him to give up his seat and avoid being hit again. She was a small Asian woman who, when offered the seat, took it thanking him profusely. The two women continued to talk. The Asian woman looked at the one talking then the other as though she was watching a tennis match. The women became aware of her and stop talking.

Positioning himself next to the back door his destination was only four stops away. As the main intersection of public transport, he knew it would be chaos when the bus arrived at that stop. He waited for the green light above the door to switch on before pushing the black rubber doors. Several passengers had assembled behind him and began to push forward. The light came on and he pushes hard on the doors, running down the steps on to the sidewalk. The other passengers followed spilling out like beans from a baked beans tin.

Another street to cross, he stood back from the curb looking around to make sure no skaters appeared from nowhere. He crossed and descended into the earth below at the Metro Station to get the underground red line train. Standing at the bottom of the escalator against one of the thick gray concrete pillars, he watched. He had done the same routine every night since the Metro red line had been opened. It was for him the quickest way to the San Fernando Valley and Burbank.

He looked at his watch. Today the time seems to be going slow. The parade of peacocks was about to begin. The Hollywood High School students would be arriving. They would walk down the escalator looking for friends or at each other. Some had expressions of aggression or even hatred. He had watched the cavalcade for months. There was a gap in the parade. Then a lone participant stepped on to the moving cold metal stairway to be carried down to the platform. He was a seventeen-year-old Asian boy with short black spiked hair. His black, plain tee shirt was cut off at the shoulders showing his only tattoo. It was a black circle with a black lightning bolt traveling vertically down in the center. It was for him a mark of his manhood and revolution. The black trousers where neither tight nor baggy and made it difficult to see if he had any concealed weapons. The trousers were tucked neatly into his brightly polished Doc Martin boots.

As he stepped off the escalator, he looked around the platform. Seeing no one he wanted to associate with he leant against the gray concrete pillar. A group of girls screeched and laughed as they travel down the escalator. They ran along the platform, their voices echoing in the cavernous station. Two young male students quickly followed them. One was plain and very nondescript, dressed like most of the high school students. Not wanting to make a statement or to bring attention to themselves. The second had white pants, the ironed crease on both legs very visible. His red trainers matched the sweater; a heavy silver chain and three-inch high crucifix finished the accessories.

The platform had become dense with students and other travelers waiting for the trains going north and south. They pushed and shouted at each other. The toot horn of the train was almost inaudible as it approached the station. The students had gathered by the yellow squares in the floor where the doors of the train usually stopped. The scream from the top of the escalator went unnoticed by those on the platform. Only when the woman hit the concrete floor at the foot of the escalator did anyone look to see what had happened.

The train arrived and the doors opened, the students pushed each other as they got on to the train before the doors closed. The doors slid noiseless together, the white pants, red sweater youth looked out on to the platform. He became agitated and began to bang on the doors, screaming something those left on the platform couldn't hear.

Malachy moved swiftly to the woman to see if he could help. She was in her forties; her ashen face had tears running down the cheeks. She lay still for a few minutes on her back looking up at the ceiling with its vaulted ironwork. She slowly rolled onto her side and began to get up. Malachy took her arm, someone had taken the other arm and together they help the woman stand. She fell against Malachy shaken by her fall.

"Thank you," she said.

"What happened?" asked Malachy.

"Someone pushed me. I felt a hand in the middle of my back."

Malachy looked at the other helper. It was the mysterious-looking Asian boy with the circle tattoo. The young man stared at Malachy, with no expression on his face. He let go of the woman's arm and walked away.

"Thank you," shouted the woman after him.

The northbound train arrived, and the red sweater boy race from the train to the woman.

"Momma, you okay?" he shouted taking over from Malachy and moving her towards a concrete bench. Malachy watched the caring young man tend to his mother. He looked around the platform for the Asian boy, but he had disappeared. The train's doors closed and the train began to pull out of the station. The pristine train had been defiled on the last carriage someone had written graffiti over the last door. The word ANT was beautifully painted. Tattooed youth was at the door window staring out of the train as it pulled into the tunnel.

CHAPTER TWO

The Artist

Anthony Soriano is a morose young man of seventeen going on forty. He dislikes the world and the disconsolate attitude was his defense against it. To his few friends he had he never talked about his family or his home life. In fact, he rarely spoke. Words can corrupt he once wrote for an English project. The teacher had given him an A plus even though he had only written three words. She felt he understood the power of the English language and therefore deserved high marks. His friends believed he was a legend, an icon of the present. A graffiti artist, a master of the spray can. His graffiti signature could be seen all over the city of Los Angeles even though he lived in Burbank. He never claimed or denied ownership. Some were thought to be forgeries as the artwork didn't have his craftsmanship. The use of color was not comparable to the one's known to have been created by him. Just using three letters he was known if not personally by every teenage in the county of Los Angeles.

His last creation on the side of an old brewery down town had made the TV news programs in Southern California because of the artistry. Using just the three letters he had created a nineteen thirties cartoon piece.

Each letter a different character, the A was an overweight woman kicking the man who made the N. He
was bending down picking up a penny. The T was a
policeman trying to stop the domestic violence the
scene exposed. He had used only black and white
paint using several gray tones to get the depth he required. At the time he liked the piece, now he felt it
was just okay. His fellow graffiti artists praised him.
It was this, which made him feel that it was not perfect
or at least his best work. He was so critical of their
work always believing it was better to be honest.
When they praised him, he felt they were sneering at
him in some way. Therefore, always looked at the
piece as mediocre.
The urge to create another piece was welling up inside
of him. He once thought the feeling he got was similar
to the kind of feeling a serial killer or rapist must feel.
This was after watching Silence of the Lambs twenty
times. Now he felt different, a visit to an art gallery in
Pasadena had convinced him it was nothing like the
same feeling. He was a true artist, a serial killer, or a
rapist they were mentally ill. When the city offered a
reward for the apprehension of the graffiti artist who
sprayed ANT all over the city, he suddenly felt he was
a wanted criminal. None of his friends told the authorities about him and nor would they. There was an
honor between graffiti artists. It was an ancient form
of expression. The Greeks, Romans even early man
had painted pictures and slogans on walls. They may
have done it for political or social reasons. He felt he
was in good company when he sprayed.
He had tried once to write an essay explaining why he
had the compulsion to create the piece he did. Finding
it hard to explain in words. To him a blank wall was

naked and should be clothed with a statement about life. He wasn't a tagger who just wrote eligible letters, he believed he was a true artist. His school notebook was full of renditions, each one carefully drawn and colored. When the local police graffiti unit gave a patronizing talk at his school about the wanton vandalism. He didn't think they were talking about him. He was an artist, not a gang member marking his territory or someone just looking for notoriety. He was a street Picasso or Rembrandt, even better he was the Burbank Dali.

He had started as a tagger, when he was ten years old, trying to fit in with his peers. The satisfaction he gained at first soon faded and he wanted to create whole pieces. He didn't care if he became famous or not. Nor would he sell himself to some entrepreneur who would exploit him.

Anthony 'ANT' Soriano was an artist and would stay pure to his art. He had called himself Ant because he hated the name Anthony. The `hony part sounded phony. It was fine for others but for him, it was what his mother called him. Ever since he could remember his mother and grandmother had called him Anthony. It made him screw up his face. Once he could talk, he would call himself Ant. His mother thought he had a learning problem and became quite worried until she realized he didn't like his name.

Everyone now called him Ant, except his mother. He had wondered why no one had put the graffiti artist being searched for by the police and his name together. He finally came to the conclusion it was like something staring you in the face and you were unable to see it. Secondly most of the adults he knew wouldn't believe he had the talent to create the art works.

Ant disliked adults, although he was becoming one, he had a problem relating to anyone over twenty. He just didn't trust them, so his actions on the platform had surprised him. For some reason he saw the woman who fell as his mother.

The Metro train pulled out of the station he stood in the last carriage looking out onto the platform. He saw the woman with her son, Jesse who was a grade below him. Then he saw the man. He'd seen him before, always dressed in a suit and tie with clean shoes. An image Ant had come to loathe, the image of greed. The man usually stood at the bottom of the escalator staring at the people traveling down to the platform. The man always followed him on to northbound train. At North Hollywood station the man would get off the train first and then disappear. Ant was convinced he and maybe others were watching him, realizing he was becoming paranoid. A stupid idea but he hadn't felt he could just dismiss the idea he was being followed. He was the notorious graffiti artist ANT.

Ant left the window and found a seat, the carriage was hot, he put his hands towards the air condition vent, there was no fresh cool air blowing. He took his note-pad out of his backpack, his latest creation, a rough drawing of a new piece of graffiti glared at him from the page. It was bright, cheerful, for him a complete sell out, a fake. Perfect for Hollywood he thought but not what he was about. He took a pencil out and drew a line across the page. He wanted something dark, threatening, like a woman, mother being pushed down the escalator. His English literary teacher had said, 'The best writers are those who write what they see around them.' He wasn't sure if she was right, he always felt it were only true of painters. The artists he liked were the ones who created what they saw even if it was their interpretation and no one else could understand it.

He had seen the gothic girl everyone called Black Bee push the woman down the escalator. Then she walked calmly down the stairs next to the escalator while watching the woman, mother and wife hit the hard-cold concrete floor. Two years earlier he had wanted to have Black Bee as his girlfriend. He was obsessed, or maybe possessed by her, then one day she belittled him in a humanities class. The bubble bust. He could see for himself that she was nothing but a vindictive sadist who got pleasure by hurting others, especially men. As a white girl he could only speculate why she was called Black Bee. She always wore black and the bee part was because she was such a bitch.

Ant's relationship with girls had been very one sided, his passion would spill out and over. While the girls were cold and aloof, he never understood why. He had sex with several of the girls, who were willing to go out with him, then after a few weeks they would just move on. He would tear himself apart trying to work out what he had done to lose yet another girlfriend. Finally, one girl who he didn't go out with told him, that they had used him. He was one of the cool guys in the school and, they wanted to be with him to make a tick on their list of the coolest in school they had slept with. He had become a sex object to a group of scheming girls. The experience had caused him to distrust any females, especially the one who was willing to give him sex.

He wasn't sure after that what kind of relationships he wanted, but he didn't want his emotions aroused only to be dumped a few weeks later. His father was always talking about at his age you find a woman, love them, and then leave them wanting more. It may have been like that in his day in the Philippines, but today in America it was the other way around. Women's rights had gone a long way.

The train pulled into Universal City station. No one left the train from his carriage. An old Hispanic construction work entered the carriage and slumped into a seat next to the door. Ant looked at the man, the lines on his face where deep as though they had been chiseled in the hard-brown leathery skin. He looked at the blank page of his notepad, the pencil poise. The image of the woman falling, black Bee's face grinning evilly and the cold silver metal escalator. The Metro train arrived at North Hollywood station. One more bus and he would be home. He had argued with his parents on several occasions as to why he couldn't go to a local school. His father had wanted him to stay at Hollywood High, saying he would get a good education there. This didn't make sense to Ant. He added it to the database of his brain another reason why he disliked adults. Irrational thinking.

Ant entered the family home, a small two-bedroom apartment in downtown Burbank. His bedroom, which he shared with his sister Susan, was the first door on the left as you entered. The room was square shaped and had been divided by a curtain six-foot-high and stretched across the whole room. They each had part of the window, but he would have to pass through her part to get to his own. He carefully stepped over her clothes and shoes, he never complained about the mess but deep down it irritated him.

His side of the curtain was worlds apart from his sister's. He had a place for everything. It wasn't only

neat but clean and there was a reason for it. If someone had been looking through his things he could tell
instantly. He knew his father had on several occasions
been looking for drugs or at least to see if there was
any evidence that Ant used them. His sister had be-
rated him several times for being like a woman in his
habitual cleanliness. He would reply to her if he were
like a woman, he would live in a mess like her.
He placed his schoolbooks on the bed, pressed the button on his CD player and picked up the headphones.
  "Anthony is that you?" called his mother from the
kitchen.
He switched off the CD player and went to the kitchen.
  "Anthony."
  "Yes," he replied in a monosyllabic tone.
His dislike of the world and most of the people in it
didn't run to his mother. Although when in the company of others, he became even more monosyllabic.
He and his mother Estefania had a very good mother
son relationship. He loved his mother, in the absence
of his father who was often away working. She had
been his strength when growing up. She was aware he
changed when others where around, especially if they
were not family. Her hope and prayers were that he
and his father would at least talk to each other. The
hope faded when Anthony and his father had fought
over the way Anthony was dressed. Now she was
grateful he hadn't got a girl pregnant and he didn't
seem to be taking drugs. The hope came back once
Anthony began to accompany her to Mass every Sunday.
  "I thought it was you who came in, good I need some
help with the cooking."

He looked at her in astonishment. She saw the look and laughed.

"No, not with the cooking, I need some lemons go down to the corner market and pick some up for me. And remember no soft ones."

He put his hand out in expectation of being given some money.

"You pay; I'll give it back later."

"Momma, you have been saying that since I was twelve. I'm still waiting."

"This time I promise."

The corner market was once a house which had been convert many years ago into a little shop. Who the owner was had become one of the great mysteries of the neighborhood? To Ant he always believed it to be either Russian or Armenian. Although the people behind the counter changed each time he went in they were usually one or the other. The market sold most things and stayed open until midnight each day.

He found the lemons and picked over them until he found three, which his mother would accept. He remembered it was only a year earlier he had bought some apples and she made him take them back because they were rotten inside. The man behind the counter nodded to him as he approached to pay for the lemons. Ant nodded back, money exchanged hands without a word being said and he left the store carrying a white plastic bag containing the lemons.

Sitting on a low wall built to divide two apartment complexes where Nickman and Chris. They were the local wannabe gang members, and often boasted they had serious gang connections. Which really translated they had been downtown Los Angeles and walked around Eighteenth Street. Ant knew who these two were, as he had observed their pathetic attempts at being gang members. They knew him by sight but had no knowledge of his infamy. Nickman nodded in Ant's direction, as he came out of the market. Chris looked up from the magazine he was reading. Nickman rose and stood on the sidewalk trying to block Ant's way. Chris joined him, a sneer creeping across his face. To anyone looking at Chris his sneer was more of a deformity. Ant looked at them, he knew they were going to play it as though he was on territory and he would have to pay to pass. He walked slowly towards them showing no emotion. They braced themselves for the confrontation. Chris rolled up the magazine as though it would be a handy weapon.

Ant walked up to them and stood a few inches from Chris's face. Nickman moved to his side. Ant and Chris stared at each. It was a battle of pent up aggression just waiting to explode. Neither Chris nor Nickman noticed Ant take the lighter out of his pocket. He flicked it and lit the magazine. A few seconds later Chris screamed as the flames engulfed his shirtsleeve. Nickman moved away and then began to laugh as Chris ran around trying to put out the flames. Ant continued up the road, a smile on his face.

Estefania and Ant sat and ate dinner together; his sister had gone to a friend's house. He enjoyed having a meal with just his mother. She would talk about her life, her childhood growing up in Daet a small town in the Philippines. How she would play tricks on her sisters and then must do the chores for her mother as punishment. He noticed she didn't mention anything about her life when his sister or his father where there.

It was as though she wanted to share with him and no one else, their secret.

Ant opened the front door to leave, after helping his mother clean the dinner dishes.

His mother called to him, "Anthony don't forget you said you'd go with me to the church festival tomorrow night."

"Sure Momma," he shouted back closing the door quietly.

As Ant stepped on the sidewalk, Nickman and Chris immediately after seeing him moved into an alley between two apartment complexes. Chris's hand was crudely bandaged and hung limply by his side. Ant could see them in his peripheral vision as he passed the alley. He debated if he should look at them but decided it would be better not to antagonize them. They peered around the edge of the buildings and saw him turn the corner.

The bus journey to Hollywood was uneventful. The usual type of passengers sat impatiently waiting for their stop. He studied each one of them looking at the lines on their faces. The clothes they were wearing and the way they sat. He knew that if he sucked in the imagery, he might be able to use it on a later piece of graffiti. He had found a new site for a piece of graffiti. This was the place where he was going to create the woman falling down the escalator after being pushed by Black Bee. It was a wall, which faced the freeway, and no one had ever sprayed it. He wondered why it was at the end of a quiet street. It would be easy to climb up the side of the building and not be seen. Standing at the entrance to the street he looked at the freeway high above. He could hear the cars speeding by, and the top of the white wall cried to him to paint a masterpiece. He felt the feeling creep over him from his fingertips he must paint on that white wall. The craving was becoming too strong, soon it would consume him and he would be obsessed with it.

He sauntered down the street. The building on each side seemed rough and aloof. They had very few windows and heavy doors. The stucco was a dirty pink and needed to be repaired. The local and wannabe gang members had crudely sprayed their logos on the lower portion of the buildings. Ant hated this type of graffiti artist. Taggers made it difficult for true artists. He stopped and looked at the quick sprayed tag, 'CREW' and 'RVW'; he knew that CREW was an older teenager call Rolland and RVW was the tag for a little Latino kid they called Dog. They had been tagging for a very long time, but it was usually not in this area.

The Street was empty, and as he approached the building with his white wall on top, the nondescript building stopped and a chain link fence began. He had realized that the buildings where not connected, inside the fence was a scrap metal yard full of old cars and rusting metal objects.

Suddenly from beneath one of the stripped-down cars two Rottweilers appeared and raced to the fence. Growling, barking, and snapping saliva dripping from their mouths. Ant jumped back into the road he had never seen such fierce animals before. He smiled to himself. So, this was what had kept anyone from marking the wall.

He looked beyond the dogs and at how easy it would be to get on the flat roof if the dogs where not there. The cars were piled like steps and would allow him to then climb onto the fire escape ladder and then up to the roof. He must befriend these savage beasts, how he didn't know, but he would tame them and the wall would be his.

He approached the fence again; "Good dogs, now calm down."

The dogs barked at him

"Sit!" he shouted.

The dogs stopped then suddenly attacked the fence again, their teeth pushing through the metal mesh. Ant retreated. He was no fool these where trained animals to protect what was really on the other side of the fence. He followed the fence along, the dogs growling on the other side. Maybe there was another way up to the roof, he thought. It was a dead end, the building with his wall on it was butted into the freeway above. The road stopped, and he couldn't see any other route to the roof.

A car entered the street and parked under the freeway. The passenger was obviously a prostitute from the way she looked. This was a place the local prostitutes took their clients. Another car entered the street and followed the first. It was hard to tell if the passenger was male or female, the driver a large white man ignored Ant and parked in the corner of the small parking lot. Ant stood looking at the two cars. He couldn't understand how anyone would allow himself or herself to be used in this way. He remembered one girl from school that turned to prostitution when her father threw her out of the house for taking drugs. She had told him it was easy, most of the time it was over in a few minutes and she could make anything from fifty to hundred dollars. She rarely had to have intercourse and didn't have to worry about small talk or fore play.

Ant found the idea repulsive, so impersonal. He needed to know the person's name and at least talk to them before he did it. Although he remembered one occasion when he was too drunk to speak and couldn't remember the next day, whom he had, had sex with the night before.

He left the street and began to make his way back to Burbank. The tag marks in this part of town indicated it was a gang area, and he would have to be on his guard. The two-block walk hadn't given him any ideas on how he was going to befriend the dogs. He put the thought out of his mind as he approached his other passion. A store selling used CD's and records at very low prices.

A feeling of suffocation enveloped him as he entered. The store was packed with Hollywood High school students. He was looking for something special, a CD of a Filipino rap group, he had one of their CD's but he wanted to listen to more.

An obese boy of fourteen passed him and said "Hey". Ant nodded and headed for the foreign import section. He flipped through the plastic CD holders obsessed with owning more of the Filipino rap groups music.

He felt the hand touch his left cheek and then slipping into his back pocket. It was a soft touch almost caressing his butt. He turned and came face to face with Kalli. She had been his friend since elementary school. Although he had at one point wanted to date her, he hadn't and now realized that if he had they would no longer be friends. She was one of the few people who knew he was ANT the graffiti artist.

"Hi."

He nodded and then asked, "Morgan or Steve with you?"

She had been Morgan's girlfriend for as long as he could remember.

"Morgan."

She pointed across the warehouse to a shaved headed man was engrossed into looking vinyl records.

Kalli wandered off, it was something she did, Ant watched her, he believed there was definitely something strange about her.

A band was playing live on the small stage in the middle of the store, the singer suddenly barked like a dog. Ant swung around and looked at him; he remembered Steve's father had Rottweiler's. It was never mentioned but Ant, Morgan and Kalli believed Steve's father was a drug dealer and that's why he had three bloodthirsty dogs.

Ant knew Steve took drugs and had on several occasions stayed with him until he came down from the high or out of the coma type state. This had only strengthened Ant's resolve never to indulge, even though the opportunity was always there.

Disappointedly he didn't find any Filipino rap; a local group 'Star Burners' had a self-promotion CD that had found its way into the warehouse. Ant knew most of the bands so he decided to buy it for a dollar. He stood in line to pay, looking around for Morgan or Kalli but they had disappeared which was nothing unusual. He was glad he really didn't feel like talking. The late twenties salesgirl took his money and handed him the CD without saying a word. She stared at him as he walked towards the exit, he turned and she continued to stare at him. The paranoia began to creep over him, he turned back to look at her, and she had disappeared. He walked into Steve Gould.

"Seen Morgan?" asked Steve.

"Yeah, he's here somewhere."

"Right, I'm late."

"Steve you have dogs?"

"Sort of."

"Are they friendly?"

"No."

"How would you befriend a Rottweiler?"

"Feed it."

"What with?"

"Cooked meat usually works, never raw."

"Right."

"Why?"

"Just something."

"There Morgan."

Morgan and Kalli were walking towards them. The three men shock hands and punched fists. Kalli stood by the side of Morgan but didn't greet Steve. Ant could tell from the uncomfortable atmosphere that Morgan and Steve had some sort of business deal to transact.

"See you," he said

"Yeah," replied Morgan.

Ant left the store, he didn't look back, he didn't want to know what they were doing.

He lay on his bed, listening to the CD his drawing pad open at the new drawing. The journey back had been uneventful, and his mind was full of the imagery of his new piece. It was a preliminary sketch of a woman being pushed down the escalator, interwoven with the letters A N T.

He turned off the CD player and listened to the muffled sounds around him. The warm air of the Santa Ana wind blew in through the window. He could smell smoke, just lightly and he assumed someone was in the alley smoking.

What was he going to do with his life? Could he get a job when he left school? Would he be like so many who took menial jobs while looking for something more permanent. His desire to be a graphic artist was on hold. He would need to go to college and he knew his parents didn't have the money to help him. The smell of smoke had increased, and he coughed several times. Maybe the building was on fire.

He jumped from the bed, ripping the headset plug out of the CD player. He grabbed his drawings and ran into the living room where his mother and sister were sitting watching the television.

"I think the buildings on fire, I can smell smoke, let's get out of here."

Estefania picked up her handbag, switched off the television and prodded Susan to get out of the apartment. Several people had gathered in the street, but they weren't looking at the apartment complex. The mountain range, which Burbank sat at its foot, was on fire. Although they were several blocks from the actual foot of the mountains, the flames and smoke could be seen and smelt.

The sirens of the fire engines could be heard racing up the hill. The wet spring followed by long summer heat had created long dry grass on the side of the mountain. With the Santa Ana type wind blowing the fire was out of control. Ant, his mother, and sister join the gathered watchers. Chris and Nickman stood on the edge of the group with another young wannabe known as Mannian Pizza Boy. To Ant this boy was far more dangerous than the other two. He would do something really dangerous to get accepted into a gang. He expected to read one day the boy had murdered someone. Ant was always on edge when he saw Mannian Pizza Boy.

"Started by someone with a lighter," said Chris
"How do you know that?" asked a woman dressed in her nightclothes.
"Obvious."
"Not to me," she replied.
Ant slowly turned and looked at the three.
"Started by stupid kids like you three, more likely," said the woman "Nothing better to do, didn't you burn your hand?"
"We didn't start it, no way man," retorted Chris
"Then I suggest you shut your mouth, before making stupid remarks. Someone will think you knew how it was started if you go around making wild comments."
"All I said…"
"We know what you said," replied the woman.
"Shit man."
"And watch your language there are small kids around," said another woman.
"We don't want any of your gang stuff around here," said another woman
"Gang, don't make me laugh, no one would want them in a gang, pathetic little boys, that's what they are."
The three wandered away from the group, Mannian Pizza Boy turned and gave the group the middle finger. No one reacted, which made him go a little crazy, the other two boys tried to calm him down. Not wanting to bring attention to themselves. Ant watched them go, a sneer crossed his face. Most of the neighbors came out into the street to look at the fire, as

darkness slowly crept across the San Fernando Valley. The sky glowed red.

Ant and his mother made several trips out into the road to look at the mountain fire. The local news had reported that several houses had caught fire from the embers drifting on the wind. Their apartment manager was standing on the roof of their complex with a water hose.

"Says he is going to stay there all night," said his wife "The owner told him too."

"Do they know who started the fire?" asked Estefania

"The police are looking for two boys one of them has an injured hand," said the manager's wife.

Estefania went inside. Ant stood looking up at the colors of the fire although transparent the colors were deep. He had brought his camera with him and took several pictures, if only he could get that effect in a piece of graffiti.

A police car drove by and stopped a little further down the street. One of the officers walked over to Chris and Nickman who were sitting on a wall. Chris suddenly pointed to Ant. The officer then spoke to his partner who joined him as they approached Ant. The smoke from the fire had become thicker and several fire alarms where calling out to the night sky from the apartments with windows open.

"The boys down there said you burnt his arm."

"No"

"He said you had a lighter in his pocket."

"Search me."

The officer did, and including the camera only found a wallet on Ant.

"Why would he tell me you did it?"

"Trying to pass the blame."

"You don't get along?"

"No, I'm not into gangs."

"He is a gang member?"

"Thinks he is."

Chris had walked up the hill to the police officers.

"He said he didn't do it."

"He did, he's got a lighter."

"I've just searched him and he doesn't have one, do you?"

"No man."

"Can I search you?"

"Why?"

"Why not."

"Okay, but I haven't got anything."

The officer searched Chris's pockets and pulled out a lighter.

'That's not mine," bleated Chris

"It's in your pocket."

"What happened to your arm?" asked the other officer.

"I burnt it."

"How?"

"I told you he set fire to my magazine while I was holding it."

"Why would he do that?"

"Because..."

"Put him in the car Tom."

The officer walked Chris over to the car and pushed him into the back seat.

"Sorry about that." Said the officer still standing with Ant. "I think we may have just found our arsonist."

Ant nodded and watched as the police car drove away.

Nickman and Mannian Pizza Boy had slowly moved up the street and as soon as the police had left, they ran to Ant.

"What happened?"

"Your homie is going to jail."

"What for?"

"Starting the mountain fire."

"How do they know we started it?"

"Because you've just told them. You got that sergeant, over," said Ant speaking into his camera.

They didn't wait for Ant to finish and started running down the road to Nickman's apartment. Ant laughed. Night covered the valley as it did every night, except tonight there was a glow of many shades of red. It was a hot night not just because of the fire, most people slept with their windows closed, and consumed electricity through there air conditioners. The smell of the smoke was able to penetrate through the many cracks and holes in the apartments. It was hard for most of Burbank to sleep peacefully. Expecting to be woken and told to leave their homes.

Dawn came. Ant lay on his bed, the fresh rays of daylight penetrating his room. His sister snored gently behind the curtain. It wasn't an irritating snore more of a soft growl.

He liked this time of day. It was almost as if only the ghosts walked the earth. Finding their way home after a night of scaring little children. For him it was a time to think without noise or distractions. Incorporating the fire in the new piece of graffiti would be a good idea, except maybe he was adding too much. It was so easy to spoil a picture by trying to add too much.

First, he had to find a way to befriend those two dogs. He couldn't ask his mother for some cooked meat.

Somehow, he would have to find another way to get some so he could feed the dogs every day.

A car horn broke the silence of his daydream, and he remembered he had promised to go the church festival with his mother. He was lucky none of his fellow students lived in Burbank, and it was because of this he always agreed to go with his mother to church events. He has heard so many of his peers made fun of at school because they had been seen with their parents at some local event.

He fell back to sleep. His mother woke him a little later reminding him of the festival. His sister had gone to see a friend and would make her own way to the festival. The day was hot and dry, the mountain fire had continued burning. The news programs had said it was only ten percent contained. Several phone calls from friends of Estefania had said the festival was off then on. A final decision being made at eleven, the festival would go ahead.

Ant and his mother walked to St. Robert Bellarmine Catholic Church in downtown Burbank. The festival took place in the schoolyard each ministry group in the church had a stall. Dunking the musical director in a tub filled with water was always a popular thing to do. Crazy golf and basketball stalls enticed the local boys to congregate. Ant passed by several of the boys who nodded at him, he returned the nod. He had seen most of them as altar servers, even though to his mother's sadness he had not been one.

Two young girls who were running knocked the bottle off the shelf stall called to him to have a go, he declined. His mother pushed him towards the stall and gave the girls a dollar for the three balls. He picked up the balls pitched the first, it just missed hitting a bottle.

The second hit the bottle and sent it crashing to the floor. Both the girls clapped and screamed. Ant blushed. A new bottle was put on the shelf and Ant took careful aim. He pitched and the bottle took flight as the ball hit it. It caressed the side of the stall before hitting the floor. The girls screamed and several people gathered around to see what had happened. One of the girls picked a large brown teddy bear and gave it to Ant. He immediately handed it to his mother. Estefania hugged it and gave him a quick peck on the cheek. The small crowd clapped and whistled. Ant blushed again.

The local band, The Fearsome Four, began to play on the small stage. Father O'Donald came over to Estefania and began to dance with her and the teddy bear. Ant watched as his mother enjoyed herself. He liked it when she smiled and had fun. His father never made her smile or made her laugh.

The Priest and Estefania stopped dancing and parted, he then chased a little girl who had escaped from her mother.

"I haven't seen Susan yet."

"I think she is over there with her friends," said Ant pointing the directions of a group of noisy girls.

"She will find me when she wants something. Let's eat."

It was no surprise to Ant that they made their way to the Filipino food stall. They always ate at this stall for as long as they had been coming to this church. They stood in line, both trying to see what was available. Susan appeared at her mother's side.

"Can I have some money, please?"

Estefania looked at her daughter. It would be hard to say no to such a sweet face. Opening her handbag, she began to look for some money.

"I'll pay for the food," said Ant.

She touched his arm and gave Susan five dollars.

"Thanks, see you," said Susan running off to join her friends.

"You spoil her."

"I know."

They collected their food and sat at one of the round tables in front of the small stage. The band continued to play while they ate. Ant looked around at the other people eating, as he turned to look the other way the body hit the table next to him. Food and soda flew into the air. The table folded in the middle. The band stop playing, then several people screamed. The food and drinks fell onto their table. Ice cubes from the sodas rained down hitting the metal tables and played an out of tune rhythm.

Father O'Donald rushed over to look at the man. A hush emanated from the table area and crept over the festival. The man's arm was six inches from Ant. He was obviously dead and very blue looking. He was wearing a tee shirt and jeans and had an Arabian appearance to him. Father O'Donald touched the man to see if he could feel a pulse.

"He's frozen, like a block of ice."

Ant looked closely at the man's hand it looked more like a piece of frozen pork than a human part. He touched the hard and very cold fingers. He had never seen a dead person so close, there wasn't any smell and for some reason he expected one. Ant stood up and looked at the man's face, the eyes where closed as though he was sleeping. The lips had begun to thaw and glistened as though someone had just put lipstick on them. He was fascinated, this was something he had to remember and put into a picture.

Several of the stall helpers began to move people away and roped off the area. A tarpaulin was found and covered the body.

Ant took his mother's arm and led her away. They slowly walked back to their apartment.

"What happened?"

"I don't know, but it will be on the news tonight."

"Poor man."

"He just fell out of the sky."

"Anthony where's your sister?"

"I don't know, you go in and I'll go back and find her."

"Tell her to come straight home.'

"Yes Momma."

"Anthony be careful."

He gave a smile and squeezed her hand.

CHAPTER THREE

WAR

Early the following morning a few blocks away from Ant and his family Malachy lay in his bed looking up at the ceiling. The crimson glow from the mountain fire washed over the walls of his bedroom. Only a few days earlier he had woken and thought the walls were closing in on him making him feel claustrophobic. He had raced out of the apartment trying to breathe as much air into his lungs as he could. One of his neighbors had seen him and from the way he looked at him, he had assumed Malachy was on drugs. This morning with the soft redness it gave him the opposite feeling. He was outside the flames lapping at his bed, as he floated across the sea of tranquilly. The siren from a fire engine brought him back to reality, he was beginning to hallucinate. He felt tired, he hadn't slept very well, and it was the events of the last two days that were responsible. Maybe the world was coming to an end and this was the epicenter. First Ricardo's wife, Fluffy, was murdered and he had seen the body in the barber's chair. He couldn't remember if he had passed anyone, if he had maybe it was the murderer. He shuddered at the thought.

Then he found out his boss was having an affair. This was followed by almost getting killed, well the woman who was standing where he normally stood was. Then if that wasn't enough there was the woman who was pushed down escalator. He shuddered again. The fall must have really hurt. Now they had the mountain fire and on the late news last night it seems a man had fallen from the sky onto a Burbank church festival. All this the week he found out he had a rare disease. He rubbed the sole of his left foot against the right leg. The pain didn't seem to go away, a dull aching pain. It felt like he had just run the marathon twice in bare feet.

He turned over maybe he could get a little more sleep, the pain in his legs continued and he shifted position several times. As he became comfortable and relax another symptom of CIDP followed. Every now and then, he received with what he described as electric shocks. They lasted only a few minutes, but they were very painful. His doctor had told him that they were one of the main symptoms of the illness and may get worse. He drifted off into a light sleep, only to be woken by an electric shock a little later. He sat up in the bed, his mind was full of conflicts, and fears he knew it was this as well as the pain, had kept him awake.

Why had his boss asked him to shred those documents? After the fuss over the shredding of documents at Enron, he would have thought his boss would have been more careful. And then when he had shredded, he was told to forget he had done it. This just didn't make sense to him, he clearly remembered when he joined the company Miss Dellman telling him to always tell the truth, now they were expecting him to lie. Did anyone see him shred the documents. No, he had been alone in the production room at the time. He wasn't sure a financial analyst who was notorious for creeping around and spying on others. He was sure no one saw him and he would lie if anyone asked there was no proof unless someone saw him.

He lay back on the pillow and tried to remember if he had been seen. Was anyone near the production room, he became anxious thinking about it. The face of Bob Cartwright, Sandra's husband, the cuckolded husband kept intruding his thought. He had seen him before, but where? Maybe he just had one of those faces, which seemed familiar. He fell asleep again.

The smell of smoke filled his room flames danced on the wall. Malachy opened his eyes, at first, he thought he was hallucinating, until he realized the mountain fire was very close. He sat up and looked out of the window, the trees and shrubs in next door gardens were on fire. The tenant of the house was desperately trying to extinguish the flame. His wife and children were climbing into the SUV. She was shouting at her husband to join her, but he fought on. The detached wooden garage next to the alley way between their property and the complex Malachy lived in exploded into flames.

Malachy jumped out of bed and quickly dressed. As he opened the front door of his apartment the heat from the fire was very intense and forced him back into the apartment. He stood for a few minutes and gathered his thoughts realizing he must get out. Stepping out onto the balcony closing his door behind him. The apartment manager was watering the side of the building his son was on the roof wetting the roof. The wife of the neighbor was now screaming at her husband, the children looked out of the SUV crying. Malachy felt helpless. Other tenants had vacated their apartments and stood on the roadside, a pathetic hopelessness surrounding them.

The fire brigade arrived and quickly extinguishes the flames. The garage was a charred frame its contents reduced to ash. The neighbor thanked the firemen then crumbled to his knees. His wife screamed and the firemen started CPR on the man. Malachy watched for a few minutes then returned to his apartment. He closed the door and leaning against it.

The smell of the fire had seeped into the apartment he felt suffocated. He searched for a tissue and blew his nose, looking out of the window at the mountain, the flames seemed to have engulfed it. A mountain of fire, the drone of water carrying helicopters and planes seemed to drag him into a depression. It flowed over his body, this 'the end of the world' or just another cock-up by man. Why was he allowing it to get to him?

The phone rang once. He looked at it, expecting it to ring again. It didn't, he had grown to hate the wretched thing, wherever you went someone was talking on the phone. He remembered when you could go to a restroom and sit in peace. Now the man in the next cubicle could be talking on the phone. He wanted to take the phone off the receiver and just lie on the sofa and vegetate watching re-runs of 'Murder She Wrote' at least Jessica Fletcher was entertaining.

The phone rang again, reluctantly he picked it up by the handset.

"Yeah."

"Malachy, its Mark, have you told anyone about the shredding?"

"No."

"Don't, I'll see you're okay, a bonus and maybe a nice long holiday."

"You're the boss."

"Yes, I am, bye."

The phone went dead, he replaced the handset. It rang again.

"Yeah."

"Did my husband just call you bitch?'

"What!"

"Who's that?"

"Malachy, who are you?"

"Lisa Thompson."

"Mark's wife?"

"Yes, who are you again?"

"Malachy Moss, Lisa."

"Oh, I am sorry Malachy I thought…" she faded away as though trying to think what to say. "Yes, well thanks Malachy I'd better be going. Thanks for calling have a good day."

He hung up the phone and jumped when it rang again.

"Hello." He said in a cautious tone.

"Malachy, it's Mark again, did my crazy wife just call you?"

"Yeah."

"What did she want?"

"I think she dialed the wrong number or just pushed the wrong button."

"Oh okay, sorry to bother you, I'll see you on Monday."

"Yeah."

Malachy hung up the phone, then pushed the button to put the phone into silent mode. He sat with his hands under his chin at his dining table, thinking about the last few days.

"What a mess the world is in." He said out loud.

"Murder, bodies falling from the sky and a mountain on fire. Now I'm talking to myself, I need to get out of this apartment, before I go completely mad."

He rose from the table and took a shower.

The car had stopped at the traffic lights. Four young-shaved headed Latino men leaned out of the windows of the Chrysler Imperial and looked warily around. This was their territory and they wanted everyone to know.

The old man stood on the corner of the street begging, his sign held in front of him read 'will work for money, I lied need money for beer. Please help.' It had been written several months earlier and had begun to fade. No one took much notice of the man. His appearance didn't demand a reaction. There was so many homeless panhandling on the streets, one more didn't attract attention. If someone had taken the time to look carefully at this beggar, they would have noticed his nicotine stained manicured fingernails. The real Rolex on his left wrist with the continuous second hand should have brought attention to this man, but no one saw. His clothes, the raincoat, second pair of trousers over a pair of jeans, and the hat with his heavy grease stains, were cosmetically made to look like a homeless man's. He was a fake not even as old as he appeared. Walking slowly between the cars, timing was the secret to his profession. He came level with the Chrysler Imperial, the driver has said something funny and turned to look at the men in the back of the car. He adjusted the woolen hat he had placed on his head, when the panhandler pulled the gun from behind

the placard and shot him in the head. Quickly the gunman repeated it on the other three, shooting each Latino in the head. As he turned to walk away, he caught
the drivers head as it began to fall onto the steering
wheel. A trickle of blood started to run down the side
of the ear from under the hat. The would-be beggar
pulled the hat down over the ear and walked back up
the line to his corner. He unscrewed the silencer from
the gun behind the placard and packed it into his backpack. He didn't look at his crime but made a hasty retreat down a side street and into the back of a small
shopping mall throwing the hat and coat into a dumpster. He ripped the trousers off and pushed them into
an already full trashcan.

The four Latino men lay in different positions, only the
driver was visible from outside the car. His head resting on his forearms as though sleeping.

Margaret Hamel was late for work, she was driving
irately to her sisters to drop her two children, Leo and
Drew. They had been willful all morning slowly driving Margaret's normal patience self away. She was
not only furious with her children but also at her husband. Who didn't listen or understand that on a Saturday he was to look after the children while she is at
work.

Her irritation was at its highest to the point where she
wanted to scream. She had gone beyond her threshold
to become this monster of womanhood, a very angry
mother and wife. It was at this moment in time she
stopped at the traffic lights behind the Chrysler Imperial. The lights were red and for some reason the vehicle in front of her had stopped a car length from the
white lines at the traffic lights. The children knew
how angry their mother was and sat silently in the back

looking out of the window. The lights changed green, the Chrysler Imperial didn't move, Margaret screamed at the windscreen "Move it." Then she began hitting the horn, her normal reaction having been brought up in New York. The Chrysler didn't move. The lights changed red.

She flung open her car door and stomped up to the car screaming "Are you going to move or stay here all day?"

Not getting a reaction she pushed her head inside the car and screamed at the driver. "I said are you going to move ... or just lay here dead."

She rapidly pulled her head out of the car and then noticed the blood running down the driver's face from beneath the woolen hat.

Margaret Hamel fainted, and it was this action, which brought others to the murder scene. Her children saw their mother fall to the ground and screamed from the back of the car.

A fluffy cotton wool cumulus cloud floated gracefully in front of the sun, sending a cold shiver over all those who had gathered.

Malachy Moss sat looking out of the window of the bus. He had decided to get away from the flaming mountain and travel to a shopping mall. The bus pulled into the side of the road as two police cars, sirens blaring raced by. Several of the passengers stood to see if they could see where the police cars were heading. The traffic began to slow down, the driver picked up his phone and spoke to someone. He turned and looked at the passengers.

"It like there has been a murder up ahead and we will have to do a detour at the next cross street."

Malachy rose from his seat and pulled the bell cord, a pre-recorded woman's voice said, "Stop requested." It would be easy for him to walk the last four blocks to the mall. The bus stopped at the stop and he descended onto the sidewalk. The traffic was at a standstill, it wouldn't be long before the drivers became angry and horns began to fill the air with noise. Malachy stopped several times the pains in his legs was getting worse and he would need to rest.

The main intersection had been closed and the police were diverting the traffic. Two police cars block the street and yellow tape was strung across the whole road stopping anyone from entering. Although the roads were wide the volume of cars and truck create a scene of chaos. For pedestrians crossing the street was normally a dangerous event. But when irate drivers, desperate to get somewhere where halted in their tracks, a slow walker could expect no mercy. Malachy crossed and walked along the yellow tape, joining others whom stared to see what had happened. Two vehicles were stopped in the center of the road and police were gathered around them. A woman and her children were being led away to a waiting police car. Not much to see thought Malachy.

The news media hovered above. Waiting for ground crews to set up, channel nine and six first on the scene. A large Asian woman spoke into the air. "Too much murder in this town." She looked around to see if anyone responded.

One of the love generation of the nineteen sixties nodded at her, her appearance a time warp to those who could remember.

The Asian woman continued having found an audience, "It every day now, I really don't know what the world is coming to."

"Never use to be like that," responded the hippie woman.

The two women slide closer together, each one sounding off about how it was and how it was the young people of today who cause the problems.

"They have no respect for their elders," said the Asian lady.

"That's true, only the other day…"

Malachy pushed passed the small crowd and looked for a way to get along the street. The police had taped off the entire street. He would have to walk the long block to the next street and with the pain in his legs coming back he didn't relish the idea.

The alleyway, which ran behind the row of shops, had not been taped off and grabbing at the chance to shorten his journey Malachy entered it.

Large blue metal dumpsters line each side of the alleyway. They had not been emptied for a few days and were overflowing with trash. Malachy passed a man scavenging through one of them. His supermarket trolley was filled with cans and bottles. The man ignored Malachy until he had passed then watched him ready to pounce if Malachy made any attempt to look in one of the un-searched dumpsters. For some people going through the trash of others had become a way of life. Although they only made a few dollars, it was enough to get one meal a day. Malachy had often wondered what he would do if he lost his job or became homeless. He had saved a little money just in case that day arrived, and he had fantasized about becoming a locksmith. He wasn't sure why he wanted that profession but for some reason it seemed romantic. He heard the car but didn't think it was traveling so fast, when the vehicle raced by, he was pushed into a narrow passageway between two of the buildings by the air pressure. He peered out of the passageway into the alley, the car had stopped, and six shaved headed Latino men climbed out. They wore the regulation gang member-clothing. Gray or brown ripped off at the knee Dockers trousers, white socks that reached the knees and white trainers. Their white tank tops allowed a display of tattoos. Two of them had 'Brown Pride' in gothic letters a word on each upper arm. Another raised his tank top and revealed 'Surenos' a Spanish word meaning southerner. They looked up and down the alleyway, before one of them cupped his hand. A thin young man in his late twenties, with 'XIII' tattooed on the back of his head put his foot in the hand. He was lifted and caught hold of the fire escape ladder, using his weight to pull it down. The other men then climbed up to the roof. Malachy watched; he had never really been this close to gang members. He watched as they collaborated with each other. They worked like a well-trained arm unit, each one knowing what they should be doing. The driver of the car drove down the alleyway once all the men had reached the roof, only to return and stand guard at the foot of the fire escape.

Malachy moved back into the narrow passageway, after thirty feet opening into a small windowless courtyard. A young man dressed in black stood looking at gray wall, making it difficult to see what he was doing. He slowly turned and looked at Malachy, his expressionless face giving now visible indicators as to whether he was going to be hostile or not. Malachy caught a quick glimpse of the graffiti on the wall. The boy looked familiar and remembering where he had seen the artist before motivated him to go closer. Standing to the boy's left Malachy looked at the small picture, clearly the letters ANT could be seen. The 'A' was a woman falling down an escalator after being pushed, then being helped up by two men. Malachy looked at the teenager. It was the young Asian youth from the Metro train station. The boy continued to work on the piece, ignoring Malachy's presence.

"That's beautiful," said Malachy.

The boy didn't answer.

"I was there when the woman fell, I didn't realize she was pushed."

The boy still didn't speak.

"Did you see who pushed her?"

The boy pointed to a half-drawn face of a girl.

"You know her?"

The boy nodded his head without looking at Malachy.

"But you didn't say anything when it happened."

"Nothing to say."

"Why?"

"No one listens."

"Yeah that's true these days, too wrapped up in making money."

The silence between them became awkward.

"My boss is cheating on his wife, who do I tell no one will listen or believe me, they won't care."

The boy didn't respond.

"The way you have drawn the figures, it looks like the word Ant."

"Yeah."

"Your name."

"Yeah."

"Ant, short for something?"

"No"

"Don't use many words do you."

"You don't speak much English, is that it."

"No."

"Don't like to talk?"

"Yeah."

"Why, because no one listens?"

"Something like that."

"Words corrupt!"

The boy turned and looked at Malachy, his face relaxing.

"Yeah."

"Not all words."

"Maybe."

"And not all adults are the enemy, but you look almost an adult yourself. How old are you? Seventeen or eighteen?"

"Seventeen, and you can't trust adults, they say one thing but mean something else. It's all crap."

"When I was a kid, I felt like you, still do in a way. Except I found this guy I could talk to, and trust. Everyone hated him, because he drank too much, but when he was sober, he always told me the truth."

"You gay?"

"No, are you?"

"No."

"Why do you ask?"

"Because only gay guys talk to guys like me."

"Does it happen often?"

"No."

"I'm talking to you because we shared an experience and you have now drawn it on a wall."

"This is only a sketch; I will try it out under the freeway near Duncan's and then it will be a big piece, later on a special white wall."

"Hope you don't get caught."

"Who care if I do?"

"Your parents."

The boy shrugged his shoulders.

"Where is it going to be?"

"Hollywood, by the freeway."

"Good luck."

The boy nodded his head.

"I'd better get going."

"Yeah."

Malachy walked down the narrow passageway. The boy called after him.

"What's your name?"

Not turning around he called back "Malachy."

He peered around the edge of the building into the alley, the Hispanic men were climbing down the fire escape ladder. The driver of the car was reversing it up the alley to where the men stood. With the same organized precision, they had when they had arrived, they climbed into the vehicle then sped down the alley. Malachy watched them leave, took one look back at Ant who was still working on his picture. The alley was now empty, and he felt he should get out of it as quickly as he could. The Latino's men's car suddenly appeared at the end of the alley and raced down towards Malachy passed and stopped. He stepped behind a dumpster, just as the car passed him. His heart was pounding. He sank to the ground and closed his eyes.

"What you do at my dumpster?" said the scavenger Malachy had seen earlier.

Malachy opened his eyes, and then stood up looking up and down the alley for the gang members had gone. "Sorry," said Malachy walking quickly away and down the alley.

At the end of the alley he turned right, the police tape was across the street, several police officers were standing looking at a Chrysler Imperial. That's why the gang guys were on the roof, they could see much better from above. He quickly crossed the street into another alley his legs were hurting now. He could see the shopping mall at the end of the alleyway. Ten yards inside the alley behind a Chinese restaurant was a bench, obviously used by the cooks when they weren't busy. He sat down and began to rub his legs. He had to try and forget his illness, disease or whatever it was called. The pain traveled from his feet up to his knees, a dull ache seemed to get more painful as he sat there.

The black mesh screen door of the Chinese restaurant kitchen opened and a small old man peered out. He saw Malachy and darted his head back inside. Moments later another head appeared, it too retreated on seeing Malachy. Malachy closed his eyes and took several deep breaths. The smell of Chinese food mixed with rotting food from the dumpster floated up his nostrils. He needed to move from here before he became nauseous. The screen door opened and a fat Chinese man stepped out and looked at Malachy. He sensed the man wanted him to move so he stood up and limped away.

Reaching the shopping mall, he found a bench just inside and flopped onto it. He looked around, and at first glance everyone seemed to walk with a limp, were on crutches or in a wheelchair. He closed his eyes and tried to shake the negative self-pity from his mind. Opening them he only saw one man with a walking stick and no one in a wheelchair.

Walking around the mall had for him lost its appeal a long time ago, he liked to people watch. He had also realized that if he sat down too long his legs hurt even more. Every shop in the mall seemed to be having a sale. Fifty to eighty percent off. This would explain why there were so many people in the mall. In the reflection of a shop window Malachy noticed someone he at first thought he knew. Then realized it was the man from the elevator who had stared at him. Malachy slid into a space between two stores, which had phones and a water fountain. For the third time that day he peered around a corner. The man had not seen him and was still talking to some woman who was holding a child.

The man ushered the woman into a shop. Malachy took this opportunity to change his vantage viewpoint. He climbed the escalator and from the second floor looked down on the shop they had entered. It was the little boy who emerges first followed by the woman chasing him. The man left the store and looked around, Malachy moved away from the handrail, so the man would not see him.

He shadowed the man and woman as they visited various shops. When the woman and child entered a lingerie shop the man stood outside. His cell phone rang, at first, the man just listened then became irritated, not angry but something was upsetting him. Malachy watched as the man tried to keep his emotions under control as he walked up and down outside the shop. When the woman and child emerged, the man relaxed as though nothing had happened.

Malachy looked at them, they were a family, only a husband and father would react the way he was, so why did he feel threatened by the man. Had paranoia taken over and he was now seeing conspiracies everywhere. The couple stood outside the department store and seemed to be hesitating as to what they should do. The little boy pulled on his mother's hand and they went into the store. Malachy entered it on the second floor. He stood behind a rack of women's blouses and watched the escalator. The woman and boy stepped off the moving stairs. He waited for the man. The woman had started to look at skirts. She was not waiting for her husband. Malachy edged his way closer to the escalator, and risking being seen walked past looking down to the floor below. The man was nowhere in sight, he checked the escalator again and still the man didn't appear.

He turned and looked for the woman and little boy, but they too had disappeared. He ran down the escalator two steps at a time. It had hurt his legs so he limped around the department store's floor, the man too had disappeared.

Leaving the store, he stood in the entrance looking around the mall, realized he had lost the man. So much for being an undercover member of the public, he was useless.

Across from the store was the restroom. Malachy entered, at the yellow stained, white tiled sink he washed his face. The toilet in a cubicle flushed and the man exited from the cubicle. Malachy stared at the man and the man stared back at Malachy. It was an awkward confrontation, neither knowing how to react.

Malachy turned and began to dry his hands and face.
The man washed his hands then took a pile of paper
towels.
"I think we should talk," said the man.
"Why?"
"Because…" he trailed off as the door opened and
boys entered the restroom. They looked at Malachy
and the man, they had realized they had stumbled on
to something, but they were not sure what. They
both pretended to wash their hands while looking at
Malachy and the man.
"What about your wife and little boy?"
"How do you know I'm with them?"
"You're not the only one who can watch."
"They've already gone home."
"Right."
"Let's get a coffee. I think you need an explanation.
I think our presence in here maybe misunderstood."
They left the restroom and walked in silence to the
food court. The man brought two coffees and joined
Malachy who was already sitting at a table.
"My name is Bruce Weaver; I work for the SEC."
"Oh!"
"We had a tip that one of your clients, sorry one of
Weinstocks and Boller Investments clients had been
trading illegally."
"Who?"
"I'm sorry I can't say."
"So why were you following me?"
"Err, I wasn't actually following you, just seeing
who worked at Weinstocks and might be willing to
talk to us."
"Well without any real information it will be hard to
say anything."

Bruce sat looking at his coffee he hadn't taken a sip and Malachy wondered if they had been spiked. He placed his coffee on the table unsure if he should continue drinking it. Bruce looked at Malachy and then took his coffee taking a long drink before returning to looking at the table.

The two boys from the restroom passed them and looked at them. The boys had come to a conclusion and even though it was a wrong one they were intrigued to see the two men again.

Neither Bruce nor Malachy noticed.

Not raising his head Bruce said, "If I tell you a name, can I trust you will not mention it at work?"

"You could try."

"Michael Mapledorf."

"Never heard of him."

"Really," said Bruce with surprise in his expression and voice. "Do you have access to all the office accounts?"

"Yes, I'm on the management team."

"I know that."

"You don't know who his sales rep is?"

"The name on the statement says Sandra Cartwright."

"Must be a new account."

"No, I think it was opened about five years ago."

"But she was only been with us for two years."

"I know that, so who gave her the account?"

"I don't know that, but Mark must know who did."

"Mark Thompson."

"Yeah, he is the regional manager."

"I know that too."

"You know a lot."

"All but the important things."

"I suppose you are going to tell me it is my duty to find out about this account and then tell you all about it."

"Something like that."

"And if I don't."

"Use your imagination."

"I could just tell Mark and Sandra about this."

"I don't think you will do that."

"Why?"

"You're not the type, you keep information to yourself just in case you can use it to your advantage in the future."

"You're one of those profilers."

"No, I just know a lot about you."

"Like what?"

"Well besides where you live and work, I know all about your credit and what you buy and where. I also know you have some rare disease."

"What?"

"I know you have a nerve disease."

"But I've only just found out."

"I saw your medical records yesterday at the FBI."

"They know?"

"Oh yes, if this thing is as big as we believe it is, they will be involved."

"Shit."

"Sure is, and someone is up to their necks in it."

"Well it's not me."

"I hope so."

Bruce's cell phone rang he searched his pockets to find where he had put it. Pulling it out of his shirt pocket he flipped it open.

"Yeah, I'm leaving now." He closed the phone and put it back into the shirt pocket.

"Malachy if you know what's right you will cooperate."

Malachy didn't answer but watched as Bruce rose and disappeared into the shopping mall crowd. The news that the FBI knew about his CIDP had shaken him. Maybe they had given it to him so he would cooperate with the SEC, they were government. He had read somewhere years ago the government had made a lot of people sick to see what the effect would be. After the study they didn't tell the people. This is what had happened to him, it was the government, he thought for a moment he was beginning to sound like a paranoid radio talk show host.

Two women in their earlier thirties sat down at his table, neither asked if the seats were taken. They were deep in conversation, one of them placed a shopping bag in front of Malachy, almost knocking over his coffee.

"Well according to Tony it was gang related, and Tony works for the coroner's office so he should know," said the blonde with a blue dress on. "Someone shot four Mexicans in the head."

"In broad day light, that's what I don't understand," said her red headed friend.

"Tony said his boss said it will start a gang war."

"Just what we need another war," said Malachy. Both women stood up and looked over the shopping bag at Malachy. He smiled at them. They ignored him gathered their bags and left, leaving him to sit alone. He sat and watched the mall fill with shoppers. It wasn't until someone bumped his table, he realized he needed to get out of the place.

The crowds of shoppers in the mall were all moving in one direction, Malachy needed to go against the flow.

He entered the stream of bodies and began to push his way towards the front entrance. He couldn't understand why they were all going in the one direction. He slid to the side wall and edged his way along, the crowd was just too strong to fight against. As he reached the front of the Burbank Town Center Shopping Mall, he could see why the hordes of shoppers were going the other way. The police had closed the road and to get to the parking structure the shoppers would now have to go through the mall. He opened the front glass door, immediately a security guard snapped "If you're trying to get to the parking lot, you'll have to go through the mall."

"No, I'm going down the alleyway," said Malachy. He walked quickly into the alley, relieved to be out of the crowd. He was always unable to cope with large crowds, he was borderline demophobic, but most people were.

His legs began to ache again, this made him walk slowly so as not to aggravate the problem. He constantly looked behind to see a car was speeding towards him, his paranoia had started again. As he crossed the intersection between the alleyway, he saw that the police activity had intensified. Was this the start of the gang war the woman had been talking about. Maybe he should think about moving to a safer neighborhood? He stopped at the entrance to the passageway, which lead to where Ant had been painting. There was no one there, the painting wasn't finished but the artistry was incredible. He looked at the detail. If this survived in a thousand years, it would be regarded as a twenty-first century cave painting.

He left the passageway and stopped as a car raced down the alleyway. Two men wearing woolen hats

pulled low over the faces sat in the car. They looked
at him as they drove by. Malachy felt his legs go
weak. He tried not to look at them, and entered the alley walking slowly his head bowed. The car turned
left at the end of the alley, he increased his pace the
bus stop was only around the corner.
A few onlookers still stood looking down the street at
the police activity, he hoped the bus wouldn't be long
he needed to sit down.
The black car drove around the corner, very slowly.
Malachy became aware of it. The windows were very
dark with illegal tinting. It was impossible to see inside, so he couldn't see who was driving. The sunroof
slid back as the car leveled with him. He prepared
himself to fall to the ground. The black poodle's head
rose from inside the car, it stared straight ahead, the
light breeze vibrating its fine fur. Malachy gave a
laugh out loud. He had seen too many horror movies
on the television.
The bus arrived and he climbed aboard relieved that he
could now relax his legs. Was this what he could expect? His life was going to be miserable and he
needed to do something to stop the process. He felt
the depression ooze over him, until the driver hit the
brakes and he was jolted out of it. It was so easy for
him to slide into a mood he would have to really work
to keep himself going. Maybe there was a support
group, or someone else to talk to, he had promised
himself he wouldn't become maudlin. A man entered
the bus wearing silly flowery hat and began to tell the
passenger joke. Malachy soon found he was laughing
and forgot his troubles.

CHAPTER FOUR

Sinners

The Soriano family sat around the dining table. Donald Soriano father and husband arrived home unexpectedly. The cutlery being crashed into the china plates broke the silence, the rhythmless noise irritated Ant. Estefania looked at her children, their miserable faces filled with food. She loved her husband, but hated the effect he had on the children, it was as though they were scared to speak. Donald sat eating. His heavy lined face aged by the constant fears he carried with him. His involvement with the National People's Army before he fled from the Philippines had made him paranoid. Always looking over his shoulder never getting into conversations with other Filipinos unless he knew something about them. Although he was now a naturalized American his nightmare of being awoken in the night by the FBI. Being dragged to the airport to be deported back to the Philippines to stand trial haunted him. He had carved a reasonable life for himself and his family. Learning how to blend in with the community, to dress and act just like anyone else. His only other little secret was his use of his son's hair dye, at forty-five he had a head of gray hairs. It wasn't vanity, which had forced him to take such steps. The other long distant drivers were all in their early thirties and made fun of anyone who looked old. He couldn't take the risk of being singled out. Bringing attention to himself would make someone ask questions and he didn't want that.

He looked at his wife. She was a good woman who had kept the family together. His children had not embarrassed the family name even though Anthony dressed strangely and rarely spoke. The recent events in the area had been playing on his mind as he drove home from his latest trip.

"I was thinking Estefania, maybe we should move to another city or even the countryside," he said.

"Why?" asked a surprised Estefania

"This city is riddled with crime, a murder every day, I read about it."

"It's not that bad."

"Oh really; men falling from the sky, who pushed him and where did he fall from? Then there is those four young men, all killed while waiting at a traffic light."

"These things happen in other places, and its worse in the Philippines."

"Let's not talk about that, but do hairdresser's wives get murdered in their husband's barber's chair all the time?"

"Oh yes I forgot about poor Fluffy."

"That Estefania is why I don't let you get your hair done. These hair salons are dangerous places. Whoever did it shaved her head."

"Well maybe it was a rival hair dresser."

"No, it's a conspiracy. The city is full of murderers," lowering his voice, "Rapes, child molestation by pedophiles. Someone is behind it all. These terrorists have even got into the priesthood, ruining our religion."

"It's not the religion that's at fault."

"I think you should look for a new church, that one is not safe attracting bodies to fall from the sky. Sounds more like some evil omen to me."

Susan yawned. Donald looked at her, his face became tense.

"You know your kids are not safe. Our President is right they are everywhere. The fires up the mountain that was government destroying their hide out. I think they started it with shredded documents. And why is the government stockpiling small pox. It's a conspiracy, I know it is."

"Don't upset set yourself Dad," said Susan

"I can't help it brings back so many memories."

Silence once again clouded over the table, Donald picked up a glass of water and drank the entire glassful in one swallow. Ant looked furtively at his father, making sure he wasn't looking, slipped the meat off his plate into a plastic bag in his lap. Susan noticed but didn't say anything. She had learned the hard way her brother could get revenge when you least expect it. The last time she had done anything, which had brought his father down on Ant, had backfired. She had been embarrassed in front of her entire class. She could never prove it was Ant who had done the deed. Who else would have access to her homework book and be able to pin a naked male picture in it? When Miss Reading had opened the book and showed the class Susan's homework the embarrassment stayed with her for a week. She still gets comments each time she hands in her homework.

"What are your plans for tonight?" asked Estefania.

"I am going to have a beer and watch the game and
you kids had better be quiet. Do your homework or
whatever you do. But no noise."
Susan and Ant didn't reply Donald looked at them expecting and answer.

"Well!"

"Yes Dad," said Susan.

"And you boy."

Ant looked at his father; his expressionless face irritated Donald.

"Yes," he mumbled.

"If you've finished you can leave the table," said
Estefania.

Susan said without thinking, "Well we can't take it
with us."

No one laughed, the joke had worn thin after being
said so many times.

Ant lay on his bed when Susan entered the bedroom.
She closed the door and stuck her head around the curtain.

"What's the meat for?"

"Stray dog."

"Really, what's it like?" she said in her early teens'
excitement.

"Pretty and still like a puppy," said Ant knowing his
sister's feelings about animals.

"Do you think Dad would let us keep it?"

"No way."

"Can I see it?"

"Not now, but soon."

"Okay as long as you promise."

"I promise," said Ant not realizing his words would
come to haunt him.

He put his Doc Martin boots on and carefully tied the fraying laces. His way of dressing had been influenced by his father's pictures of the rebels he ran with in the NPA. He could never tell his father this, even though he had wanted to talk to his father about it. After hours of thinking why he was a graffiti artist he had come to the conclusion it was his way of being a rebel, protesting the status quo.

He poked his head around the kitchen door and saw his mother washing the dishes. He wished he had a job so he could buy her a dishwasher. She would never let either he or Susan do the dishes, they had schoolwork which was more important.

"I'm going out, I'll be back by ten thirty."
Estefania turned and smiled then blew him a kiss. He caught it and pressed it against his heart. He had been doing this little ritual since he was a small child. Leaving the apartment, he closed the front door quietly.

Arriving at the street where the dogs lived took him about an hour. He stood at the entrance to the street he felt uncomfortable in the neighborhood. Even though most of the gang members around here he knew from school, he didn't want to test that association.

The owner of the yard where the dogs roamed was locking up the yard as Ant approached. He didn't look at Ant, climbed into a black Lexus and drove down the street. The freeway above was loud and fast. He looked up and wondered if he could get on the freeway then jump onto the roof. The gap was too big. It wasn't worth the risk, this was going to be his last piece in public.

He stepped towards the wire mesh fence, one of the Rottweilers lunged at him. The dog's teeth gnawing at the wire fence, the saliva dripping onto the ground. "Good dog."

The dog growled even more and was joined by the other dog, which paced up and down looking angrily at Ant.

The first dog began to mimic the other and paced up and down. He would then stop and lunge at the fence. Ant wondered how strong the fence was, dogs less fierce than these two had killed a woman in San Francisco.

A large black bird swooped down into the yard, the dogs ignored it, they had their eye on a bigger prey.

Ant took the plastic bag out of his pocket. Both dogs stopped and looked at him. He threw a piece of meat over the fence. The prettier of the two dogs jumped and caught it. Ant thought it was prettier because his eyes had softness to them.

He threw a second piece of meat, expecting the second dog to jump for it. He didn't, but kept pacing up and down leaving the morsel of beef to be eaten by the other dog.

Ant made a mental note about how the two dogs had reacted. He would need to understand them a lot better if he was going to befriend them. He threw a piece of meat to the back of the yard, the prettier of the two raced to find it. The other just growled at Ant. He threw it a piece of meat at the dog that was pacing up and down. He had a thin strip of white fur on his head just above his eyes running at a slight angle. The dog let the meat fall in front of him before picking it up. He immediately spat it out, the other dog scooping it up.

Ant sat down on the curb opposite and looked at the
dogs, which had settled down as though lying in front
of an open fire. With their black and brown soft fur,
they looked so placid and harmless.
A car drove up the street and parked in the far corner
under the freeway, the dogs didn't react. They were
obviously oblivious to the constant traffic, unless
someone threatened their domain.
The squeak of the shopping cart could be heard before
the man pushing it appeared. The dogs became excited and began to race around the yard. The cart was
overloaded with plastic bags and newspapers; it was
old and rusting. The man was thin and, in his fifties,
his face, weather beaten and hard after the many years
of living on the street. His clothes were dirty and old,
his hair cut short was almost all gone. Ant took out his
small sketchpad and began to draw him. The dogs
barked but didn't growl or attack the fence. The man
ignored Ant as he stopped the cart at the yard's gate.
He began to look through his shopping cart, the dogs
barked even louder.
    "Shurr... let me find it first, you're just like my wife,
    stop making all this noise."
He took a Styrofoam take-out food tray out of the cart
and opened it.
    "Meat, this one is for you Bill."
The prettier dog became very excited and ran around
in a circle. The man tipped the food carefully over the
fence trying to avoid the barbed wire on the top. Bill
ran forward and began to eat furiously at the food as it
dropped to the floor.
    "Now what about you Kaiser, you want your food?"
The other dog stared at him and watched as the man
tipped the contents of another Styrofoam tray over a

different part of the fence. Ant could just see what looked like Chinese food fall to the ground. It was all vegetables. Kaiser was a vegetarian. It somehow seemed wrong, a vicious Rottweiler not eating meat. The food hit the floor, but unlike the other dog Kaiser didn't pounce and begin eating. He circled it and sniffed at it before tasting it. As he ate the white fur above his eyes disappeared making him look less fierce.

The scream from the far corner where the car was parked didn't make the man or the dogs look up. Ant turned to see what all the noise was, a woman was screaming at the car.

"I want my fucking money," she screamed as the car reversed and drove out of the parking lot. It clipped the shopping cart as the driver turned into the street.

The woman strutted across the parking lot, pulling her skirt down while trying to straighten her hair.

Ant returned to look at the dogs, the man had his hand through the wire mesh and was stroking Kaiser's head. The dog obviously likes the contact as he kept turning his head so the man could scratch another part.

The woman had reached Ant and as she walked past, he looked at her. Her legs where naked, the short skirt covered her butt and she wasn't wearing any underwear. The heels of her feet where white and cracked and the strap of the shoes dug into the heel as she walked.

She suddenly turned and screamed at Ant.

"What you looking at? Want a freebie?" she then continued to walk down the street.

Ant looked at her or was it him. It was hard to tell from what Ant had seen but something in the face and made him rethink. If it had been a man why hadn't he

seen the genitals from where he was sitting, after all he
or she had walked very close to him.

The prostitute stopped and bent down to fix the strap
on his or her shoe, Ant smiled it was a man. He could
just make out the genitals, which had fallen out of a
very tiny G-string.

The man with the shopping cart packed his things up
and began to run after the prostitute shouting "You
giving freebies?"

A car turned into the street and drove up the parking
lot, making the man with the cart and the prostitute
step to the side.

She screamed at the car "Get your money first."

Ant watched the car park before returning to watch the
dogs. Bill and Kaiser, he had heard those names before but couldn't remember where. The dogs continued to eat, Ant went to the fence maybe he could put
his hand through and stroke Kaiser, after all the dog
didn't really know who had given him the food. The
dogs looked up as he approached the fence, they both
returned to eating. Ant relaxed, he was going to put
his hand through the wire fence and touch the enemy.
Bill continued to eat as Ant touched the fence. Kaiser
lunged pushing the fence out. His teeth wrapped in the
wire mesh, food and saliva dripping from the mouth.
Ant jumped back, the shock of the dog's actions making him feel shaky. He walked quickly away and
across the parking lot to the other side. The noise of
the freeway was very loud the deeper he went under
the freeway. The building around must be deflecting
the sound, someone could get raped down here and no
one would hear.

He approached the car in the corner, he could see a
pair of legs resting against the roof of the car. From

this distance it was the movement of the car, which
told him that someone was fornicating. He didn't really care, it didn't disgust him or anger him, he had an
indifference to it. Prostitution had been around for as
long as man had been on the earth, why everyone got
upset by it he couldn't understand but that was adults.
They took pleasure in the sex with prostitutes, then
tried to stop it. Why these two were so blatant about it
he could understand, if the police came, they would
immediately know what is happening. He couldn't see
if it was two men, a man and women or a transvestite.
He had once dressed up as a girl. A girlfriend had
done it to him, he liked the feel of the girl's clothes on
his body, but he didn't want to wear them all the time.
He had become so indifferent to so many things. His
generation was forced to accept so much that was in
his opinion wrong. Murder was everywhere, his father
had been right about that and it was mostly the young
killing the young. At school violence was common,
even the campus police had a difficulty trying to keep
it under control. If you looked at someone the wrong
way or spoke to someone in the wrong way, you could
get knifed or beaten. That is why he didn't speak
much. He rarely looked at others in the school unless
he was far enough away for them not to see him looking.
He watched as the man's white pimply buttocks went
up and down. It reminded him of the time he had
caught his parents having sex. He was seven years old
and stood in the doorway of his parent's bedroom. His
father was rough and crude with his mother, she cried
out several times in pain. Ant didn't understand what
his father was saying but he knew it was bad. The
words had stayed in his mind and every time he heard

them, he flinched. Cunt, bitch, and slut. He had grown up thinking that sex was a rough game where men inflicted pain on women and women enjoyed it. After the sex, his mother had kissed his father thanking him. Although now he had learnt differently, it still was an image which came to mind when he thought about sex.

As he looked at the fornication in the back seat of the car he was surprised when the face of the recipient appeared over the shoulder of the customer. The hair was array and the make-up, especially around the eyes was smudged. Creating black holes in the face with two small white spots in the middle. The face disappeared and the man stopped pounding away. After a few adjustments of his clothing the man climbed out of the back seat of the car. Beads of sweat had formed on his forehead. His receding hair was wet and stuck out in different directions. He looked at Ant and then indicated to the prostitute with is index finger to get out of the car. The prostitute began to straighten her appearance, while the man walked briskly around the car to the driver's side. Once inside the car he pressed the door locking mechanism and started the engine. The prostitute stopped preening herself and tried to open the door. The car moved and the driver opened the window enough to throw a condom out. It fell to the floor and joined the others that littered the parking lot. The car drove off, Ant and the prostitute watched as it accelerated down the street. Ant turned his attention to the prostitute she was staring back at him.

"What?" she screamed.

Ant didn't reply but continued to look at her, it was a 'her' he was sure. She looked like a girl and acted like a girl; therefore, she must be a girl. The prostitute

took a pair of white panties out of her tiny pink handbag. She carefully stepped into them, lifting her skirt
as she did. Ant's mouth dropped open as he caught a
glimpse of a shaved scrotum. It was a man, a transvestite. He had been convinced it was a woman. These
days you couldn't tell, what was the world coming too.
He was beginning to sound like his father and the
thought scared him. Was this the transformation from
boy to man, when you suddenly started to sound like
your parents? He was brought out of this thought suddenly when the prostitute shouted at him.

"Something wrong kid?" he continued to straighten
out his clothes, "never seen a woman get fucked before, no you wouldn't have, you still a virgin."
Ant stared at him. He found it hard to think of him as
a 'him', he looked so female.
The prostitute was fixing the panties in the crease of
his buttocks. The white flesh of his right cheek clearly
visible, the skin was translucent with blue veins zig-
zagging its surface. He suddenly realized that Ant was
staring at his butt, at first, he tried to ignore and continued to adjust his panties.

The stare became too much, and the prostitute exploded, "have a good look kid, you will never be able
to afford this beautiful piece of meat."
He stopped adjusting his panties, straightens his skirt
and leant towards Ant.

"You don't speak much, what's the problem, got a
cock stuck in your throat? Shit kid I haven't got the
time to waste waiting for you to say something, I got
the rent to pay."
Ant watched as the prostitute walked across the parking lot and onto the road. He stopped by the fence neither dog growled nor barked. Bending down to move

the strap of his shoe placing a hand to steady himself on the wire mesh fence. The dogs ignore him. Only when he began to walk down the road did Kaiser look at him.

Ant stood in the center of the parking lot looking at the two dogs, why hadn't they attacked when the transvestite had put his hand on the fence. Kaiser was lying down as if he was asleep. Bill was prowling up and down, as if he was a lion in a cage at the zoo.

Three cars raced up the road and into the parking lot. They went to different parts of the lot as though it had been orchestrated. One driver opened the back door of his car, then took his trousers off, exposing his crisp blue boxer shorts.

Ant had seen enough for one day and slowly walked out of the parking lot. Kaiser continued to sleep while Bill prowled observing Ant as he came close to the fence. Kaiser woke and snarled at him before arching his back ready to pounce.

"See you tomorrow Kaiser, and you Bill."

Kaiser's ears flickered at the sound of his name. Bill stopped and waged his tail at the sound of his name. Two more cars came up the road, forcing Ant to step closer to the fence. Kaiser lunged and through the wire mesh his teeth caught hold of Ant's left leg of his jeans. He pulled hard to release the grip, ripping the material as he did. Kaiser barked and growled at his victory, saliva dripping to the floor. Ant ran.

As he approached the bus stop, he could hear the two women talking. They were dressed conservatively in middle aged type clothing even though they looked in their early thirties.

"Well I told him, if he wants me to work late, I expect a taxi home," said the taller of the two as she pushed her dyed blonde hair from her face.
"I wouldn't expect anything more, so what did he say?"
"He said and would you believe it 'I don't need a taxi as he would take me home after we have had dinner'. I said my husband wouldn't like that and he had the nerve to say then don't tell him."
"Really, I'm not surprised. You know Karen in accounting she said he had tried it on with her."
"Well she would, she thinks every man is after her."
They both laughed and Ant smiled as though he knew what they were talking about.
"Did you hear about that man who fell from the sky over in Burbank?"
"Frozen, wasn't he?"
"Yes, and my Wayne said it was aliens who abducted him."
"Well your Wayne was in the Military he would know about those things."
"Anyway, according to the news, he was an alien and an illegal one who stowed away on the plane."
"No."
"Didn't say where he had come from but landed in the middle of a church festival."
"You know that girl who works in the production room?"
The tall blonde woman gave a quizzical look at the other woman.
"You know, Oh what's her name?"
"Barbara."
"No not her, the tall thin one who smokes, well she smells as though she does."

"Jo Anne."

"Yes her, well she is telling everyone she was there and saw the whole thing."

"She does live in Burbank."

Ant stood leaning against the blue pillar of the bus shelter. He looked straight-ahead listening to the two women. He smiled to himself when he heard the woman say 'Jo Anne had seen the whole thing.' He had been sitting at the next table, but now it was just a memory an image glued his imagination.

He slid back into listening to the women's conversation.

"That's it like our Wayne said the other night its them terrorists, I said you're right those terrorists are terrible people. They are blowing up everything and killing everyone."

"Yeah" replied the other woman looking suspiciously at Ant.

"Wayne said we should put all those terrorists against a wall and kill the lot of them."

"What Terrorists does he mean?"

"All terrorists, I think."

"I know they are all terrorists, but there are two types of terrorists, foreign and the ones who are American. I mean you can't kill Americans, can you? They're American."

"True."

"You can't put them against the wall and shoot them, you have to have a trial and then you can execute them."

"Right, or could hang them."

"Yes."

Both ladies stared off into the distance. Ant smiled, it was conversations like this, which made him realize how uninformed the adult world he was entering really was. He thought for a few moments, was he falling into the same pattern. He didn't read much or watch television. His information came from the street and the schoolyard and how accurate could that be.

The bus arrived. Ant boarded the bus and found a seat halfway down, next to a window. The two ladies stayed at the front and continued to converse. He stared out of the window, everyone on the street seemed to have a cell phone. He suddenly felt the urge to have one. All the other students at school had cell phones. They would arrange to meet each other and talk about homework. Maybe that is why he didn't have friends. It wasn't anything to do with the fact his school was so far away from his home.

The bus stopped abruptly and the driver, a large over weight woman, left the bus to walk over to a doughnut stand. Her huge obese butt stuck out as she leaned forward to speak into the small window of the doughnut stand. She returned to the bus carrying a bag of doughnuts and a large Styrofoam cup of coffee.

She closed the doors and took a doughnut out of the bag before driving off. Stopping at a regular bus stop a man entered, he had a strange smell emanating from his body as he passed Ant. He found a seat at the back of the bus and flopped down in it. The man was extremely thin and his shoulders where hunched over. His clothes were old and dirty, his left shoe was cut in half the sock worn away and the skin on his heel very hard and dry.

"The lord says you are all sinners," he shouted, "you will all go to hell, the lord has told me."

Several passengers looked around at the man before returning to stare forward. Some tried to make themselves invisible, or at least unnoticeable, so the man wouldn't pick on them if he began to pick on individuals. It was known that mentally ill people like this man would single out one person and make their journey hell itself.

"That's right turn your back on God, I am his servant and bring you all a message."

The man sat down and stared out of the window. Silence engulfed the bus, the other passengers bracing themselves for the man to continue.

Ant turned and looked at the man, who sat with his head resting on his hands. The rest of the bus returned to the normal activity the two ladies continued to talk about the threat of terrorists on the bus. Their conversation was just audible and had unnerved some of the passengers.

Ant watched the man waiting for him to explode again with some religious rhetoric. The man just sat there resting his head on his soft clean hands. The nails were manicured and had been buffed to shine. The mark of a very large ring could be seen on the left third finger. It didn't fit the image of a crazy homeless person. Ant searched the man features looking for other inconsistencies. His hair had been dyed black and recently the scalp still had dye on it. This was strange, but nothing to do with him. Ant returned to look out of the window. It was odd that a homeless man had manicured nails and dyed hair and if he was his father it would be a conspiracy. Terrorists as the woman up the front of the bus where still talking about. He refocused his attention to the street and his mouth dropped open, as everyone seemed to have a cell phone it was an epidemic.

He needed one, but whom would he call? Morgan, he doesn't have a cell phone nor does Steve. Kalli she didn't have a cell phone, she said they were the cause of so much trouble. People being too accessible. Maybe he needed new friends, but he had always found it hard to make new ones. He just didn't trust many people and a friend needed to be trustworthy. Still he wanted a phone, he would ask his mother, if he could have one. He would say he could make new friends, be able to keep in touch with the family. If his mother called him up and asked him to buy something from the grocery store on the way home, it would be okay. No, that would not be cool if the other dudes found out. The desire to have a cell phone had become very strong. It had become an obsession, the obsession.

The preaching homeless man suddenly jumped to his feet and ran to the back doors.

"The lord says stop the bus," he shouted.

"We're not at the stop," shouted the driver back to the man.

"The lord says stop the bus, I need to get off, away from all this sin, sex and drugs."

"Next stop coming up," shouted the driver, "please keep calm sir."

The bus pulled into the curb and the green light above the door came on. The homeless man opened the door but didn't get off the bus. He turned and looked back at the passengers.

"You will all die in hell," he shouted, "God can see your sins, the sex and drugs, women who prostitute themselves wearing short skirts and no stockings. Bare legs are a sin to God."

"Are you getting off sir?" asked the driver.

"I will when the Lord tells me too. He just wanted me to add that men are the most sinful. When they play with themselves, destroying all those little babies. God can see you and you will all burn in hell." The man then left the bus, the driver moved away from the stop quickly. Most of the passengers were looking out of the window at the man. He had now fallen to his knees and was praying with his hands clasped together in the prayer position.

Silence fell on the bus, only to be broken by one of the two women at the front of the bus.

"Poor man must have a mental problem."

"My Wayne says they should be in a hospital away from the normal people," replied the other woman.

"I suppose you could put them with the terrorists, somewhere."

"Now that's a good idea I'll tell Wayne that when I get home."

This was the signal for the rest of the bus to start talking.

Ant sat silently looking out of the window, why had the man been like that, he was obviously not homeless or poor. He arrived at this bus stop and rang the bell. He needed to find a supply of meat and Chinese food so he could feed Kaiser and Bill. Kaiser Bill of course he remembered he had read something about him. Something to do with a war, which one he couldn't remember there was always some war going on somewhere. Maybe he could drug the dogs with sleeping pills and then get by them. He would ask Morgan or Steve to get him some sleeping pills for a dog. He would have to make sure they both understood he only wanted to put the dogs to sleep not kill them. Steve had the habit of getting carried away.

The woman who had been sitting in front of Ant left her seat and exited the bus by the back door. As the bus pulled away from the bus stop a man who had been staring at the woman in a lustful way shouted. "She has left a bag of shopping."
The driver ignored the man and continued to drive down the street. She was fed up with all the shouting and had decided not to listen.
The man opened the bag and looked inside, then threw it back onto the seat. "Bones." He said in disgust.
Ant reached up and pulled the cord to ring the bell. As the bus pulled into the curb he reached over and grabbed the bag left by the woman and made a quick exit by the rear door.
He turned his back to the bus; not wanting to see any of the passenger's face as the bus drove away. Once it had driven away, he slowly opened the bag and looked inside. The bag contained bones from a butcher's shop, the sort you give to a dog to chew on.
Ant smiled to himself, he had a good start and now he had to find a regular supply and some Chinese food for Kaiser.
He knocked on the apartment door his parents had never given him a key of his own. His sister opened the door, when she saw him, her face broke into a de-monic smile.
   "I've got a cell phone." She said and producing from her back a shining silver colored cell phone.
Ant pushed past her and made his way straight to the kitchen. His mother was at the stove cooking. She turned and smiled at him, then indicated with her pursed lips that someone was in the corner by the kitchen table. Ant opened the refrigerator and put the bones in the bottom drawer. As he turned to look back

into the kitchen, he saw his father sitting at the table
reading a free Filipino American newspaper. Donald
looked up at his son then returned to reading the paper.
Susan entered the kitchen she looked at Ant then at her
father. The demonic smile still on her face.

"Oh, daddy thank you so much for the cell phone,
now I can call all my friends."

"You'd better not run large telephone bills," said
Estefania.

"Mommy if you call a cell phone to a cell phone it's
free. I'm was the only girl in our class without one
all my friends and I can now talk."

"Well just remember it's really for emergencies, so
you can tell us where you are and who you are with."

"Of course, mommy and thank you again daddy,"
she said in a sycophantic tone.

Donald looked up at his daughter and gave a weak em-
barrassing smile, he looked across at Ant who showed
little sign of being hurt.

"I suppose you want one," said Donald "Well if you
want one you can go out and get yourself a job and
buy yourself one."

Ant didn't react, he was used to his father playing fa-
vorites, and he had been doing that most of Ant's life.
His mother put her arm around her son's shoulders.

"A job what a good idea. Your Uncle Caesar said
they were looking for a dishwasher at the restaurant.
They needed someone every Monday, Tuesday, and
Wednesday night from five till eleven. I think he
said it was four dollars an hour, cash."

"There you are, you had better go and see Caesar before the job goes," said Donald as though the sugges-
tion had been his.

Ant looked at his father, a slight resentment appearing a snarl in the corner of his mouth.

"Off you go Anthony, and tell Caesar I will see him and Jean tomorrow as planned," said Estefania.

Ant entered the bedroom; his sister was sitting on the bed talking on the cell phone with one of her friends. He ignored her and looked for a pencil, which had fallen under the bed.

"Wait, what are you looking for? Sorry it's my brother he is sulking because he hasn't got a cell phone."

Ant left the room having found the pencil taking his sketchpad with him. As he closed the front door he called "Bye Mom." He didn't wait for a reply.

Uncle Caesar was his mother's oldest brother, often called 'jack the lad' because he had so many jobs. He didn't have any children of his own and had always been generous to Ant and his sister. His latest job was working in a Chinese restaurant. Ant stood looking at the front of the restaurant. It was an expensive looking establishment, a Chinese restaurant with valet parking in this part of town would only encourage the wealthier of the area to visit.

Ant wandered around the back, several waiters and cooks sat on plastic crates smoking. A thin Chinese cook who was a few years older than Ant smiled.

"You come looking for Caesar, yes?"

Ant nodded and the cook disappeared into the kitchen of the restaurant.

Uncle Caesar burst out of the screen door smiling. He was a very fat man with an infectious smile and laugh. He was dressed in a suit and bow tie, although he had bits of food around the corner of his mouth.

"Anthony, my favorite nephew."

Ant nodded.

"How are you, how is my sister? What brings you here?"

"I heard you needed a dish washer."

"We do yes, are you interested?"

Ant nodded.

"It's only three days a week and four dollars an hour, but we pay cash on the day."

"I need the money."

"My brother in law being mean, again, is he?"

Ant lowered his head; even though he had issues with his father he would never say anything against him.

"We will give free food though, when do you want to start, next Monday?"

Ant nodded.

"Good, just get here ten minutes before five, and say high to your Momma for me."

"She said she'll see you tomorrow."

A voice from inside the kitchen called out, "Hey Caesar."

"Got to go, see you on Monday."

Caesar returned to the kitchen almost walking into a bus boy carrying a tray of plates.

A kitchen worker opened the door and carried a plastic bin fall of left-over meals and poured them into a round oil drum which was already overflowing. The other workers all looked and smiled to Ant before going back into the kitchen. Ant went over to the oil drum and looked at the food, a huge smile appeared on his face and he said out loud, "For you Kaiser." The smile stayed on his face until he went to sleep that night his sister became quite worried and hid her cell phone under her pillow.

CHAPTER FIVE

Janice Smart

Malachy sat at his desk. The view of Beverly Hills stretched out in front of him on a cloud free day. The tops of houses poking through a sea of green trees. The auspicious club house of the elite golf club surrounded by trees and imposing island between the fairways. He turned to his left and looked at Santa Monica and the Sea. He could just make out the shape of Santa Barbara Island, almost hidden by a mist of lace. This was one of the perks of working in an office tower; he could walk around the floor and see Los Angeles, Hollywood to downtown and the infamous Staples Center.

His phone rang several times before he picked it up. The caller ID said zero, meaning it was reception.

"Yes" he said in an irritated tone.

"The visitors for Mister Thompson have arrived."

"What visitors?"

"I don't know, they said they have an appointment with him."

"Well there is nothing on his calendar, do you have their names."

"One moment."

Malachy clicked on Marks calendar; the morning was clear he had an appointment at his hairdressers NoNo Men's Salon at three but that was all.

Michelle from reception spoke, making Malachy jump he didn't expect him to be so loud.

"Tell him it's regarding the Fahey account."

"Okay, I will be down in a minute."

Malachy rang Mark, although he sat outside of Mark's office the door was closed and therefore it was difficult for him to communicate any messages.

"Yes Malachy," said Mark in a brusque voice.

"Sorry to bother you, but some people have arrived. There is nothing on your calendar, the receptionist said it was to do with the Fahey account."

"They're early. Malachy put them in a conference room on the 26th floor."

"But there is nothing on your calendar!"

"Yes, well you must have forgotten to put it on."

Mark closed the connection leaving Malachy, unable to correct him. But this was not the first time he was blamed for something he knew nothing about.

As he descended the gray marble stairs, which led to the reception on the floor below the pain in his legs began to get stronger. Going up stairs wasn't a problem but going down he had found it seemed to somehow inflame his problem.

At the foot of the stairs were three men and a very striking looking woman. The men were dressed in pin stripe corporate regulation suits. Two of them were the sort who would disappear quite easily in a crowd. They didn't have any real distinguishing features. The third man stood out not just because he was considerably overweight, but the suit fit so tightly as he moved the seams of it where stretched to the point of ripping.

The man sank into one of the chairs his body just fitting into the oversized seat. He taped his fingers impatiently, then his left leg began to beat up and down. In contrast the woman was thin, almost on the border of anorexia. Her brunette colored hair seemed to flow down her back the waves and curls in unison like a small stream rolling over the powder blue suit. She wore a fluffy white blouse, which gave the impression of white foam on water, completing the outfit. Except her black leather shoes, which didn't match. The two-inch high heels were a strain on her feet as she changed her weight from one foot to the other. Malachy felt she wanted to take the shoes off, they weren't hers or they were brand new and hadn't been worn in. As he approached the woman, she looked at him and smiled.

"Sorry to keep you waiting, Mr. Thompson will be down in a moment. I'm Malachy Moss his assistant."

He held out his hand to shake her hand. Her thin boned hand shot forward and he noticed the scar, which stretched from her little finger to her wrist. Before he could make a comment one of the men slid ungraciously between them. He had to change his small brief case to his left hand in order to shake Malachy hand. The hand was cold and damp, the short stubby fingers fitting uncomfortably into Malachy's.

He looked the man in the face, the skin was smooth over the bone framework. This was not the man's original face, how many faces lifts, it was difficult to determine but Malachy was convinced there had been at least three.

Then the man put an arm around the woman and guided her back toward the obese man who was now trying to easy himself out of the seat.

Malachy turned to the receptionist. "Michelle is conference room twenty-six available?"

"Yes, Mister Moss," she replied with a slight resentment in her voice.

She hadn't forgiven Malachy for rejecting her invitation for dinner and then to go on to a club. She had refused to believe one of her girlfriend's suggestions that he might be gay. She knew he wasn't she could tell. She'd seen enough gay men to be able to spot them.

"Thank you, Michelle. Would you like to follow me?"

Malachy said to the waiting clients.

He opened the door and let them pass him into the conference room. The obese man immediately sat himself down on one of the ten chairs around the oval table. The woman moved to the other end of the room and looked out of the window onto one of the movie studio's below. Her shoulders relaxed as she peered at the ant like people below rushing from one studio to another.

Malachy stood in the doorway, "would any one..."

He didn't finish as Mark Thompson pushed past him into the room.

"Thank you, Malachy."

"Do you need any drinks?"

"No need we won't be that long."

Mark then closed the door leaving Malachy looking at it.

"Are they going to be long?" asked Michelle.

"According to Mark no, but who knows. I didn't even know they were coming."

"Well I hope they won't be too long we have a meeting in there in half an hour."

"If it's a problem just call me," said Malachy as he ran up the stairs two at a time, only to regret his actions as he reached the top.

His legs began to hurt. He really must remember running is something he must do in moderation.

"Are you okay?"

The voice boomed from the solid built Tony Elliot, as he stalked the 27th floor with the air of a wan-a-bee sales representative. It was this claim to self-importance, which made Malachy dislike him along with the fact he dragged his feet as he walked creating an irritating sound.

"Yes, thank you. I must remember not to take the stairs two at a time."

"Why?" The question was irritating, as Malachy had spoken about his disease several times with Tony.

"A. G. E."

"What's that?"

"Something I don't think you will reach."

Malachy passed the puzzled Tony and returned to his desk. As he began to sort through the paperwork on his desk, the meeting Mark was in begun to play on his mind. He had never heard of the Fahey account and he knew the name of most of the accounts. He opened the company account software and typed in Fahey. As was normal he waited for the result. A computer company may claim its product is fast but if the software is so complex then it can take time to receive an answer. A gray message window appeared telling him he had insufficient authority to access this account. He tried again and received the same message. He leant back in his chair. Access to all the accounts in the office had been granted to him, he was part of the management team. He sat up and typed the names of several accounts he knew where restricted access only. The accounts opened without a window message. He tried the Fahey again, and he was refused access. He had learnt a little computer trick, which would allow him to see who has access to that account. The usual window opened and told him that only Mark Thompson had access to that account. The appearance of Mark quickly put the search for account information out of his mind.

"I'm going to San Diego. I will be away for the rest of the day. If anyone needs to contact me, they can call me on my cell phone."

"Yes sir," said Malachy looking quickly at Mark's calendar.

"I know there is nothing about these meeting on my calendar I have only just been told about them myself."

"Do you have the addresses?"

"No, I'm driving down with the client."

"What about the company policy regarding knowing where the senior management is, security will want to know."

"I'll deal with that later. You just tell anyone who calls I'm with a client"

"If that's what you want," said Malachy a resigned tone in his voice.

"Bye Malachy."

"Mark your hair."

"What about it."

"NoNo today."

"Cancel it."

Mark left the office. The day continued slowly. Malachy tried Mark's cell phone several times but was unable to make contact. And made excuses as to why he couldn't be contacted.

The conversation around him soon changed from the sports game last night to one of office intrigue. Was Mark Thompson having an affair and if so who with? They're many suggestions as who was Mark's mistress but according to the consensus the paramour was Sandra Cartwright. Malachy had no doubt in his mind. His sense of loyalty to Mark made him wish others would not be so flippant with their comments. As with all gossip it soon changed and after lunch the conversation turned to money laundering. It seems a former employee who had moved to a rival firm had been arrested for laundering drug money. A meeting was convened by the sales representatives to discuss the fall out and if it would affect Weinstocks and Boller. Malachy had tried to contact Mark but his cell was either out of range or switched off. The tension in the office rose, as sales representatives became anxious. Malachy looked at the digital clock, as it clicked over, the minutes seemed to take forever. At five minutes to two, his phone rang. He didn't recognize the call ID number and spoke in his usual non-committal voice.

"Weinstocks and Boller Investments, Malachy speaking how can I help you?"

"Malachy, its Mark."

"Hi Mark we have been trying to contact you."

"Is there a problem?"

"Well not really, more of an iceberg. "

"Meaning?"

"Some of the sales reps want to speak to you about money laundering."

"Money laundering! Why what has happened?"
"Jim Brocklestone at Willieman's has been arrested on money laundering charges."
"Who needs me?"
"I think Peter Mindoff seems to be the most worried, he thinks he has found a connection to us."
"He was always a drama queen, put me through to him."
"No problem and I'm leaving in a few minutes do you need anything else?"
"I don't think so. You can leave and have a good night."
"Thanks, you too."
Malachy listened for a few seconds after he had connected the two men, then released his phone from the call.
It had long been his practice to ritually close his computer and then lock his drawers. Today he followed this custom but as he was leaving, he placed a little piece of sticky tape over one of the drawers. Something made him feel it was the right thing to do. Too many strange things had been happening in his life and he wanted to make sure that someone wasn't messing in his personal things.
Inside the stainless lined elevator, he pushed the lobby button. The doors closed slowly and the elevator began to descend, stopping four floors below to become filled with passengers. The doors began to close and another man who Malachy was convinced had been watching him for the last few weeks stepped into the elevator making the doors reopen, to the annoyance of some of the impatient passengers. The man stood facing the doors. If he had seen Malachy, he made no indication, maybe he was one of Bruce Weavers SEC

guys. The elevator stopped at several other floors, no one entered or left. Malachy looked at the man he seemed younger; something had changed. He smiled, the man's hair was no longer gray, he had dyed it a soft brown color. If the man's desire was to look younger, it had worked, he looked a lot younger. Only his clothes had not changed he really needed to update his attire, he stood out in the suited crowd.

The doors opened on to the lobby as the elevator arrived. The passengers on mass poured out. Malachy tried to see where the man was, he had simply disappeared. The walk down the hill to the bus stop didn't spring any surprises. He lost himself in his own thoughts about the office and his colleagues. The man stood by the square metal pole the bus stop sign hung from. He looked at Malachy as he approached it. Hoping Malachy was so engrossed in thought he wouldn't see him standing there. More people arrived and as the bus pulled up to the stopped, they surged forward trying to be the first on the bus. A small man pushes in front of a Hispanic woman who looked as though she was going to have her baby at any moment. It was one of the things, which annoyed Malachy how today most men do not have manners. He had noticed that today most American's lack any real consideration for others it really was becoming a selfish society. And he could count himself among the offenders.

He stood at the front of the bus looking down its length, there were only a few seats left at the front of the bus. He sat heavily down on the brown plastic seat. The man sat opposite him and deliberately not making eye contact with Malachy, staring to the back of the bus. Malachy looked at him, was this man following him and if so why? What was really going on?

Malachy felt he had been watching too many films and had started to live in one. The young woman sitting next to him had a problem sitting still, this fidgeting flowed over to Malachy. This brought him out of his paranoid daydream.

Her anxiousness coupled with the desire to help was unbearable to those who encountered Janice Smart. She had grown accustomed to introducing herself as 'Janice Smart, smart by nature that's me' this was followed by a girlish giggle. Today she wore jeans with bleached patches and an oversized sweater which had been pulled out of shape so much that the arms reached the ground. She had to keep pulling up the woolen sleeve, so she could use her hands.

Her hair was blonde and always kept clean. She had never seen a hairdresser in her life. The hair spewed out and over a red Alice band, in every direction. Her big blue eyes stared through the owl size rose tinted glasses. She wore no makeup and her greasy face always seemed as though she had been through a car wash and been waxed. Sitting on her lap was a large handbag filled with Metro bus guides.

Born in Van Nuys, California she had acquired a Brooklyn accent from watching too much television as a child. Even to this day she talked back to the television screen because of the lack of parental interest and communication. Her mother had tired of her at an early age and once Janice began to talk her mother grew more despondent towards her and the endless chatter. To eliminate her guilt her mother sat Janice in front of a black and white television. To Janice it became the substitute mother. She watched the television from the moment she woke in the morning to her eyes closing at night. She didn't stop talking and began to imitate what she saw and heard. As a teenager the school authorities though she might have a multi-personality problem. It was because of the way she would go from one-character accent to another. Janice finally settled on a Brooklyn accent after a boy she became obsessed with told her he liked girls from Brooklyn. The relationship never matured into anything, but Janice continued to twang away in the accent.

Her mother had died seven months early and had left a gap in Janice's life. It wasn't that her mother did much for her, but now the house was empty and there was no one to talk to when she got home. To fill this chasm Janice began to ride the bus and talked to total strangers. To anyone who would make eye contact with her. Some tried to ignore and hoped she would disappear, others allowed her to talk during the journey if only to eliminate the boredom and time of the journey.

Janice had found herself employment after leaving school in a large upscale department store. She worked in the basement of the store, by herself sorting the returns so they could be placed back on display. While others would have hated the solidarity of the work, she embraced it as if it was paradise. With only the store display mannequins to talk to, she could chatter away without anyone telling her to shut up or complain to the management.

Today had started as normal, after her shower and breakfast of toast and canned orange juice she had run to catch the early morning bus. Picking it up one block from her home and being delivered outside the department store, she saw no reason to use her mother's car, which was locked away, in the garage.

It had been a slow day and she was grateful when it
was over. She hadn't talked too much and this had
disturbed her, she had something on her mind. What it
was she didn't know only something was making her
think and not talk. As she left work, she had said to
herself "when I get home, I will have some dinner then
go to bed early." This was a euphemism for watching
the television while lying in bed.

At the bus stop she had pushed her way onto the bus so
she could get home quickly. She sat at the front of the
bus. Her mother had told her when she was a little girl
on one of the very rare occasions, she took her out.
Only murderers and gangsters sat at the back of buses,
nice people sat at the front of the bus. As she grew up
and began to ride public transport she would stare at
the men at the back of the bus. To her the dirty
clothed worker on his way home from a very hard
day's work looked like murderers and gangsters. She
had never ventured towards the back and glanced there
every now and then expecting to see someone being
murdered.

She began to talk out loud, most of the other passengers knew her and avoided eye contact.

   Today she became very excited and her verbal drivel
   grew louder and louder until the bus driver JoAnnie
   Frank shouted, "Janice calm yourself down."

   "Sorry, I'm so sorry JoAnnie, I really don't know
   what has come over me today."

   "That's okay just don't talk to loud, remember there
   are other people on the bus."

Janice sat quietly for about five minutes looking at the
man opposite her.

Malachy sunk back into his seat relieved the constant
torrent of noise from the young girl next to him had

stopped. He turned his attention to the dyed hair man. Something about the man made him feel very uncomfortable. It was as though the man was spying on people, and not just people him particularly. The man continued to avoid eye contact with him, what was he hiding, why wouldn't he acknowledge his existence. Janice leaned forward the feeling of wanting to speak suddenly was too much to control and she burst forth.

"Don't I know you from somewhere, you look very familiar?"

The man had mistakenly made eye contact with Janice in his attempt to avoid eye contact with Malachy. He shook his head desperately trying to find somewhere else to look.

"We have met, but you were older."

"I don't think so," replied the man hoping to kill the conversation.

"Yes, I just can't remember where, but I have seen you before."

"I'm sorry to disillusion you but we have never met before," said the man raising his left hand to pull the cord to ring the bell.

The electronic voice activated by the cord said, "Stop requested."

The bus stopped and the man ran down the stairs so quickly that he almost stumbled.

As the bus pulled away Malachy thought he saw the man get into a car.

"I have seen him before, he looks like an undercover cop."

The words emanating from her mouth jolted Malachy. She was right he did look like a cop or someone who worked for a government agency.

As the bus stopped at a red traffic light JoAnnie turned to look at Janice, she had a soft spot for this young woman. She remembered the morning the young woman had sat silently looking ahead. The silence from her had unsettled the other passengers who had grown accustomed to her talking. As she left the bus that morning, she had asked her what was wrong. Janice answer still haunted her, "My mother died this morning." Is all she said, as though she was giving a matter of fact piece of information. It was obvious that Janice was upset, but just didn't want to show it. She had internalized the emotion and JoAnnie had from that moment had a special liking for her.

"Janice what's wrong today you seem very agitated?"

"I know, something is wrong, but I can't just seem to understand what it is.

"Well try and keep calm."

"Sorry JoAnnie, I didn't mean to make the police man run away."

"It's okay just settle down."

Janice sat staring in front of her at the empty seat. Malachy also looked at the empty seat. The woman was right, the man did look like an undercover policeman, and he too had seen the man several times. That is why he recognized him, but he didn't look like one of the men from the SEC. His thoughts were interrupted by Janice talking to the driver.

"It's been a strange day. Someone, I don't know who, has moved my mannequins. They must have done that last night. Maybe we are going to have another sale and they need the space. Oh no I shall be so busy if we have another sale."

"Well if you do have a sale, Janice please let me
know, Davidson and Day have the best sales in
town."

"Okay I'll know tomorrow."

As the bus arrived at her stop, Janice jumped up the
excitement flowing over her again. Malachy watched
as she descended from the bus, he had the urge to follow, it was only a few stops from his and maybe the
walk would do him good.

The bus drove on. Malachy stood next to Janice and
began to walk beside her.

She suddenly stopped and looked at him.

"You following me?" she said her face set firmly in a
quizzical expression.

'No not really, I just wanted to know why you
thought that man was a policeman."

"The man on the bus?"

"Yes."

She thought for a moment and turning completely to
face Malachy looked straight into his eyes.

"I'm not sure, he just looked like one. His clothes,
the way he looked at you as though he was watching
everything you do and mentally making notes."

"Yes, you're right that exactly what he looked like he
was doing."

"He was watching you."

"Are you sure?"

"Yes I am."

"Oh, what makes you say that? What was it he did to
make you think he was watching me?"

"He wouldn't make eye contact with you, when I talk
most of the passengers look at each other. Especially
when I confront them. He just wouldn't look at you,
and on the Discovery Channel a program I watched

said that it was a sign of someone who was deliberately avoiding someone else."

"Yes, I saw that program too."

"Have you done something wrong?"

"I don't think so."

"That's okay then."

She then ran down the road and around the corner. Malachy watched and wondered how many people would dismiss her as having a mental problem. She was very intelligent just wanted company. Obviously, she was lonely. Sadness began to creep over him. He too was lonely more so now than ever before.

A blue car drove slowly by him. He looked inside to see if the dyed hair man from the bus was one of them. The passengers in the car were staring straight ahead, as though looking for a store.

Malachy began to walk a little quicker down the road, he glanced into the shops as he did. He hadn't been in this part of Burbank for some time, even though he lived only a few blocks away.

The explosion of glass on to the sidewalk just ahead of him seemed unreal. The explosion's force and heat suddenly reached him forcing him towards the wall of a dentist's surgery store. He had been daydreaming about winning the lottery when the blast occurred.

The blue car with the two men in it had stopped a little ahead of the store. The men now wore ski masks and where looking back at the explosion. A man appeared from an alley by the side of the store his ski mask pulled up and sitting on his head. He looked at Malachy before running to the blue car, which as soon as he was inside accelerated away.

A man appeared from the store, which Malachy realized was a hair salon. His white barbers coat was torn and heavily blood stained. He seemed dazed and small whiffs of smoke came from the white coat. A woman came out of the salon, her head covered with a plastic dying cap. Black smoldering lumps covered the cap, any hair that had been sticking through the cap and burnt.

The distant sound of sirens could be heard.

Malachy rushed to help the man who was sitting down away from the broken glass. He took the arm of the woman and guided her to sit down next to the man.

He then went to the salon and entered the place. Inside he tried to see if there was anyone else inside. The black smoke emanating from the back of the salon was thick. It was difficult to see if anyone was there.

He came outside and shouted to the hairdresser. "Anyone else inside."

The man looked up and shook his head. The woman had become very hysterical Malachy stooped down by her and began to calm her down.

"Robbers," said the hairdresser looking at Malachy as the blood from a head wound trickled down his face.

"Please robbers," he repeated.

Malachy looked at the man and then nodded in agreement.

The paramedics arrived and began to attend to the hairdresser and woman. The fire brigade began to unravel the hosepipes. It didn't take then long to get the fire at the back of the salon under control. The police had taped off the area. A policeman approached Malachy; he looked suspiciously at him. "Did you see what happened sir?" The way he said sir indicated to Malachy the officer had little or no respect for the general public.

"Only the ending of it from out here. I think it was a robbery because the men had black ski masks on then sped away in a gold colored car."

Malachy could see the hairdresser behind the officer looking at him trying to hear what he was saying. Seeing this he raised his voice so the hairdresser could hear what he was saying.

"I see sir, so you didn't get a good look at the men?"

"Not sure they were both men, one could have been a woman in men's clothing. With ski masks on it's hard to work out the sexes."

"Really, what about the car?"

"Gold, didn't see the license plate, not sure it had one at the back. I was trying to help these two." He said pointing to the hairdresser and the woman.

The hairdresser was helped on to a gurney and as he was being wheeled away, he called over to Malachy.

"Thank you, what's your name."

"Malachy Moss."

"Malachy how do I contact you to thank you properly."

He took a card out of his pocket and gave it to the man.

"My cell phone number is on there."

"I'll call you later."

"That's okay, no need to do that."

"I will."

The hairdresser was wheeled into the waiting ambulance. The woman who was still a little hysterical was being taken to another ambulance.

"If I could have your name and address sir, so we could get a formal statement later."

"No problem," Malachy wrote his name and address on the officer's note pad.

"Thank you sir and we will be in touch."
Malachy left the scene relieved to be going home. As he walked, he began to wonder what it was all about, and maybe the Fluffy McRae murder was connected to this. He stopped at a traffic light his feet and legs had begun to hurt and he wished he hadn't got off the bus when he did. Why he was constantly making such silly choices he didn't know and he didn't believe it was anything to do with his illness. Later as he sat quietly eating his dinner at home, his mood had changed and he felt depressed. The day seemed to have been very long and his desire now was to rest. He stood at the kitchen sink washing his dinner plate. The meal hadn't been an exciting cordon bleu meal he wasn't a very good cook. He had noticed he had become very picky about his food. The window of the kitchen was open a few inches and the sound of the apartment complex and street interrupted his thoughts. Someone had thrown something made of glass into the dumpster and the sound of shattering glass made him jump. The memory of the glass window of the hair salon came into his head. He had never seen an explosion and it was an incredible sight. What was it all about, and what did the man in the ski mask shout? He suddenly stopped himself that was right the man in the mask who came from the alleyway had shouted something. He sat down at the kitchen table. He had to remember, something about Fluffy. He remembered the man had shouted "Another fucking Fluffy." Who was Fluffy? And why had the hairdresser insisted on it being a robbery. It looked more like an attack from some rival gang, and if what the man had shouted meant anything then it was a gang attack.

He finished cleaning the kitchen then checked to make sure the front door was locked. He had always been a nervous person but tonight he felt even more scared. He lay on his bed, turning this way then the other; he just couldn't get comfortable. Just as he was dozing off, his cell phone came to life and rang. He stretched out his hand and picked it up from the bedside table. He flipped it open and in a sleepy voice said. "Yeah."

"Malachy, this is Jonathan Puller, the hairdresser you helped today. Thank you for not saying too much to the police. A friend of mine will come and see you and explain what's happening and if you need a haircut, it's free for the rest of your life from me."

"Yes, thank you."

"I'm sorry if I woke you up, please go back to sleep and we will talk again soon."

The phone call ended and he closed the phone replacing it on the bedside table. He fell asleep waking several times in the night with electric shock type pain, once it had subsided, he fell back to sleep.

He woke from the dream with the doorbell rings, he sprang out of bed, his legs hitting the floor and pain traveling up his legs. He looked at the clock and wondered who it was at four thirty in the morning, waking him up. He was still sleepy as he unlocked the door and peered through the screen door at the two people outside. A young man maybe a little younger than himself and a girl who was no more than fourteen or fifteen dressed in very thin material dress stood shivering.

"Mr. Moss?"

"Yes."

"Could we talk to you for a moment?"

"Why, at this time?"

"It's about what happened today at the hairdressers."

"Who are you?"

"Friends of Mr. Puller."

Unthinkingly he opened the screen door and let them enter. Once inside the young man took a gun out of his pocket and pointed it at him.

"You have to come with us."

"Why?"

"I think it's best you don't ask any more questions but just do as we ask."

The girl opened the screen door and the young man pushed him outside. The cold night air hit his body through the thin material of his pajamas and made him shiver. The coldness of the ground penetrated his bare feet. He knew he would suffer electric shocks at some point for this. He turned to see where the girl was but she had stayed in the apartment. As he walked past the other apartments, he looked and hoped someone was looking out of their window and would see him being kidnapped. At this time in the morning it was unlikely and he stopped looking.

The young man pushed him into the back seat of the car. The girl suddenly opened the door to the back seat, and slide in.

"You locked the place," asked the young man.

"Yeah and got his keys for him."

They drove in silence, Malachy trying to remember the route they were taking. But realized he was being driven around in circles. The car turned into an alley-way, which ran behind some house on one side and warehouse on the other. They pulled up in front of one of the warehouses. The girl got out of the car and opened two large doors, just enough for the car to drive inside. Once inside the doors where closed and the girl appeared at his car door and opened it. He stepped out of the car, it was dark inside and he could just make piles of boxes. The young man indicated with the gun to walk to the right and then up some stairs to an office. When the door of the office was opened a bright light illuminated the warehouse showing him the boxes of electrical appliances. As he entered, he saw two men sitting on a sofa at the other end of the office. They both stood up and approached him; Malachy's mouth dropped open as Ricardo McRae crossed the room.

"Mr. Moss I am sorry for this little game of intrigue but once you have heard the story about what is happening. I am sure you will understand."

Malachy didn't answer he shivered.

"Please come over here and have a seat, I and my colleague will explain. Would you like a coffee or tea to warm you up? Steven you really should have let Mr. Moss get dressed before you asked him to come and see us. At least let him put on a pair of shoes. Lisa would you go down to the warehouse and see if you can find a nice warm coat and a pair of shoes for Malachy."

The other man stood up and looked at a wall chart.

"You should find something over by the kitchen and I think Mr. Moss would be size forty-four and a shoe size I think would be nine."

Malachy looked at him and made a little nod in agreement.

"Good well once you are warm and had something to drink, I will explain," said Ricardo "Thank you for helping Jonathan today, such a nasty business and him working on one of his old clients at the time."

Malachy sat back on the sofa and closed his eyes. This was a dream and he would wake up in a moment in his own bed. The sound of the door opening made him realize this wasn't a dream. He was sitting in an office and in his pajamas with no shoes on his feet. He was beginning to feel the cold and small electric shock had begun in his toes. The girl who had brought him to the warehouse was standing in front of him. She has a sheepskin-lined coat and a pair of beautiful Italian looking shoes. He stood up and took the coat it fit him perfectly. Slipping his feet into the shoes the warmth of the soft brown leather quickly penetrated his feet. The coat soon warmed his body and he felt a little better.

"Mister Moss please may I call you Malachy, such a good biblical name." Without waiting for an answer, he continued. "My name as you may know is Ricardo McRae and this is my colleague Peter DuVella. I am sorry the younger members of our company felt it necessary to bring you here in such a dramatic way."

At that moment the young man entered the office he was carrying a tray with mugs of coffee on. He handed a mug to Malachy and asked "Milk or sugar?"

"Just milk."

The young man poured some milk into the mug and then retreat to join the girl on the other side of the office. Ricardo and Peter sat down on the sofa one on each side of Malachy.

"Now Malachy, let me tell you a story, I am really sorry you got involved in this yesterday, but if you hadn't maybe it could have been worse."

"You see we are having a little problem between local hair dressers," said Peter

"Several months ago, a gentleman, if that's what we can call him and may I add will remain nameless opened a hair dressing salon here in Burbank," said Ricardo

"He began to lure the customers away from other salons by lying and making up dreadful stories," said Peter

"Well as you can imagine we objected to this newcomer and got very upset and then things started to get out of control," continued Ricardo "It became very violent and what happened yesterday was all part of it."

"What about your wife?" asked Malachy.

"Oh, you know about that, well that has nothing to do with the war."

"The war?"

"The war between hairdressers."

"Mister McRae's wife was murdered by her ex-husband," said Peter.

"Ex-husband?" questioned Malachy.

"Yes, the police are looking for him and I'm sure they will find him."

"At first, we thought she was murdered because of the war, but when the police found a fingerprint of Scott, that was dear Fluffy's ex-husband, in the salon. I knew it was him who had killed her. I told the police about the phone calls she had from Scott threatening to kill her if she didn't come back to him," said Ricardo wiping away tears with a paper tissue.

"I'm sorry, why did he cut her hair."

"He was my business partner before, and so it was a way at getting at me."

"I hope you understand about the war, and why we don't want the police involved," said Peter

"It really is not in their best interest to know about it," said Ricardo

"So, we are hoping you will not say anything, and I'm sure we can come to some understanding."

"What about the newcomer, won't he keep fighting until he has won?"

"I don't think we will have any more problems from him, not after tonight. What he did yesterday at Jonathan salon was going too far."

"I don't think he will be staying in Burbank."

"I see, and have you told me everything."

"I think so, we had better get you home and back to your nice warm bed. I really am glad you came to see us Malachy."

"I didn't really have a choice."

"The guns fake," said the young man reaching over to take Malachy's mug.

"It looks real."

"It does, doesn't it?" said Peter a smile on his face. "I have a box full of them made in China or was it, Korea."

"Steven, I want you to take Malachy home and make sure he gets safely into his apartment."

Steven nodded his head.

Malachy stood up and began to take off the coat.

"No, you don't need to take it off, it's a present for being so understanding," said Ricardo.

"That's right and if we can ever do anything for you, just come and see Ricardo at his salon."

"Thanks, the shoes too?"

"Of course."

"Well good bye Malachy it really has been a pleasure meeting and talking with you."

They all shook hands.

Steven led Malachy down the stairs from the office and opened the car door for him to get inside. He slid into the back seat expecting the young girl to join him. Steven opened the large doors before driving the car out of the warehouse. Malachy didn't see who closed the doors but when he looked back, they were closed and the place was in darkness.

They drove in silence, when they arrived at his apartment, Steven jumped out of the car and ran around to open his door. Malachy stepped out onto the road; dawn was just breaking through.

"Good night sir and thank you," said Steven handing him his door keys before getting back into the car and driving away at speed.

Malachy looked up and down the road, several people were getting into their cars and to drive off to work. As he walked through the complex to his apartment, he felt like he was the keeper of some great secret. He knew what many didn't and would never know. In a strange way he felt he had not only helped solve the mystery of Fluffy McRae's murder but also the hair-dresser's war. His little fantasy, playing detective.

As he closed the door of his apartment, he suddenly had a panic attack. What day was it? Should he be on his way to work? He turned on the television; it wasn't the normal morning news programs it must be Saturday. Then he heard the newspaper landing on the floor outside the apartment. It must be Saturday. He sank onto his sofa and fell asleep, exhausted.

CHAPTER SIX

Graffiti Murder

Ant stood on the third step of the fire escape ladder. He looked down at the two dogs Kaiser and Bill sleeping. After days of feeding them with food from the Chinese restaurant he had been working at he had done what no other graffiti artist had been able to. It had been easy to place the sleeping pills Steve got for him into today's canine feast. He wasn't convinced they were just sleeping pills until Steve tried them on his father's two dogs. They slept and when they woke wandered around as if they were drunk. Steve's father thought the dogs had found a stash of drugs and eaten them. Over the last few days Bill had become very friendly and had on two occasions allowed Ant to put a hand through the wire mesh and to pat him on the head. Kaiser had remained mean. The food he brought was obviously to the dogs liking, as Bill now became very excited when Ant appeared.

Before climbing the ladder, he had touched both sleeping dogs, their brown and black fur was soft and velvety. Though both dogs were very vicious, it reminded Ant of a television program he had once seen about lions who had been tranquilized. The lions where like little kittens and these two dogs were like little puppies as they slept. He had wanted to touch the dogs for some time, but only Bill had allowed a quick pat. Kaiser still attacked the fence if you got to close to it. Ant thinking, he had won them over a few days earlier had learnt this. When having patted Bill, he tried to touch Kaiser, only his quick reaction saved him from a very bad bite.

The prostitutes and their clients ignored Ant he had become part of the scenery in the small street and parking lot. Even the local police officers would wave to him as they patrolled the area. The police had stopped him on one of his first visits to the street.

He had produced an animal rights membership card and explained his concern for the safety and wellbeing of the dogs. They accepted his story and openly encouraged him to visit and check on the dogs.

He looked out into the parking lot; it was empty, too early for any activity. At least another hour before the early birds would start to arrive. He couldn't see if anyone was watching him and there was no sign of the police, he continued up the ladder. Climbing on to the flat roof, he was surprised to see how big the space was. The usual air conditioner units were sporadically placed across it. The door to the fire escape inside the building had been pad locked from the outside. Ant wondered why anyone would do such a dangerous thing, if there were a fire it would be impossible for anyone to get out. Or what was stored inside so secretive they didn't want anyone to get inside and find it. The scrap yard where the dogs lived was never used, and he had not seen an entrance into the building. Maybe the whole thing was a front. Other than the air conditioner units, which looked as though they had not been used for many years, there was an air filter unit, which hummed away. Ant assumed it was filtering the air going into the building. As he passed the large air duct, he felt the breeze of warm air coming out, he thought he smelt a slight smell of marijuana plants. When he was in twelfth grade, he remembers a grounds man at the school being arrested for growing marijuana in the school's greenhouse. It had been the smell, which had given the authorities the tip off. And he had wondered what that smell was during those classes in the greenhouse.

The white wall, his great desire was on the right running at right angles to the freeway. The freeway parapet would help hide his activity from the drivers, who were more concerned about getting home than watching a kid spray a wall. He stood watching the cars and trucks speed by, life had become too fast. Maybe if the unrest in the world continued then gas prices would reach five dollars a gallon and there would be fewer cars on the road. More people on public transport, and it would take the city ten years to cope with an increase in passengers. It really was a no-win situation. Life was going to race by and he was soon to be caught up in the madness. For this moment he felt he had reached the top of Mount Everest, the air was in his mind clean and refreshing.

He was king of his castle and as he walked around the top, he peered over the parapet at the street below. A car drove up and parked in the parking lot, he couldn't see if there were one or two people in it. As he drew close to the fire escape ladder a bird flew up and almost hit him in the face. He looked over to see how the dogs were doing, like children they slept. It was as though after a day of fun and games they had just fallen asleep exhausted.

He returned to the wall and unpacked his backpack. He had created an inner lining where he could hide the cans and markers. He laid the cans of spray paint in a neat line from a dark color to light. Rolling out the drawing, he used the bag and the plastic containers the dog food had been in to keep drawing from rolling closed. He sat facing the wall. He felt it must be like a marathon runner feels just before the race. You know what you must do and roughly how long it is going to take. The anticipation to start, he looked at the drawing and then the wall. He mentally drew squares on the wall in the same way there was pencil drawn squares on the sketch.

He stood up and took a black marker and approached the wall. Using the brickwork, he marked the squares before roughly sketching the first letter. He stood back and looked at the letter A, it was correct in proportion, so he quick drew the other two letters. The T needed a little correction before he was able to stand back and look the beginning of his piece of art.

Someone was shouting in the street below, he turned and looked over the parapet. Two transvestite prostitutes were arguing and a small crowd had gathered to watch, they screamed at every insult, which was being shouted. The crowd hoped it would turn into a vicious fight and encouraged the two transvestites to 'get at it'. A car had parked a little way from the excitement but the back seat tinted window and been lowered. Ant watched, he despised violence, but like most people he would watch. After several pushes and a few slaps one of the transvestites grabbed the others dress and pulled. The dress made of thin cotton ripped off the thin boy's body leaving him standing in a padded bra and girl's black panties. The on-lookers screamed and

applauded this display of violence. The semi naked
transvestite attacked the other and pulled off his
blonde wig. The crowd roared again with approval. In
retaliation the wig less boy slapped the other, which
led to a slapping match, only stopping when the padded bra was wrenched from the naked transvestite's
body. The small-developed breasts looked like those
of a young pubescent girl. Several of the on-looker's
whistled and others clapped in delight. The crying naked boy transvestite picked up his bra and dress, before walking away and down the street. He began to
wail and scream as though he had just been whipped to
near death.

The back door of the expensive Mercedes Benz
opened and a man dressed in a gray suit with gold jewelry around his neck and rings on his fingers stepped
out. He approached the other transvestite who was
now trying to rearrange his blonde wig. They spoke,
the transvestite using his hands to gesticulate and point
to the other transvestite. The man removed an envelope from his inside jacket pocket and handed it to the
boy. The boy thanked him and kissed the man's hand.
The man with the intention to wipe his hand from the
kiss patted the boy on the back wiping his hand as he
did. He returned to his car and drove down the street.
The other on-lookers had dispersed leaving the blonde
wig transvestite alone in the parking lot. The other naked transvestite who had run down the street returned
and approached. They hugged each other, and then the
blonde one hand over the envelope the man had given
him. Several of the on-lookers had returned, hoping
the two were going to fight again. They were disap-
pointed as the transvestites holding hands walked
down the street. Ant looked back at his wall; he was

ready to continue the piece. Suddenly a noise below made him look back. Two men had begun to fight unlike the transvestite one this was for real and the fists where making their marks on each man's face. Blood poured from one man's nose splashing onto his and the other man's white tank top. A police car raced up the street and stopped just in front of the men. Ant slid behind the parapet before peering over it to see what was happening. A policeman and woman broke up the fight putting both men in handcuffs. Not before the female officer was punched in the breast by one of the men. She kneed him in groin as a response then twisting his arm up his back put the handcuffs on. The officers pushed the men into the police car and without speaking to anyone else drove down the street and away from the area. Ant had not realized how busy the street and parking lot was, every time he had been to the area, only a few prostitutes and their clients entered the street. He looked back over the parapet to see the area was now empty.

He returned to his wall and began to spray paint his piece. The letters where clear A N and T but so was the cartoon characters which sprang out of each letter. The woman being pushed down the escalator by the girl.

He stopped when he heard a car drive up the road to the parking lot. Crouching behind the parapet he watched as a man with gray hair and expensive Italian suit opened the door to allow a long-legged brunette woman step out. The two stood close talking intimately, the girl ran her slender hand down the side of the man's face. He tilted his head to enjoy the pleasure this simple gesture was giving him.

Ant smiled to himself he remembered the days his parents had been affectionate to each other. It was no longer the case, and he had on several occasions wondered why they had drifted apart. He even suspected his father of having an affair. Only to find out he really was working overtime so the family could buy a house in a nice neighborhood. To Ant his mother was sacred and he felt it was his duty to protect her from the horrors of the world. This thought started when he was a little boy and had on occasions caused arguments between his parents. Hence his father's belief that 'Anthony must be a mommy's boy'.

He returned to his terminus ad quem and began to fill in the body of the letters, the woman who had been pushed down the escalator was the tee and he spent time giving the tee shaped depth. This was a poor woman who was a victim and therefore entitled to be presented in the best possible way. He would leave the face until the end; he had been in China Town and watched, as they would paint the pupil of the eye on the dragon last. A symbolic act and for him putting the woman's face were going to be his symbolic end. The N was the escalator, as he stood back and looked at his work it looked more like a car than moving stairs. Putting the yellow strip down the side would give it a sense of movement and therefore the image of an escalator.

The girl Black Bee who had pushed the woman was only an outline; this was made easy because she never wore a dress or skirt. He began to give the figure black jeans, giving it depth with gray spray paint. The first scream didn't make him react but once the second one occurred and seemed to continue, he walked over to the parapet and looked down into the parking lot. The woman who earlier had shown the man some affection was being strangled by the expensive suited man. The woman was looking straight up at Ant, her left hand let go of the man and pointed up to him. Her expression of bulging eyes and open mouth infused itself on his mind. He quickly pulled back, and then slowly looked back over the parapet, only to see the man push the woman's dead body against the chain link fence. Her head was still facing him; the eyes less bulging and the face had become less tightly stretched.

Ant watched as the man kicked her legs together, then picked up her handbag and threw it into his car. The woman's hand still pointed up and her index finger was extended while the rest of the fingers curled into the palm. Ant sensed the man would follow the finger and drew back, he moved to the corner by the fire escape and through a hole which rainwater would drain off the roof. He looked down at the man, who was staring up to where the woman was pointing. The man stared hoping to see if anyone would peer over the parapet. From this position Ant watched the man give up staring and get into his car. The car sped down the road to brake screeching to a halt. The man stood by the driver's door and looked about, especially at the roof. Ant stayed hidden behind the parapet not knowing if the man had seen him. He crawled to the white wall and leaning against it too scared to peer down into the street below. For the first time in his brief life he had just witnessed a murder.

He closed his eyes and the woman's face reappeared looking at him. The decision to change the picture happened quickly and without any mental discussion.

He worked quickly to change the color of the woman's dress and hair. He altered the direction of the right arm and made it point upwards. Spraying the previous one with white paint to hide it.

The escalator became a car, the man's car, he was glad he hadn't painted the yellow stripe. On the side of the car he added the letters from the man's license plate. He stood back and looked at the picture, the escalator had never looked right, he must remember to work on it just in case he wants to use the image in the future. The A Black Bee figure soon became a man in a black suit. He worked fast on the man's face, he had only seen it briefly and wanted to make sure he remembered the way he looked. Feeling exhausted he stepped back and looked at the wall again, only the murdered woman's face left to do. He closed his eyes and seeing her face, began to transpose the image onto the wall. The eyes haunted him and he carefully worked to make the eyes of the picture as haunting as he could do.

Finally, he finished and stood back to look at his masterpiece. He shuddered, this was what he had really seen a murder and now it was captured for everyone to see.

One of the dogs below barked. He looked over the parapet by the escape ladder. Kaiser had woken and was barking at a man trying to get into the yard. He didn't recognize the man, but a little way down the road the car was parked and the murderer stood by the side of it. The murderer called to the other man who ran back to the car. Kaiser although still a little drugged was racing around the yard. Bill slowly woke and began to bark, not sure what at.

Ant realized he would have to find another way off the roof. He gathered his things, even taking the empty spray cans in case the police found them and his finger prints where all over them.

He stood looking at the roof, trying the door which was padlocked on the outside he dismissed it as a possible way down. He would have to find another escape route; he hadn't expected this kind of a problem but had been prepared if the dogs had woken. He didn't want to put the dogs back to sleep, as this was now a line of defense he really needed.

On the freeway side of the roof the parapet wall continued against the brick wall of the central building. Leaning over he could just see another flat roof on the other side of the brick building. He would need something to hold. Two pipes stretched the length of the brick building but where too high for him to get hold of. He would have to walk on tiptoe to hold them and touch the parapet wall. His hand found a wire, which had become embedded in the mortar between the bricks. It seemed to be strong as he tested its strength by pulling on it. The wire pinged out of the mortar, and ran across the brick wall. He would have to risk it, he could hear Kaiser and Bill barking and growling even louder. His backpack was lighter than when he had arrived so he didn't think this would cause him any problems. He placed a foot on the four-inch wide parapet wall and edged himself into position. He tested the wire one more time, before launching himself on this dangerous journey.

He slowly moved along the ledge, he grew more confident and once he was halfway between the two roofs, he stopped and relaxed for a few moments. The pop sound and a howl from one of the dogs woke Ant from

this brief rest. The black car slowed down on the freeway and Ant caught sight of it in his peripheral vision.
He wasn't sure if it was the murderer's car but he
wasn't going to wait and find out. He continued to
move along the ledge seeing the car drive off.
He was about three feet from the safety of the other
roof when he realized a man standing on the roof, he
had left was looking over at him. The man climbed
onto the ledge but after two steps he retreated to the
roof. The man grabbed the wire and taking a knife
from his pocket cut it, letting it fly into the air. Ant
felt the tension on the wire give and managed to grab
hold of the corner of the building. He scrambled on to
the roof not looking back to see if the man was following. He raced for the fire escape ladder and his heart
pounding began to slide down it, the soles of his feet
held against the edge. The friction on his hand began
to burn and he slowed himself and climbed down the
last few steps onto a platform. The street below was
empty, and he slid the extension ladder onto the sidewalk. He climbed down and watched as the ladder
slide back into position, expecting the man who was
up on the other roof to suddenly appear. He looked
one way then the other, he was trembling, and for the
first time in his life he was really scared. This was no
game, these men were serious, and he had unwittingly
seen a murder. A car turned into the street to the left
of him, Ant began to run to the right. He raced down
the road and at the cross street he ran straight across
making several cars brake and honk their car horns.
He arrived at the bus stop he had waited at for weeks,
and he now felt exposed and vulnerable. He entered a
small grocery shop and hovered by the door. The
owner behind the counter looked at him suspiciously,

as he kept peering out of the door into the street. Unable to just watch the shop owner circled around the counter and stood looking at Ant. Just as the owner was about to ask him what he was doing, the bus arrived. Ant quickly exited from the store and onto the bus, once again his heart pounded as though it was about to explode.

He found a seat near the back and slide down into it, before peering out of the window. He couldn't see any cars, which could be the murderers, but what if they had changed cars how would he know.

The bus stopped and a man in a gray suit entered, as he walked down the bus, he looked at each of the passengers. As he came level with Ant he stared and still stared as he took a seat a little way from Ant.

Ant slid lower into the seat and peered over the seat in front at the man. Why had he stared at him, he must be one of the murder's homies. They had found him and so quickly, he was going to be murdered on the bus in front of all the other passengers. He began to sweat and breathe heavily, looking anxiously from one passenger to another. He needed help, if he was going to be murdered. None of the other bus riders seemed the sort who would help, he was alone. The man in the suit rose from his seat and walked towards Ant. Staring straight at him. Ant's heart pounded he was not ready to die not this way at least. The bus stopped and the man passed Ant and descend the bus by the rear door. Ant took a deep breath and sighed out loud. A Latino woman sitting opposite looked at him intently. She sensed he had a problem and not wanting to get involved she turned to the front staring straight ahead. He tried to calm himself down, he was beginning to become stressed. Was he overreacting, and had his father's conspiracy theories taken control? The man, the murderer was after him, to kill him, had he imagined it? Was this what happens when you are so scared you start to invent problems? His mind raced trying to think and at the same time sift through the information it was being bombarded with. He had not realized he was such a panic merchant, always boasting how calm he is in a crisis and yet he was in full panic mode.

He had to get a grip on reality before he made a mistake and was murdered. The other passengers all seemed innocent people but looks could be deceptive. He looked for a friendly face someone he may have seen on his many visits to the area. He didn't recognize anyone, for the first time on this bus route he didn't see a single person he had seen before. Why today of all days, why had everyone he knew or had seen before chosen not to travel on this bus?

The bus slowed down and finally stopped. Several police cars had blocked the roadway ahead. Officers hiding behind their car doors guns pointing at a car, which had been stopped in the middle of the road.

"It looks like we are here for a little time, if you want to get off and walk let me know," said the driver.

A large woman carrying several grocery paper and plastic bags went to the driver.

"How long?" she asked in abrupt tone.

"Who knows I had one of these last year in Glendale and it lasted three hours," replied the driver ignoring her manner.

"Well in that case I will get off," she replied.

"If we get moving and I see you I'll pick you up you aren't hard to see," said the driver in a sarcastic tone.

The doors of the bus opened and several of the passengers alighted. Ant hesitated. He was about four blocks from the train station. If he walked up the back alleyways, he could make it quite quickly.

He looked at his watch. "Shit, I will be late for work." He whispered to himself.

He ran down the steps and onto the sidewalk, the road a head was blocked by policemen. He ran back to the cross street and down until he reached an alleyway. He looked behind, to see if anyone was following him. But the attention was focused on the police activity. The noise from the police and news stations helicopters drown out any normal street sound. People had abandoned their cars in the side street and made their way to the main road to see what was happening.

He entered the alleyway and ran until he reached the next cross street. He looked to the right and left before crossing the street, but like the street, before everyone's attention was on the police activity.

Feeling a little relaxed he slowed down and walked up the alleyway. From behind a blue dumpster three shaved hair young men appeared. They were about his age but he had never seen them before. Ant stopped, expecting trouble he thought about running back and quickly looked behind.

"Hey Ant man, what's happening?" said an acned face Latino youth.

"Mario," replied Ant relived to see someone he knew.

Mario looked at the three young men in front of Ant.

"He's cool," said Mario.

The three young men relaxed and joined Ant and Mario. The smell of marijuana emanated from the group, they were high and looking for fun. To them

causing grievous bodily harm was fun, the people
liked it or they wouldn't enter their territory would
they. Lucky for Ant he knew one of them or he may
have had trouble.

"Hey man what's happen in the street?" asked the
tallest and meanest of the young men.

"Cops," replied Ant

"Thought so," said Mario who began to sway and
then giggle.

"Looks like you guys are on some good stuff," said
Ant aware that you needed to pacify marijuana ad-
dicts.

"Yeah" is all one of the group could say before they
all burst into laughter.

"Sorry but I need to get to work," said Ant and ran
down the alleyway.

"You need anything," shouted Mario after him.
Ant stopped and turned and shouted back. "Stop anyone following me."

"You've got it man," called Mario before falling to
the ground laughing.
Ant had indulged in the weed, at one time he thought
he was becoming a real pot head. This like so many
other teenage things faded from his mind. He just
didn't see the need any more to get high by artificial
means. He had realized that the spray paint acted as an
agent to get high. That was why he wore a mask if he
was in a confined space doing a graffiti piece. He had
passed the drug phase of his life, now he was into art
to get a euphoric feeling.
He continued to run until he reached the station, at the
entrance he once again checked behind himself. It was
always wise to have your guard up. Well that is what

his father had verbally beaten into him as he grew up.
And for once he agreed.

He descended towards the platform taking the steps
two at a time. The platform was empty, but he quickly
walked the length of it to make sure.

Positioning against one of the gray concrete pillars at
the foot of the down escalator he took several deep
breaths and relaxed a little. Watching the travelers
pour onto the platform, he scrutinized each person.
When a well-dressed man, particularly in a suit regardless of race descended, he tensed and watched them
walk along the platform. This man was taller than
Ant, his suit was new and Italian looking, and only the
shoes gave the hint that the man had been through
some dust. As he rode the escalator down, he stared at
Ant, the corner of his mouth turned up in sneer. Ant
watched the man as he walked directly towards him.
Clenching his fist Ant knew it would do little damage
but at least in his mind he would have put up a fight.
As the man grew closer Ant could smell the over
whelming cologne the man was wearing. The man
brushed past Ant deliberately touching him.

The man said very quietly "Love to fuck your butt."
Ant smiled, he would have normally realized the man
was gay, and stepped out of his way when he approached. But the heighten stress had lowered his
street-smart senses. Ant contemplated calling after the
man saying, 'Nice cologne but did you have to mari-
nate in it.' But he chose not to, he needed to be anony-
mous today.

The southbound train slowly entered the station, the
train driver leaning out of his cab window and shouted,
    "Get back from the edge."

Several tourists of unknown origin had moved close to the edge to take photographs of the train entering the station.

The northbound train blew its whistle as it entered the tunnel.

Ant didn't move until everyone had boarded the southbound train. He stepped on to the carriage looking at the passengers. As the buzzer sounded and the doors began to close, he stepped out onto the platform and ran onto the northbound train, just as its doors were closing.

As the train pulled out of the station, he looked at the platform to see if anyone had exited the southbound train. The platform was empty.

The train thundered through the tunnels. Ant looked at each passenger. They seemed innocent enough, but a baby face is no indication of a monster underneath. He had read that somewhere and today it felt appropriate.

The train arrived at his station, the doors seemed to take forever to open and, in his impatience, he tapped the door window. He ran up the concrete stairs and onto the escalator taking them two at a time. His bus had just arrived, and he quickly found a seat at the back so he could peer out of the window at the travelers leaving the station. The bus pulled away before many of the people had exited the station, so for the first time that afternoon he relaxed. He had felt the paranoia grow inside of his head. It was stupid he kept telling himself, but it wouldn't go away. He suddenly felt cold and took the light black jacket his father had owned out of his backpack. His sister had claimed it was hers and for several weeks she would steal it and wear it until he began to hide it.

With only a few minutes to spare he arrived at the restaurant, the cooks and waiters sitting outside the kitchen door nodded or said 'hi' to him. Whether this was because they knew his uncle ran the place or that they liked him he wasn't sure. Before putting the backpack into the locker, he took out the empty spray cans, he had found he could dump them in the trash bin behind the restaurant. The room was small and only had enough room for one person. He locked the locker and unfolded the clean apron he found inside. His aunt had taken the task of always making sure her nephew had a clean apron. The door open and his Uncle Caesar entered. Ant was pushed against the wall so they both could stand inside the room.

"Anthony."

"Hi Uncle Caesar," said Ant in a depressed tone.

"You okay, you look pale as though you have seen a ghost."

"I'm fine, I had to run, so I wouldn't be late, I didn't want to let you down."

"That's a good boy, well you take it easy. I can't have you falling ill on me; your mother would never let me hear the last of it."

"I'll be okay."

"If you're sure, you had better get to the kitchen, I know they have a lot of pans and woks which need washing."

Ant entered the kitchen, the other workers all looked at him some smiled and nodded hello, and others just looked. The corner where he washed the pans and dishes was separate from the main kitchen. Two stainless steel sinks filled with water where piled high with pans and dishes. To the left of this area was the men's restroom and Ant had seen it used many times during his shift at washing up. He opened the dishwasher to see if it was empty so he could place the dishes he pre-washed into it. Several large cooking pans needed to be cleaned and he knew they took priority over the dishes. He began to scrub them, the restroom door open and an elderly man exited. He looked at Ant then returned to the dining room, walking into a busboy carrying a tray full of dishes.

"Hi," he said, "I'm Jon the new busboy."
He was a tall youth of mixed race, with his black hair dyed blond at the ends. Ant nodded and then took the plates from him and rinsed them before placing them into the industrial dishwasher. Ant returned to the pots.

Jon returned with more dishes and placed them on the metal table next to the sinks.

"Caesar your uncle?"
Ant nodded.

"Don't tell me you can't speak, had your tongue cut out by drug dealers while you were in prison for murdering the President."
Ant smiled then nodded.

Jon laughed, "At least you have a sense of humor, unlike some here. Got to go."
He rushed out of the kitchen into the restaurant.

Ant stop washing and a gray depressing cloud seemed to flow over him. If only Jon hadn't mentioned murder, he would have been okay. He had been trying to keep the image of the woman out of his mind, and now it flooded back.

The door from the restaurant opened and a very drunken man staggered in. The man stopped and looked at Ant obviously not knowing where he was going. Ant pulled from his melancholy pointed to the restroom. The man followed Ant's arm and stumbled into the rest room. The restaurant door opened again and a well-dressed man entered Ant tensed and kept the man in his side view. The man walked straight to the restroom and entered, then quickly withdrew saying

"Sorry."

He stood awkwardly by the restroom door, his embarrassment manifesting in his fidgety posture. This was interrupted by a little cough, as though he was trying to get someone attention.

"He should have locked the door," said the man hoping to get an agreement from Ant.

Who nodded, and the man smiled.

Jon returned with more plates.

"I just said to your friend the man in there should have locked the door."

"Drunk I think, what do you say?" said Jon looking in Ant's direction.

Ant nodded.

"He is such a talker this one,' said Jon indicating with his head in Ant's direction. "Got to go."

"So, have I," said the man.

"You want me to get the drunk out of there," asked Ant.

"Oh yes please, or someone will have to mop this floor."

Ant dried his hand on the apron and opened the restroom door. The drunken man had fallen asleep fully clothed on the toilet seat. Ant tried to wake him and then helped him to stand up. He guided the man out of the restroom, the other man rushed in and locked the door.

The drunk stood by the restaurant door when Jon burst out carrying a pile of plates. He swerved around the man and placed the plates on the metal table. Ant pushed the drunk through the doors and returned to his sink. If he didn't have to waste so much time with the customers, he would get the washing done in half the time he thought to himself.

"So, what's happening?"

"Drunk fell asleep."

"Figures, going."

Ant watched as Jon raced back into the restaurant. He placed a pile of plates into the dishwasher and started it. The man placed a hand on his shoulder, made him jump, he felt his bladder release and his underwear became wet. He turned slowly and saw it was the man who had been desperate to use the restroom.

"Here take this and thanks," said the man giving Ant five dollars.

"Thank you, sir," replied Ant remembered his Uncle telling him always 'thank' the customers if they give you something.

He watched as the man left, he felt his jeans under his apron the urine hadn't penetrated, but the now cold wetness felt uncomfortable.

Jon returned carrying more plates. "The place is buzzing tonight. What's your name?"

"Ant."

"Ants aren't they little annoying creatures that are everywhere you look?"

"Yeah."

"Figures. Got to go."

Ant moved some of the pots and pans he had cleaned to a wire shelf. With all these interruptions he was getting behind with his work. He continued to rinse the plates and was unaware of the man standing by the restroom looking at him. Ant wasn't sure why he turned and looked, except he had that feeling you sometimes get when you know someone is staring at you.

The man was staring and didn't move. Ant became uncomfortable and kept turning to look, all the while holding a large pan in his hand just in case, he needed it. The man continued to stare. Ant stopped what he was doing and stood looking at the man. He was in his early fifties looked as though he had a modicum income, from the clothes he was wearing. Jon entered from the restaurant and the man ran rushed into the restroom.

"Hey Ant, what's wrong?"

"That man who has just gone into the restroom, just stood there and looked at me."

"What was he wearing?"

"Black suit and yellow shirt and tie."

"Fag, I was watching him earlier he looks at all the young men."

"That's okay then, I got scared he looked as though he wanted to kill me."

"Why would he want to do that? Your just paranoid too much television kid," said Jon laughing as he left.

The restroom door opened, and the man looked out into the area. He looked at Ant then blushed before returning to the restaurant.

The night continued and Ant became tense whenever a suited man entered the area. He was paranoid because he had witnessed death.

Tonight, the conveyer belt of dishes from Jon slowed down, and he finally finished washing.

He collected his backpack threw the spray cans into
the dumpster and said goodnight to his fellow workers.

"Your Uncle has gone," said one of the waiters as he
opened the kitchen door onto the alleyway.

"Okay, have a good night," he said and left the restaurant.

The street was full of cars. It was as though the people
didn't recognize the difference from day and night. He
began to walk down the street, the thought of the murder reentered his head. If the men had seen him, then
he was sure they would be looking for him.

The car slowed and moved at his pace. He wasn't sure
if he should just run back to the restaurant. The window opened and the man who had been staring at him
from the restroom looked out. He smiled and said,

"can I give you a ride?"

Before Ant could reply Jon had appeared and putting
his arm around Ant squeezed his butt so the man could
see.

"Sorry man this one is mine."

The man nodded and the window closed as the car
drove away.

"Told you he was gay."

"Thanks, I think I'm a little paranoid tonight."

"No problem, you get use to them most are just looking for a pretty boy to play with."

"I'm not gay."

"Nor am I, but they are everywhere these days and
they look just like you and me."

"I know that."

"Good. I just didn't want you to stereotype that's all.
Any way I must get going, my wife will kill me if
I'm late. I have to be up early for my day job."

"You married?"

"Yes, two years and I have a beautiful little princess. My baby girl."

"How old are you?"

"Nineteen next Wednesday."

"Happy birthday," said Ant as Jon ran across the road to a car parked on the other side.

Ant watched him leave. He couldn't believe someone so young could be married. It must have been a mistake, he realized he was thinking about Jon rather than what he was going to do about the murder.

He had always believed he was street smart because the other kids at school thought he was a cool guy. He now began to understand he knew nothing about survival and wished he had spent more time with his father learning that stuff. He walked in the shadows, checking each car that passed, only relaxing as he turned into his own street. Nickman and Chris were weightlifting outside the apartment complex, seeing Ant they stared at him. Maybe they felt strong because they had been lifting weights, he wasn't sure, but he just gave them one of his stares and they went back to the weights.

Ant smiled after he had passed them, but his relax state disappeared as a car backfired and the horror of his situation returned.

He fell back onto his bed his breathing was heavy and irregular. Every sound he heard made him become tense. He felt he was going to burst.

His sister entered her side of the room and began to open drawers moaning that she couldn't find what she was looking for. She noticed Ant's jacket on the chair by the door and took it as she left the room.

Ant was scared, he didn't know if the killers had followed him and now knew where he worked and lived.

If they did then his parents and sister wherein danger,
all because of what he had seen. He remembered the
film 'Witness' and what that little boy had gone
through and that was only a film.

He sat up sharply in bed and opened his eyes the face
of the woman murdered was staring at him every time
he closed his eyes. He had to get away to protect his
family, he would have to hide until they found the killers. He hoped they would, but with so many unsolved
murders he wasn't sure they would.

The doorbell rang and he sprang out of bed, he needed
to answer it before his sister or mother did. He slowly
opened the door and looked outside. A small round
woman who was as round as she was tall stood looking
at him.

His mother gently pushed him to one side and opened
the screen door.

"Alice come in, you will have to excuse my son, but
he has been working all night and I think he is now
sleep walking."

The woman passed Ant and looked at him as though
he was a zombie.

Ant stood looking out into the street it seemed quiet
and peaceful, but as he knew looks are deceptive. He
returned to his room he had to get away just to protect
his family. It's what his father would do.

He took his backpack and emptied it so he could fill it
with essential items. His CD player and his case of
CDs to him life without it wouldn't be worth living. A
toothbrush and paste, hair bush and gel. His graffiti
note pad and a selection of pens and pencils.

He stripped and changed his underwear remembering
what had happened at the restaurant. He thought if he
was going to be on the run for a few days he needed to

start with clean ones. He looked at his bed and then the rest of his things, he would be back. He changed his shoes and socks he would need warm things if he was going to be sleeping on the streets.

He pondered if he should leave his parents a note, and after a mental discussion with himself he hastily wrote a note:

'Gone to Simon's for tonight and tomorrow to study for the exam. Will call you. Ant."

He placed it on the small table by the door in the hall under the statue of the Virgin Mary and the Holy Child. He knew his mother would always touch it before she left the apartment. He looked for his jacket but couldn't find it, his sister had taken it again, but he picked a thicker one. The nights can be very cold and he hated the cold.

He peered out expecting someone to attack him, but the street was empty. He closed the door quietly and ran across the street. He stood in the sunken parking lot of the apartment opposite and turned and looked back at his apartment. Susan came out of the door and was wearing his jacket with is distinctive yellow circle and lightning bolt motif on the back. For the first time realized how much they looked alike. He had spiked her hair and wore the same type of clothes he did. Maybe she was trying to copy him. The car had driven up the street without its headlight on. He watched as the gunfire erupted and Susan danced to each bullet that hit her. He screamed he wanted to run out but knew that if he did, he would be next. Why did she have to wear his clothes? He hit his head against the wall of the apartment he couldn't do anything and he had just caused his sister to be shot. He saw another car enter the street and he ran to the alleyway. Tears running down his face.

CHAPTER SEVEN

Investments

It always surprised Malachy when the bus turned onto the freeway on ramp. The bus only traveled a short distance on the freeway, this only happened at specific times of the day. The reason was never given and even the drivers didn't know why, or just didn't want to say. Most of the drivers were friendly but he occasionally came across one whose attitude was so bad they made the crazy passengers seem almost human. He sat looking out of the window, watching the cars drive by. One car, one person inside was obviously the reason why Los Angeles had a traffic problem. If only the public transport system could rival other cities, then there was a chance the congestion would ease. He looked around the bus the dirt and smell, not just of the bus but some of the passengers made him wish he hadn't sold his car. He could be out on the freeway driving by himself listening to his favorite music program on the radio. It had been an impulsive act, one he now regrets and wished he could turn the clocks back. He was still angry with himself. The car was a wreck and needed a lot of repairs. He wasn't even sure if it would have passed the smog test, not without a little bit of bribery.

His attention returned to the outside world, a little way ahead the usually white wall, which seemed so out of place, as everywhere else in the area had been gratified. He saw the picture any art gallery would have been proud to hang. He looked at it as the bus drove slowly by, he instantly knew who had created the piece, well something like it, and it was the same but somehow different. It was no longer an escalator but a car and a woman lying on the ground pointing up towards the sky. The bus stopped as the traffic came to a halt, there was never a reason for the stoppage, yet it happened every morning in the same spot. He stared at the faces they were different from the sketch he had seen. The woman pointing to the sky looked familiar, he had seen her before, and she wasn't the woman who had fallen down the escalator. He wasn't sure where, and it wasn't a face type, the artist had captured a real likeness of a woman he had seen. It would come to him. he would remember, he never forgot a face.

The bus started to move and collected speed as it drove down the off ramp. Its journey on the freeway was over until another day. He sat deep in thought, why couldn't he remember where he had seen the pointing woman. The whole graffiti piece had been changed. He wondered what had happened to the young artist who created the art to change it. Had it been changed, or did he just remember the piece wrong, he would have to go and look at the original small drawing.

As a child his grandfather had taken him to many art galleries, 'to see famous works of art' his grandfather would say. At first, he reluctantly accompanied him, but as time went on, he began to appreciate what his grandfather was doing. Several years later when his fifth-grade class had a field trip to an art gallery he became a star pupil for his knowledge of the paintings and their painters. As a result, he was able to ask Lisa Marie Baldwin out on a date. It was only once but she was in love with his knowledge, until she realized he knew nothing about literature. He spent the summer reading and trying to understand the grand scheme of things. His grandfather was amazed he didn't want to go outside and goof around with his friends. For him he had one ambition to win back the love of his life. Sadly, when he did it wasn't the same, she had changed, and he had changed. Once again, he was glad of the experience, he had become a bookworm because of love and now he loved books.

He continued to daydream as he entered the office, it was different something had changed, there was no enthusiasm and energy. This made the beginning of the day miserable and as his legs began to hurt, he wished he could sleep for a whole week. The morning dragged on. He didn't dislike his job only on days like this did he wish he were somewhere else. The melancholy was like a cloud hovering over him. His colleagues sensing his mood and kept their distance. They had learnt from experience to give him space.

The picture of the graffiti he had seen on the white wall was on the office televisions suddenly caught his attention. He turned the small speaker on his desk up so he could hear the news item.

"Police are not sure if the graffiti has anything to do with the murder of the prostitute found in the street below. Now for the weather in your area." Malachy turned the speaker off. What murder, there had been no murder. He smiled at his own stupidity in a city when every day someone die's violently most wouldn't be considered murder.

He went to the mail room and found a copy of the local daily newspaper, scanning the front page and several inside before he found a picture of the graffiti and then read the article.

"What are you reading?" asked Vernon the mailroom operative.

"About a murder, some prostitute was murdered last night."

"Yeah I read about that, two dogs were shot as well."

"Interesting."

"What is?"

"I know them."

"You know the prostitute?"

"No, Vernon get your mind out of your pants, I know who did the graffiti. Well I've seen others by him. Thanks Vernon can I keep the paper?"

"Sure," said Vernon adjusting his pants a little petulant after being told to get his mind out of them.

Malachy slide into his seat, he had been away from his desk a little too long and hoped no one noticed. A picture of a woman he thought he knew appeared on the television monitor. He turned the speaker knob on as the news item changed.

"Who was that woman?" he asked Rosemary who had been standing at a printer looking at the television screen.

"The prostitute who was murdered last night."

"Really she reminds me of someone, but I'm can't remember who."

"She looks like that actress who always plays prostitutes on Law and Order."

"No, I've seen her recently, and she didn't look like a prostitute."

"Malachy you're just dreaming again."

"Maybe."

He continued to work but kept one eye on the television monitor looking for the news item to appear again. He had the speaker on his desk turned low. Forty-five minutes later the picture of the woman appeared on the screen he turned up the speaker and listened.

"Police today are looking for anyone who may have seen this woman last night. She was found murdered in a roadway under the freeway, a location used by transvestite prostitutes and their clients. Police would also like the graffiti artist who spray painted this last night to come forward as they may have vital information regarding this murder. The police are not sure if the killing of the two dogs close to where the woman was found is related. Now today's other news..."

He continued to look at the screen his mind wandering, he felt he was involved, not only because he knew who the artist was but because he also had seen the woman before.

"Malachy." He jumped and turned to face Marie Rossi a young client analyst. "That information you wanted on the Fahey account, I didn't find much it was opened about three years ago and has a P.O. Box address. There are three names attached to the account. Oh, and it was made restricted access about two years ago but doesn't say who ordered it. Sorry it's not much."

"That's it she was the woman who came here yesterday."

"Which woman?"

"The one who was murdered last night."

"The prostitute?"

"She wasn't a prostitute, not when she came here."
Marie looked at him, she sniffed the air wondering if
he had been drinking.

"If you say so Malachy." She returned to her desk a
puzzled expression on her face.

He looked at the information she had given him on the
Fahey account, the three names on the account where
Anthony Drongotti, Helmet Von Davian and Monica
Trystwold. He picked the handset and dialed the re-
ception desk.

"Reception, how can I help you?" said the bright eager young voice of Michelle Greengrass.

"Malachy here, yesterday Mister Thompson had
three guests, did you get their names."

"Let me look," there was a pause and Malachy heard
the soft breathing of Michelle and the turning of
pages. "No, I don't have anything written down, are
you sure he had guests?"

"But three people came you must remember, two
men and woman."

"Sorry Malachy I don't remember in fact we had no
visitors yesterday."

He replaced the handset, stood up to see if Mark was
in his office. Mark was bending over his round conference table in the center of the room. He was reading the Wall Street Journal unaware Malachy now
standing in his doorway.

He suddenly looked up, a suspicious look on his face.

"Malachy, what can I do for you?"

"Yesterday you had four visitors regarding the Fahey
account."

"I don't remember seeing anyone yesterday, are you
sure it was on my calendar?"

"Yes, but there was nothing on your calendar and you know how I like to keep things up to date."

"I'm sorry Malachy I don't think I saw anyone yesterday I went to San Diego all day if you remember, because you cancelled my hair appointment at NoNo's. Did you ask the receptionist maybe they came to see someone else and asked for me as head of the office?"

"The front desk said there were no visitors yesterday."

"There you are then, and the Fahey account is restricted access only, it's the account of a famous person who doesn't want people to know who they are."

"But Mark they came, I saw them, and the woman is now dead, murdered and they say she was a prostitute."

"Your imagination is working overtime again. You have been reading too many murder books. I have a lunch appointment with a client, so try to keep the office going and no more fantasies about dead people please."

Mark stood up put his jacket on and briskly pushed past Malachy, exiting the floor via one of the side doors. Malachy watched him go. Mark had changed, he had transformed into a secret hoarding employer. Something wasn't right. He had seen the woman and the three men, and the woman was the murder victim. It somehow all fit together, the three people, Mark, the murder, and Ant the graffiti artist. The woman who came to the office yesterday and the one in the graffiti piece where the same person. He just couldn't get it out of his mind. The rest of the day went slowly by, Mark didn't return from his lunch. To Malachy it wasn't the denial of those around him, but the man he had come to trust and admire suddenly had lied to him. He felt nauseous and watched the digital clock change the minutes until he could leave.

The news item repeated it endlessly during the remaining day. Each time Malachy saw it he was positive the woman who had been murdered was the woman who he had seen in the office the day before. His irritation had distracted him so much when it as time for him to leave he didn't notice the time.

"You still here?" asked Rosemary.

He looked at the clock, he was twenty minutes late in leaving and there would be no chance of putting the extra time down to overtime.

"Just leaving Rosemary, some of us don't watch the clock."

"Really I always thought you did. Remember it's the long weekend."

"Oh yes, thanks I forgot, I hope Mark remembers he didn't last time and came into the office the last long weekend."

Malachy collected his things together and closed his computer. As he passed Elizabeth Dellman's office he waved and shouted "Good night."

She turned and looked at him her face set in a hard-non-responsive look.

The elevator was as usual slow, the doors opened and a woman in a vivid green cotton suit stood in one of the corners. She looked at him then repositioning her feet said, "I didn't realize it was going up."

Malachy nodded and pressed the lobby button. The elevator descended and stopped several floors below. The woman exited. Bruce Weaver entered he gave Malachy a nod of the head before turning to face the elevator doors. Malachy looked at him, what was this man really doing? He seemed to always be there watching and waiting. In the lobby the man walked briskly away without looking back at Malachy. The walk from the office to the bus stop took about ten minutes, today it seemed to take longer. The reasoning voice in Malachy's head began to argue with him what he should do. Having convinced himself he couldn't let the situation just go. He planned to go to the police station to let them know what he thought he knew. It was a long journey from this bus stop to the police station and Malachy knew he would spend the whole time debating what he should do.

Elizabeth Dellman had been the administrator of the office for seventeen years. She had seen a great many people employed and then leave, some because they wanted to, others where, to use the company's word, terminated.

She had over the years learnt not to be affected by the changes. In some of the terminations she had been the instigator in the firing. You either play her game or she would find a way to get rid of you. Her collection of personal secrets about the employees, although never mentioned in public, was known by most of the office. To some she had become the evil Ms. Dellman, blackmailer. In her own mind she didn't see it as blackmail, just another business deal to pay for her expensive vacation and luxury items.

She had been threatened several times by those who were fired, but always laughed it off as *just meaningless words*. Why would anyone want to hurt her, is what she would say when someone asked if she feared the threats.

Monica Budarbin's threats earlier in the day when she was fired from her client analyst position didn't worry

Elizabeth. So as not to deal with the constant questions from the other employees as to what had taken place. She had closed the blinds on her large window, which gave an extensive view of the sales floor.

She was busy typing a reply to an email when her door opened and closed, she didn't hear it.

Her phone rang, she picked up the handset, straighten the spiral cord in her usual manner. She hated the cord to be twisted and therefore difficult to deal with.

"Hello." She bellowed into the mouthpiece. The only reply was static and silence.

As she went to replace the hand set a hand took it from her.

Unthinkingly she said, "Thank you."

The cord was around her neck and being pulled tight before she realized there was anyone else in her office. As the cord unwound from the spiral shape the murderer had to pull harder and harder to get the required effect on Elizabeth.

Taken by surprise she had died quicker than the killer had expected. She hadn't stuck her tongue out or her eyes bulged. It was as though she had just fallen asleep. The Killer checked to see if she was dead before removing the cord from around her neck. They straightened the cord before replacing the handset on the cradle.

The murderer placed Elizabeth's hands on the keyboard and propped her to face the monitor. Then bending over they picked the infamous notebook out of her handbag, flicked though it before tearing each page out and placing them into Elizabeth's shredder under her desk.

Once the murderer had finished shredding the secrets of the office. The hard cover had been placed into the regular trash bin. The killer wiped everything they had touched with a cloth. At the door they gave the blind cord a little pull to open them just enough for anyone who is looking in to see Elizabeth at her computer. Flicking the lock switch on the doorknob, so as they closed it from the outside it would be locked, the murderer left the office closing the door behind them. Malachy Moss had no clue as to what had just happened at the office as he climbed the steps to the Burbank Police Station. The steps were made of gray concrete with dark brown stains trailing up or down. He hoped that it wasn't blood. As he entered the station, he was amazed how cold and uninviting the place was. If the police really wanted the public to help solve crimes, then they needed to make the place more welcoming. The large thick sheets of glass, which dominated the communication area, meant most people would shout at the police officers behind it. Malachy looked at the woman officer behind the glass.

"Yes sir."

She had that hard as nails look, which most television cops showed as stereotyped.

"I would like to speak to someone about the murder of the woman under the freeway."

He slowly shouted the words in hope that she heard him through the glass.

"No need to shout sir, I can hear you quite well."

"Sorry, but this glass is so thick."

"But there is a microphone in the wooden base."

"That would be the woman who died yesterday sir?"

"Yes, I think I know who she is."

"If you would like to take a seat over there sir, I will find someone who can help you sir."

"I don't need help! I want to help you."

The officer ignored this comment and went into the back area of the station. Malachy looked at the line of benches she had indicated, they were fixed to the floor and set against the wall.

"As if someone would want to steal the benches."
He said loudly to himself.

A young man with a woman who was obviously his mother sat nervously on one of the benches. He wrung his hands several times before drying them on his oversized jeans. He looked at Malachy, the face of someone who wanted to be anywhere but here. Malachy nodded and sat at the other end of the bench. He didn't want to get into conversation with either the son or the mother. And he wasn't sure if they spoke much English, as they looked Hispanic but could have been from the Middle East.

He sat on the hard-wooden seat, electric shock pain surged in his feet, the usual effect when he relaxed himself. He has become so used to the pain he didn't really notice it only flinching when it became very intense. He needed to find out more about his condition, but the Internet hadn't really yielded much information about CIDP.

The door at the end of the entrance hall opened and a tall thin man in a soft olive-green suit crossed to the front desk. The female officer behind the glass indicated with her head towards Malachy.

The man approached him seemed to get bigger the closer he came. The man towered over Malachy who had not realized how tall the man was. Whoever had designed the paint work inside the station had created an illusion of size.

"Good evening Sir, I believe you may have some information regarding the murder of a young woman."

"Yes, I think I know who she is."

"Would you like to follow me sir into an interview room and I will get all the relevant information."

He stood and walked behind the detective, who was about six foot seven inches tall. They waited at the door for someone to buzz them in after the detective had pressed a button, which was covered in dirt and the words press to enter had faded with the constant use.

The waiting room was a cold pastel blue color with two chairs and table, and like the bench outside, was fixed to the floor.

The detective sat down and faced Malachy staring at him as though he was waiting for him to confess to the murder, or at least any murder.

"I'm Detective Campbell, now how can I help you sir?"

"I think I know who the woman was."

"Which woman Mister...?"

"Malachy Moss, the woman who was found murdered under the freeway today."

"The prostitute?"

"She wasn't one, and I think her name was Monica Trystwold and she lives in Santa Barbara."

"I see sir and why do you think that?"

"Well she came to our office yesterday, I think."

"You're not sure?"

"Well I know the woman who was murdered came to the office, I think."

"You seem very vague about it."

"When I asked others at the office about seeing her in the office, they said they hadn't. But I am sure, she was the woman or a woman very much like her."

Malachy jumped in his chair a violent electric shock pain attacked his left foot. Detective Campbell looked at him inquisitively.

"Is there a problem sir?"

"No problem, I have a rare disease which sometimes gives me electric shock type pains."

"I see." Said Detective Campbell looking at the door as though he wanted to make a quick escape. "If you would excuse me, I will be back in a moment I need to check up on something."

Malachy nodded his head and watched as the detective left the room. He sat looking around the room and wondered how many people had been questioned in this room. There didn't seem to be any blood stains, but the room had recently been painted. He stood up and began to pace around the room. At first it was normal steps but then he started to take small then long steps, this soon changed to a few hops on one leg then with both knees close together. The pain returned to his legs, he stopped hopping as the pain grew worse. For some that had never experienced this type of pain it would be hard for them to understand what it felt like he thought.

He began to hop lightly from one foot to the other as the detective returned. Detective Campbell stopped at the door and looked at Malachy as though he had gone mad.

"Mister Moss we checked up on Monica Trystwold in Santa Barbara, she died several years ago five to be precise."

"Oh, I just thought…"

"Thank you for taking the time to telling us the information we really appreciate your help."

"I wasn't much help."

"That is what most people think, but we have been
able to eliminate Ms. Trystwold from our inquiries
because of your information."
"Well yes there is that I suppose."
Detective Campbell held out his hand, "Thank you
again Mister Moss."
Malachy shook the officer's hand, but something was
not right with the way he had spoken. He wasn't sure
if it was the tone or the words he used, why did people
in authority always use the word we and ours. Who
were they speaking on behalf of?
"I know she came to our office."
"If you find out any other information please don't
hesitate to contact us."
"I will. I know she came I'm not blind and I am not
stupid either."
The detective led Malachy back to the reception area,
shook his hand and opened the door on to the street.
He gave a little push, as he shook Malachy's hand
again which seemed to force Malachy to run down the
steps and onto the sidewalk.
Looking back at the building he noticed the blinds on a
window on the second-floor snap closed. Was he becoming paranoid or was something odd about what
had just occurred? He needed to think, or at least go
over in his mind the events. He also needed to drink
something he felt dry as though he was starved of water.
One thing he could count on was the endless coffee
shops in the city, it was as though every corner had
one. He sat down in the first one he came too, began
to replay his encounter with the law. The police Detective Campbell didn't ask him a lot of questions, it
was as if he already knew the answer and just wanted

to know how much he knew. Then he was dismissed so quickly or was it because the officer thought he might have been a lunatic. One of the many crazy people on the streets. No, there was definitely something wrong, if he could only put his finger on it. He would go back to the police station and confront the officer.

Opening the station door, he was surprised to see the place empty, a smiling police officer stood behind the thick glass reception counter.

"Good evening sir how can I help you."

"I would like to see Detective Campbell please."

"Detective Campbell, I don't think we have a Detective Campbell at this station sir."

"I just met him here about an hour ago."

"Really, let me ask someone he may be a visiting officer from another station."

The officer picked up the phone on the counter and dialed a number. He turned his back on Malachy so he couldn't hear what was being said.

The officer returned to face Malachy.

"Sir I checked we have no Detective Campbell at the station nor has one been here in the last few days answering to that name."

"But I just met him an hour ago; he took me through that door into an interview room."

"Sir I'm sorry as I have said we do not have a Detective Campbell at this station."

Malachy stood staring at the officer; he didn't know what to say. The officer stared back and gave a weak smile. Malachy smiled back and said, "Maybe I should file a missing person report."

The officer laughed "Goodbye sir and I am sorry not to be able to help you."

"You may have already. It's what is not said that gives the clues into solving the case of the missing police officer."

He turned and walked briskly out of the station and across the street. He stood in the doorway of the Bail Bond Company. He was even more convinced that something wasn't right and he was going to find out what it was.

As he crosses the street, he looks up the side of the police station, two men were talking at a side door. He was sure he recognized them but at a distance it was hard to be completely positive.

Running back to the traffic lights; pain surged up his legs. He kept forgetting he now had a problem and there was a lot he could no longer do. Running was something he had enjoyed at school. Even had hopes of competing in national track events but like so much in his life it faded. Stopping at the corner of the building and peered around to look closer at the two men. He knew them, the first was Detective Campbell, he recognized him by the repulsive suit he was wearing. The second man to his shock was none other than Bruce Weaver. Malachy slide back around the corner so something was going on and it had to do with the Weinstocks and Boller Investments.

He returned to look at the men just as they were shaking hands. Bruce Weaver reentered the police station. Detective Campbell ran across the street and began to walk up the sidewalk. Malachy waited, he wants to get a little distance between them so he could follow and not be recognized easily. He started to follow, keeping close to the building just in case he had to dart into a doorway or pretend to be shopping. The cat and mouse adventure stretched several blocks, he was surprised Campbell hadn't turned around. He was too far behind to be seen in any shop window.

The detective had stopped at a traffic light and Malachy realized he was now very close to the man. He pretended to look in a shop window as the detective looked about him. If he noticed Malachy then he didn't show it. The light changed and the detective ran into a larger department store.

Janice Smart was just finishing her afternoon break, and as she did every day, she was looking at the leather handbags. She had developed a fetish for handbags at a very early age, but the cost of these had made it so she could only look. Detective Campbell approached her. He didn't say anything but just looked at her. She looked up and saw him giving a weak smile.

She had always aspired to be a sales associate so in her best-spoken manner she asked, "Can I help you sir?"

Malachy entered the department store and saw Campbell and Janice Smart talking together. He watched as Janice animatedly pointed this way then the other. The detective took a piece of paper out of his pocket and began to search for a pen. Janice handed him her white plastic pen she always carried in her pocket. He made a few notes folded the paper and returned it with the pen into his pocket. He thanked Janice and left the store by a side exit.

"Can I help you sir?" Said a woman dressed in a dark blue two-piece suit, with a gold name badge precariously pinned just above her left breast.

Malachy looked at the badge and read Annette Jordan Assistant Manager First Floor. She took a deep breath, which made the badge raise higher his eyes followed it. As she exhaled the air, he slowly looked her in the face.

"No thank you, I..." he trailed off and rapidly chased after Detective Campbell into the street.

Campbell was climbing to a black sedan, with a uniformed driver. The car pulled into the traffic flow before speeding off up the road. Malachy began to follow the car after running a short distance he suddenly realized the futility of his action. He returned to the department store, if he couldn't catch the detective then he would speak to the girl.

Walking around the floor looking for the young girl, unable to find her after two circuits he spotted Annette Jordan walking towards him. He picked up a leather handbag and turned it over in his hand as Annette slid herself next to him.

Without looking at her he said, "I'm really sorry about that I thought I saw someone from work."

"Where you looking for something in particular sir, for your wife may be?"

"The sales assistant my friend was talking to disappeared."

"Sir which Sales Associate do you mean?"

"She had on one of your uniforms except she wore trainers on her feet."

"Oh, that will be Janice sir, she's not a sales associate, she doesn't work on this floor sir."

"Where does she work then?"

"In the basement sir, in returns."

"The basement."

"Where you looking for anything in particular?"

"Yes, shoes black shoes."

"Men's shoes are on the second floor turn left once you step off the escalator."

"Thank you, Annette."

"My pleasure sir, the escalator is this way sir." She began to walk towards it.

Malachy followed and as he traveled to the next floor he looked back at Annette. She was looking up at him her expression had changed and a cloud of suspicion had enveloped her face.

He walked aimlessly around the second floor passing the shoe department several times. He needed a reason to go down to the basement.

His third passing of the shoe department he stopped and picked up a brown leather casual shoe. It smelt new, but not the real leather smell he knew shoes should have. He turned it over and looked at the label underneath. Made of leather composite, he wondered what that was. His attention went to the man behind him who was talking to the sales associate. "Do you think you have some in you warehouse?"

"I'm sorry sir we no longer carry that style, it was last summer's collection. Their maybe an odd pair in the returns department."

"You know what style I'm talking about?" The man handed the sales associate a picture of the shoes he had cut from a glossy magazine. He continued his description; "They are square across the front with black tassels."

"Yes sir, I know the ones you mean, as I said we had them last year, but let me show you the latest style."

The associate placed the glossy page into a small bin, which was under one of the display tables.

Malachy grinned to himself, luck was on his side to-day. The sort of day he should do the lottery. He moved over the display table with the bin under it and picked up a shoe, he looked around the floor to see if anyone was watching him. He looked back at the shoe he was holding, a pink plastic high heel with a fluffy bobble on the front he replaced it on the display table. He gave a little laugh quickly bent down and retrieved the glossy page from the bin.

At the top of the escalator he peered down to the floor below. Annette Jordan stood at the foot of the moving stairway. He took several steps back; he didn't want her to see him. He needed the elevator to avoid the nosy Ms. Jordan. At the far end of one of the aisles a sign hung from the ceiling with an arrow pointing to the right with the word elevator in bright blue letters. A large group of women with baby buggies crowded around the elevator entrance, he would have to be patient. The mothers and their babies began to be transported to the different floors. Malachy followed a woman with a crying baby into the elevator; she pushed the first-floor button.

"What floor?" she called.

"Basement" replied Malachy.

"Sorry no basement button here."

The elevator doors slowly closed and it traveled at a very slow pace down to the floor below. The door opened even slower, the woman and her crying baby walked briskly out, he began to follow and then saw Annette Jordan standing with her back just outside. He quickly pulled himself into the elevator and pushed the second-floor button. An old man began to enter as the doors closed, they stopped closing as a female arm shot across them.

"Let me hold the doors for you sir," said Annette Jordan.

Malachy forced himself against the wall of the elevator; if Annette looked inside, she would see him. Her hand slithered out from holding the door, she had not seen him. He gave a large sigh of relief, as he waited for the doors to close. The old man suddenly stuck his walking stick out so the doors wouldn't close. Malachy stop breathing.

"Which floor for men?" asked the old man.

Annette Jordan stepped forward and looked in to the steel box.

"The second-floor sir."

"Okay," said the old man who pressed the button for the second floor, it lit a soft amber.

Malachy had lowered his head hoping she wouldn't see him. He chanced a look and slowly raised his head. It was moments like this he wished he had long hair and he could look through it without being seen. Annette was staring straight at him, a glare of fury intertwined with a look of pleasure having caught the murderous villain. They made eye contact, but the doors closed before she could react.

When the doors opened on the second floor a small crowd of mothers and babies in their buggies had gathered outside the elevator. Malachy slipped out of the elevator, he could see Annette pounding her way to the elevator, the mothers and babies had blocked her from seeing him. He looked around to see if there was any where he could hide, a white door marked 'employees only' and been left open. He pushed open the door and walked into the passage and closed the door. One of the faults Malachy had which he had been told about all his life was he could never leave anything alone. He opened the door and peered out on to the shopping floor. Annette Jordan was trying to see into the elevator, but it was full of crying babies and the even louder mothers. She had not seen him enter the employee area.

The service elevator a little way along the passageway opened and an old man pushed an empty cloth side skip out into the passageway. He then tried to pull a full skip into the elevator, Malachy pushed from the other side, and the old man looked up and gave a toothless smile. Once they were inside the elevator the old man stood up slowly from his bent over position.

"Thanks," said the old man, "which floor do you want?"

"Basement please."

"Basement." Repeated the old man as though he was astonished anyone would want to go down there.

"Yes, I need to see Janice."

"Oh Janice, crazy Janice who talks to herself."

"Yes, that Janice."

"She a nice girl really but they do treat her as though she is mad, I think she's just lonely. I talk to her sometimes and you would be very surprised at the things she knows. I think she would be good on that Jeopardy program."

The elevator arrived at the first floor and Malachy helped the old man push the skip out into the corridor.

"Thanks again, say hi to Janice for me."

"I will..." He looked at the old man's name badge and read it, "...Bert."

Malachy stepped back into the elevator as the doors began to close and descended into the basement.

It contrasted with the public floors, quite a different world. The fading yellow paint on the walls was not helped by the dirty beige colored linoleum floor covering. The ceiling lights where placed at twenty feet apart and was obviously very low wattage. On the

wall opposite the elevator a sign with an arrow read
'returns'. He followed the sign until he found an open
door, which had a large sign hanging precariously by
one nail above the door. It read "returns department."
Malachy entered and found himself in a large room
full of shelves, which had boxes neatly placed on
them. Just inside the door and to the right was a table
piled high with clothes.
Janice appeared out one of the isles between the racks
of shelves. She was talking to herself. "I know I've
seen him before, and not just on the bus. I don't think
he is a nice man..." She stopped talking when she saw
Malachy standing just inside the room.
"Hello, I don't normally get visitors."
"I'm sorry for interrupting your discussion, but I'm
trying to find a size eleven in a particular style of
shoe. The girl on the second floor said you might
have a pair down here in returns."
"She shouldn't have sent you down here, what do the
shoes look like?"
"Well they were all the crazy last year, low heel and
square toed, black with brown trim." He handed her
the picture he had retrieved from the trash bin.
"Size eleven." She looked at the picture and entered
one of the aisles. "He wants a size eleven, big feet
for a man his size." She suddenly shouted to Malachy. "I will be with you in a moment sir."
"Take your time."
"This must be them, what do you think?"
Malachy was wondering whom she was talking to.
She returned empty-handed and gave him the picture
back.
"Sorry sir we only have a nine and half size and they
were a display pair."

"That's that then, I'm sorry for interrupting your conversation."

"I wasn't talking to anyone; I work down here on my
own."

"Oh, I thought you were talking to someone."

"No just me on my own."

"Don't you get lonely?"

"No not really, I talk to my friends." She pointed to
the four mannequins and then gave a girlish giggle.

"A one-sided conversation."

"That's true, but those poor dears don't have much to
say and now there are only four left last week we had
over thirty. But I do listen sometimes and hear the
most unbelievable things."

"Listen?"

"Yes, if I move this board, I can hear what's being
said somewhere upstairs."

She moved a small twelve-inch square board from an
old heating vent. Malachy moved closer to the vent.
Janice pointed and whispered "Listen."

"Miss Pingham, I'm not sure what you are imply-
ing," said a man voice.

"Well, let me put it plain and simple Mister Brandish
unless you start to take care of me financially, I will
go to Mister Lewis with my evidence."

"What evidence do you have?"

"I have printouts, which show how you have been
stealing money from the company to take your mistress out."

"I don't know what you are talking about."

"Don't play dumb with me Mister Brandish, or may I
call you Darren? Or better still how about 'My big
bad wolf'."

"Where did you get that from?"

"I have hard evidence and I will go to Mister Lewis and your wife unless you pay up."

"Carol my dear I will need to think this over."

"Talk to your mistress more like."

"That too, let me get back to you."

"Well don't take too long."

Somewhere out in the corridor a door opened, Janice and Malachy looked at each other. Janice replaced the board.

"Rehearsal for a play, that's what they were doing."

"Possibly, do you know who they were?"

"No, we don't have anyone called Darren Brandish or Carol Pingham. I know everyone who works here, that's why I think it must be a rehearsal for a play."

A voice echoed down the corridor. "Janice who are you talking to?"

Janice put her index finger to her lips, and then said, "Hello who's there?"

Annette Jordan appeared in the doorway she looked at Malachy then at Janice. A sneer of disapproval washed over her face.

"Janice what are you doing and who is this gentleman."

"He came looking for a pair of shoes, he has a picture of the ones he wants, and they are last summer's style."

"That may be so but what is he doing down here."

"The sales girl in the men's department on the second floor said there might be some in the returns section in the basement so I came down to find out."

"The sales associate on the second-floor men's department sent you down are you sure?"

"Positive, she said I might find a pair if I go down to the basement."

"Did they, I will speak to them later, I'm sorry sir but
customers are not allowed in this area."
"We didn't have his size, so I wasn't able to help
him."
"Yes Janice, now you get on with your work."
"It wasn't this young lady's fault. I was sent down
by the girl on the second floor. Janice here has been
most helpful a credit to the store."
"Yes sir, thank you. I'm sorry we couldn't find the
shoes you wanted. You might want to try one of our
other stores."
"I will."
"Now if you follow me, I will show you the way
back to the shopping floor." She turned and walked
out into the corridor. She shouted over her shoulder,
"Janice I will be back in a moment to talk to you."
"Yes Misses Jordan."
Malachy looked at Janice and gave her a smile and a
little wave. Janice waved back a little girl look on her
face.
Annette Jordan was waiting at the service elevator; she
was one of those women who enjoyed being a supervi-
sor. It made her feel she had power over others; it
gave her a sense of being in control. Her mother had
always ordered her and her sisters around and it was
Annette's turn to order people of less standing around.
It wasn't she felt superior to others but she knew she
was, her father had always said they were not an ordinary family.
They stood in silence looking at the elevator doors
both wishing they would open. Malachy hated this
feeling of awkwardness and began to move his balance
from one foot to the other. Annette looked at him; she
wasn't sure why he was so fidgety.

"She really was trying to be helpful."

"Yes sir, but we can't have customers wandering around down here. I'm sorry the sales associate in the men's department misled you. But Janice should have known better."

"Why is Janice at fault?"

"She should have called to say a customer was down here, so they are both at fault."

"Oh, I see collective guilt, so you blame everyone that way you do not single out anyone. I really hate that attitude, if the girl on the second floor had not told me to go to the basement I wouldn't have gone, it is her fault. But if you run this store by blaming everyone then that's what you do."

He felt the anger and frustration rise inside him this is what happens at his company and it was so unfair.

"Sir how we run this company is really none of your business."

Her tone had shown him that she was nothing but a dictator.

"What is your name?"

"Miss Jordan, why?"

"Well, when I make a complaint about what has happened, I want to make sure I get your name right."

The elevator arrived and as the door opened Bert was standing just inside, he looked at Annette then at Malachy who put a finger to his lips. He hoped Bert understood the gesture and wouldn't acknowledge him.

"Hello Misses Jordan how are we today?"

"Very well Bert."

"That's good."

The elevator arrived at the first floor and Annette and Malachy exited it. She walked briskly on to the shopping floor.

"Do you need to buy anything else sir?"

"No, I don't think so."

"Let me show you the quickest way out on to the street."

She led the way out into the street. After Malachy had exited, she closed the glass door and stood looking at him. He walked down the street, he wanted to get away as quickly as he could, and he could feel her eyes still on him. At the corner he turned and leant against the building and took a deep breath. He needed a coffee and somewhere to sit down.

CHAPTER EIGHT

Something is Wrong

Malachy sat in the coffee shop. The vanilla white chocolate mocha was too hot to drink so he just stared at it. He wasn't much of an investigator, he had failed to find out from Janice what detective Campbell had asked her. Was it anything to do with the murdered woman, if so, what did Janice know about her? There was so much he wanted to know. What was the connection between the victim and the Fahey account? He had too many questions and no answers and this would drive him crazy.

He stared out of the window and watched Annette Jordan leave the department store by a side entrance. She climbed into a waiting car. He looked to see if he recognized the driver a long black haired Asian looking woman. He didn't, nor did the woman look like a police officer.

After she had gone, he stared at the door she had exited. There was a sign in the middle of the door, it had begun to fade so he strained his eyes to read what it said. 'Associates only' was all he could make out. The green letters had worn thin from all the people who had leant against the door.

It was as though a light bulb had been switched on in his head if he watched the door. He would see Janice leave the department store. Annette Jordan had already left he needn't worry about anyone seeing him talking to Janice. He sipped at his mocha, a self-congratulation feeling flowing over him.

This feeling dissipated as he watched the employees leave one by one. What if Janice worked until ten at night, no she wouldn't work that long. The frustration grew, he wished he could get his impatient mood under control. Janice must have left by another door. He had been watching for over an hour and there had been no sign of her. He became irritable and sank into a depression. He had been doing this a lot lately and had wondered if it had something to do with his disease. Janice was familiar he had seen her before. It was her voice he recognized from the bus when she thought the man was a policeman.

The door across the street opened and a man stepped out, he held the door open until Janice emerged into the early evening light. The man and Janice talked, she smiled and laughed, her whole body enjoying whatever they were talking about. Janice may seem strange but there was something about her, which made you feel warm towards her. The man and Janice parted. She ran across the street towards the coffee shop. Malachy sank in the seat and hoped she didn't look in. Janice quickly walked past the window without looking inside.

Malachy quickly left the coffee shop, then stopped and remembered he should be cautious. Janice was about twenty yards ahead of him. He looked around to see if anyone was following them. Confident no one was he walked fast to catch up with her. When he was a few steps behind her, he could hear her humming. She had stopped at a road junction waiting for the light to change. He tapped her lightly on the shoulder; she turned looked at him then gave a little girlish giggle.

"Keep away or I'll call the cops."

"I only want to ask you one thing Janice."

"How do you know my name?"

"Annette Jordan told me."

"Well she shouldn't have, I'm going to tell her next time I see her. You're the man looking for those shoes from last year."

"Sorry Janice. All I want to know is what the man asked you."

"What man?"

"The man who stopped you when you were looking at the handbags."

"The handbags, oh after my break. He told me not to talk to you."

"Did he say why you shouldn't talk to me?"

"Yes, he said you killed little girls and ate little boys."

"Janice, he didn't say that."

"Well misses Jordan told me not to talk to strange men or any man because they were only after one thing."

"That's not fair, what about your boyfriend?"

"I don't have one."

"I can't believe that."

"It's true."

"What did the man really say?"

"He asked me where he could buy spray paint, I told him we are a department store and he needed a hardware store. So, I sent him to Spright Brothers up the street."

"Why did he ask you?"

"He had this sweater with paint on it, and we are the only ones selling the sweater. The paint was a nice purple color."

"Well that was very nice of you, I mean to help the man."

"Just doing my customer service thingy which old fancy pants Jordan keeps telling us."

"Fancy pants?"

"Yeah that what the girls on the floor call her."

"Thank you, Janice, I don't want to ask you any more questions."

"Why not? I like talking to you, you're cool," she said trying to sound hip.

"The man said I killed little girls."

"Oh yeah he did, what do you do with them?"

"I plant them in the garden, so they grow and I can eat then when they are big," said Malachy smiling and walking away from her.

Janice mouth dropped open, then closed. "What do they taste like?"

"Chocolate," shouted Malachy.

"I don't believe you," shouted Janice watching him disappear up an alley behind some shops.

She walked towards her bus stop and turned around shouting, "what's your name?"

"Arrh…" came back the reply.

"That's an odd name." She ran back to the entrance to the alley way to see Malachy being attacked by three men.

"Hey what are you doing I'm gonna call the cops," she shouted.

The men stopped looked at her gave a few more punches before running off in the other direction.

Janice approached Malachy she hadn't seen the violence firsthand. It had always been on the television, so seeing someone being beaten had shaken her. Malachy was trying to stand up, he vomited. The vanilla white chocolate mocha gushed up from his stomach, which felt like a train had just hit it. Janice came very close and looked at his pale white face.

"You okay Arrh?" she asked looking down at the vomit.

"I will be when I get my breath."

"What happened?"

"They were trying to rob me."

"There is a seat at the bus stop, let's get you there."

"Good idea."

"Do you think you can walk that far, or do I need to call the paramedics? I could call them."

"No, I don't need them, the seat will do."

They walked slowly, Janice looking at him. She wasn't sure what she should do. Her only medical knowledge came from one of the many television programs she had watched over the years and most of them were soaps. She felt a glow inside her it was the first time in her life she was able to help someone. He hadn't told her not to fuss and go away.

They arrived at the bus stop Malachy sat down the hard-brown plastic seat. He felt sick.

"Did they steal anything?"

"I don't think so, no here is my wallet," he said checking his pockets.

"That's good, but they didn't look as though they were trying to rob you. I've seen it on television they looked like they were roughing you up."

"I think I need a restroom."

"There is a Chinese restaurant around the corner, well not quite around the corner. The food's good, not that I eat there but my mother took me once a long time ago and I enjoyed it. But I was only six"
"Let's go."
"Only if you think you can make it."
"If I fall you can pick me up."
"Okay."
"Janice I was just joking."
"Oh."
They walked slowly, Janice hopping from one side of him to the other. She was scared he would fall over and she would be on the other side and he would hit the ground. It wasn't just that he would hurt himself but she would laugh and he wouldn't understand why. She didn't really know why, but whenever she saw an accident she would laugh.
"You know the more I think about it I really don't think they were robbing you. It looked more like a gang beating. Are you in a gang Arrah?"
  "Why do you keep calling me Arrah?"
  "When I shouted what's you name you shouted back Arrah."
Malachy smiled then laughed out loud.
  "Are you in pain?"
  "No, Oh Janice. I didn't shout my name back. You must have heard me scream when they first attacked me."
  "Really, so what is you real name?"
  "Malachy."
  "Malachy like in Charles Dickens films."
  "Yes."

"That's a nice name. I'm Janice Smart, smart by
name and nature. Well not really I'm a little stupid
and very gullible so I have been told."

"Janice don't be negative, you are not stupid."

"Just doing my customer service thingy. Here's the
restaurant."

She opened the glass door and stepped aside so he
could enter first.

"You take a seat and look at the menu, I'll clean up
and we will have dinner."

"I can't afford it."

"My treat for saving me from death."

"Not really, but don't be too long I get nervous and
then have to leave."

Malachy smiled and left for the washroom. Janice sat
nervously looking around the restaurant and then at the
menu.

Malachy locked the door and looked at himself in the
mirror above the sink. The color had drained from his
face he wanted to vomit. He turned and wrenched the
contents of his stomach into the toilet bowl. He
washed his face in the cold water, which gushed out of
the faucet marked hot. Looking back into the mirror
he watched as the water ran from his face. He took the
paper towel from the wall holder and dried himself.
His face was beginning to hurt from the several
punches it had taken.

Why had he been attacked, Janice was right they
weren't there to steal anything they had come to give
him a warning. About what, he couldn't say, but he
had stirred something up.

On returning from the rest room he saw that Janice had
left. On the table was a note, the writing was childlike
big bold letters. 'Sorry I couldn't wait, I told you I get

nervous. If you really want to buy me dinner you can call me at eight one eight, five five seven eight two four six. Sorry, Janice Smart.'

He put the notepaper into his pocket and looked at the waiter who was hovering a few paces from the table. His little note pad and pencil ready to take an order. "Sorry, I've been stood up," said Malachy and left the restaurant without looking back at the waiter.

The night was a cold one and Malachy's sleep was broken by pain in his feet. He wished he could just get a full night's sleep, slowly he dosed off and woke at nine thirty. He lay in bed the pain had become bearable and he contemplated if he should try and sleep longer. His mind had become active and he knew he couldn't just lie in bed and do nothing. After a shower he sat looking at the walls of his apartment, the coldness of the off-white color was beginning to irritate him, and he would need to get out the place before he exploded in anger. He would go to the Burbank mall and get something to eat.

An hour later he sat in the food court of the mall, eating a Greek gyro and French-fries. He smiled to himself for the first time since waking, he was pretending to be European. He still couldn't understand why they were called French fries but at that moment in time he really didn't care. He sat munching on his food looking straight ahead at a young boy dressed in clothes, which were several sizes too big for him. The boy was writing graffiti on a metal seat with a large felt tip pen. The boy's disregard for anyone around him made Malachy feel angry. If he or any other person wrote on a table, chair or wall the mall security would be on top of them in seconds. The boy looked at Malachy, gave a sneering grin and gave him the finger, before running off into the mall shopping area.

Malachy felt secure, a comfortable feeling sitting surrounded by strangers. He wasn't alone, after the attack the night before he had become aware that something wasn't right. The fear of something worse happening to him began to rise inside his mind. It was a strange sick feeling as though something was pressing down on his stomach. This made it difficult for him to eat, he pushed the food around his plate. He should have called Janice at least to say thank you for her help.

An old woman carrying a pile of newspapers passed him, as she passed one of the papers under her arm fell to the floor. The woman didn't stop but continued her journey. A serious look on her face, she was aiming for her destination and nothing was going to stop her. He bent down and picked up the paper, it was yesterdays. On the front page was a picture of the graffiti he had seen from the bus. He looked at the picture, it was the same but somehow different from the one he had seen the young man drawing. At least it was in the same style. He ripped the picture out of the paper, he felt guilty for doing it. As a young high school student, he had been caught at the local library ripping articles out of the papers. He was banned from the library, until the head librarian was sacked for molesting female readers in the romance section.

"Don't I know you? My name is Janice Smart, smart by nature, smart by name." The words seemed to float towards him. He turned and saw Janice trying to sit down next to a young couple, who was obviously trying to avoid this altercation.

"Janice," shouted Malachy "I'm over here." Janice turned and saw him, her face lifted into a big smile.

"Oh, there is my friend, sorry I can't sit with you.
Nice to meet you both." She shuffled across the
floor carrying a tray full of food.
"Hello, fancy meeting you here," she said sitting
down opposite Malachy.
She arranged her plate of food carefully in the center
of the tray. Wiping her plastic knife and fork and then
placed then precisely each side of her plate. The cup
of soda was positioned to the right of the plate. Then
she bowed her head and said a silent prayer. When she
had finished, she lifted her head and then opened her
eyes. Malachy was staring at her, she gave a little giggle.
"My mother always said you should thank someone
for your food. She never said whom, just someone,
so today I thanked Mrs. Jordan."
"Why her?"
"Well I thanked God first, then Mrs. Jordan. I don't
know why here, maybe one day I will thank you."
Janice began to eat as she did, she emitted a low humming sound as she did. Becoming aware that he was
looking at her, she gave one of her infectious giggles.
"Sorry I always make a sound when I eat, when I
was little it would drown out the noise of people arguing. Then after that I would eat alone and continued to hum."
"It's okay Janice, you do whatever you want to."
She smiled at him, then noticed the newspaper clip-
ping on the table.
"What's that?"
"This is a picture of a piece of graffiti, well more of a
work of art. It's wrong though I saw the original and
this looks nothing like it."

"Well that's what happens when people paint over other people's pictures, don't they?"

"This hasn't been painted over. I saw a little version of it when the boy who drew it was working on it. Only this is different, like he was telling us something."

"Like what?"

"I'm not sure, I think I need to see the original."

"Where is it?"

"Back of Duncan's in the alley way that runs under the freeway."

"I know that place, let's go when I finish my food."

"You want to go with me."

"Yeah, it's like a mystery on the television."

They dumped their empty plates in the trash bin and left the mall.

"You have a car?"

"No."

"Can you drive?"

"Yes, but I sold my car a few weeks ago."

"I have a car, well it's not really mine, it is now but it belongs to my mother. She's dead now."

"I'm sorry to hear that."

"Oh, it okay, I miss her, but she wasn't very nice to me."

"Let's get a bus and go and see this graffiti."

They stood at the bus stop. The silence between them felt comforting and somehow reassuring. Malachy liked it when he could be with someone and they didn't have to spend time always talking. He looked at Janice she may not be the most attractive woman around. Her inquisitiveness, although child like her reasoning, was that of a very mature woman. She needed a makeover not just her face but her clothes as

well, he wondered if he was being cruel to think this
way. If Janice wanted to conform, fit in, she would
need to change, but maybe she was content with the
way she looked. She turned and looked at him, the
smile was innocent and warm.

"Janice what are you thinking?"

"Now?"

"Yes."

"About my mother, why do you think she was so
horrible to me? She once said I was ugly, a plain and
ugly girl. No man will ever want me she said I
would die a lonely old woman. It really made me
cry, I was thirteen years old and just getting interested in boys."

"I don't know why she said it but maybe it was because she didn't want you to get involved with boys.
Janice you're not ugly."

"You don't have to be nice. I know I'm not beautiful. Once some boys at school made a bet and the
one who lost would have to go to bed with me. I
found out what they were up to, I didn't let on I knew
nor would I have sex with someone under those cir-
cumstances."

"Janice beauty is in the eye of the beholder. Look
around you, you will see a beautiful woman with an
overweight not good-looking man and vice versa.
Yet if you get to know them you will find out they
are really in love. It has nothing to do with the way
they look. Love is a very hard thing to understand,
and I'm sure some day you will meet a man and he
will take one look at you and fall in love."

"Oh yeah. You sound like one of those agony aunts
in the paper."

"I mean it, I believe it. I have too, I'm not married yet, don't even have a girlfriend."

"You could be gay. There is a man at the place I work who was married for twenty-three years and then found out he really liked men and left his wife. The whole place talked about it for weeks."

Malachy didn't answer as the bus arrived. The thought had crossed his mind, but he didn't think he was, he just couldn't see men as being desirable. They once again slipped into silence, he wondered what memory Janice was thinking. The pains in his legs had started again. He pondered how long it would be before he would end up in a wheelchair or worse confined to a bed. The constant pain and electric shock type pain had become worse over the last few weeks. He had tried not to acknowledge it, if he didn't think about it maybe it would go away, and he then didn't have a problem. It was one of his weaknesses. Burying his head in the sand, his mother would say, whenever he didn't admit something to himself. He was so engrossed in thought he jumped when Janice touched him on the arm.

"Sorry I didn't mean to make you jump but I think this is our stop."

They stood and watched the bus continue its route.

"Do you have a mother and father?"

"Yes."

"I know you have them, I mean I know how babies are made, but are they alive?"

"Yes, they live in Kansas now."

"With Dorothy and Toto."

"Who?"

"Dorothy and Toto, you know the Wizard of Oz."

"Oh yes, I liked that movie."

"You know, I'm really stupid."

"I wouldn't say that."

"I am, I found a piece of paper on a copier at work, it said, 'are you dead or think you are then ring this number'. So, I did, it was the people from the third-floor accounting. They laughed at me for weeks, even now when some of them see me they laugh. I cried for a week and had a really difficult time going into work."

"Janice I'm sorry, that must have been horrible."

"My mother said I deserved it as I was a very stupid girl."

"You're not stupid, only gullible, and the people from accounting are cruel and very pathetic if they think it is normal to play such an un-cool game."

As they reached the pedestrian walkway, which ran under the freeway the sunlight from the other side, shone on the sidewall. The graffiti stood out from the wall as though on show on a gallery wall. Malachy and Janice stood and stared at the painting. If some-one had taken a picture, they would have surmised they were looking at a Rembrandt or Leonardo Da Vinci.

"It's beautiful, just like a photo."

"It has changed since I first saw it and Ant, that's the artist, painting it. He told me he would draw a life size on the wall before the real picture was created."

"Ant, what a strange name," said Janice giving a lit-tle giggle.

"The rough sketch was smaller about two foot by three foot."

"This is huge I'd say ten feet and about fifteen feet long. And it doesn't look like the picture in the pa-per you showed me."

Malachy took the folded piece of newspaper out of his pocket and opened it. He and Janice compared the picture on the wall with the paper one.

"It's almost the same but now in the paper the man's face is very clear."

"I don't understand it, what is the picture about?"

"I think I do, the woman has been murdered and by this man," said Malachy pointing to the male figure in the wall painting

"Murdered!"

"Yes, look here is a picture of the woman murdered, she was found below the graffiti on the street."

"Oh yeah, you're right that's her, so who is the man who killed her, is he her boyfriend?"

"I don't know, but I think I need to find Ant, he obviously has some of the answers."

Janice stared at the wall painting she had a puzzled expression on her face.

"What's the car doing in the picture?"

"Well on the newspaper version it doesn't have a proper number plate but here it has JJ 1000 D."

"That's a clue."

"Janice who ever said you were stupid didn't know you."

He took a piece of paper and pencil out of his pocket. It had become a habit to carry something to write with, for as long as he could remember. He wrote down the number, maybe he could find out whom the car belonged to.

"You're bit like me aren't you, carrying odd bits and pieces just in case you need them."

"In some ways we are alike."

"So, let's go and find this Ant man, this is a real adventure. I've always wanted to solve a mystery."

"Janice, don't think this is a game."

"I know. But it is fun. So, where do we find Ant, under a stone."

"No." laughed Malachy.

Janice began to giggle which became a laugh. Her whole body began to shake with the laughter, which made Malachy laugh even more. "I don't know where he is, but I think I know someone who does."

The problem with a public transport system in a city, which had been made for cars, was it was slow.

Nearly everyone had a car and in some cases two, so the roads where always full. It took them an hour to reach the mall and Malachy vowed he was going to buy another car.

The mall was a magnet for the young, a place where they could meet. It took him very little time to find the graffiti artist he had seen earlier. As Malachy and Janice approached the young boy, he recognized the man, but couldn't remember where from. They stopped in front of him, Janice to the left side to stop him from running she smiled which caused the young boy to tense.

"Do you know Ant?" asked Malachy

"Not really."

"What does that mean?"

"I know who he is, but his not my friend."

"Do you know where I can find him?"

"No."

"Thanks."

"Why do you want him?"

"I want him to paint a wall for me."

"Ant's cool, you could ask Morgan." Malachy looked at the boy it was obvious the young boy has an admiration for Ant.

"Who's Morgan?"

"His Ant's homie."

"And where do I find Morgan?"

"Last time I saw him he was on the DDR machine."

"DDR machine?"

"Yeah."

"What's that?"

The boy looked at Malachy with disbelief.

"The Dance, Dance Revolution Machine, it's in the basement of the mall by the arcade."

Malachy looked blankly at the boy. Janice didn't seem to know what the boy was talking about. The young boy suddenly began to hop on one foot, his feet touching the floor in four different places.

Malachy smile, "that's what that machine is called. Thanks, and next time don't give me the finger."

The boy looked puzzled then remembered where he had seen Malachy before.

"Yeah, sorry" said the boy running off into the mall.

Malachy and Janice took the escalator to the basement. Malachy kept smiling to himself at the way the boy had explained what the DDR machine was. The mall wasn't one of the biggest shopping places in the area, it didn't take long to get to the basement. At the foot of the escalator Janice stopped.

"I need the restroom; it's up there you go find this Morgan and I will come and find you."

"Janice you're not running out on me, again are you?"

"No, I really have to go."

He watched her as she travelled up the escalator, he wasn't sure if he was going to see her again. He walked towards the video machines, several kids where hanging around them. He looked up and saw

Janice walking on the floor above. She looked over
the balustrade and saw him. She waved and he
pointed towards the video machines, she nodded her
head.

He approached the machines, looking from one young
man to another. Dressed in black a youth was dancing
on one of the machines. He looked about Ant's age
and had the same look on his face Ant usually had. He
was watching a screen, and an arrow traveled up the
screen he would tap or stamp on the corresponding pad
on the metal platform. The music was loud and fast,
the young man jumped and hopped trying to keep up
with it. Beads of sweat ran down his teenage face, he
didn't wipe them away but continued to dance. Malachy looked at him, some envy stirred inside. He
wished he could dance like this but his legs no longer
had any muscle strength.

The music stopped and the young man wiped his face
on his tee shirt.

"Are you Morgan?"

"Maybe."

"Do you know Ant?"

"Maybe."

The music started again and he began to dance once
more.

"I'm looking for him it's urgent," shouted Malachy.

"Haven't seen him for days, what you want him
for?"

"I need him to paint a picture."

"Why?"

"Because I think he is good."

"You going to pay him?"

"Of course."

"Haven't seen him sorry."

"Look if you see him, or speak to him, tell him Malachy is looking for him about the picture."
Morgan didn't answer, continuing to dance this time faster than before.
"Will you tell him?" Shouted Malachy.
"Yeah, if I speak to him."
"Thanks."
He stood back and looked at the young man, who was now concentrated on the machine. It was as if the machine was consuming the boy, drop by drop of his sweat. Malachy didn't know if the boy would pass on the message, but he needed to let Ant know he was looking for him.
Janice left the ladies restroom, as she leaned over the balcony looking down to where Malachy was. It was hard to tell if he was talking to someone. She looked to the right then the left trying to gauge which escalator she should take. The two men suddenly stood out, they seemed out of place. Not because of what they were wearing it was as though they were searching for someone or something. The realization she knew who the men were shot into her mind, she had seen them before. The night before when they were trying to beat up Malachy, these where the same men. She looked desperately for Malachy she needed to warn him, he hadn't seen them. She had to tell him, but how.
The high pitch squeal and the strange body movements of Janice bought the attention of all those around on both levels of the shopping mall towards her. She was in their eyes having a fit and this was something they didn't really want to see but couldn't take their stare off her. Whether it was the body jerking and her odd

arm movement no one was sure. Her right arm bent at the elbow, her index finger jabbing the air.

Malachy looked up at first, he panicked and didn't know if to run towards the stairs to get to her. She was staring at him, her eyes seem wild and then he noticed her right arm and finger, she was pointing. He looked towards where she was indicating and saw the two men, who like everyone else had stopped to look at Janice. It was the men who had attacked him the night before. He took several steps backwards and then turned and ran. One of the men spotted him and tapped the other on the shoulder who immediately started to chase Malachy. Janice peered over the balustrade and down at the men as she hopped from one leg to the other.

Malachy ran for the escalator, but as he approached, he could see a woman trying to push her baby buggy onto the moving stairs. Janice was at the top of the escalator and could see that he didn't have a chance getting past the woman. She could see the men getting closer and closer towards him and her excitement went out of control. She squealed again, Malachy didn't look up and realizing his predicament ran into the department store. He dodged past several shoppers trying out expensive looking perfumes and colognes and ran through a mist of different smells. The two men where close behind and pushed the shoppers and sales assistants out of the way. A display stand holding cheap jewelry came crashing to the floor as the men ran past. Malachy reached the stores escalator and began to climb the stairs two at a time. One of the men reached it just after him and began to run up the moving stairs. The other man slight fatter than the first and desperately out of breath arrived and climbed onto the moving stairs.

The pain in Malachy's legs grew steadily worse. He had no strength to run any more, the men would catch him before he reached the top. He was a few steps from the top of the escalator one of the men was only three steps behind him. Malachy kicked the metal side panel of the escalator with his heel. Immediately the moving stair stopped and the man behind him lost his balance fell backwards on to the other chaser. They tumbled down the stairs, rolling each other as they did. A small crowd quickly gathered at the bottom of the escalator and watched as the men fell. The fall disoriented the two men and it took them a few minutes to untangle themselves and remember what they were doing.

Malachy ran towards the exit of the department store not daring to look behind him, just in case one of the men had managed to not fall down the escalator. In front of him he could see Janice race out onto the bridge which connected the store to the second level of the parking structure. He swung the glass door open and ran onto the bridge, he peered into the parking structure he couldn't see Janice anywhere. He limped into the structure and went behind two SUV's and stopped to catch his breath. His breathing was hard and he seemed to have difficulty controlling it. He could feel and hear his heart pounding inside him. The pain in his legs was now an intense burning sensation. He carefully looked through the windows of the vehicle he was hiding behind. The two men had reached the parking structure and had begun to search between the cars and vans. It wouldn't be very long before they reached him, he needed to find somewhere else to hide and he needed to find Janice. To the left of him was a stairway, which leads to the floor below. He made his way towards it constantly looking where the two men were. Standing behind a twelve-seat black van it was a short dash to the stairway. He lay on the floor and looked under the cars and trucks he could see the men's feet as they searched between the vehicles. He saw the wheels of a truck traveling down the aisle towards him, hoping it would turn right when it reached the bottom of the aisle. He could then use it as cover to run the short distance to the stairs. He stood waiting for it to arrive, as the truck reached the end of the aisle the driver hesitated. Malachy not waiting for him to turn ran towards the stairs. The driver turned towards him and stopped abruptly so as not to hit him, honking his horn as he did. Malachy looked behind him and caught sight of the two men who had looked up as the driver had hit his horn. They began to run, Malachy ran down the stairs, once on the first floor he ran and hid behind a large sedan. He really needed to find a safe place to hide. What had happened to Janice where was she? From behind the car he looked at the stairway and watched as the two men descended the stairs. They stopped and tried to work out which way he had run.

He moved further into the parking structure if he could get to the other side he would be on the street. Maybe he could disappear into a crowd of shoppers if there was some. As he ran between the parked cars, he stopped at each aisle to check it before crossing. He stopped to catch his breath, from somewhere behind he heard someone shouting. He peered over the truck he was behind and saw three security guards approaching the two men. They didn't seem in the mood for a

friendly chat. He hoped this would keep the men oc-
cupied while he made his escape. The hand touched
his shoulder and made him jump. He had always had a
problem with people scaring him. His whole-body
shock with fear as he turned to see who was behind
him.

Janice stood smiling at him, he grabbed her and gave
her a hug, she squealed.

"Thank God you're safe, I was worried about you."

"I'm fine just wondering why it took you so long."

"Janice! I had two men chasing me."

He pointed to where the two men were, the security
men had surrounded them, and some sort of argument
was taking place. Janice pointed the other way towards the street, which was only about twenty yards
away.

She began to run, he tried but his legs had become
heavy and somehow seemed to lose their mobility.
She stopped and looked at him, came back, took hold
of his hand and pulled him out onto the street. At the
corner was a bus stop, and driving up the road was a
bus, Janice franticly began to wave the bus down. The
driver stopped and picked them up, Janice helping
Malachy up the metal stairs.

He sat down and began to rub his legs.

"Are you hurting?" whispered Janice

"Sort of."

They travelled several stops when Janice gave one of
her infamous little squeals.

"What's wrong?"

"We're going the wrong way."

"Where are we going?"

"My place if those men know who you are, they will
go to your home."

206 | EDWARD ARNO

"I'm not sure they know who I am or where I live."

"Oh, I think they do. I don't believe in coincidences, my mother told me there was no such thing."

"You may be right. It was strange they should turn up in the mall and began to chase me."

"That's true."

Janice rang the bell and they both disembarked the bus, crossing the street and stood waiting on the other side of the road.

"When we pass the mall let's keep our heads down just in case."

"I'm not really sure they were looking for me Janice."

"Oh, I think they were, who else?"

"Maybe Ant, remember that's who we were looking for."

"Oh yeah, I forgot about him."

"Janice thank you the diversion and telling me the men where there."

"When I was a kid if I wanted some attention, I usually faked a fit and got what I wanted."

"I thought at first you were really having one, it looked so real."

"Plenty of practice."

The bus arrived and as it passed the mall they slid down in their seats and peered out of the window. The two men were on the sidewalk, still arguing with several security men, it looked as though they would be there for some time.

Janice slipped further down in her seat and giggled.

CHAPTER NINE

Washing Money

The house had been built in the nineteen thirties, it had an impressive veranda with square stone pillars thick at the bottom tapering upwards, holding up the roof. All the windows had decorative metal grills encasing them, for the prevention of burglaries. The olive-green paintwork on the building was several years old and had begun to peel on the sunny side of the house.

Janice led Malachy towards the back of the house. He saw the double door garage at the bottom of the garden. The garden itself needed some work, although the pathways were reasonably clear, the dry almost brown lawn and flowerbeds needed tending too.

"I always use the back door, creature of habit that's me. It was my mom's house, she left it to me. I thought she should have had a lot of money and jewelry but I didn't find any and the lawyer said there wasn't any."

"At least you have a roof over your head."

"I suppose."

Malachy noticed the sourness in her voice and wondered what sort of relationship Janice and her mother really had. The back door opened onto the kitchen, he looked around the spotlessly clean room.

"You don't cook?"

"Yes, I love to cook, Momma wouldn't let me, but I do now," she said pushing open a door and disappearing as the door swung silently back.

Malachy followed and entered a large room with an invisible divide between the dining room area and the living room area. The furniture had been made for the house, and although it was old was in very good condition.

"You keep the place very clean."

"It was my job when Momma was here, so I just keep doing it. I like the place tidy."

"Janice this is a really nice home."

"Do you mean that?"

"Yes, I'd be very proud if this was my place."

"You're the first person I've ever brought here."

"Wow, thanks. Can I sit down now, my legs are beginning to hurt again."

"Did you hurt yourself in the shopping mall?"

"No, I have this ... disability."

"You don't look disabled."

"It's an illness where my legs, feet and hands have a lot of pain. I've only just found out I have it."

"Oh, I am sorry to hear that."

"If I rest a little the pain will go away."

"Would you like to have something to drink, tea coffee, I don't have any soda, sorry."

"Are you going to have something?"

"Tea, I like tea with milk in it."

"Sounds good to me."

"Then you rest, and I'll make some tea, it's like having a real guest."

Malachy smiled at Janice's comment and watched as she entered the kitchen. He sat down on the sofa and was amazed at how soft and comfortable it was for something that was fifty years old. He slowly looked around the room. It was more of a showplace than a place people lived in.

Everything in the room was simple, nothing cluttered. Over the year's people collect things, dust catchers', items that don't really have any practical purpose. In this house there were none, on a small sideboard behind the front door was a vase. On the shelf over the fireplace was a clock and two brass candlesticks. The only pictures where on a small table next to a lazy boy chair. The pictures were old and of adults, there were none of Janice either as a child or adult. There were no other object d'art, it was as though no one had ever lived in the house.

The kitchen door swung open and Janice entered carrying a large wooden tray.

"You will be careful won't you, this is my mother's best china and I don't want to break it. It has been through five big earthquakes and never been broken."

"You didn't need to go to all this trouble a mug would have been sufficient."

"Oh no, you are my first guest and I want everything done properly."

"I feel privileged, a real honor, thank you Janice."

"I found some cookies, they maybe a little hard but they should be fine. I'll let the tea stew, that's what you are supposed to do."

"Janice why aren't there any pictures of you as a baby?"

"I don't think any were taken my mother said I was so ugly as a baby she didn't want to break the camera."

"That must have hurt you."

"Not at first but as you grow up and other kids show off their photos it gets to you, I'm not sure if my mother loved me, she never said."

"I'm sure she did."

"I'll never know, but I loved her, and I miss her."

Janice's eyes filled with tears. She took a paper napkin from her dress pocket and wiped her eyes and then blew her nose.

"Well you pour the tea I'm really looking forward to it."

She carefully picked up the teapot and poured the hot brown liquid into the cups. Malachy added a dash of milk into his and offered to do the same for Janice. She nodded her head.

They sat in silence sipping the tea. She sat her legs together tightly and stared ahead, lost in deep thought. Malachy looked at her, she must have had a very miserable life growing up with a mother who either regretted having her or worse was jealous of her.

Janice put down her cup and pours herself more tea. She took Malachy's and automatically pouring him another cup of tea.

"I've been thinking," she said not looking at him but staring at the fireplace.

She continued to stare. Malachy waited to see if she was going to finish her sentence, but as it became clear she wasn't he asked. "What have you been thinking?"

"Oh yeah sorry, we need to work out what's really going on."

"With what?"

"Well why where those men chasing you for a start, then who killed that woman and why?"

"I think it's all mixed together, if we solve one part, we will have the answer or maybe a clue to what's really going on."

"So, where do we start?"

"We?"

"Yes, this is the best fun I've ever had and nothing or no one is going to stop me now."

"It could be very dangerous."

"You can protect me."

"I would but I don't think I am much good anymore."

"Then we will look out for each other, partners in crime."

They sat in silence, the thought was exciting, but at the same time scary.

"In all the mystery books I've read, the detectives start to solve the crime by working out first what they do know."

"So, I'll start at the beginning and go on 'til I stop."

"Alice in Wonderland."

"What?"

"You just quoted something from Alice in Wonderland, almost quoted, I think it was a little different in the book."

"I didn't realize, so this is what I know so far."

"Stop I need to get a paper and pen to take notes."

She ran to a sideboard, opened a drawer, and took out a small note pad and several pencils. She inspected them to make sure the leads were sharpened.

"Okay I'm ready begin."

212 | EDWARD ARNO

"This is what I know so far, the woman who came to the office was the murder victim, even though everyone tells me she didn't come to the office."

"That means it's a larger conspiracy, if several people will cover up something. Why do you think they did that?"

"I think it's because my boss is up to no good."

"What are his name and the woman's too?"

"Mark Thompson and her name was Monica Trystwold, if that is who she is."

"What do you think your boss Mark is doing?"

"Money laundering."

"Money laundering, you mean he washes money?"

"No, not exactly. Money laundering is the conversion or transfer of property. Knowing that such property is derived from serious crime activities, for the purpose of concealing or disguising the illicit origin of the property. Or assisting any person who is involved in committing such an offence to evade the legal consequences of his action. The concealment or disguises of the true nature, source, location, dispositions, movement rights with respect to or ownership of the property. Knowing that such property is derived from serious crime. I think I have said that right, it is what the textbooks say money laundering is."

"What does it mean?"

"Basically, moving money from one bank to another until you can't tell where the money originally came from, then giving it back to the criminal."

"And you think your boss is doing that?"

"I'm not sure he is actually money laundering but he is doing something like that and his mistress is helping him."

"His mistress?"

"Yes, she's one of the investment professionals at work."

"Really this is more like a script for a daytime soap."

"That's why I think it going to be hard to get anyone to believe it."

"Where does the bug come into it?"

"Bug?"

"The bug you were trying to find."

Malachy looked at her and then burst out laughing.

"You mean Ant, that's his street name, I think. He saw the murder and put clues in his picture up on the freeway."

Janice wrote on her note pad and then stared into the fireplace. Malachy followed her stare and drifted off into thoughts. If he could at least find someone who had seen the woman in the office, he would know he wasn't mistaken.

"Shouldn't we go to the police?"

"I've tried that, but they don't want to know."

"Strange. So, what's our next step?"

"I think we should go to my office and look around there may be some clues. Then I think we should try and find Ant."

"Where's your office?"

"Century City."

"I suppose we could take the bus or use my mother's car. You said you could drive."

"I do, where is the car?"

"In the garage."

Janice rose, collected the teacups and carried the tray back into the kitchen. She placed the crockery into the sink and put the tray with a stack of others.

"I'll wash them later," she said while she was looking through a bundle of keys she had taken out of an oversized bag.

She opened the back door and let Malachy leave the house. Then looked around to see if anything was burning before closing and locking the door behind her.

"The light is still on."

"Yes, I always leave one on, I'm not sure if anyone really thinks someone is in the house but at least it makes them think before breaking in."

Malachy smiled as he looked at the oversized padlock on the garage door. Janice fumbled through the bunch of keys and finding one tried it in the lock. She stood back as Malachy swung open the door. Inside the neat and clean garage was a new four door Ford car.

"Nice car."

"Yeah mother never took it out except when she wanted to show off to one of her friends."

Malachy walked around it, like the house it was immaculately clean and polished.

"What's in the trunk?"

"A dead body," replied Janice

"What?"

"I don't know I was never allowed to go near it. After mom died, I was too scared too. But I kept the insurance up even changed the name on it to me."

"You drive then?"

"I took the lesson and test at school, even passed but I've never really driven a car."

Malachy opened the trunk, Janice peered in cautiously not knowing what to expect. The trunk was filled with shoeboxes.

"What are these?"

She picked one up and opened it almost expecting
something to jump out. It was filled with money, she
opened another it too was full of money.

"I wonder why she put it here."

"Possibly didn't trust banks or was trying not to pay
taxes on it."

"Whose is it now?"

"Janice this is now yours to keep."

"She did love me."

"Why do you say that?"

"Well just before she died, she made me come very
close to her mouth and whispered in my ear 'the
body is in the trunk' then laughed. It scared me at
the time."

"She was telling you where the money was."

"Yes, thanks mom. I think I need to hide it now so
we can take the car out."

"Any ideas?"

"Oh yes, close the garage doors please."

"I'll put the light on."

Malachy closed the garage door as a light came on.
He turned back towards the car. Janice had disappeared.

"Janice, where are you?"

"Down here."

At the back of the car Malachy found a trapdoor open
and Janice standing at the bottom of a wooden set of
stairs.

"Could you pass down the boxes to me please?"

He passed the boxes down to her, and then watched as
she disappeared in the room below. He closed the
trunk and climbed into the car. It was as clean on the
inside as it was on the outside and had a slight smell of
gardenias. He looked at the mileage clock, which

registered only three thousand miles. He lay back in the driver's seat and waited for Janice. He closed his eyes. The pain in his legs began to increase, he knew it was because he had begun to relax.

The front passenger door opened, and he awoke with a start.

"Sorry to wake you."

"I was just resting my eyes."

"Snore when you just rest your eyes do you?"

"Was I snoring?"

"Yes, very loudly."

"Sorry."

"So, I put the money away, closed the trap door you can't see it even when there is no car in the garage. I don't know why it was built but my mother would hide things down there and even threaten me with being put down there if I didn't behave."

"If you put the money in the bank remember to do it a little at a time, banks report to the IRS if too much money goes into an account all at once."

"I'll be careful, but I think I will buy myself a cell phone first. I've always wanted one."

"Who will you call?"

"Well I'd call you for a start."

Malachy found his own cell phone in his pocket and switched it on. He had the habit of not using it at night and weekends.

"You drive, I need to take some more lessons before I get behind the wheel."

She handed him a key and he turned the ignition. The car sputtered and then died.

"Batteries dead."

He flipped a level and the hood of the car opened. Janice grabbed some cables from the wall and connected then to the car battery. She then flicked a switch and a battery charger came to life.

"Try it now. I would do this for my mother."

He tried again and the car came to life. She switched off the machine and disconnected the charge wires. Then indicated to him to drive the car out of the garage. She swung the door open and stepped aside to allow him to drive the car out.

He slowly drove up the driveway adjusting the mirrors and seat as he did. Janice closed and padlockeds the garage door. She ran along the driveway her heels high kicking up behind. It looked strange to Malachy in the rearview mirror. He dismissed it as something Janice had done all her life and he was just to accept it. She opened the car door and slip onto the passenger seat her face was that of a child who had just been given the treat of a lifetime.

"This is the first time I've ever been in this car."

"Are you telling the truth?"

"Yes," she said indignantly. "Mom would never let me sit in it said I would make a mess."

"Well Miss Janice Smart sit back, and imagine I'm your chauffeur and we are going out for a Sunday drive."

"But its Saturday."

"I know but just imagine it's Sunday afternoon, and the sun is burning down on the poor folks of Los Angeles as little miss rich girl Janice goes for a drive."

"Okay I'll try."

Malachy slowly drove the car out of the driveway onto the street. It had been several months since he had driven a car, so he was taking no chance and carefully guided the car along the streets.

"I think we should take the surface streets, rather than go on the freeway."

"If you say so my man," said Janice and then gave one of her little girl giggles.

He soon found he hadn't lost the ability to drive and vowed to get himself another car. There were quite a lot of cars on the surface streets, but as they passed close to the freeway, they could see it was packed solid with Saturday travelers.

As they approached Century City and onto the street in which Malachy worked, he began to look for a space to park. If this had been a weekday it would have been impossible to find anywhere. As it was a Saturday of a three-day weekend, he had no difficulty in finding somewhere.

"Janice when we get inside the building let me do all the talking."

"Why?"

"The security is very tight, and they will ask a lot of questions."

"Okay. I really enjoyed the ride."

"Me too, it's a nice car."

They entered the building from the west side. Malachy braced himself to answer the questions he knew the security company men would fire at him. He stood at the security officer's console, but no one came to speak to him. He quickly left and taking Janice's hand entered the corridor of elevators. He pressed the up button, and a door open, he and Janice entered. He quickly put his access card on the pad and pressed the twenty-sixth floor. The doors closed and he felt relieved, they traveled quickly to the twenty-sixth floor.

"I actually work on the twenty-seventh floor but on the weekends we don't have access, by elevators."

"So how do we get to the twenty-seventh floor?"

"We walk up the stairs."

"These are nice offices."

"They're okay we need more space. but they are not going to get any."

The main lobby was in darkness, just a few emergency lights, illuminated the area. It gave the impression of a deserted film set. Janice shuddered and stepped closer to Malachy.

"This place is a little scary for me."

"Don't worry I'm here," he said the words, then thought about what he had said. He was as scared as she was.

"We will use the back stairs, sometimes the financial analyst works at the weekend and I really don't want to explain to them what we are doing."

They walked down a gray impersonal corridor and climbed the solid concrete steps and stood looking at the floor to ceiling wooden door. Malachy produced another plastic card and swiped it over a red light, which turned green, and the door mechanism clicked. They entered an open plan office. Janice looked around an expression of puzzlement slid over her face.

"Don't you have an office? she whispered.

"Only the managing director has an office."

"It must be nice to be able to see all the other workers and to be able to talk to them."

"It's okay."

The sound of laughter came from around the L shaped office. Malachy grabbed Janice and pulled her into a recess and then through a door marked 'Mail Room'. He closed the door carefully and guided Janice across the room and behind a large cupboard workbench situated in the center of the room. The room was lit by safety lights, which didn't illuminate the whole room. The mailroom door opened. Malachy tensed, he hoped whoever it was wouldn't switch on the overhead lights.

A heavyset male voice said, "Mark just keep shredding the papers and I'll go and find out where Helmet is."

Janice squeezed Malachy hand.

"Get back to it and I'll get back to you later, make sure your cell phone is open."

A door closed and the sound of soft rubber soled shoes squeaked across the mailroom floor. Janice squeezed Malachy's hand even tighter.

Another door opened and then closed.

Malachy peered slowly over the top of the workbench. From where he was, he could see the room was empty except for himself and Janice. He sat down next to Janice and gave her a weak smile.

"Helmet was one of the people who came with the murdered woman."

"You were right about your boss, he is washing money, or something like that"

"Money laundering."

"Yeah that's it, I knew it had to do with cleaning the money."

"I wonder what papers he is shredding."

"Let's go and find out."

Malachy gave Janice a look of surprise. She never seemed to fight shy of danger.

"Let's get close to his office and see what he is doing."

He opened the mailroom door and peered into the office. He couldn't see anyone, so they crept half-crouching across the room to a pod of fifteen work-stations.

"Squeeze under this desk, and I will go and see what's happening."

Janice moved the chair and crawled under the desk making herself as comfortable as she could. It reminded her of her childhood games of hiding from her mother. She gave a little giggle in remembrance.

Malachy moved on all fours behind the pod of desks. At the end of the pod he peered around the corner and raised his head slowly. At the far end of the room he could see Mark standing at the conference table in his office pushing papers into a shredder.

A door at the other end of the office, near to Mark's office opened, the two men who had been with Monica Trystwold the murdered woman entered the office. He knew them as Helmet Von Davian and Anthony Drongotti, they were dressed in a slightly out of date charcoal gray silk suits. Helmet entered Mark's office carrying a black plastic bag and emptied the shredding into it.

A door banging from the other end of the room made Malachy and the three men turn sharply to see who had entered the office. A small man and woman entered. Malachy had forgotten the cleaners came about this time.

He crept back to Janice who was still hiding under the desk. She smiled as she saw him.

They both froze as the voice the deep male voice spoke, "What do you want?"

"We've come to clean," said a Hispanic male voice.

"Right, get on with it then."

Malachy indicated to Janice to follow him and they crawled along the pod towards Mark's office. Mark and the two other men were leaving as Malachy peered over the top of the desk pod. He watched as they exited, one of the men was carrying a black plastic bag.

"They have gone, so let's go and see if we can find anything around Mark's office."

They were still on their hands and knees as they approached the office. Looking into the office through the large floor to ceiling window they could see the file drawers and cabinets where open and empty. The portable shredder was back under Marks desk.

Malachy tried the office door it was locked.

"Strange he never locks his door."

"He has this time."

"I think we should get of here I don't think we will find anything of use now."

He continued to crawl until he reached a small corridor, which led to the administration and legal departments. Once they were out of sight of the cleaners they stood up.

"I really don't know how babies can crawl so much it really hurts the knees."

"You're just getting old."

"We go this way back to the stairs and then down to the twenty-sixth floor."

They walked past Elizabeth Dellman's office. Malachy was looking ahead and was surprised when Janice gave a little squeak. She grabbed his arm.

"There's a woman in that office."

"What"

"There's a woman in that office," said Janice pointing into an office.

Malachy retraced his steps and looked into Elizabeth Dellman's office. He could see Elizabeth sitting at her desk.

"Shit I think she is dead."

"Dead? Why?"

"I don't know why."

"No, why do you think she is dead?"

"Because her head had fallen against the computer monitor."

"Poor thing."

"Let's get out of here before something happens to us."

They quickly descend to the first floor via the elevator and cautiously stepped out. There was no sign of a security guard, so they exited by one of the side doors. It would mean walking around the building to where they had parked Janice's car. Malachy thought it was the best thing they could do. If Elizabeth Dellman had been murdered, they didn't want anyone to know they had been in the building. He then remembered he had used his card to get into the office. He would have to come up with a reason why it was used if anyone asked. He searched his pockets but couldn't find his card.

As they turned the corner of the building and walked on to the street where they had parked Janice's car, he saw a black plastic bag sticking out of a trash bin. He picked it up and open it, inside it was full of shredded papers.

"I don't believe it they had just thrown it away."

"Maybe they thought no one would look inside and if they did, seeing it was shredded papers, they would just leave it there."

"Let's take it I'm good at jigsaw puzzles."

"Well I know they did put shredded material back together years ago in Iran, but this could take forever."

They crossed to the car and Malachy checked around and under it before he opened the door and got inside. He put the key in the ignition and started the car. It jumped into life.

"I think we charged the battery enough when we drove here."

"Let's go back to my place," said Janice.

"Okay but I think I should go home later I need to change my clothes and check things are still there."

"I never asked which was your desk," she drifted off into a thought.

They sat in silence for the first few miles, Malachy became aware Janice was beginning to act a little strange and pulled the car into the curb. He looked at her she was staring straight ahead and was shaking.

"What's wrong?"

Janice gave a deep sobbing sigh.

"That woman was dead, wasn't she?"

"I think so."

Janice gave a few more deep sighs. Malachy put his arm around her and gave a little hug.

"That's the first time I have seen a dead body."

"Me too, but today is also your first day as a private detective."

"She turned and looked at him and gave one of her girlish little giggles.

"Janice, I think this is a very dangerous thing we have stumbled into and maybe you shouldn't be involved anymore."

"And you should, no way we just have to be a lot more careful. I will play at being stupid most people ignore me when I do. But I am only playing to get attention."

"You're good at it too."

"And today was the first time I was in this car, well riding in it."

"Are you okay now?"

"Yep, who do you think murdered her?"

"How do we know she was murdered?"

"Well you could see the bruising around her neck from where we stood. She had been strangled with something that left those strange bruise marks."

"Quite the detective."

"Not really too much Court TV."

Malachy started the car and eased it into the flow of traffic.

"I don't think we have been followed," said Janice.

He looked at her and gave a little laugh.

"You really like doing this, don't you?"

"I think I've always wanted to be a Private Investigator. Although I do get scared very easily."

"Me too. But we must remember to be careful and once we have some real evidence then we go to the police. Agreed?"

"Certainly captain."

They drove in silence only to be broken when Janice lunched into "Did you know when the Iranian's threw out us Americans, way back the Iranians put together all the shredded paper we had left behind?"

"No, I didn't know that," he replied not wanting to destroy her eagerness even though he had just mentioned it.

"History channel program. Well I am going to see if I can do the same."

"It may take you forever."

"Oh, I like a good puzzle. I would spend hours putting together jigsaw puzzles with the picture facing the table."

"If you think you can do it, I'll go home and change."

"You will come back tonight?"

"I'm not sure, what will your neighbors and friends say."

"I don't have any friends and the neighbors can go to hell."

"I'm told it's nice and warm there."

"My place?"

"No hell."

They arrived at Janice's house and he drove the car up to the garage.

"Don't you need the car to get home?"

"No, I'll walk, it's not far, anyway this is your car."

"I know but I thought you could use it."

"We will use it when we need it."

Janice jumped out of the car and opened the garage doors. He drove slowly into the space, switched off the engine. He wiped his face with his hand before giving his head a little massage.

Janice opened the trunk and took out the black plastic bag.

She stood just inside the garage waiting for him. Out in the street one of her neighbors was surreptitiously beginning to work on his dried earthen lawn. Giving a little glance at Janice's house when he thought she wasn't looking.

She was watching him and gave a giggle of excitement. She watched for the man to look again and gave him a wave. The man's body stiffened, not knowing if he should wave back to pretend not to have seen her. Janice laughed out loud as Malachy climbed out of the car.

"What's wrong?"

"Nothing wrong, Mister Sanchez from across the street has come to have a nose. And I caught him staring so I gave him a wave and now he's not sure what he should do."

Mister Sanchez looked at Janice and Malachy. She gave him another wave, then turned and closed the garage door. Malachy picked up the black plastic bag. Janice began to walk up the path. Malachy quickly came beside her and slipped his hand into hers. She grabbed it and then looked at Mister Sanchez, as the man looked again, she gave him a big wave. They both went into the house.

"Thanks, you have given them something to gossip about."

"I didn't do it for that reason it was my way of saying thank you."

"What for?"

"For being my friend."

Janice looked at him, her mouth dropped open.

"You're thanking me for being your friend?"

"Yes, I realized today I don't really have many, in fact I don't have any."

"Why not?"

"Not sure."

"You have a girlfriend?"

"No"

"Boyfriend?"

"No, you're the second person to ask me that. Do I look gay?"

"No, but you do stare at people a lot and I saw this program on Court TV. It was about how rapists and killers sometimes stalk their prey with their eyes. That doesn't sound right, what I mean they stare at people, trying to find their next victim."

"Now you're staring. Do I look like a rapist or killer?"

"No, but people who stare at other people usually do for some reason."

"But the gay bit?"

"Oh, I've seen men and women on the bus look at each other in a strange way. I can't describe it except it looks like they want to eat the person."

"Maybe they were just hungry."

"Funny, you look at people as though you're trying to get inside their heads. As though you were trying to feel and think like them."

"That's a little deep Janice."

"I told you I watched too much Television."

"I love to people watch. We had this seminar at work, and it included body language. Since then I've read a lot about it and so I look at people to see if I can read them from their actions."

"So, what do you read about me?"

"Your kind, honest and sadly a little gullible, but when you find the right man, you'll make a wonderful wife."

"You can read that in me?"

"No, the last bit comes from getting to know you."

"I don't want sex with you."

"I didn't ask for it."

"Sorry that came out wrong, I don't want you as my boyfriend, I want you as my friend. You know what I mean."

"Yes."

"You don't mind."

"No. And here am I looking forward to a lot of hot steamy sex."

Janice gave him a look of surprise.

"I'm just kidding. Janice, I want you as my friend anything else will spoil what we have."

"Me to, so you go home and change I'll get stuck into putting the papers back together."

"Good luck."

"I don't need that just a lot of patience and some nice music."

Malachy took a piece of paper and wrote down his phone numbers.

"Janice my cell and home numbers if you need to call me."

"Thanks, let me give you mine, well it's still in my mother's name."

Janice stood on the top step of her home and waved to Malachy as he walked down the path. Mister Sanchez was still working on his garden.

"By the way honey remember to bring your tooth-brush when you come return," she shouted.

"Okay sweetheart," retorted Malachy.

Mister Sanchez dropped his spade and ran into his house.

Malachy walked back to his apartment he wished he had taken the car his legs and feet were hurting.

He checked around to see if anyone was following him. When a car drove by, he checked to see if he could be in danger. He then looked for a place to run to. As he turned into his street he wondered if he should enter via the back alleyway. The street seemed calm and he couldn't see any strange cars around.

He opened the screen door on his apartment, the front door was open. He entered slowly someone had ran-sacked the place. Every cupboard and drawer had been searched. He checked each room someone had been looking for something. The appliances, which would normally be taken in a burglary, were still in place. He returned to the living room and checked the front door lock. It had not been forced who ever entered and used a set of keys or picked the lock. He closed and locked the door.

He turned and looked at the devastation not sure where he should start. The phone rang and he jumped. He began to franticly search for the phone and found it under the sofa.

"Hello."

"Hi it's Janice."

"Oh hi."

"What's wrong?"

"Nothing I'm fine."

"Good I was just checking you got home safely."

"I'm fine."

"Okay I'll see you later."

He hung up the phone and began to pick up the cushions from the floor. He cleaned the apartment room by room for the next two hours. Then took a shower, the water running down his body seemed to wash away the feeling of being invaded. After he dried and dressed, he sat on the sofa and drank a glass of coffee flavored Soya milk. He put the glass down lay back and closed his eyes. He drifted off into a sleep and dreamt.

'He was being chased by a panther that was always at his heels. He could see his boss Mark on an elephant dragging Elizabeth Dellman's dead body in a child's Radio Flyer cart. He ran and jumped over a wall, which had been painted to look like a country field. The panther ran into it and knocked itself out. He leaned against the wall on the other side and could hear bells.

He woke to his front doorbell ringing.

He sat for a few seconds unable to move. Then he crept to the front door and peered through the spy hole. He could make out the shape of two men standing on the other side. He stood to the left side of the door.

"Who's there?"

"Police."

"How do I know you're the police?"

"Open up Mister Moss and we will show you our ID Cards."

"Wait a moment I need to get dressed."

He moved away from the door, what he needed was time to think what to do.

CHAPTER TEN

Where is Ant

Malachy opened the door cautiously he couldn't remember if he had put the lock on the screen door. Although it wouldn't really stop an intruder from entering it might give a few seconds to shut and lock the front door. He had stood wondering what he should do in his state of tiredness, which had clouded his reasoning. He had decided to open the door.

The two men standing on the doorstep both held the police ID cards so he could read them.

"Sorry to bother you Mister Moss, but we do need to ask you a few questions"

Malachy unlocked the screen door and was relieved he had locked it instinctively. He stood aside to allow the two men to enter looking at them as they passed him. As he closed and locked the screen door the phone rang. He picked up the handset.

"Hello."

"Hi how are you."

"Hello, sorry I can't talk just at the moment I have visitors I will call you back."

He returned the handset to the telephone cradle.

The two police officers sat down and stared at him intensely.

"Mister Moss."

"Oh, please call me Malachy."

"If you wish sir, do you know Elizabeth Dellman?"

"Why yes she's the admin at work."

"Admin?" asked the smaller of the two officers.

"The office Administrator."

"When did you last see her?"

Malachy thought for a few minutes, he wanted to say a few hours ago dead in her office.

"Friday as I was leaving work, why what's happened to her?"

The officers ignored his questioning.

"And that was the last time you saw her?"

He nodded.

"Did you go to your office today? Asked the smaller of the two officers.

"No, look what's happened."

The taller and fatter of the officers took a small note pad out of his pocket.

"Did you ever give her presents or money?"

"No why would I do that?"

"She didn't suggest it would be in your best interest to be very nice to her."

"No, we hardly saw each other."

"You look after Mark Thompson correct?"

"Yes, I am his administrative assistant."

"When was the last time you saw him?"

"Friday as he was leaving."

"Do you have any other phone numbers for him other than his home or cell phone number?"

"No, he does have a second cell, but I was never given that number."

"And you have no other way of contacting him."

"No, I'm not even sure where he lives, he is a very secretive man."

"Well if he contacts you please give me a call," said the small officer handing Malachy a business card.

The door rang and made Malachy jump.

"You're a little nervous sir."

Malachy ignored the statement and went and opened the door. Janice stood looking at him waiting for the screen door to be unlocked. After he had unlocked it, she marched into the room and said "Hello" to the two officers.

"This is my friend…" said Malachy who was interrupted by Janice.

"Actually, I'm his girlfriend and you are?"

"I'm Detective Wallace and this is Detective Gazon and your name is miss?"

"Janice Smart."

"Well we have nearly finished asking our questions, Malachy do you have your office access card?"

"Yes, it's here on this table." He looked on the small table behind the door.

"Strange I thought I put it there."

"When did you last have it sir?"

"Friday morning, to get into work I don't need it to leave the building. I suppose I could have left it on my desk, I've done that before. It really annoys the security people."

"Did you use it today?"

"No, I haven't been to work today. It's the long weekend."

"For some sir," retorted Detective Gazon.

"What's going on?"

The detectives looked at each other, then Detective Gazon nodded and spoke.

"Elizabeth Dellman was found dead in her office and we have been unable to contact Mister Thompson. His wife says she hasn't seen or heard from him for two days."

"Elizabeth dead? What did she die of?"

"She was murdered."

"Murdered! Why would anyone murder her?"

"We think she may have been blackmailing some of the employees."

"Blackmail."

Malachy sat on the arm of the chair. The news seemed to have shaken him. This was the impression Detective Wallace interrupted from his actions.

Janice hopped from one foot to the other. She wanted to say something but knew this was not the time. The little side glance from Malachy she thought she saw told her to keep quiet.

"Miss Dellman, we believe was blackmailing several of the employees having learnt information from the company's background checks and from the personnel files."

"Like who?"

"I can't really tell who at this time, but we are trying to find out how many people were being blackmailed. Mister Moss was she blackmailing you?"

"No, I've nothing to hide. Mark, what's happened to him, I don't remember any trips he was taking this weekend?"

"His wife said if anyone should know where he is it would be you as you keep his calendar."

"Sorry I don't know, have you tried his cell phone?"

"Yes sir, a woman answered when we did get through and now it doesn't get answered when we call."

"My access card, what was that all about?"

"Your access card was used earlier today to enter the building."

"Did the security guards see who came in?"

"Unfortunately, they seemed to have been a little distracted and the video recording cameras were being used for something else."

"You mean the security guards where watching porn."

"Something like that sir."

"When was she murdered?" asked Janice The police office that had introduced himself as Detective Wallace looked at Janice then replied. "The actual time of death hasn't been determined, but the coroner's preliminary report says sometime on Friday night."

"Why didn't the cleaners see her on Friday?"

"We haven't spoken to them yet."

"Who found the body?"

Detective Gazon looked at his note pad he flipped a few pages before looking up.

"Martin Farland, says he had come into the office to finish a client presentation. Does he often work on the weekends?"

"The F.A,'s work whenever they need to, they are on call twenty-four seven."

"F.A.'s?"

"Financial Analyst, they do all the work for the sales reps."

"I see."

Detective Wallace made a coughing sound in his throat, Detective Gazon put his book away.

"Mister Moss if you think of anything which might help us or Mister Thompson contacts you please give me a call." Detective Wallace handed him his business card.

"Sure."

The two officers moved further into the room making wide sweep of the room and then walked around the sofa before heading for the front door.

Janice and Malachy stood at the screen door watching the two men walk down the steps. Once they had reached the garden gate, Malachy pulled Janice into the apartment and closed the wooden door. They sat down on the sofa and stared at each other. The process of collecting the thoughts was evident.

"Why did they walk in that strange way around the room before they left?"

"I think they were checking out your place just in case you had something they could get a search warrant to check the place over. Or they were looking for your access pass."

"No, I think they have found that I really have lost it. I think I left in the office just before we left."

Janice stared at the wall lost in thought. Malachy looked at her.

"When they were here you were hopping from one foot to the other, what did you want to say?"

"Can't remember, wasn't anything important."

"Why are you here?"

"When we talked on the phone you sounded so suspicious, I thought you were in danger and you were giving me a clue"

"How did you know where I lived?"

"It's in the phone book, I looked you up."

"I'm glad it was there."

Janice looked at him had she just understood what he said, did he mean he was glad to see her or was she fantasizing again. Before she could continue the thought, she was interrupted.

"So, they found another body and Mark is missing, I wonder what's really going on."

"It's like a murder mystery from the television."

"Except this is real, I'm feeling hungry."

"That's what thinking does, makes you hungry."

"What!"

"My mom told me not to think, it would make me hungry and I would become fat."

"Your mother had some strange ideas, she said things to you that are not really true, but only to make you shut up."

"That's what I think I mean I never felt hungry thinking."

"See, but I am hungry so let's go and get something to eat."

"Okay, you're not really my boyfriend I just wanted to say it to those police officers. You're not angry about it are you?"

"No Janice I'm not angry, you're my friend and it did make the police officer lighten up a little."

"You need to tidy up in here."

"I was burglarized last night. I came home and found someone had ransacked the place."

"Oh, I'm sorry I thought you were just a messy man."

"Another thing you mother told you."

"Yes, did they steal anything?"

"That's the odd thing nothing seems to have been taken."

"Lucky."

As Malachy locked the front door, he hoped that no one else would enter his home and ransack it. He wondered if he had left it unlocked the last time and that is how the intruder broke in. He knew his short-term memory had been playing tricks on him lately. It was either due to stress or the illness. He knew the pains which kept attacking him was due to the situation he was in now, the stress of the solving a murder. It had occurred to him that maybe he should not be so foolish and just take life as easy as possible. The little demon in his head began to talk and argued he would get bored and would wither and fade to dust. But your health the other voice in his head said.

"Hang my health." He shouted.

"Sorry."

"Oh, nothing Janice just a little conflict in my head."

"I have them, people said I was going mad when I told someone. Now I keep it to myself."

"You're not going mad. Our brains talk out the problems and it seems as though we have little voice in our heads. And like I just did in frustration you shout out to stop the process."

"You really understand don't you."

"Understand what?"

"Me."

"Janice you are just like the rest of us only you have a better way of showing how kind and nice you are."

"Wow, do you mean that?"

"Of course, I don't say things unless I mean them."

They continue to walk in silence to the fast food restaurant. Janice began to look about her.

"Do you think we are being followed or watched?"

"Maybe but I too hungry to worry about that now."

They sat in silence as they ate and looking out of the window. The sudden thump on the window made them both jump. The teenager who had hit the window and his friends stood laughing before running off. Janice gave one of her giggles, which transported itself to Malachy who began to laugh. They both sat laughing for a few minutes, the rest of the customers and staff in the fast food restaurant looking at them. This made Janice laugh even louder. Once they had calmed down with only sporadic out bursts Janice said "I love watching people I just wish I could understand what some of the things they do mean."

Malachy looked at her. To most people this girl was a simple child but every now and then she asked question or had a thought, which amazed him. He must never underestimate her.

"Sorry it just came out, I was just thinking why do people sit the way they do? Or talk with their hands? Have you noticed how some people touch your elbow or arm when they talk to you?"

"It's called body language."

"Body language, you mean bodies talk?"

"Sort of, well yes bodies do talk. People react to others in a series of gestures. Those movements are in general the same and have the same meanings."

"Really it's like a foreign language."

"Well there are always cultural differences like some races are more tactile than others."

"Tactile?"

"Touchy, they will touch you when they are speaking to you. Let's say a young man likes you he will start to touch you on your arm or hand. Testing the water to see if you like him."

"Wow."

"Elizabeth Dellman would never allow anyone to touch her. While Mark my boss would always touch you on the elbow or shoulder. People have even

been known to pass on secrets without realizing they
are doing it."

"Like what?"

"Well say you could see someone coming up behind
me but couldn't say their Miss so and so. You might
rub the side of your nose and as long as I understood
what that meant then I would know."

"You could even work out in advance a secret language that only you and the other person know."

"Let's say the man coming up behind me has a gun,
you could make you fingers look like a gun and put
then over your mouth. If you and I had arranged this
as a sign, then you could save my life."

"Right and it would only work if we had agreed in
advance. But what about the other things like crossing the legs and the way people look at you and do
things with their lips, like biting them?"

"Each movement means something and there are
books which explain in general what they mean."

"I think I need to read those."

"Me too."

"Maybe that's why we are both still single."

"Right. I think we should go home it will be dark
soon and we need to get some sleep."

"Aye, Aye Sir," said Janice giving him a salute.
Outside the air had cooled down and a light breeze was
drifting from the nearby mountains. The traffic was
light on the road and very few people walked the Burbank streets.

Malachy and Janice walked looking at the houses the
few people that were out and the cars, which passed
by. As they came to the cross street a car full of young
boys sped around the corner. One of the boys threw a

can of soda at them it missed and hit a parked car setting off an alarm.

"Kids." Said Janice.

From down one of the back alleyways a loud bang echoed from one building to another. This was followed by a group of teenage girls running down the alleyway laughing.

Malachy and Janice looked at each other and in unison said, "Kids." They both laughed.

Turning into the street Janice lived on Malachy checked to see if anyone seems to be watching her home. All the cars seemed empty and no one was standing suspicious by a building. He was scared and he could feel the tension in Janice.

"You going to be okay?" he asked.

"Oh yes, I'm just a little cold and I don't mind being on my own."

"Let me check inside first."

"No, you don't need to do that."

"I think I do, if only to make me feel relaxed that you're safe."

Janice relaxed a little she was hoping he would do that. Malachy entered the house and checked each room. He found nothing and as he returned to the living room Janice visibly relaxed.

"No one is here."

"See I told you."

"Okay I'll get going but call me if you need something."

"Do you mean that?"

"Yes, I wouldn't have said it otherwise."

Janice sat on the sofa and drifted off into thought.

"Janice are you okay?" a slight sound of panic entering his voice.

"I've never had any one really care about me before,
a friend I mean."
He looked at her, he wanted to hug her and kiss her on
the cheek but knew it might be misunderstood.
"I'll get going and remember to call if you need me
but I think you're going to be safe."
"Okay thanks and you take care."
Malachy turned and looked back at Janice's house as
he turned the corner, she was still standing on the top
step watching him go. He waved and continued down
the street. He was tired and knew he must keep his
wits about him, watching the cars as they passed him.
He walked past the entrance to his street and headed
for the back alley behind the apartment complex.
He slipped into the darkness of the alleyway and was
shocked to see a man carrying a gun run across the alleyway at his complex. He stepped into a side entrance of another apartment, his heart pounding inside
and his legs beginning to shake. He peered around the
edge of the recess and looked into the alleyway. No
one was there so he walked quickly out onto the street.
He needed to get away from the area as fast as he
could. The next corner a council owned parking structure had recently been built. Once inside he climbed
up to the open roof on the sixth floor. He could clearly
see into his street from this vantage point. His apartment was under siege with armed paramilitary men
crawling over the complex.
A police helicopter flew low overhead, he sank down
behind the parapet. The light from the helicopter was
illuminating the streets around his complex. He
needed to move away from this area as soon as he
could. Crawling back to the stairs and descending to

the floor below he peered over the parapet to see if the street below as empty.

The last rays of day faded, and the parking structure lights flicked on. He descended to the street level and then out onto the street. Crossing the road, he began to mingle with the moviegoers who had either just arrived to see a film or were leaving after seeing the latest blockbuster.

Lost in the crowd he relaxed, but his problems were not over he needed somewhere to sleep or at least rest so he could think. He needed to find the graffiti artist. Ant had the key to what was going on even though he didn't realize it. The boy was also in great danger if anyone put together that it was him who had drawn the graffiti.

After bumping into several people some whom seemed to want to escalate the situation he stepped into an alleyway behind the cinema. He would go and see Janice she at least knew what was going on and would let him sleep on her sofa. The alleyway was lit by a few streetlamps and was deserted. He was scared that someone might follow him or would jump out and grab him. He was becoming paranoid and knew he must get a grip on reality. The alleyway light suddenly switched off and he froze expecting something to happen, after a few minutes the lights flickered and came back on. He raced down the alleyway across the street and into another one. The alleyway didn't have a streetlight and was lit by the apartments above.

A motion sensor light suddenly switches on which illuminates the alleyway. Malachy jumped, his heart raced with fear and his breathing became rapid. He looked around and then realized it was a motion sensor, which had switched the light on. Continuing up

the alleyway and on the edge of the light he could just
see a piece of graffiti. The light went out.

He ran back to engage the sensor and the light sprang
into life. He quickly moved to look at the graffiti. It
was an Ant piece, although it was very rough and obviously had been executed in a rush.

The graffiti was only a sketch with no fill in, the letter
Ant was made of two men leaning against each other
only touching at their heads. The faces of the two men
had been very meticulously drawn. They both carried
guns and it was the guns, which touched creating the
cross on the letter A.

He wished he had a camera with him it would be good
to have a copy of this piece. Maybe he could buy one
of those disposable ones at the seven eleven. The light
went out and he ran into the range of the motion sensor
again. He looked at the second letter, which if it were
a true Ant piece would be the letter "N". It was a letter
"N" a picture of a dead woman, with a magnifying
glass on her face giving an almost photographic image
of the face. The rest of the "N" was her limp body
shaped into the "N".

The light went out again and once again he raced back
to the light sensor. The last letter of the piece was a
self-portrait of Ant. He was tied to a wooden cross
with bullet holes in his chest and blood trickling from
his mouth. Malachy step forward and looked at the
face more clearly. A tear was just leaving the face and
the eyes where cast down. He looked down at the foot
of the cross a little girl was lying dead on the floor,
bullet wounds all over her body.

The light went out, he stood staring at the image until
he could no longer make it out.

"Ant said what do you want?" said a voice from deep in the shadows.

Malachy jumped and swung around to see where the voice had come from.

"I need to talk to him about his pictures."

"Why?"

"Who are you?"

"I'm a friend of the Man."

Malachy could just make out the shape of the man. If the motion sensor light came on, he would be able to see who it was.

"Tell him I understand and know who she was."

"What's that mean?"

"Just tell him he will understand."

"Is that it?"

"Tell him, no wait, tell him I can help. No that won't work either."

"Make your mind up."

"Tell Ant I believe he is a true artist and paints what he sees, I too see it."

"Ya what," said the voice and then took a step forward. Malachy could just make whom it was who was speaking.

The motion light came on, Malachy spun around to see who had activated the light. It was a group of wild cats attacking a small rodent, which had already been torn apart. As he returned to where the voice had come from, he saw the figure of Morgan stepping back into the shadows. Morgan turned and ran down the passageway between the two apartment complexes. Malachy stood watching him, if he didn't have problems with his legs he would have run after him.

The light went out then came back on again as the cats began to fight each other. A man at one of the

apartment windows stuck his head and shouted,
"Who's playing with those lights."
He looked down into the alleyway and saw the cats.
Malachy took this opportunity to continue down the alleyway and onto the road, where Janice lived.
He stood in the shadow looking up the street. He felt
the vibration of his cell phone. He fumbled in his trouser pocket to recover it. He looked at the caller ID and
saw it was Mark Thompson's cell phone number.
"Hello Mark," he said opening the connection.
"Malachy it's Sandra, Mark has disappeared."
"What?"
"Mark has gone, we were supposed to have a dinner
with a client. My husband and I turned up at the restaurant and we waited but he didn't turn up. I had to
deal with the client on my own."
"I see."
"I called his home and his wife said he had not been
home since Thursday."
"I don't know where he is."
"If he calls you, tell him to call me as soon as he can,
I really need to talk to him."
"Okay."
"Bye."
"Bye, why are you calling on Mark's cell phone?"
The line had gone dead.
He pondered if he should call her back but decided not
to. He slipped the cell phone back into his pocket and
not looking up he turned into another alleyway behind
an apartment complex. When he looked up, he saw
just ahead of him, Morgan in a light from an underground parking structure beneath the apartment complex. He was leaning against a telegraph pole smoking
and trying to blow smoke rings. He was unsuccessful.

Malachy crept along the edge of the alleyway keeping in the shadows. As he reached the edge of the light Morgan was standing in, he realized that Morgan was talking to someone on his cell phone. Malachy slide back into the shadows and listened.

"Okay man, take care," said Morgan closing his cell phone.

He took a long drag on his cigarette and then flicked the remaining butt down into the parking structure. He walked towards where Malachy was but didn't see him in the shadow.

Once he had passed Morgan stopped to light another cigarette. Malachy moved out of the shadows and behind Morgan. Using his fingers as though they were a gun. He stuck them in Morgan's back

"Freeze."

Morgan stopped and let the cigarette fall from his mouth, he slowly began to turn around.

"Face forward."

"I don't have money man."

"I don't want your money, where's Ant?"

"Who?"

"Don't mess with me Morgan, where is Ant?"

"I don't know."

"You've just spoken to him on your cell phone."

"Shit man, I don't know where he is."

"Yes you do and if you don't tell me, I'll put a bullet up your arse."

Malachy lowered the gun and placed it between the cheeks of Morgan's butt.

"The Man didn't tell me man."

"Don't lie either you tell me or I'm gonna shoot."

He pushed his imaginary gun deep into the crack of Morgan's butt.

"Look man I don't know where he actually is, he said he was at his art place that's all. Please don't shoot me, at least not there."

"If you're lying, I'll come and find you. And don't call Ant if I find out you did. I'll blow your dick off when I find you."

"I won't man shit please."

"Okay keep walking."

Malachy pushed him with the finger gun and watched Morgan move very slowly away. Morgan had for some reason raised his hands and as he walked on to the street a woman passing looked at him as though he was crazy.

Keeping in the shadows Malachy ran up the alleyway laughing to himself. He was close to Janice's house and relished the idea of telling her what had been happening.

It took a lot of self-control to stop laughing. He busted out into a fit of giggles and then stopped trying to control himself. He could see Janice's house from where he stood and was about to cross the street when he saw a dark figure by the side of her house. He watched trying to find a way to get closer to the building. The dark figure was joined by several others. All were dressed in black jump suits and some wore helmets with visors. He wasn't sure but it looked as though they were carrying automatic rifles.

He was grateful the streetlight was out it allowed him to become invisible. It also made it difficult to see what was happening at Janice's house. He needed to get closer to see what was happening and to see if Janice was okay.

A little way up the street, across from Janice's, there was an underground parking structure that didn't have

a security gate. He had noticed it the last time he had
been there. At the time he wondered why the owner
had not put in a secure gate like the other complexes.
He would have to go back down the alleyway and then
cross between two complexes to get to the alleyway
and the underground structure.

Creeping down the alleyway suddenly the streetlight
next to where he had been standing came on. If he had
been standing there, he would have been illuminated.
As he walked, he thought about the street lighting, it
was completely unpredictable. Someone should tell
the council to do something about it.

Seeing a passageway between two aging apartment
complexes, he tried to run, then slowed down to a hob-
ble, down it out, into the street and across into the garden of an empty house. The garden was littered with
building materials and gave the impression as though
someone was trying to restore the house, even if it was
taking a long time.

The wire mesh fence at the bottom of the back yard
had a hole in it and looked as though it had become a
short cut for someone. He climbed through carefully
not to catch his clothing as he did. He quickly walked
into the sunken parking structure opposite Janice's
house. One forty-watt bulb flicked in the middle of
the structure. Several cars were haphazardly parked
some looking as though they had been abandoned a
long time ago. He moved from one car to another trying to keep in the dark as much as possible hoping the
men at Janice's house wouldn't see him.

The light bulb flickered and then died. He conjectured
if it was like the streetlight and once it had cooled
down would relight itself. But this bulb was dead and
wouldn't be replaced in a hurry. In the darkness he

quickens his pace, at the entrance to the structure on the street side he peered around the wall and looked across the street to Janice's house.

The men had made entry into the house, the porch light came on and for a few seconds Malachy could see one of the men standing outside. He stared ardently he couldn't believe it. He knew the man, he'd seen him before, several times. It was the man from work the one he had seen in the elevator. The man who had watched him in the office building lobby. The man Janice said was a police officer. What was he doing here at Janice's house and where was Janice now? These questions flooded his mind. He pulled back behind the wall closed his eyes, placing the palms of his hands over his face. For the first time he really felt scared, he became hot and began to shake.

He returned to look at the house, the light was now off, and he could only just make out the shape of several men standing outside the front door.

The hands came from nowhere and covered his eyes. They were small boney hands cold as porcelain but with a soft touch and they dug into his eye sockets. He didn't move but froze from fear. The hands pulled him back slowly behind the wall before releasing him. Gathering his senses, he turned and saw Janice's smiling face. He grabbed her and gave her a hug. She was surprised and pushed him away.

"Sorry," he whispered.

She just smiled and indicated for him to follow her to the back of the parking structure. Once they were in the alleyway and out of sight of her house, she gave him a hug.

"I didn't mean to push you away, you just surprised me."

"I was so glad to see you. There are men all over your house."

"Not just men, some of those black figures are women."

"I think it's my fault."

"I know it's connected to you because I heard one of them mention your name."

"How did you get out?"

"When I was a kid and my mom had one of her boyfriends over. I would sneak out of the house by falling into the next-door garden from my bedroom window. When I heard them coming, I ran into my old bedroom and slipped out of the window."

"Thank God you did."

"Then when I crossed the road, I saw you and came up behind you."

"You scared me to death, well nearly."

"Sorry."

"I wonder why he was there?"

"Who?"

"A man I've seen in the building I work in, the man you said was a police officer."

"He was in my house?"

"Yes, another piece of the jigsaw puzzle."

"I like doing those."

"We need to find Ant and I think I know where he is."

"Let's go, I don't think we should stay around here too long."

The light of the car switched on, neither of them had heard it enter the alleyway. Janice grabbed Malachy, and began to kiss him, they fell against the wall as the police car drove slowly past them. The car's front window searchlight scanned the dark areas. Janice's hand came up and shielded Malachy face as the light panned over them.

The passenger police officer lowered his window and shouted, "Get a room." Then turning to the driver, they both laughed.

Janice stopped kissing Malachy and shouted back at the officer "we can't afford one."

Looking into Malachy's eyes she said "Sorry it was the only thing I could think of doing. I saw it once in a movie and it just came into my head"

"It's okay. I think I saw that movie too."

"We should go now."

She took hold of his hand and they ran down the alleyway away from the police car. They kept running until Malachy stopped, his legs were hurting, and his breathing had become difficult.

"Sorry I need to catch my breath."

"No problem, where are we going?"

"To the walkway under the freeway by Duncan's, I think that is where we will find Ant."

"Ant the graffiti boy?"

"Yes," said Malachy trying to control his breathing while rubbing his legs and ankles.

"Why?"

"Because I think he is the link to the whole thing, not sure if he knows it but I saw a picture of his and it gave a new slant on this thing."

"Okay." She began to walk slowly and took his arm acting like a walking stick support.

"I don't understand what's wrong with you but if this helps."

"Oh, Janice it helps."

The tunnel under the freeway was once a road but had been closed to vehicle traffic. It was often used by the

homeless to sleep in at night and school kids during
the day as a place to take drugs. The lights, which
were clamped to the ceiling of the tunnel were black
and rusty, long forgotten by the city that worked on the
premise 'out of sight, out of mind'.
They stood in the entrance. It was hard to see if anyone was inside, lying on the floor asleep. The streetlight from each end of the tunnel didn't penetrate all
the way and left a black hole in the middle.
 "I don't think anyone is here," said Janice hoping
they didn't have to go inside.
 "Let's check."
 "Must we?"
Malachy didn't answer but entered the tunnel appre-
hensively. He needed to find Ant he wasn't sure why.
His world was being changed upside down and now he
felt he needed some answers. He already had too
many questions left unanswered.
Janice stood looking at him. It wasn't long ago she
had been kissing him and now he was walking into a
black hole not knowing what was there. A noise from
behind her made her follow him at a rapid pace.
The tunnel stank, of what was hard to differentiate, but
it wasn't a pleasant smell. Each step took them deeper
into the darkness, and their eyes desperately tried to re-
focus. Slowly allowing them to see more and more.
Something ran along the ground in front of them. It
then stopped and turned and looked at them, its two
bright eyes piercing the darkness. They had invaded
its territory and it wanted them to know they were the
intruders. The white strip down its back had become
visible as their eyes readjusted.
 "Skunk."

The creature turned away from them and ran down the tunnel and into the street at the other end.

"At least it didn't spray us."

"Good, I hate that smell."

Janice stopped and gave a little squeal she fumbled in her pockets and took out her house keys. She pressed a button on a black square piece of plastic and a small beam of light shone out from one corner. It illuminated a piece of graffiti the one they had seen before. Janice scanned the wall showing other newer pieces by Ant. The light left the wall and scanned the rest of the tunnel. Their eyes had now become completely accustomed to the darkness and they could see no one was inside the tunnel.

"He's not here."

"I know, but he has added more pictures and another figure has appeared in this piece. Malachy went closer to get a better look he peered at the picture.

"I think this is my boss."

"How do you know in this light?"

"I just know, bring your little light over here."

Janice shone the light on the face of the figure Malachy was looking at. It was the face of Mark.

They both turned and saw a line of men standing at the entrance to the tunnel to their left. Their head swiveled and they looked the other way, the streetlight was stronger at this end and they could make out the men were carrying guns.

The skunk returned and as one of the men kicked at it with the barrel of the gun he was carrying, the skunk lifted its tail and sprayed the line of men.

Janice and Malachy moved to the wall opposite. A metal door built into the wall felt cold against Janice's back. She turned and searched for a handle. If she could get the door open, they could maybe hide inside. The men began to move into the tunnel Malachy stretched his hand out groping for Janice, but she seemed to have disappeared. A hand grabbed at his sleeve and pulled him backwards through the metal door. He stood in complete darkness unaware where he was. The sound of a metal door closing and the squeak of a wheel turning sounded surreal. The smell of dampness permeated the air. He felt like cold wet wisps of air race around his body. He shivered from the cold.

"Janice."

"I'm here."

"You okay."

"Yes, but I not sure what brought us here."

"What do you mean? You didn't open the door?"

"No, the door wouldn't open there wasn't any handle. Then this hand grabbed me and pulled me inside."

"Whose hand?"

"I don't know I can't see."

A softer hand clasped Malachy's left wrist and he was led deep into the darkness. He could hear dripping water and his feet were splashing in water as he was dragged along.

"Janice could you let go a little, your grip it is hurting my wrist."

"I don't have your wrist, I thought you had mine."

The hand let go of Malachy's hand. He stood still wondering what was going to happen next. The hand gripped his wrist again this time a little softer. Another hand pushed his head down and then propelled him forward. His foot hit a step and he had to lift his foot quite high to step through a doorway. Once on the other side he bumped into Janice who grabbed his arm and wouldn't let go.

The sound of the metal door closing and the squeak of the wheel could be heard again. This was repeated.

"I think we maybe in a submarine."

"What in Burbank?"

"Just kidding Janice."

The noise of a level being pulled down with a gushing sound was followed by a light being switched on.

They were in a concrete walled room the ceiling was so high it was hard to see it. A few woolen blanks lay in the corner.

Malachy turned around and saw Ant standing looking at them. His black clothes were very dirty. His face was gaunt, his eyes deep in their sockets were tired. His soft skin beneath the dirt was pale and dry.

"We can't stay here they will work out what we did and find the other entrances," said Ant.

"What did you do?"

"I flooded the chamber between them and us.

There's a small reservoir of water which the fire department uses for freeway emergency. If it rains, they can store water in the chamber we have just gone through."

"Thanks."

"Don't thank me yet."

Ant gathered his few things and placed them in a black backpack.

"Follow me, I hope you don't mind heights, just don't look down."

He crossed to the corner of the room and began to climb a metal ladder, which seemed to go up and up. Janice looked up.

"I feel like Jack in Jack and the Beanstalk."
Ant continued to climb, Malachy pushed Janice to follow, and she reluctantly began to climb.
"How high is it?" she asked trying not to look down.
Ant didn't reply. As they got higher, a cool breeze could be felt. Malachy feet felt strange on the metal rungs of the ladder. He hoped his legs didn't give out.
"Stop" commanded Ant
Janice stopped and wondered if Malachy had heard.
When he didn't walk into her, she relaxed.
Malachy looked down and immediately wished he hadn't. They had left the light on in the room and he wondered if they should have turned it off.
A gust of cold air rushed past him this was followed by Ant shouting "Okay you can come up now."
As they emerged out of the shaft, realizing they were standing on the side of the freeway, Janice helped Malachy climb the last few steps. Ant leaned down, flicked a switch and replaced the metal lid of the shaft.
"What about the light on in the room?" asked Janice.
"I've just switched it off. We have to walk a little to get to the ramp and off the freeway."
The cars of the freeway flashed by, a few articulated trucks, thundered by, a gust of wind sucking the three adventures slight towards the traffic. Malachy took Janice's hand, the warmth felt comforting. The danger was not over, and they needed to find somewhere safe to hide. Ant trudged ahead of them, his shoulder bent down and his head looking at the ground. He had just saved them from who knows what.

CHAPTER ELEVEN

On the Run

Malachy, Janice, and Ant sat in the corner of the all-night coffee shop. Ant held a plastic cup with both hands clasped around it. He stared at it, the white surface of the inside beckoning him to paint on it.
They had sat in silence for at least ten minutes only Malachy had spoken when they arrived, to order.
Janice had taken money out of her bag to pay but Malachy had motioned she put it away and to find a table.
Malachy stared at his cohorts as he sipped his vanilla caramel latte. Janice looked tired, the lines under her eyes were deep and dark. For someone on the run, Ant didn't look too bad and Malachy put this down to his age.
Janice looked up from the floor and stared at Ant then Malachy. She coughed hard, deep from her throat.
Malachy looked at her then, as though he suddenly came alive.
  "Oh sorry, Janice this is Ant. Ant this is Janice."
They looked at each other and nodded. Silence then descend on the group once more it was a cloud of un-comfortableness.
Malachy looked around the coffee shop they were the only customers, and they weren't making the owner

rich. The man behind the counter had returned to his book. His thick rubbery looking lips spoke the words as he read, as his dark sunken eyes scanned the page. Malachy had surmised he was from the European eastern bloc countries. His accent was heavy and his English limited. Malachy picked up his coffee cup and took a drink, slowly he craned his neck backwards expecting there to be coffee inside. He looked inside the cup it was empty. He rose from the table and went to the counter.

"Yep," asked the man behind the counter without looking up from his book.

"Same again please."

"Two latte's and a glass of milk."

"Yes please."

Malachy placed the drinks in front of Janice and Ant.

"I think we will be safe here for the time being"

"Why did you want to see me?" asked Ant

"Because I think you saw the murder. I know who she is and maybe why she was murdered."

"They are looking for me."

"Who are?"

"The guys who murdered the girl."

"So, you did see the murder?"

"Yes, then they came after me and tried to kill me. They shot at me and then at home, my sister wearing my jacket, was hit and I think she's dead. I ran, I was so scared. If I had stayed maybe they would have killed my whole family."

"Who was the woman who got murdered again?" asked Janice

"She was something to do with a client at work, but everyone tells me she didn't exist."

"Well she did he saw her murdered."

"True Janice, also I think the government are investigating my boss and he had something to do with her."

"Is that why you wanted to see me?"

"Yes, no, my boss has gone missing according to his wife and his mistress."

"Sounds like one of my mother's soaps. Why do they call you Ant?" asked Janice.

"I don't like my name and when I was little, I could just say Ant. Everyone called me that from then on."

"I see, I quite like it."

"Where do you fit into all this?"

"I am not sure. I meet Malachy at the department store I work at and now we have armed men chasing us."

"So, what do we do next?"

"I'm not sure, have you told your parents you're safe?"

"My friend Morgan rang them. My dad won't care but my mother will."

Malachy's cell phone rang.

"Yes."

"Malachy, its Sandra, have you heard anything?"

"No."

"I just don't understand why his cell phone is always busy."

"Because you're using it."

"What?"

"You have Mark's phone and he must have yours."

"Oh, no wonder no one is calling me."

"Call your number and maybe Mark will answer."

"Yes, I'll do that. My husband is missing too."

"Maybe he is with Mark."

"Do you think so, Malachy? I'll call you later thanks."

"Who was that?"

"Sandra, she is the mistress."

The back door of the coffee shop opened, and two tall bulky police officers entered. They looked at the three sitting in the corner. All three looked back and the officers nodded. At the counter the fatter of the two, his uniform straining at the seams leaned on the counter and looked again at the three in the corner. Malachy stared back. The officer was in his mid-thirties but had already achieved the weather-beaten hard man look. The officer's slight brown mustache needed trimming and dying to match the dyed black hair. His eyes were brown and piecing.

Malachy whispered to the others "let's keep on talking we don't want to seem suspicious"

"What shall we talk about?" asked Janice

Ant shrugged his shoulders.

"I saw this film once," said Malachy just loud enough for the officer to hear. 'The problem with the film was you never really got all the pieces."

Ant and Janice stared at him. Janice wondered if Malachy had gone mad or was on drugs.

"It was about this man who had murdered someone, and a boy had seen him do it."

"I think I saw that one, wasn't the boy a Mormon or something religious?"

The policeman lost interest in them and began to talk to the man behind the counter who was now making their drinks. The way the officer was standing and his body gestures it looked like he was flirting with the guy behind the counter. The other officer had gone over to the window and sat down looking out on to the street.

"So, what happens now?" asked Ant, the lines of worry developing on his young face.

"I think we need to work out the facts as we have them between us."

"Oh, oh I have something," said Janice excitedly

A high pitch squawk sound emulated from the radio of the officer by the window. He spoke into the speaker extension, which was fixed, to his shirt near his left ear. Intently he listened before picking up coffee and joined the other officer at the counter. The two of them spoke in a whisper and turned to leave the coffee shop. The officer who had been standing at the counter twisted around and blew a kiss to the man behind the counter before leaving.

"Did you see that?" asked Janice her face showing her shock.

Ant gave a loud sigh of relief and sank back into the chair.

"Another drink?"

Ant nodded.

"Stop," shouted Janice as she rummaged in her pockets. "I have this." She handed Malachy several pieces of paper which had been taped together.

"What? How? That was quick."

"They hadn't been properly shredded and had stuck together so it was easy to put them back together. You see they are four pages together and for some reason the shredder didn't completely shred them. The last sixteenth of an inch stayed intact."

"Good one Janice."

"Drinks?" asked Ant who felt out of the conversation.

"Oh yes. Here, some money."
Ant looked relieved, he only had a few dollars left and he wasn't sure how long he was going to be living on the street.
Malachy began to read the papers. It wasn't very easy because of the way they had been shredded but it started to get the gist of the material.
He looked up from the papers, "what if the police find the rest of the papers?"
"I put them in a box as though they were packing."
"Clever one Janice." He raised his hand and gave her a high five.
"Thanks. I'm not just a pretty face." She gave one of her little giggles as she said it.
Ant returned to the table carrying the drinks.
"I hope you don't mind but I got some muffins as well I am hungry."
"No problem."
"I don't understand, where did these papers come from and why were they shredded?"
"My bosses office, he was shredding them, and I can see why now."
"Why?"
"Because it has account names and numbers and other restricted information. This is interesting."
"What is?" asked Janice trying to see what he was reading.
"One of the names on the account was with the woman who was murdered when she came to the office and the man lives quite close to here."
"Who?"
"Anthony Drongotti."
"You've lost me," said Ant.

"Sorry let me explain, you saw a woman murdered, she was in our office the day before and was involved in a restricted account. In fact, an account that everyone denies exists."

"Meaning?"

"I think my boss was involved with money laundering and this was one of the accounts he was using for it."

"Money laundering doesn't mean washing money and hanging it out to dry. It means taking bad money and making it look legal. That's right, isn't it Malachy?"

"That's a good way to put it."

"A lot of money?" asked Ant moving forward so he could hear every word.

"Usually in the millions, because of the creative way how they launder the money, it really has become an art form."

"What money is it?"

"Drugs, terrorist and the type of crimes where the source of the money needs to be concealed."

"Good job my dad doesn't know about it. For him everything that's corrupt is part of a big conspiracy."

"I think what we really should do now is go and see this man, he may even talk to us."

"Won't that be dangerous?"

"Maybe but it's better than sitting here waiting for something to happen. If we tell Anthony about the murder, he may help us."

"You got a car?" asked Ant

"No."

"I do."

"Janice your place is swarming with the police, the feds, who knows what else."

"I don't have cockroaches."
"I don't mean insects, just people."
"I moved the car."
"Why did you do that?"
"Not sure, I wanted to drive it, so I parked it at the
mall."
"Drink up, let's go."
"Do you think I should call my mother?" asked Ant
Malachy handed him his cell phone.
"Don't tell her what happened or who you are with.
Just tell her you're sorry and need to sort out a few
things first. Well something like that," said Janice.
Malachy and Ant looked at her.
"Well I know what mothers are like, they push ask-
ing questions, until you told them everything and
don't mean too."
Ant nodded he understood exactly what Janice meant.
He went and sat by the window. Malachy returned to
reading the shredded papers, he kept making sighing
noises as he read.
Janice stared at Ant as he talked on the phone. She
wasn't sure about him and she need to have an opinion, she always did. He had a strange name, looked
odd in the way he dressed and didn't say much. But
something inside made her feel he was an okay guy.
Malachy gave another deep sigh and she looked at
him. She had grown to like this man. She didn't want
him as a lover and there was never any question of it.
He was like a big older brother. But why was he so involved in this mystery. Most people in his position
would have just walked away, he was running towards
it.
She hadn't told him she had been fired from her job.
Well they had said she was laid off. Her returns

department was no longer needed. She didn't care at this moment of time, she was on an adventure, however strange it all was. Should she tell him, if only to tell someone.

Her eyes refocused and she saw Malachy staring at her because she was staring at him.

She looked away in embarrassment, but when she quickly glanced back, she caught Malachy staring at her. Then she realized he wasn't staring at her. He was in deep thought. She broke the silence.

"He's a little strange."

"They say that about you."

"I know I got fired today."

"What? Because of me?"

"No, they said they didn't need me anymore."

"I'm sorry."

"I'm not, I hated the job."

"What are you going to do?"

"I'm not sure, take a break, I have some money of my own and then there is the money my mother left me. I really need to find out what I want to do with my life."

"Don't we all."

Ant returned and flopped down in the chair.

"Not go well?"

"Oh, mom was fine and the family, said I had to do what I needed to. My father is blaming himself. Said they were after him for things he did when he was younger in the Philippines."

"But that's not true."

"I know but you don't know my dad. Some men came around and they said they were police. My father knew they weren't, so he told them I had gone to see my grandparents in the Philippines."

"Your dad sounds okay."

"Mom said he missed me."

"Oh, he will, once when I was little, I went to stay with an aunt and my mother made me come back after a week. She said she missed me. I think she really did."

"But my dad hates me."

"That's what you think, sounds like he loves you, but just can't show it. Just like my mother," said Janice dismissing the self-pity in Ant's voice.

Malachy looked at Janice she really was a smart woman. It was at moments like this she seemed to shine.

"What about your sister?" asked Malachy.

"She's dead. The police think she was caught in crossfire of a gang war."

"In Burbank? said Janice.

"Burbank High is not all Gee club and dancing these days," stated Ant.

"I'm sorry," said Janice.

"I think it's my fault."

Malachy looked from one to the other and before Janice could reply said, "So let's go and see Anthony Drongotti."

Janice had parked the car in the corner of the parking structure at the Burbank mall. From the way she had parked it Malachy took a few minutes to back out and leave the parking lot. As they drove along the street Janice relaxed in the passenger seat. She was in a movie, the female star. She had drifted off into a fantasy *'The FBI or was it the CIA had asked her to solve a major crime and here she was being driven by her personal bodyguard.'*

Ant sat in the back of the car looking at the two in front, he wasn't sure why he was there but for some strange reason he trusted them. They seemed to understand, give him the space he liked without too many questions. They made no judgment of him, and this was something new. He wasn't sure he could handle it. He had been beaten down by everyone in authority he encountered, even some of his peers at school. They don't like his hair, his clothes, he was to most, just another crazy tagger. These two, who he hardly knew, took him for what he was, and they had even complimented him on his pictures.

"What are we going to do after we have seen this man?"
The silence was broken by Janice who had come out of her dream.

"We need somewhere to stay."
"A motel."
"Not a bad idea Janice."
Ant sat in the back looking at them, he wanted to join in the conversation but felt inadequate. As if the thought he had suddenly woke up, he bust out saying "Shouldn't we book a room before we go to the house in case, we are a very long time talking to this man."
Janice turned around and looked at Ant. "Now that is a very good idea, I don't fancy sleeping in the car."
"Okay look out for a motel we're not far from the airport so there must be one around here somewhere."
Janice and Ant stared out of the window searching the darkened building looking for a motel. Janice's competitive edge began to well up inside her. She wanted to find it first and began to push her face against the

side window. She remembered a trip she took with her mother. She would tell Janice to look and see if she could spot the place they were going. Sadly, Janice came to realize it was just a game her mother used to shut her up.

Janice sank back into her seat, the feeling of being childish made her blush. Hoping it was too dark for the others to see her red face. She sat silently looking forward, why did she behave like this, she was a woman now, old enough to have children of her own.

"What's wrong Janice?" asked Malachy

"Nothing."

"You sure?"

"I was being childish, and I don't know why. I wanted to find the motel first."

"Me too," said Ant.

Janice looked at Ant, he nodded his head.

"Well my children keep looking and the first one to find a motel will get a candy."

Ant laughed, which prompted Janice to follow. Looking back at Ant she mouthed 'thank you'

He smiled and said, "If you are looking at me, you'll not find the motel first."

Janice laughed out loud and began to look for the motel.

The light bulb behind the motel sign flickered as they drove on to the forecourt. All three had shouted 'Motel' as they had seen it ahead of them.

Malachy jumped out of the car and ran into the glass-fronted lobby. He began to talk to the balding little man behind the counter. Janice and Ant sat silently watching, each one wondering what to say. They both relaxed when they saw Malachy take his wallet out of his back pocket.

"I thought he wasn't going to get somewhere, I could really do with a good sleep," said Janice"

"I need a shower and some sleep."

"Have you been living under the freeway since you ran away?"

"I didn't really run away I went into hiding because of those men after me."

"Who are they?"

"Not sure."

"None of this seems real. I keep thinking I'm in a film, an old nineteen thirties spy mystery movie."

"I don't think I've ever seen an old movie."

"Oh, you must have, my mother would sit me in front of the television, and I'd watch whatever was on. It took me a long time to realize I could change the channels. Then I only watched what I wanted to."

"We didn't have television until two years ago."

"No way."

"Yeah way, my dad said the government could see into your living room through the TV monitor."

"Did you believe him?"

"At first, as I grew older, I found out it wasn't true and was just his paranoia about being watched by big brother. Now they say smart TVs have cameras in them"

"What?"

"I think my dad is illegal, even though he has lived here for twenty-four years."

"I won't tell."

"It doesn't matter if you do. My mom is legal so I don't think they can throw him out. Anyway, I was born here so I'm an American and he is my legal guardian."

"I see, where's Malachy?"
They looked into the glass-fronted lobby, but there
was no sign of him or the baldheaded desk clerk.
They searched the motel building for signs of him, and
when the desk clerk suddenly appeared in front of the
car, Janice gave a little squeal.
  "Okay kids all set, thanks Mister Jenkins we will see
  you later."
Malachy climbed into the car and drove out of the
forecourt. Before anyone had a chance to say anything.
  "We have a room with two beds, one king size for
  Ant and me and a full for little baby Janice."
Janice looked at him and stuck her tongue out then put
her thumb in her mouth. Malachy laughed.
  "According to Mister Jenkins the house we want is
  only three blocks away."
The three-story house was set back from the road, the
garden in the light available looked perfectly manicured. Looking like a film star's Hollywood home, the
center roof section was shaped like a pyramid. Above
the front door with its Greek columns on either side
was a brass shield with the letter 'D' in old English
typeface. A light from a lower room spilled out onto
the garden.
  "Wow, should we all go?" asked Janice a slight trace
  of fear in her voice.
  "Yes," said Ant firmly.
  "Better to stick together, I agree with Ant, we don't
  want anything to happen to our little baby girl."
Janice playfully punched Malachy on the arm.
They walked up the faded red brick pathway, which
was lit by square glass encased lamps.

"I feel like Dorothy and we are on the road to Oz,"
giggled Janice.

"It really looks more like a film set than a house
where people live."

"It would be great for a Halloween party," said Ant.
Ant lifted the brass knocker and made two loud knocks
on the oak door. Janice became impatient as no one
opened the door.

"I don't think anyone is in."
The door opened and a white-haired old lady peered
around the edge. She was dressed in a neck to floor
flowery patterned dressing grown.

"No thank you," she said as he began to close the
door.

Janice stuck her foot on the doorstep preventing her
from closing the door.

"We need to talk to Mr. Anthony Drongotti," said
Janice.

"He's not here."

"When will he be back?"
The old lady stood looking at the three eclectic characters as she decided to answer the question.

"He is dead."

"Sorry."

"He died last year."

"Then we really need to talk to you, are you his
wife," asked Malachy.
The door opened a little further.

"Why do you need to talk to him?"

"I'm from Weinstocks and Boller Investments."

"You need to talk to the accountant Mr. Fahey."

"I would prefer to talk to you. I think you know
what about."

"I don't know anything."

She began to close the door.

"Mrs. Drongotti we are trying to find out why a woman was murdered, and I think you know something which may help us."

The old lady paused again from closing the door.

"Please Mrs. Drongotti we believe you really can help us," said Ant in a very respectful tone.

"Just the three of you?"

"Yes."

"I can only spare you a few minutes I was on my way to bed."

"That's all we need."

"Come in quickly then."

The door opened wider and Janice rushed in followed by the other two. Mrs. Drongotti closed the door and slip a bolt into place.

The hallway was round with a staircase, which hung out of the wall and spiraled up to the next floor. The old lady led them into a marble kitchen. Like the outside of the building it looked more like a film set than the real thing. The highly polished marble surfaces had very few kitchen appliances on it. Glass fronted wall cupboards were full of expensive china and glassware.

The old lady indicated for them to sit down at an old-fashioned kitchen table at the other end of the room.

"This kitchen is as big as our whole apartment," whispered Ant to Janice who nodded.

As they sat down Mrs. Drongotti looked at each of them, Janice smiled then gave one of her little giggles.

"I wouldn't have let you in if this young man hadn't been so polite. Obviously, he came from a very good family."

Ant smiled.

"What's your name?"

"An... Anthony, this is Janice and Malachy."

"Malachy as in Dickens, how nice."

"Mrs. Drongotti I'm sorry to hear your husband has died. We needed to talk to him about an account he had with Weinstocks and Boller Investments."

"My husband didn't have an account with them I would have known about it."

"Are you sure I've seen his name on the account papers."

"Oh he signed some papers for Mr. Fahey before he died, which I think came from Weinstocks and Boller Investments, but he didn't have an account with them."

"Mr. Fahey."

"Yes, he was our accountant, he had been with Tony's and my accountant for many years a very nice man."

"How did your husband die?" asked Ant.

The question stopped Mrs. Drongotti for a moment. She stared at Ant searching his face wondering why he had asked that question.

"He fell asleep driving."

"Where?"

Malachy and Janice looked astonished at Ant. Mrs. Drongotti flickered eyelids as she stared at him.

"On the way back from Santa Barbara."

"Why was he there?"

"That's just it I'm not sure, he told me he was going to see some old friends in Santa Monica. And we had friends down there, so I wasn't worried. Then when the police came and told me he had died near Santa Barbara I couldn't understand what he was doing there."

"Maybe he had gone to see Monica Trystwold," said Malachy.

"He had I found some notes in an old jacket he was going to wear that day. I made him change it into something more descent."

"Had he been to see her?" asked Ant.

"I rang and asked if he had and was told she was dead, been dead for years. And you know what's strange, she died while driving too, fell asleep at the wheel."

"That's more than strange. Did they do an autopsy on your husband?"

Mrs. Drongotti slide round in her chair to face Ant fully.

"Yes, and they found he had taken sleeping pills or something like that. That's odd too as Tony didn't believe in pills and we don't have any in the house."

"Do you think he was murdered?"

"I do," said Mrs. Drongotti, "And that's why you're here."

"Sort of," said Malachy.

Speaking directly to Ant she asked, "How can I help you?"

"Tell us all you know about Monica Trystwold, Mister Fahey and Weinstocks and Boller Investments," said Malachy.

She ignored him until Ant had nodded his head.

"My husband was a good man, so I really don't know why he got involved. I came home from the shops one day to find Joshua Fahey and Tony signing some papers. Another man was with them, but I was never told his name."

"Pity," commented Malachy.

"After they had gone, I asked Tony what it was all about, and he said Joshua wanted him as a witness to some papers."

"Wouldn't they have done that at Fahey's office?" asked Ant.

"That is what I thought, but I didn't say anything, then one day a package arrived full of money, hundreds dollar bills. Tony said he'd lent someone some money and they were paying him back."

"You didn't believe him?" asked Ant.

"Tony had never lied to me all our married life, but I knew this was a lie."

"Then what happened?"

"We argued about it until he admitted that the money had come from Joshua Fahey for signing those papers."

"Sounds fishy to me," said Janice who had been just sitting and listening.

"Me too," said Mrs. Drongotti, "And that's not all every month a package came."

"Do they still come?" asked Ant.

"No, they stopped after a few months, then Joshua Fahey came and told me Tony had made arrangements for the money to be paid into my bank account each month. And it has been without missing a month."

"I'm not sure I like Joshua Fahey," said Janice.

"Oh, he's alright, a little greasy if you get my meaning. He also told me to tell him if anyone came asking questions about Tony and the papers he signed."

"Did he say signed?" asked Ant.

"Yes, and I said Tony had witnessed surely and he said oh yes that was right."

"Mrs. Drongotti, you have been a great help and I
don't think your husband's name needs to be mentioned again."

"If Tony did something wrong, then it should come
out."

Malachy stood up, "Well thank you again for your
help." Janice stood up.

Ant didn't stand up, he stared at the white-haired old
lady.

"There is something you've not told us isn't there?"

Mrs. Drongotti looked deep into Ant's eyes.

"I've seen you in church with your mother, haven't
I?"

"Maybe, I go every Sunday to Mass."

"I knew I had seen you, you have a funny name,
cockroach or something."

"They call me Ant but my name is Anthony."

"Yes, your right I haven't told you everything I'm
scared."

"Me too ever since I saw that woman murdered but
we need to find out the truth, if we don't no one
will."

Malachy sat down, followed by Janice. Ant had sudden grown in his respect. This young unconventional
man was not a shallow self-centered lazy youth. He
had morals and believed in the truth regardless.

"The daughter of Monica Trystwold came to see me.
She told me she thought her mother had been murdered."

"Did she say why her mother was murdered?"

"Because she asked too many questions."

"Just like me," said Ant

"We talked for about five hours, after a while I asked
to see her ID, not sure why, but she was who she said
she was."

"Did she say anything else?"

"At the end, she said Tony had said he was scared
because he knew it was to do with money laundering.
At first, I didn't believe then as I put two and two together, I realized she had been right."

"Then what happened?"

"Well two, no three days later this woman arrived
said she was Monica Trystwold daughter. I knew
she wasn't, and she asked a lot of questions, but I
gave very vague answers. I didn't like her."

Malachy slide to the end of his seat eager to hear more.

"After she had left, I called Joshua and told him, he
said I did the right thing."

"Which was?" asked Janice.

"Oh, I didn't tell him about the first lady, only the
imposter."

Ant open his backpack and took out his sketchpad, he
flipped through the pages until he came to a picture.

"Is this the woman?" He handed Mrs. Drongotti the
pad, it was a pencil drawing of he murdered woman.

"Oh, my yes it looks just like her, did you draw
this?"

"Yes."

"You're very good." She continued to flip through
the sketchpad.

"Who was she?"

"She is the woman I saw murdered."

"I see."

"You should go to art college Anthony or can I also
call you Ant?"

"If you want to, I just don't like my name."

"Why ever not? Anthony is just a strong name.
What does your mother call you?
"Anthony."
"Don't you have a little sister?"
"Err," he didn't want to go into what happened, so he
just answered, "Yes."
She closed the Sketchpad and handed it back to him.
"Now you be careful, I don't think those people are
very nice."
"We will," replied Malachy.
"Are you going to call Fahey?" asked Ant.
"No, I don't think so he doesn't need to know about
this but let me know what happens."
"We will," said Ant standing up.
"Do you have a back door?" asked Malachy.
She led them through a family room out into a patio
area and then into the back garden.
"Just go down this garden path through the gate and
then into the alley behind."
"Thank you" said Ant and gave the white-haired old
lady a peck on the check.
"You may look strange young man, but I can see you
have a heart of gold."
Ant smiled, Janice and Malachy shook her hand before
setting off down the path.
At the garden gate they all looked back at the old lady.
"Do you think she going to be okay?"
"Yes, she's a lot smarter than that she looks and
knows how to look after herself. Think about it why
did she open the door. She's in the house on her
own."
"That's true."
"So why did she open the door?"

"Because she knew me from church and that's why she said no thank you then she tried to close the door."

"Right."

They sat in silence on the way back to the motel each in their own thought.

"The motel for some sleep."

"We shouldn't park the car in the motel parking lot," warned Janice.

"Good thinking."

"You were good in there you really handled her very well," said Malachy.

"She reminded me of my Lola."

"Lola?" quizzed Janice.

"Grandmother."

"Well she liked you."

They parked the car up a side street from the motel. Malachy had realized how important having them both along was, each one thinking of things for the combined security. He supposed that was what friends were for.

"I need a shower," said Janice scratching at her arm.

"We all do especially Ant."

"Do I stink?"

"No but you look browner than you did when I first saw you."

"I'm very tired," yawned Janice.

Once inside the motel room Janice headed for the bathroom. Ant and Malachy sat on the edge of the beds looking at each other.

"It's just my facade."

"The way you look."

"You have to do your own thing without appearing to be a geek."

"What's wrong with looking like a geek?"

"Malachy it may work for you and really there is nothing wrong with it if you don't want attention."

"And you like the attention?"

"No, but it makes people leave me alone, by dressing and looking the way I do."

"Don't you get lonely?"

"Sometimes but each time I've let people into my world I get hurt, better to be alone than be hurt."

"You can't be on your own all the time."

"I'm not now."

The bathroom door opened a cloud of steam preceded by Janice dressed in her underwear entered the room. She quickly climbed into the full-size bed, pulling the bed clothes up around her neck.

"Who's next?" she asked.

"You go Malachy I will take a long time. We should also make sure we have everything packed and ready to go just in case someone comes. Janice make sure your clothes are handy so you can jump into them if need be."

Malachy entered the bathroom and closed the door.

"Oh, I feel so much better funny I really don't like taking showers every day but when you don't, you really miss them."

Ant nodded, he suddenly felt uncomfortable being alone with Janice.

"Today has gone so slow, normally my day's race by."

"It's because you have broken your routine. Everything we do is routine. In your case you get up, go to work, get on the bus, seeing the same people, come home and then watch television. It's not really going fast it only seems that way because your mind isn't really focused on what's happening."

"I never thought of it that way, but how do you break it?"

"Change your routine, however small the change you'd be surprised how much it alters your day and the pace of time."

"I'll try that."

Silence fell between them and wasn't long before a soft breathing sound could be heard from Janice. Ant took out his sketchpad and began to draw a picture of the sleeping Janice.

Malachy came out of the bathroom and climbed into bed.

"Your turn," he whispered to Ant.

Ant put away his sketchpad and before entering the bathroom closed the bedroom light.

Malachy slipped into a deep sleep.

CHAPTER TWELVE

Janice in Love

Ant's hand squeezed Malachy's shoulder, Janice sat on the edge of the bed, she was searching for her clothes in the subdued light from the curtain window.

"Malachy wake up, someone is trying to get into the room."

Malachy became instantly alert and looked at his watch six thirty in the morning. The three of them dressed in silence, each making sure the other had everything together.

"Make the bed," whispered Ant.

Janice reluctantly made the bed, wondering why she needed to do it as this was a motel and they had staff that did these things.

After Malachy and Ant had made their bed, they moved a chest of drawers in front of the outside door. This was followed by a thin wooden wardrobe, which didn't take much moving. Behind the wardrobe was a door covered in dust and dirt. Malachy tried the doorknob and found it opened into the next room. Putting his index finger to his lips he indicated the other two should follow him into the next room.

A newly married couple lay asleep in the king size bed. Ant closed the door and they crept around the bed. Janice scared she might knock it and wake up the couple. The shadow of several men could be seen silhouetted through the curtains of the big window. Unlike their room the exit door to the room was on the side, as Malachy opened a cool morning breeze blew inside.

All three quickly exited the room and Ant closed the door.

An armed police officer came around the corner and approached them.

"Anyone else in this room?"

"No we just came out as ordered."

"Go stand with the other guests." He pointed towards the soda machine.

As they moved towards the other guests the police officer stuck a red sticker on the door.

"What's that sticker mean?" asked Janice.

A man dressed in his pajamas said, "The room's empty"

Janice nodded to him and joined Ant and Malachy with the other guests.

Another police officer arrived and looking at the crowd of guests standing by the soda machine approached and whispered to them.

"You people need to move around the corner please." Slowly and reluctantly the crowd moved around the corner of the building.

"What's going on?" said a small woman who was dressed only in her imitation Victoria Secret's silk underwear.

"Drugs, that's what the officer told me some big-time drug dealer, his wife and a little baby girl."

"Oh yes I saw them arrive, in an expensive car, she had a fur coat on or was it leopard skin, something like that," said another woman.

"Sweet little girl thought her name was Janice," said a woman dressed in a skintight leather outfit.

Malachy grabbed Janice's arm before she had a chance to say anything, he led her to back of the crowd. Ant followed he too was worried that Janice would say something. Once behind the crowd who were now trying to make their way back around the corner to see what was happening. Malachy led the others into a passageway, which took them to the back of the motel, and into an alleyway. A police car stood at the entrance to the alleyway but there was no sign of any police officers near it. The three decided to make a run for it and quickly walked down the alleyway and out into the street turning right away from the motel.

"I'm glad we parked the car here," said Janice as they sat in the car watching the serious crime unit arrive. "What now?" continued Janice.

"Why are the police so interested in us?" asked Ant.

"Yes, that is peculiar, there is something we don't know, and does this radio work?"

"I think so, I've never used it."

"Let's move from here, I don't like being too close to the enemy. And then we can listen to the radio.

"I think we should find Joshua Fahey," said Janice.

Malachy's phone rang then died.

"Batteries dead."

"Mine too," said Ant.

"If we had one of those car chargers, we could charge them while we drive."

"One of these?" said Janice producing a car cell phone charger from the glove compartment. "I found

it on the bus one day didn't know what it was and
stuck it in here one day, in case my mother found it."
"Where do you keep the kitchen sink?" asked Ant.
Janice and Malachy looked at each other then burst out
laughing.
"In the trunk," said Janice "with the queen size bed
and the seventy-two-inch television."
As they drove, their high spirits made them unaware of
the car following them.
Malachy pulled into the parking structure of the Mall.
He was tired and just wanted to park in some dark corner and sleep. He found a relatively dark area, the
light fixture was very faint, and with any luck would
shortly die. He wasn't sure if he had parked in between the white painted lines of the parking space, but
he didn't care.
Ant stretched out on the back seat, Malachy lowered
the seat into a reclining position and lay down. Janice
reclined her seat lay back then raised the seat a little
before getting comfortable she wanted to be able to see
out of the window a little. They all fell quickly into a
deep sleep.
The time between night and day in this part of America didn't have the luxury of a beautiful dawn. The
grey drabness, which emerged from the orange tinged
blackness, was dawn. The concrete pillars of the parking structure seemed to blend in with the evolving daylight.
Henry Lopez had been a night security guard at this
mall for seven months and he had become accustomed
to the occasional parked car at night. Some driver who
was too drunk to drive home and stopped in the mall to
sleep the effect off. Others had been a little more out-
rageous in their actions. From the full sex act with the

rear door of the car open so the long-legged man didn't get cramps while humping his lover for the night. There was once a woman with a full-size blow-up plastic man with over size penis. It was her grunts and groans what made Henry look inside the back seat of the car. When she wouldn't stop, he had to report it and call the police. She told the officer who arrived she wasn't going to stop until she had had an orgasm. It took two female officers to drag her off the doll and only after one of the officers had deflated it. When he had told his boss, the man was furious for not calling him at home so he could come down and watch. Henry from that moment on never told his boss what he saw, and the man had lost all the respect he had earned from Henry.

He had seen the two cars arrive and assumed they were together until looking at the CCTV he saw them park at different ends of the parking structure. He wondered if he should call the police, it had all the drama of a drug deal. As no one got out of either car he changed his mind and decided to go down and investigate.

He stood just inside the parking structure, he could see both cars and mentally tossed a coin to see which one he should go to first. The black sedan was the furthest away he decided to take that one. He felt uncomfortable as he walked towards it. His imagination and the old film he had been watching the day before began to raise his fear level. A mad gunman could be inside, waiting for some fool to come looking in at the window.

A gust of wind evolved out of nowhere and took a plastic soda cup rolling across the floor. Henry gave a slight jump of fright he must stop watching horror movies. The parking structure was full of the previous day's trash; the cleaning crew didn't arrive until seven. He trod on a fast food container and the remains of someone Chinese meal oozed out he checked his foot to see if any had stuck to the sole. It was clean, and he relaxed a little as he cautiously approached the black sedan. He expected to find someone inside sleeping but the car was empty.

He stood looking around the structure, it felt like an old Clint Eastwood western film. Somewhere was the driver of the car waiting to jump out at him. His imagination had always been vivid, but since working at the night security job it had intensified. He took another look inside the car he tried the door, but it was locked. He started to walk towards the other car looking back every now and then just in case the driver returned. Janice woke from her sleep to see a man's face pressing against the window of the car. She gave a squeal, which woke Malachy from his sleep. Henry tapped the window. Janice looked at him then at Malachy.

"Roll down your window a little," said Malachy. Janice slowly turned the handle of the window and watched it open a few inches.

"What are you doing here?" asked Henry. Janice looked again at Malachy hoping he had an answer, he shrugged his shoulders.

"We are here for the sale." blurted out Janice spraying the window with spittle.

"Sale!" repeated Henry.

"Yes, it starts today, and we don't want to miss it."

"My mom liked sales," said Henry.

"Mine did too," replied Janice relaxing a little.

"Your mom dead too?"

"Yes a few months ago."

"Sorry to hear that, mine died three years ago, day after Christmas. I miss her."

"Sorry, I sort of miss my mom too."

"What's your name?"

"Why do you want to know?"

"I might want to ask you out on a date."

"Really, well my name is Lana, what's yours?"

"Clint."

"What like Clint Eastwood?"

"Yeah."

"I like him."

"Me tōo, maybe we could go and see a movie together with him in it that is if you don't already have a boyfriend."

"I don't this is my cousin and that's just a friend in the back."

Henry looked in the rear window and saw Ant sleeping like a baby on the back seat.

"You got a phone number."

"No, you give me yours and I will call you, if that's okay."

"Yes great, err I've got a piece of paper somewhere here."

"I have one," said Janice rolling down the window and handing him a piece of a paper and a pen.

"Thanks Lana."

Janice gave a girlish giggle, which made Henry give a nervous grunt. He handed the paper back making sure he touched her hand and slowly removing his from hers.

"Thanks Clint I will call you I promise." She put the paper in her handbag, which was lying in the well of the car.

"I hope you get what you want in the sale, the mall doesn't open until nine."

"Thanks Clint, I will call you."

"Promise?"

"Yes."

"Bye then Lana." And he walked away from the car back towards the Mall.

Janice rolled up the window and watched him go, after he was out of sight she turned and looked at Malachy who gave her a weak smile.

"What?" she retorted feeling her whole body begin to blush.

"Nothing," said Malachy returning to sleep.

She looked out of the window hoping Clint would re-appear. She had never had this strange feeling before her whole body was tingling and she had a fluffy feeling inside her stomach.

The driver of the other car had returned, he settled into the driver's seat adjusting his position several times before he felt comfortable. His large size hands clothed in light brown leather gloves caressed the steering wheel. The white cuffs of his starched laundered shirt were slightly soiled, and he pushed them back up inside the coat sleeves.

He looked at the clock on the dashboard and then at his Rolex, one of them was wrong and this annoyed him. Time was a precious commodity and therefore it had to be accurate. Switching on the radio he flipped through the stations until he found one broadcasting the news.

'Police are looking for several people tonight in connection with the two murders at Weinstocks and Boller Investments. Mark Thompson CEO and Chairman was found dead in an elevator shaft after

*several people said they had heard a cell phone ring-
ing from below the elevator. Earlier in the week the
company administrator Elizabeth Dellman was found
strangled in her office. An unknown police source
said the company was under investigation for fraud,
tax evasion and large-scale money laundering operation.*
The time is now...'
The man looked at his Rolex and then at the dashboard
clock, he took off the right-hand glove and adjusted
the Rolex. Peering at the watch and then helped it up
to his face. He had paid a lot for the watch and if it
wasn't going to keep good time, he wanted his money
back. He looked at the face and watched the second-
hand tick each second. A strange feeling came over
him he hoped he hadn't been sold a fake watch. Now
he came to think of it something didn't look right, it
didn't look the same as his bosses. He just couldn't
work out what the difference was.

He replaced his glove and pulled the level on the side
of the chair so he could lie back in the seat. As he
closed his eyes, he mumbled to himself "Rolex's don't
tick."

Janice became restless, her emotions had just been
aroused and she wasn't sure how to handle her feelings. She sat in the seat, it felt lumpy and very uncomfortable, and she was fully awake. Her body was
tingling, and she had this strange sensation of excitement. Here she was sitting in her mother's car, having
lost her job, then made new friends and met this man
who made her feel warm, no, hot deep inside.

She looked at Malachy, who was sleeping his nostrils
and mouth giving off a very faint snore. She wanted to
wake him and ask him what it was she was feeling,

was this an emotion she should ignore or one she should embrace. His opinion was important to her, she felt he was like having an older brother and needed his wise advice. Swiveling around in the seat she looked at Ant who was curled up like a little baby on the back seat. He appeared so vulnerable, and maybe he was but his persona was that of a street-smart kid who took no shit.

She turned and sank back into her seat. Being confined like a tiger in a cage desperate to escape and run free. Staring out of the window she began to study the car at the other end of the parking structure. She was sure someone was in the car, but again she wasn't certain. She stared intently her face moving closer to the windscreen until she hit it. At that moment a flash of light happened again in the car. She was positive now someone was in the car and watching them.

"I wonder why?" she said softly to herself.

She turned the radio on very quietly, at first all she heard was static, then turning the tuning knob she found a new station. She put her head beneath the dashboard. Her left ear pressed against one speaker. She listened as the news report was read Mark Thompson's death and the search for several people by the police. It was though it was all part of a television show. She made no expression on her face or any reaction by her body. Years of being alone had made her devoid of any public exhibition of her feelings, unless she was trying to get someone's attention.

Turning off the radio she sat back in her seat and looked out into the parking structure. She wondered if Henry would patrol the parking structure again, she hoped he would. A panic feeling gripped her as she desperately tried to remember what he looked like. He had bright shining eyes with a gentle soft look. Janice never really noticed noses but his was of a man who is in charge, strong and firm. His baby soft looking lips, which made her want to nibble on them while they kissed. She began to fantasize Clint and Lana in a romantic movie.

Malachy gave a violent twitch with his right leg, Janice jumped in her seat.

"Sorry," she said looking at him. Malachy was still in a deep sleep.

In the distance she could hear a rumbling noise, at first, she wasn't sure what it was until she saw the cause of the rumble. A miniature road sweeper was cleaning the parking structure. It had never occurred to Janice the parking lot was cleaned. She, like so many, just took it for granted it was always clean when she had been to the mall with her mother.

The sweeper made a large circle around the car parked at the other end of the structure. The man perched on the sweeper, driving it around and around made no gesture towards the other car. Janice had wanted him to wave or make some sort of movement towards the car indicating to her that there was someone inside the car. She was still convinced there was someone inside and they were spying on them.

Her attention moved from the car towards a side door of the mall. Clint stepped outside and waved at the sweeper driver. Then looked over towards Janice. She sat up and prayed he would come over to her. She wanted to see if she got the same feeling again. She wanted to speak to him, oh she couldn't remember what his voice sounded like. Clint went back inside the mall closing the door behind him. Janice's heart hit her stomach as the pangs of disappointment

298 | EDWARD ARNO

traveled up her body. She sank into the car seat giving
a deep long sigh.
Malachy jerked again and this time he woke up and
immediately began to rub his legs.

"What's happening?" he asked.

"Well while you have been sleeping like a baby there
has been another murder."

"What?! Who? When?"

"Someone called. Now what was the name, oh yes
Mark something or other."

"Mark Thompson."

"Yes, that's the name, he was found at the bottom of
an elevator shaft. People using the elevator could
hear a cell phone ringing, so they reported it and the
police found the body."

"We need to think."

"Do you think we need to talk to someone about
this?"

"Yes, Janice I think we do, this is beginning to scare
me."

"I'm always scared, I'm scared of my own shadow
when I have one that is."

"I'm hungry," said Ant from the back seat.
Malachy and Janice turned and looked at him. He
gave them a smile, which made them both give a little
laugh.

"Another half hour and we should be able to go inside the mall and get something to eat."

"I wish we could go to the restroom and have a little
wash."

"Anything happened while I was sleeping?"

"My boss was found dead."

"Nice," said Ant.

"Not for him," uttered Janice.

Malachy looked at her then burst out laughing.

"I think someone is in that car, parked on the other side."

"Janice you're just paranoid."

"No, I'm not," said Janice who then gave a scream as Henry Lopez tapped on her window. She rolled down the window and gave a very girlish smile.

"The food court is open if you want to get something to eat before the shops open."

"Good," said Ant. "I'm really starving."

Janice opened the door and Henry held it while she climbed out of the car.

"Thank you," she said. "What's your real name?"

"Henry and yours?"

"Janice."

"That's a nice name for such a pretty girl."

"Oh, thank you," said Janice blushing from head to toe.

Malachy and Ant climbed out of the car on the other side, Ant putting his finger in his mouth as though to throw up.

"Be nice, you'll be in love one day."

"If I live that long."

"Not all the places are open, but Valley Faire does a great breakfast menu," said Henry.

"Oh, that sounds good," said Janice falling in next to Henry as he walked towards the mall.

"I thought you two were together," said Ant as he and Malachy followed behind at a short distance.

"No, we are just friends."

"She can be very annoying, but at the same time she can be very sweet, as my Mom would say."

"True she grows on you."

"Are you scared?"

"Sort of, it's hard to be really scared because we don't know what we are up against."

"I know what I'm up against and why I am wanted."

"Because you saw the murder?"

"Yes." Ant fell silent and gave a sudden shudder. "It really didn't affect me until the men came after me and shot my sister. I killed her."

"We will have to go to the police."

"Yeah, I know and they scare me more."

"You should ask for immunity before you tell them anything."

"I was thinking about something like that, maybe I need a lawyer."

Henry had led them to Valley Faire, a fast food service station in the food court. He was explaining the menu to Janice who was looking up at him as though he was a movie star.

He turned and looked at the others, giving a weak smile.

"I see you all in a moment, the food is good, and they give good portions." He looked at Janice and then left. She turned and watched him walk out of the food court area.

"He's gone to do some more patrolling and then he said he would take a break and rejoin us."

"Nice," said Ant. "I'm hungry."

"Order what you want, I want a number three breakfast with an extra coffee. I'm going to the rest room. Here's some money."

He handed Janice a twenty-dollar bill and left walking toward the rest room. He looked around to see if any one else was in the place, only the shopping mall employees in their various uniforms seemed to be strolling around.

"I'll have a number three too," said Ant and rushed after Malachy.

The water ran over Malachy's hands it felt soothing and he relaxed a little, Ant stood next to him and splashed water over his face and everything else around. Malachy slowly lowered his face towards the faucet and refreshed his face. He wanted to sink deep into a pool of water because of the feeling the water had on his face. Ant grabbed his arm and pointing his pouted lips at one of the cubicles. They both bent down and looked under the door. A pair of brown work boots and dirty blue jeans pulled down to the ankles could be seen. Standing up Malachy nodded at Ant who turned off the faucets and dried himself on the paper towels.

Janice was sitting at a table talking to Henry. She continued to talk to him when they sat down. Henry acknowledged them with a nod of the head and returned to listening to Janice. Malachy went to the counter to wait for the food. Ant stared at Janice, she was so animated, and it was as though her whole life had just begun. Henry became aware of Ant staring and thinking he was staring at him, coughed several times out of nervousness.

He looked at his watch.

"Janice, I have to get back to work, I hope you don't mind."

"No, I understand, been there done that."

"You have my phone number, give me a call some time."

"Thanks, I promise I'll call you."

"See you later."

Janice looked at Henry as he walked away.

"He likes you and he has given you his number"

"I like him, and I know he has."

Malachy joined them "The food will be ready in a few minutes, I am starving."

"Me too," said Ant.

"What about you Janice?"

"I'm fine."

"She's in love," commented Ant with a hint of teasing in his voice.

"No, I'm not." Snapped Janice looking at Malachy and Ant who were both nodding their heads. "Well not in love, I just like him a lot and who knows."

"Good for you Janice, go for it."

The food arrived and silence descended on the table as they ate with gourmet passion. It was obvious they were all hungry unaware of the pairs of eyes watching them.

The gloved hands gripped hard the brass colored rail above them on the second floor. The owner of these hands was making a conscious effort not to be seen from below. Only his hands gave any indication of his presence. On the other side of the balcony Henry stood looking down at the diners. The side door to the nonpublic corridor was slightly ajar just in case he had to make a quick retreat from the prying eyes of his manager. He found hard to accept that a girl like Janice would be interested in him, let alone talk to him. He was beginning to worry she wouldn't call him and began to think of ways he could meet her again.

"I've been thinking about all that's happened," said Ant waving a piece of bacon in the air as he spoke.

"The murder and things, how we met, and I think

there must be some real connection. A thread and
something or someone must link them together."
"People kill for different reasons," explained Janice
in a nonchalant matter of fact way.
"True but with this case I think it was for not just
money," said Ant still waving the bacon as he spoke.
"They seemed to have messed up, by making too
much noise," replied Janice.
Ant looked at her and then Malachy.
"I think what Janice is trying to say is they are bringing to much attention on to themselves by what they
are doing."
Ant nodded and lulled back into silence consuming the
remaining bacon and savoring the taste in his mouth.
Janice sipped at her coffee she was deep in thought of
a white or cream wedding dress. She would have to
clean the house if they were going to live there together. She came back to reality as she stared at the
roof of the mall and saw first the gloved hands and
then a quick glimpse of the man behind the gloves.
Something about what she saw reminded her of the car
in the parking structure. The sparkle of light from his
watch was what she had seen in the car, which had
made her think someone was in the car.
"Don't look now but there is a man up on the second
floor looking down on us."
Malachy stretched across the table to take the sugar
bowl, which he didn't want so he could whisper to
Janice. "Where?"
"Above Ant."
"I can see him in the reflection from the other side of
the balcony. He looks very suspicious," said Ant.
"What should we do?

"Let's all go to the rest room, that way I can get a
better look at him and see if he follows us."
Outside the restroom Malachy turned and looked up at
the balcony, by this time the Mall was beginning to fill
with shoppers and several men stood looking over the
balcony.
    "Which one is he?" whispering out of the corner of
    his mouth.
    "The one with dark glasses and gloves on," whis-
    pered Janice back.
    "Oh yes I see him all in black."
    "Yes, that's him, sorry I've got to go," said Janice
    rushing into the ladies' restroom.
Eric Swan sat on the toilet his pants and boxer shorts
down around his ankles. The smell emanating from
the white porcelain toilet bowl beneath him didn't
make his feel sick. He liked the smell it was his smell.
He felt comfortable and secure, this was the one place
he could be alone, no one to criticize him if he farted
or made a smell. He was lost in his own thoughts unaware of what was happening outside the restroom. He
began to read the graffiti, which had been scratched
into the cubicle paintwork. His favorite was 'If voting
could really change things, it would be illegal'. He
smiled to himself again as he read it, the others on the
wall were of a sexual nature and even though he found
some of them amusing he couldn't understand why
people had the urge to deface public property.
Eric didn't hear the heavily armed SWAT team enter
the white and blue tiled restroom. He didn't even hear
then as they crept along the wall and past the washbasins. He didn't see them in the cracked mirror with its
faded scratched graffiti. He only became aware of
them when the cubicle door busts open and three men

dressed head to toe in black wearing ski masks pointed assault rifles at him. He stood up and then fell against the cold wall. He suddenly realized his genitals where exposed.

"What the f...?" He screamed but before he had a chance to finish his sentence someone screamed at him.

"Keep your hands up and move slowly forward out of the cubicle."

"You've got to be kidding, I need to wipe my butt and pull my pants up," shouted Eric.

"Move forward slowly." repeated the police officer that seemed to be in control of the situation.

Eric didn't move.

"Move," screamed the officer.

"No," shouted Eric. "I'm going to wipe by butt hole and then pull my pants up. If you want to shoot me go ahead."

He turned his back on them and took some toilet paper and bending over wiped himself. He showed the results to the three police officers looking at him. He felt violated and he wanted to show his feelings. He took another few sheets of toilet paper and wiped again and then pulled up his boxers and pants. He pushed the lever to flush the toilet.

Slowly he walked out of the cubicle and over to the washbasins. Two more officers pointed their guns at him. Using plenty of soap he washed and then rinsed his hands. He took a few paper towels from beside the basin and looking into the mirror he asked. "Now what's the problem officers, my ex-wife not paid her parking tickets again?"

"On your knees," screamed the lead police officer.

"No need to shout, I don't think I'm deaf."

"Now."

Eric slowly went to his knees and put his hands behind his head. Two officers grabbed his wrists before lowering them behind his back and handcuffing him. The lead officer searched his pockets and threw his belongings into a plastic bag another officer was holding. He was grabbed under the arms and pulled to his feet and quickly marched out of the restroom.

A crowd had gathered and he was rushed across the mall's food court. Eric looked at the staring face hoping he would recognize someone. But today everyone seemed like a stranger.

The doors of the police wagon closed and Eric sat on the cold metal seat. Wondering if he was in some kind of dream and had not woken up yet. Was this some giant April fool joke out of season by one of those television reality shows or someone from the office having a laugh? Maybe it was just a mistaken identity sighting from the most wanted program. He had never in his whole life done anything, which deserved such treatment.

Malachy, Janice, and Ant peered over the back of the booth in the food court watching as the police van drove away. Once it had disappeared, they slide down into the imitation leather seats.

"That's not him, the man who was watching us," said Janice.

"I know."

Ant just nodded his head bemused by what had just happened.

"You saw him follow you into the restroom?"

"I saw him go into one of the cubicles and he hasn't come out of the restroom."

"So, he must still be in there."

All three rose and ran into the men's restroom no one was at the washbasins or urinals. Malachy pushed open each cubicle door, the place was empty.

"Look," said Janice pointing to the ceiling, "one of the tiles has been pushed aside."

He must have been hiding up there and once the police had left, he climbed down while we were all looking out of the window and sneaked out of here."

"We've lost him," said Janice disappointedly.

"Maybe."

"If we knew where he came from, it would be possible to find out who he is," said Ant putting a protective sound in his voice to make Janice feel relaxed.

A mall security man entered the rest room stopped and looked at the three of them.

"This is the men's restroom Miss I must ask you to leave at once."

Janice gulped but kept her face serious. She looked straight at him and in a deep voice replied. "I am a man if you don't mind." Then walked out of the restroom.

Malachy and Ant began to wash their hands trying not to laugh. The security man stood looking at them his mouth wide open.

Outside in the food court they looked around to see where Janice had retreated. At first, they couldn't see her because of the man she was talking to was obscuring her from their sight.

Ant spotted her and pointed to where she was. Janice exploded into a loud scream and then continued to scream bringing the food courts attention on her. The man backed away and joined three other suited men who had been circling around the food court.

Malachy and Ant ran toward her, as she moved backwards towards the sidewall of the food court. From
where they were, she suddenly vanished. As they
reached the spot where she was, they could see a hand
sticking out of a door, which wasn't really a door, a
panel in the wall that opened. The hand beckoned
them to follow.

The panel in the wall opened wider and they both slide
quickly through to the other side. Janice emotionally
gave them a hug each. Henry was behind them putting
a metal bar across the panel.

"This will stop them for a short time."

"This is becoming a habit squeezing through holes in
the wall," said Malachy.

"Oh, thank you," said Janice in her girlish voice.

"My pleasure, anything to help you. A princess in
distress."

"Thanks Henry. Janice who was the man you were
talking to?"

"He wanted to know where you were and said you
were a dangerous killer and I had to go with him."

"Who was he?"

"He didn't say, but he had a gun under his arm."

"We need to get away from here and find some
where to hide."

"Let's get to the car."

"Mistake," said Henry.

"Why?" said all three in unison.

"I was watching on the CCTV monitor and they
looked at your car before coming into the mall."

"I wonder who they are?"

"I know," answered Ant. "Well not the one talking
to Janice but one of the others was the one of the

men who tried to kill me the other night when I saw you know what."

"I've moved the car." interrupted Henry. "Well not very far but the brake wasn't on properly so I pushed a little way from where it was to confuse the men."

"Oh, that must have been me I think I knocked it when I got out of the car."

"Good job you did Janice."

"Give me the keys," said Henry "I will drive to the other side of the mall. You can take this passageway to the end. Turn right when you get to some steps go down them and follow the passage until you come to a door. Don't open it I will from the other side, I have a key, if you open it, it will set off the alarm."

Malachy hesitated for a few seconds before handing over the key. They were trusting a stranger with their lives and all because Janice liked him.

"Thanks," said Janice.

"Wait here about five minutes then set off."

"You be careful."

"Janice don't worry about me and when this is all over you and I can have dinner and you can explain what it is all about."

"Oh yes I would like that."

Henry left going in the opposite direction from the one he had told them to go.

"I hope we can trust him."

"Oh yes we can."

"Janice you are smitten, you would trust your worst enemy at this moment."

"One thing I do know is when someone is lying to me and he wasn't lying to me, to us."

"Okay we trust him we really don't have a choice."

Ant began to walk along the passage and disappeared around a corner. When the other two realized he had gone they followed to find him peering through a hole in the wall. He saw them and put his finger to his lips, then beckoned them over to join him. Several holes had been drilled into the wall. Malachy looked through one and could see into the men's restroom. Several men were standing in the middle talking, he recognized them as the suited men who were after them. Ant taped him on the shoulder and pointed to his ear. Malachy put his ear against the hole and could just hear the men talking.

"John, my friend it's simple, the girl and older man we need to find out what they know. The lad has to be eliminated, if that kid ever talks to the police, we are all dead."

"I think the girl already knows, she's not stupid, she may sound it but underneath that little girl routine is a very clever woman."

"Maybe, I'm more worried about Moss, if he starts to put two and two together with what he already knows we can all kiss our freedom good-bye."

The rest room door opened and another one of the be-suited men entered. The man Malachy hadn't seen before turned to the urinals as the man entered so he couldn't see his face properly.

"I think they are heading for the parking structure and their car."

"Okay you and the others see if you can find them, I'll join you in a moment."

"Right boss."

After the man had left the unknown man turned back from the urinal, he was clearly worried.

"John clean this mess up, I want nothing left to cause anyone a problem and do it quickly."

"Okay Mister Adamson.

Ant and Malachy looked at each other. They both had understood what the Adamson had just said. Janice was still looking into the men's restroom.

"Janice don't be a peeping tom."

She stood back from the wall her face red with embarrassment, she too had understood. She wanted to cherish the comment the man had said about her being intelligent but knew this wasn't the time to mention it.

"I think we had better get going if we are to meet Henry."

The passageway stretched the length of the mall and was very dimly lit. Pipes and cables and other metal tubes ran along the ceiling making it look very low. They passed two doors and they were both locked Malachy checking each time. At the end they turned right and found themselves at the top of some steep stairs. Ant who was leading slowly descended them, the passageway again turned right. Ant stopped the other two walked into him. Someone was standing in the shadow just ahead of them, Ant pointed to them and they watched as the person moved into the light. Henry was pacing a worried expression on his face. They walked cautiously towards him expecting someone to jump out at them.

"Where have you been?"

"We took a little longer than five minutes," said Malachy hoping Janice wouldn't explain what they had just seen and heard.

"Your car is straight ahead in the parking structure about the seventh car on the left."

He handed Malachy the keys and then looked at Janice who gave him a weak smile.

"I'll check no one is about, but Janice let me know you are safe."

"I will and we still have to have dinner."

Henry looked at her, he wanted to take her in his arms and kiss her. He quickly composed himself and opened the door to check, no one was around.

"All clear."

"Thanks," said Malachy stepping out into the sun light, Ant followed, but turned to see Janice push a piece of paper into Henry's hand before giving him a kiss on the cheek.

They sat in the car for a few minutes checking to see if anyone was watching them.

"We need to do something to change how we look."

"I'm not dressing up as a woman," said Ant.

"No one suggested it."

"I think it's all clear let's go I'm getting a little scared."

They left the mall's parking structure each of them checking to see if anyone was following them.

"See Janice I'm not the only one who thinks you're intelligent."

She just smiled and looked out of the window.

"I think I know how we can change how we look. I have friends," said Malachy.

Bob, Mike and Stan

The barber's chair swung round Malachy looked in
the mirror at the new him. His hair was now a soft
light brown and had been cut close to his head. The
eyebrows had been dyed to match the hair.
Peter Duvelle and Ricardo had been true to their word,
when he called to say he and two friends needed a
makeover. He was told no problem go straight to Ricardo's salon in the high street. The blinds had been
down when they arrived, and the closed sign was still
on the door. Ricardo had not opened the salon since
his wife's death.
  "You like the new look?"
  "Yes, very much, thank you. When will you open
again?"
  "Monday. My customers keep on calling, I'm not
sure if they want a haircut or a look at where Fluffy
died. The police removed the chair, but I won't tell
them that. I will say it's that chair over there the broken one."
  "Funny how people like to look at murder scenes, do
you remember when Simpson's wife died, and people drove by in Brentwood to have a look at the
sight."

"Right and I wonder what they thought they would see."

"Me too."

"Now you go into the back and Peter's wife will help you find some new clothes."

Ricardo was cleaning up the hair from the floor when Janice stepped from behind a curtain at the side of the salon. Her new hairstyle made her look thinner and less geeky. The clothes accentuated her figure and made her look sexier. She was now looking at a woman in the mirror not a child in adult clothes. Janice liked what she saw she had never realized how beautiful she could look.

Malachy slide out of the back room. The clothes were not to his taste, but they altered his appearance. The college jock look had always been for the other guys, he had always liked to blend in, not stand out looking for attention. As he looked in the mirror, he could see why he had disliked the jocks so much. The automatic assumption you were athletic, while being expected to be a complete party animal.

He turned and looked at Janice, his mouth dropped open, the expression 'clothes make the man or in this case the woman' was really true.

"You look so beautiful," he said unthinkingly.

Janice gave one of her little girlish giggles. "I hope Henry likes it."

"He is a fool if he doesn't, Janice where have you been hiding."

"Girl's learn from their mother and mine didn't like me, so she never told me anything except I was use-less."

"Which you're not, wow I bet Henry will ask you to marry him."

"Don't be daft we hardly know each other."

"You'll see."

"I hope they can help Ant he is the one who really needs to change."

"He has to change it is the only way he will save his life."

They hadn't notice Ant enter from the washroom of the salon. His black shoulder length hair was now blond and braided into stripes across his head. He wore white jeans and a blue and yellow patterned Hawaiian shirt. He smiled at them, which sent a shudder up Malachy's back.

"I think that may just save your life Ant."

"I'm not Ant, my name is Anthony. Ant is a black haired, black clothes boy I left behind in the restroom."

"We should really get a picture no one will ever believe us."

"I've got a camera here somewhere," said Ricardo who began to search the cupboards below his salon station.

Malachy had plugged his cell phone into the charger when he arrived at the salon, it suddenly rang. Janice grabbed at it before anyone else could move.

"Hello, oh hi, we are okay. Thanks."

"Who is it?"

Janice didn't reply but continued to listen.

"Who is it?" repeated Malachy

"Henry."

"Henry how did he get my number?"

"I gave it to him," said Janice. "Yes, I'm still here, so what happened?"

"I saw her give him a piece of paper as we left the mall."

"But why my phone number?"

"One moment Henry." Janice cupped her hand over the mouthpiece. "Because if I gave him my phone number, I wouldn't be home to hear it ring and answer it. Sorry Henry, now, where were we?"

"That makes sense," said Anthony who was staring at himself in the mirror.

Janice listened interrupting frequently with "Right."

"Does it really make me look different?"

"Anthony, I almost didn't recognize you."

"My mother would love it, well maybe not the hair, but the clothes."

"Sometimes you have to do what you have to do to stay alive," said Ricardo returning from the back of the salon with a camera.

"Ricardo how much do we owe you?"

"Nothing friend, you helped Peter and myself we are just repaying you."

"Thanks, I'm a little worried what happens now, but this change I hope will help us get things sorted out."

"Bye, I'll see you soon and Henry thanks. Me too."

They all turned and looked at Janice as she closed the cell phone.

"Ant..hony I didn't recognize you."

"Tell us what Henry said or life is going to be a little miserable as we keep asking you. I'm sure you don't want that."

"Okay, Henry said after we left the men who were chasing us started to search the mall and finally broke through one of the panels and into the corridor. The police were called and arrested two of them. Henry made out he didn't know what was going on. He's worried about me, about us."

"Did he find out who the men were?"

"They were local crooks, according to the police, but Henry thinks the police only said that and they knew who they really were."

"Why would local crooks go after us?" said Malachy sitting down in the barber chair.

"After me?" said Anthony.

"I think we need to get to the bottom of this, or none of us is going to be safe. Janice won't be able to marry Henry and have six children, and you Anthony won't become a world-famous artist."

"Who said I was going to marry Henry and have six children?"

"Well Janice it always happens in movies and TV."

"Malachy don't you know, it's not real in Films and on TV, just pretend."

"As long as you do Janice you won't get hurt anymore."

"So, what happens now?"

"I think we should have our picture taken then go and see Sandra Cartwright. I think she may know what's really going on, well as far as the company is concerned."

"Picture everyone," said Ricardo who was joined by Peter and his wife for a group picture.

After leaving the salon by the back door they checked the road as they drove to Sandra Cartwright's condominium. Parking a street way from the actual address had been Janice's idea. Malachy showed visible signs of being nervous as they ascend in the elevator. He was worried what he was going to find out, and maybe put their lives in even more danger. What had really unnerved him was the street door being wedged open just a little and the security man who usually sat behind the imposing desk was missing. Even when the lobby desk phone rang as they enter the building.

The elevator doors opened on the second floor; the corridor was empty and eerily silent. Malachy wasn't sure what he had expected but this silence made his senses sharpen with fear.

The condominium door was open and as Malachy pushed the door a little more. He could see Sandra moving from room to room carrying clothes and books.

She was unaware of him and the others standing in the doorway, he gave a light knock. She didn't stop her packing, so he knocked again hard this time.

Sandra came out of a bedroom carrying an armful of panties.

"Malachy! What are you doing here?"

He and Janice entered the living room and watched Sandra place the panties into a suitcase.

"And you have a girlfriend with you."

"Sandra, I need some answers."

"Don't we all."

"No, I'm serious, something has happened, and I need to know what it is."

"Okay what do you know?"

Ant had stayed outside the door until they had moved deeper into the living room. He then crept into the bedroom to the right of the front door. Once inside he found a small cupboard and hid. He wasn't sure why he did this, but his instincts told him something wasn't right and for him to hide.

"So, Malachy what's so serious, for you to come and see me at my home?"

"Mark's dead."

"I know that."

"Someone has been shredding papers at the office
and a man or maybe several persons from the SEC
have been investigating the company."

"Really? I didn't know that."

"But you and Mark were…"

"Lovers. Hardly, no Malachy everyone thought we
were. But I am married."

"So was Mark."

"True, but have you met his wife."

"Mark and I worked together that's all, even if that
evil bitch Liz Dellman told everyone we were having
a mad passionate affair."

"She's dead too."

"Didn't know that, when?"

"I think Friday evening in her office, while on the
phone."

"Nasty."

"Did you know she was a blackmailer?"

"I guessed as much from what has been said about
her."

"I'm not sure if her death had anything to do with
Mark's."

"Mark had mentioned something about her having
too many secrets. But I didn't really know for sure if
she was really a blackmailer."

"I think she must have had something on Mark for
him not to have sacked her."

"Malachy, who's your friend?"

"Oh, sorry this is Janice and…" he stopped speaking
when he realized that Ant wasn't in the room.

"Well that's nice, now what was it you wanted to
know?"

"What's happening? Why was Mark killed?

"I don't know."

"But you and Mark were so..."

"So, what? Close? Not really, he would have liked to have been, but I had other ideas and plans," said Sandra an irritation forming in her words. "Oh, who cares now. Yes Mark and I had an affair but he wasn't very good in bed, a little small for my taste, so I went back to my husband."

"So, I wonder who knows."

"That a difficult one as most of the management team is dead. Malachy I would be very careful you could be next."

"You know who killed them."

"No, not really, but I can guess."

"Who?"

"Malachy I really don't have time for this."

"Sorry Sandra I am just trying to understand."

"What is there to understand?" snapped Sandra her irritation boiling over.

"Who's the murderer and why they did it."

Sandra stared at him, she was trying to control her temper, but as she stared at him and then at Janice she exploded.

"Shit, what the heck? Get real Malachy and stop worrying about your stupid little disease. It's over and everyone is trying to cash in, especially the rich. This isn't a free country, it never was. It's controlled by corporations and businessmen who only see the bottom line, which is money. They tell you what to watch on the TV, what to eat and when to eat it. God, they even tell you what to think."

"That's not true," shouted Janice.

Malachy turned and looked at her. She had become very animated at what Sandra was saying.

Sandra looked at them both then continued. "I just want a share of the pie, I'm no different from everyone else."

"I'm not like that," shouted Janice hopping from one foot to the other.

"Tell your stupid little girlfriend to shut up."

"Sandra there is no need to be rude."

"Malachy, you know you were the joke of the office, just a tame lap dog. We used to joke, Mark and I. He was sure if he had said sit, roll over you would have done it."

"I was just doing my job."

"Well now you will have to find another one, I am off, so close the door behind you when you leave."

"So, you don't know who did these murders?"

"No and I'm not staying around to find out."

"What about your husband."

"Him? It's all his and Mark's fault."

"I don't understand."

"No, you don't do you? Well I'll tell you what you want to know what's been happening at Weinstocks and Boller Investments. I got Mark drunk one-night, Bob made me. He then put Mark in bed naked with a transvestite. One of Bob's friends knew several, so it was easy to find a good looking one. Anyway, Bob took pictures and blackmailed Mark into helping with some money transactions. Mark got hooked on the transvestite, it was really she or is it he, Mark was having the affaire with. He or she didn't mind his small dick."

"What transactions?" asked Malachy ignoring her comment.

"Bob had a company which sold pills over the Internet."

"Drugs you mean?" asked Janice who had now calmed down.

"No narcotics, drugs to enlarge your penis or breasts and the infamous fake Viagra."

"I see."

"Do you? Bob made millions. Mark helped dispose of all the money and then they set up a company to sell other more pleasurable drugs."

"Like ecstasy."

"Something like that."

"Your husband was a drug dealer."

"That and other businesses."

"So, where's your husband now."

"I don't know, but I'm not stopping to find out, I don't think the killing stopped yet."

"Why? Who do you think is going to get murdered next?" asked Janice.

"I don't know but I think Bob murdered Mark to keep him quiet."

"What about Monica Trystwold or whoever she was, the first victim."

"He murdered her, she was an actress who suddenly wanted more money, so Bob dealt with it."

"Why did you marry him?" asked Janice.

"Sweet little girl he was good in bed and gave me everything I wanted. I've told you it's all about money and what you can get out of life."

"You don't care, do you?"

"Not really. So, if there is nothing else, I'm off."

She picked up two suitcases and left the room. Malachy sat down on the sofa, he needed to take in what had been said. He couldn't ignore the political and sexual diatribe, but the information about the murders need to sorted if they were now going to the police or someone in authority.

Janice stood against a wall as Ant appeared. He was in some other world as he looked around the room. Janice watched him as he touched and picked up objects. He stood staring at the pictures on the wall and even ran his fingers over the surface of several of the oil paints. It was as if he was sucking in the room for ideas. Janice wished she was artistic, once her mother had given her a paint by numbers set. She had loved it except she hated the color of the paint, so she changed them by mixing her own. The picture looked the same, but the colors seemed strange and didn't match what the objects were supposed to be. She was proud of it because she had kept inside the black lines and for her that was a big achievement.

Ant was looking at the only collection of photos in the room. They had been neatly arranged on a small table by the window. The largest picture was of two teenagers a boy and a girl holding two smaller children. He could see Sandra's likeness in the teenage girl and surmised that the other must be her siblings. The next picture was in a silver frame and was of a woman in her forties and looked as though it had been taken in the sixties. The clothes and hairstyle date from back then, if he remembered the picture books, he had been looking at Ricardo's while waiting for his hair to dye.

"This must be her mother," he said out loud but the other two were lost in their own thoughts and didn't reply.

As he picked up the next picture the hairs on the back of his neck stood up. It was a picture of Sandra and her husband Bob. Ant stared at the picture and was convinced he knew the man. The glass was very dusty on the inside of the frame. The frames little clips on the back had been bent over inwardly and so made it very difficult for him to take the cover off. He went into the kitchen looking for a knife to pry open the back.

Janice had joined Malachy on the sofa and they both stared at the blank wall in front of them. They didn't notice the three men enter the condominium until they stood between them and the blank wall. Malachy looked at the taller of the men and immediately gave a weak smile.

"Err Bob." Bob looked at him and recognized him and relaxed.

Bob was a handsome six-foot three fair haired man. It was his natural light blue eyes, which made the females, go weak at the knees when they met him. The look was just a façade the man underneath was cold, calculating and to some just plain evil.

"I forgot your name."

"Malachy Moss, I work with your wife Sandra."

"Yes, Malachy, of course you're waiting for Sandra."

"Yes, she called me and asked me to come and pick up some papers for Mark."

"Mark, I don't think he'll need any papers now once I get hold of him."

"Why?"

"We were looking for your wife," said Janice as though she was coming out of a dream.

"Me too," said Bob giving Janice a quizzical look.

"Stan you look in the bedroom to see if her clothes are still there."

Stan was a failed personal trainer the suit he wore didn't fit very well and made him look like a small-time gangster. He went towards the kitchen.

"Not that way the bedroom is upstairs idiot."

Bob returned his stare to Malachy and Janice.

"So, Malachy where is Mark? I've been trying to find him all day."

"Dead," said Janice.

"Dead," retorted Bob.

"Yes, he was murdered."

"Murdered, who by?"

"We don't know, but I know the police were looking for Sandra. She and Mark had picked up the wrong cell phone and Mark had hers in his pocket when they found the body."

"How was he killed?"

"I don't know," replied Janice.

"I think you should look for another job Malachy working at Weinstocks and Boller Investments isn't safe with two deaths in one week."

"Two deaths?"

"Yeah Sandra told me the woman she is always arguing with was murdered."

"Oh Liz Dellman, the administrator."

Stan reappeared and stood next to Mike the other badly suited man with Bob.

Without looking at Stan, Bob shouted, "Well."

"Yes Boss."

"Yes what? Are her clothes upstairs in the bedroom closet?"

"No just yours."

"She's done a bunk, the bitch and I think I will too, until this blows over. Malachy if you see my wife tell her I'm looking for her."

"Sure, where will you be?"

"Around or at the beach house."

Bob crossed to the small table and looked at the pictures on it.

"The bitch has taken the picture, let's go before the cops arrive. Malachy close the door before you leave and remember if my wife comes back tell her I need to speak to her."

"Okay."

Bob, Stan, and Mike left as quietly as they arrived. Janice rushed after them closing the front door once she heard the elevator doors close and locked it.

When she returned Malachy was no longer sitting on the sofa. The glass door of the balcony was open and she could see him standing in the shadows trying to peer over the balustrade.

He returned to the living room and slumped back onto the sofa.

"That guy is a real idiot, did you hear what he said, honestly some people."

"No," said Malachy who was still deep in thought.

"He told you to close the door before you leave. If you close the door before you leave you can't leave."

"Right"

"Funny isn't it?"

"Right."

"Malachy you haven't been listening."

"Right."

"Malachy…"

"Sorry he didn't murder Mark."

"He didn't?"

"No, he was surprised when I told him, at first I thought he had when he said Mark wouldn't need the papers anymore. But I think he was referring to something else."

"I see I was so sure he had."

"He said she, Sandra, told him about the woman in
your office who died at her computer, was dead. She
said she didn't know she was dead."

"So, one of them is lying."

"Her, she was full of it and she never looked you
straight in the face when she talked to you. That was
on the Discovery channel once."

"You may be right a compulsive liar."

"Where's Ant?"

"Anthony is here."

"Sorry Anthony."

"That's okay," he looked pale and the fear in his eyes
had returned.

"What's wrong you look like you've seen a murderer."

"I have."

"Who? Which one?"

"The man who was here is the murderer."

"Which man?"

"Which murderer?"

"This one." Ant produced the picture from his
pocket having successfully removed it from the
frame.

Malachy and Janice looked closely at the picture.

"Bob."

"Yes, if that's his name and the other two were with
him. It was one of them that fired at me when I was
on the roof and I am sure they are the ones who
killed the two dogs."

Neither Malachy nor Janice questioned his certainty it
was obvious from his tone. As Malachy stared at the
picture, he recalled Ant's graffiti, the man's face was
the same.

"You really captured the way he looked in your graffiti piece. I only saw him briefly once and I could only just remember what he looked like. You possibly saw him less than me. You must have a really good photogenic memory."

"Thanks, I did my best."

"It was a good job you hid yourself when they were here. I don't think any of us would be alive if they had seen you."

"I wasn't sure at first, but when I saw his profile I knew. Then one of the others was standing so I could see him in the mirror. I was sure he had seen me especially when he came into the kitchen."

"I'm glad you hid."

"Years of hiding from the police when I was doing my pieces had helped me just disappear when I need to."

They stared at each other the realization of how close they had come to being murdered if Ant had been seen dawned on each of them.

"I found something else in the back of the picture frame."

He handed a piece of paper to Malachy. It had a list of names and numbers followed by telephone numbers neatly printed on it.

"It could be a list of dealers and/or accounts they laundered the money through."

"It must be important to hid it," said Janice taking the paper, folding it and placed it in her pocket.

"So, what now?"

"I think we are safe here for the time being, so why don't we just rest awhile and think."

Malachy made himself comfortable on the sofa and relaxed.

Janice mumbled to herself she was hungry and wandered off in the kitchen search for food.

Ant produce a small sketch pad out of his pocket, he stepped out on the balcony and sat on the white plastic chair. He looked out at the manicured lawn and sanitized swimming pool. He wanted to go home, he missed his mother and his father even though he knew his welcome would be difficult. He wanted to know if his sister was really dead. There had been nothing on the news about a little girl dying in Burbank. He began to draw a picture of his sister. She had all the beauty of their mother.

Malachy lay back on the sofa and looked at the ceiling it was the first time in days he felt he could relax. Although like a dog asleep he had one sense alert for anything that might happen. What had he gotten himself into, what had he dragged Ant and Janice into they were innocent bystanders, well not Ant, he had seen the murder? If Bob had murdered Monica, could he also have murdered Mark and Liz Dellman? Why would he kill them?

Was Bob's reaction to being told of Mark's murder genuine? I t looked like it, so if Bob didn't murder Mark and Liz then who did?

These thoughts raced around his brain creating enough electricity to light an entire city block. He could feel himself become anxious and sat up right and took several deep breaths and whispered 'relax, relax, relax.' The desired effect may have been achieved he fell back into the sofa exhausted and drifted off into a light sleep.

Janice opened the cupboards in the kitchen, it was barely stocked with food, but she felt there was enough to make something for them to eat. The freezer had two items in it, a pack of chicken breasts and Italian sausage. She took them both and placed them in the microwave to defrost. She continued looking in the cupboards for other ingredients, it was obvious who ever lived here dined out most nights. She took cans of sweet corn, mushrooms, and potatoes, she would make a stew.

The largest cooking pot was hidden behind a large red candy jar. The jar was very big and it was difficult to get the jar out of the cupboard. She placed it on the counter and returned it to the cupboard to retrieve the cooking pot. The department store label was still stuck on the inside of the pot. It had never been used. She washed it and placing it on the stove adding all the ingredients. After covering with water, she needed some seasoning to make the stew taste good. She opened the red candy jar and closed it. In a small cupboard above the stove she found a few herbs and added them to the pot.

She sat down on a wood stool and looked at the heat beneath the pot as it began to cook the food.

Janice had been in a daze, she hadn't really taken in what she was doing, she just wanted to lie down and sleep. She looked at the red candy jar something hadn't registered in her mind properly. She cautiously opened the jar again and looked inside. It was filled with rolls of what looked like hundred-dollar bills. She counted one of the bundles there were a hundred, hundred-dollar bills. She replaced it into the jar, she needed something to put the money in her bag was too small. A few plastic bags had been left in a drawer but they wouldn't really do. She opened the broom cupboard, which was behind the door. So, this is where Ant had hidden when the men had been in the condominium. Inside she found a bag she recognized from her department store, if it were the same type it would have an extra compartment in the bottom. She found the zip and opened it. Yes, it was the same one they had sold. Most people who brought the bag had to be shown the secret compartment, a good place to hide things from your husband, she heard one assistant tell a customer.

She counted the bundles as she placed them in the bag. Never had she seen so much money in all her life. It was so much more than what her mother had left her. She zipped the bag up to hide the little tag which gave away the compartment's whereabouts.

Sitting at the kitchen table with a pen and paper taken from one of the drawers she wrote 'one hundred times one hundred is ten thousand, one hundred and twenty times ten thousand is...'

She paused while she worked it out, one million two hundred thousand.

"Wow that's a lot of money," she said out load, "divide that by three and we would each get." She wrote four hundred thousand on the paper.

She placed her elbows on the table and stared at the pot on the stove, which had just begun to boil. Fantasizing what she would do with her share of the money. On the balcony Ant looked at his drawing, it was no longer a sketch for a graffiti piece. He wanted to be a real artist, he wanted to paint pictures and have proper exhibitions. He wanted to go to Art College, to develop what he had. The pencil drawing in front of him was a little girl lying on her back on the banks of a stream her long hair floating in the stream. She wasn't dead, her eyes and face showed life and happiness. He looked at the face of his sister and the feeling of homesickness returned. His life had changed forever, and he wanted to go home and start a fresh. No longer be a secret graffiti artist but someone who was recognized for his work. Graffiti was for kids, he wanted to paint, that was it, he wanted to paint in oils, watercolors, and other things. He had advanced in his perception of life, and therefore his art. He had grown up and become a man.

He shivered at this new thought, a brief moment of fear crossed his mind, was he safe with this new world. He dispelled the horror and began to embrace the new Ant, no Anthony. Even though he didn't like the name it was what he was to be called and he would grow to like it. He looked down at the picture, the face looked back at him and was smiling, and he shook his head and looked again. No, the face wasn't smiling but she did look beautiful. He took a deep breath and sighed. Malachy Rolling Moss sat on the edge of the sofa, his mind was un-clouding. They had relaxed and he now had to drag his consciousness into the present and think what they should do next.

He looked towards the window and saw Ant looking at his drawing. He strained his neck to see if he could see Janice. She must be in the kitchen from the aroma of food, which came, floating his way. Tomorrow was a workday he would return to work if he had a job. No one had called to tell him what to do, the company usually dispatched information to their employees via a phone ring around system. But wasn't that for emergencies and were the boss and the administrator being murdered an emergency, or a tragic act. The emergency call round had been set up for natural disasters, like earthquakes. He would go to work and see what happens maybe someone from New York would come and take over.

Janice appeared at the kitchen door "Food's ready, I hope you like it."

Ant looked into the room, Malachy motioned him to come in and get something to eat. They sat around the table. The stew stood on a ceramic tile in the middle of the table. Janice lifted the lid the smell and sight of the stew made everyone feel even hungrier.

They ate in silence, until Malachy remembered "Janice this is really good thanks."

"Oh, it's nothing really I threw everything into the pot. Anyway, I think we would have eaten anything, I know I was starving."

"Me too," said Anthony.

"So, what happens now?"

If ever a cue for something dramatic to happen this was the time thought Malachy.

Ten SWAT team members stormed the apartment, M16 pointing at the three diners.

"I think I have an idea," said Anthony trying not to laugh.

Janice slipped her arm into the bag strap before complying with the commands being shouted to raise their arms.

An Officer handcuffed each of them and then checked to see if they had any weapons on them. The rest of the police team spread out and began to check the rest of the condominium.

An officer with three thin stripes on his arm picked up Ant's sketchpad from the table and flicked through it. He stopped at the pictures of the murdered woman.

"You do this?" he asked while continuing to look through the book.

Ant didn't reply.

The officer continued, "I think we have found the notorious graffiti tagger ANT." He said this without addressing it to no one in particular.

He closed the pad and placed it in his pocket.

"Let's go."

"Anthony do not say a word," shouted Janice

"Quiet," shouted the officer.

"Not without your parents or a lawyer present."

The officer stopped and stood in front of Janice and shouted into her face "Shut up."

Janice unperturbed shouted back "You've got bad breath."

The officer quickly marched all three out of the apartment.

Janice was taken down in the elevator first with the senior officer.

"Anthony, Janice is right, demand a bargain first before you say anything."

"Okay."

Neither officers with them made a comment, and as they emerged from the building, they were taken to different police cars and driven away.

Sandra Cartwright stood by the tennis court of the condominium complex and watched as the cars raced away. She didn't notice the first rays of sun reflecting on the binoculars on the twenty-seventh floor of the company's building opposite.

CHAPTER FOURTEEN

Mountain Lions

Malachy stood on the sidewalk outside the police station. It was one of those humid nights, when regardless of what you were wearing your clothes stuck to your body. He felt a tear of sweat run down his back, to disappear into the waistband of his boxer briefs. He felt dirty and sticky from sitting in the interview room for so long. He was sure the brown stains on the wall were blood not coffee as the police interrogator had told him. He was convinced they had been put there to intimidate the person being interviewed. Why hadn't they cleaned them up. The other thing he noticed was the station itself was cool from the air conditioning system, but the interrogation room had no air conditioning. They told him it wasn't working in the building. Another lie to add to the many they gave him. There was no ventilation grill in the room. If only there was a breeze or even some rain to cool the humid air down. He looked around aimlessly hoping to see Janice or Anthony.

The police had asked hundreds of questions mostly about Anthony. Did he know Anthony Soriano was the main graffiti artist in the city? Did he know they had been searching for him for years? Did he know where Anthony obtained his paints? Did he, Malachy help him get the paints or help him with the graffiti? Malachy had become monosyllabic in his answers. He did know some of the answers, but he wasn't going to tell them. When he had asked them about Mark and Liz Dellman's murders they had changed the subject. They were not willing to discuss the matter with him. At last they had finally allowed him to leave. Almost pushing him out of the police station, after he had asked if he could see Janice or Anthony.

Now he was outside, standing waiting for something to happen. The car stopped abruptly at the curb next to him. The dark tainted windows made it impossible for him to see inside. The passenger's side window silently slides down. He expected a gun to be pointing out at him. He stepped away from the car, preparing to run or drop to the floor if he needed to. When no gun appeared, he came forward and peered into the car. He was surprised when he saw Rosa Peronine a financial Analyst from the office smiling at him.

"Rosa?"

"Malachy get in quickly I'm on a red zone."

As he climbed into the car, she began to drive away before he had closed the door. He struggled to get the seat belt lock and heard the door locking mechanism click. The side window closed, and he felt himself a prisoner for a few seconds.

Janice left the police station and saw Malachy climb into the car. She called to him, but he didn't turn around and see her. She ran down the steps of the police station but was too late to grab his attention as the car drove off before he could even close the door. She stood on the curbside hoping in and out of the gutter. She didn't see Sandra Cartwright cross the street heading towards her. It wasn't until Sandra was standing next to her that Janice realized she was there.

"Hello, your Malachy's little friend."

"I'm a friend of Malachy, yes. I thought you had run away."

"Oh no that's not my style, anyway I've done nothing wrong. It was my S.O.B. of a husband and Mark 'Mister self-important' Thompson."

"Malachy just drove off in a car."

"I know, Rosa Peronine's car."

"Who's she?"

"A Financial Analyst in the office, I'm not sure why she picked him up. I didn't think she liked him. In fact, I don't think she liked many people."

"Where will she take him?"

"I don't know, but I wouldn't trust her. She has always given me the creeps as though she was hiding something that would kill you if you knew."

"Oh, do you think Malachy will be safe."

"That my little friend I can't say. Now if you would excuse me, I'll go and see some handsome sexy police detective, if they have one."

Sandra ran up the steps stopping half way and called to Janice.

"She lives in Burbank with her mother, near the golf course, up in the hills."

"Thanks," said Janice watching as Sandra entered the police station.

She had always disliked women like that who were overconfident. They could always get what they wanted. Janice felt awkward not sure what she should do. After a moment's thought she crossed the street and walked to the bus stop. She would go home, have a shower and then see if she could find Malachy or should she call Henry.

Malachy fiddled with the seat belt, he hated when the strap was twisted. So, he didn't notice Janice run down the police station steps as Rosa drove away. It took a few minutes to straighten the belt before settling down in the passenger seat.

The car's air conditioner blew cold air into his face, and after the humidity of the night air outside it was a refreshing relief.

Rosa drove with speed along the roads away from the police station. She glanced nervously in her mirrors, acting paranoid. Malachy became aware of her erratic driving and constant mirror checking. He didn't say anything at first, he too was concerned about what might happen next. As she continued to race, he decided to make a comment.

"I think you should slow down Rosa, or the police are going to pull you over and give you a ticket."

"Right, sorry. I thought we were being followed, you know they haven't found Bob or his friends."

She eased off the gas pedal and the car slowed down.

"I didn't know that how do you know?"

"I saw Sandra earlier and she is very worried."

"Why Rosa?"

"Well Bob is a very violent man, when he gets angry."

Malachy nodded his head he was sure Bob could be very violent if he chose to. He looked out of the window as the street flashed by.

"Where are we going?"

"Somewhere safe, somewhere no one will find you."

He sat contemplating what she had just said.

"Rosa who would be after me now, I've been to the

police and they weren't interested in anything I had to say."

"That's just it, Bob said you could be a witness and therefore you needed to go away."

"Oh, I'm not going to be a witness I really don't know anything."

Rosa put her foot on the brake and the car came to an abrupt stop.

"What do you mean you don't know anything?" screamed Rosa. "You know everything. It's because of you this has happened. If you hadn't been snooping this would never have happened."

"Me? What did I do?"

"Oh Malachy Moss don't play the little innocent lost boy with me. If you hadn't gone on and on about Monica Trystwold being in the office being the same woman who was murdered beneath the freeway none of this would have come out."

"If someone had just said yes, she does look like the woman who came into the office, instead of denying it I would have kept my mouth shut."

Rosa started the car and began to drive slowly. Malachy looked at her hands gripping the steering wheel so tight they were white.

"Rosa the woman was murdered."

"She needed to be, demanding this and that. She was a worthless actress Bob found in a diner."

"She may have been an actress, but that was no reason to get murdered."

Rosa didn't answer but began to drive faster.

"So, you were involved?"

"Involved, Bob and I were in love, he is going to leave Sandra and marry me. We had a brilliant plan

until Monica, Elizabeth and you started to mess
things up."

"Liz Dellman?"

"That bitch tried to blackmail us about our affair. I
mean whom does she think she is messing with. But
it wasn't because she was going to tell sweet boring
Sandra about Bob and Me. She somehow found out
about the money, so she had to go away too."

"The money?"

"Yes, the money, Bob got Mark to launder the
money for our boys in Columbia."

"Your boys in Columbia?"

"The boys."

"Malachy stop repeating everything I am saying, you
really are becoming a bore."

"Sorry, but the way you said boys it sounded like
they were family."

"They are, my brothers and cousins."

"I see."

"I don't think you really do, when Bob and I had a
vacation in Columbia two years ago he met my family and they became business partners.'

"To launder the money?"

"If that's what you want to call it."

"Well that what it is, and now several people are
dead because of it."

"I prefer to call it a money exchanging operation."
Malachy sank into silence, thinking about the confession Rosa had just given. He hadn't realized they even
knew each other. She had been Sandra's financial analyst for a time so maybe that's how they meet. If Bob
and Rosa had murdered Monica and Elizabeth then
they must have murdered Mark, it stands to reason."

"Who murdered Mark?"

"Bob."

"Why?"

"He found out Bob murdered Monica. He really was a very stupid man. Did you know he sprayed his bald patch black so it looked like he had hair? Anyway, he threatened to go to the police, so Bob put him away. I thought you knew all this."

"Not everything, where are we?"

"Oh shit, I've gone too far."

She made a U turn in front of the oncoming traffic. Several cars had to brake or swerve to avoid hitting the car.

"Watch out Rosa you almost go us killed."

It was at this moment that Malachy realized he was going to be murdered.

"Look Rosa I'm not going to tell anyone, nor do I want a share of the money. So, if you would just stop the car and let me out, I'll go home and you can go and meet Bob."

"Sorry Malachy you know too much, any way I'm beginning to enjoy this."

"Enjoy what?"

"Murder, it is such a high."

Rosa suddenly turned left and took one of the roads that led up the hill. The streetlights had stopped several streets back and the road was lit by her headlights. The car swung to the right, then the left. Her headlights illuminated the entrance to Wildwood Canyon Park. The name of the park was embedded into a low brick wall.

Malachy grabbed his seat as Rosa pushed on the accelerator pedal and the car raced up the twisting road.

He wasn't sure where he was but from the glimpse of the roadside, he was in a hill park with brown picnic

seats and tables along the roadside. He searched in
hope of seeing someone, walking their dog, trying to
find a quiet place for a cuddle. But on this night no
one seemed around. The park was empty.

Rosa suddenly turned the car to right and hit closed
gates of the Police Shooting range. Both of them continued moving forward in their seats until the seat belt
halted them.

"Shit it's closed."

She reversed the car and continued up the hill. Slowing
down when she thought she had found a suitable place
to stop. Each time she came to a place, which looked
possible, she stopped the car briefly before continuing.
They reached the top of the road and drove around the
small roundabout island twice before she parked the
car. Rosa leant forward and looked out of the windscreen. Malachy unbuckled his seat belt and carefully
moved the strap from across his body. He turned and
tried to open the door.

"Sit still until I tell you to move," screamed Rosa not
altering her stare out of the windscreen.

He sank back into his seat, was this 'the end' he
thought.

"You will move when I tell you to and not before,"
she repeated in a mechanical sounding tone.

He looked at her. The manic expression on her face
gave him shivers up his spine. She was mad.

"I can't just kill someone like Bob I need to prepare
myself. I have to make sure you have given me all
the information."

"Rosa I don't know anything."

"Don't lie to me, you and mister high and mighty
Mark Thompson were always talking. He told you
everything, so don't lie."

"I'm not lying Mark never told me anything. He didn't trust me."

"I don't believe you now get out of the car and no funny tricks." She produced a gun from under her seat and pointed at him.

He opened the door and slowly stepped out, once outside Rosa shouted. "Stop and don't move anymore." She opened her door and climbed out pointing the gun at him though the car. Once she was outside, she brought the gun over the top of the car and pointed at his head.

Still pointing the gun at him she ordered him to, "Walk around the car slowly and don't make a dash for it." He made his way around the car and stood at the trunk on the driver's side. Rosa still pointing the gun at him bent down and began to search under the seat with her left hand. She found the flashlight, but it seemed stuck and she pulled and pulled but it wouldn't move. Unthinkingly she placed the gun on the seat and using both hands tried to free the flashlight.

Malachy seeing her put the gun down ran off up the hill and through the concrete pillars, which adorned the entrance to the hill trails. Unable to clearly see, he ran as hard as he could. The pain from his illness soon began to take over in his legs and he started to slow down. Behind him he could hear Rosa shouting at him. The path was steep and then turned to the left once around the corner he stopped. He needed a good place to hide and as there was very little light. It was going to be hard. He could see the flashlight illuminating the sky as Rosa scanned the hillside. He could hear her footsteps on the gravel path.

He grabbed a tree root and pulled himself up off the path. Even though his legs and feet hurt he kept pulling himself up the bank. He stopped and looked back to see if Rosa had found out where he was and was climbing up behind him.

He was about twenty feet above the path now and saw the flashlight turn the corner. Rosa had stooped and was trying to listen to hear where he was.

"Malachy stop hiding I'm going to find you," she shouted.

She shone the light along the path then began to scan the hillside. Malachy continued to climb slowly, looking back to see where the light was in relation to him. Something on his left side made a movement as the lights illuminated it. Rosa fired at it, that moment the grip he had on the tufted of grass gave away and he slipped down the hillside. He gave an "ahrrr" sound as he fell.

"Got you," shouted Rosa.

He grabbed at a root as he slid down the hillside, stopping himself from falling anymore. He looked down onto the path below he had fallen about ten feet and assumed Rosa had spotted him. She had the flashlight on something in a clump of bushes to his left.

"Malachy," she shouted.

A sort of grunt sound came from the clump of bushes. Rosa fired several times more until the grunt sound stopped.

He held onto the root his arms and wrists becoming as weak as his legs. From down on the roadway the noise of a car starting made Rosa react and she began to run down the path back to where she had parked the car. Malachy slowly and painfully let himself slide down the hillside and onto the pathway. He stood and tried to listen to see if he could hear anything from the roadway. He heard Rosa scream, "That's my car."

The bushes, which Rosa had shot at, gave way and whatever she had shot at fell onto the pathway. He limped over to see what it was, cautiously checking just in case the animal was still alive. The eyes of a young male mountain lion stared at him. It was dead. He took a deep breath. This lion had saved his life from Rosa and she had possibly saved his life from the mountain lion. A sound from the bushes the lion had been hiding in motivated Malachy to creep towards the bend in the path. He peered around the corner expecting Rosa to appear with the flashlight in his face.

A roar behind made him turn the corner and walk quickly down the path. Without light it was difficult. It was a very rough pathway and the ruts and unevenness of the surface made it hard for him to walk fast. He wondered how he had run up the path without hurting himself. He reached the concrete pillars and the roadway.

Rosa's car was gone but had Rosa. Maybe someone had stolen her car while she was trying to murder him. It was too late to think or care he needed to get away from the place.

The road was steep and it hurt his legs as he walked rapidly, but at least the surface of the road was smooth. The mountain pathways had been very hard on his feet and legs. He peered ahead trying to make out what the strange shapes, which appeared were. He was hoping to meet someone, but not Rosa who he assumed had left the area. Maybe there would be a car parked hidden in the darkness. As long as it wasn't Rosa's, he would be fine. He hadn't seen any cars or trucks when they drove up the hill, but if some lustful young couple had decided to consummate their relationship in the wild, he could interrupt and ask for help.

No cars, trucks or lovers appeared at the next bend and no Rosa either.

The road became less steep and he was able to slow down his pace. He really wanted to sit down and rest, he knew if he did that, he could have more problems. It was important for him to get out of the park and back onto the streets of Burbank.

A picnic bench by the side of the road gave him reason to stop. He sat down. The cold brown colored metal penetrated his clothing. For a few seconds it was refreshing taking away the encroaching pain, which was beginning to seize his whole body. No one really understood what he felt from the disease. It was moments like this he wished he could cut off his legs just to lose the chronic pain.

He started to mull over what Rosa had confessed, she had killed Mark and Elizabeth because she was in love with Bob and because he had told her to. Bob was money laundering through the company for her brothers and cousins. He smiled to himself, if he had walked into any film company office and told then the scenario, they would have shown him the door. It was just too cheesy for words.

Something small, black, and white scurried along the roadway. Malachy stood up and after stretching his legs continued down the road. He hadn't realized how far they had driven up the mountainside. It was a mountain. He was sure of that even though he had heard locals refer to it as a hill range. Turning the next bend, he saw the gates of the Police shooting range Rosa had hit, they were damaged beyond repair. She had hit it with such force he wondered why her air bags had not deployed.

Just his luck there were no policemen doing night maneuvers, funny how when you need a policeman they are never around. Then when you don't want one to stroll or drive by there are several in a pack. Looking for innocent citizens who are just about to break some minor law or infringement. His thoughts wandered and he wondered if the police did night practice as not all crimes happen during the day.

He had been walking on the left-hand side of the roadway and crossed over to the right side. He wasn't sure why he did this, but he felt it was the right thing to do. A tree up on a slope reminded him of Janice, he wasn't sure why, but it looked like her. He hoped she was okay, and Rosa hadn't got to her first. He must go and see Janice first to see if she has not been hurt. Then he could share with her the confession of Rosa. Janice would be surprised he was certain.

He could just make out the bend in the road ahead and didn't hear the car rolling towards him. Rosa hadn't turned the lights or the engine on, she hadn't been convinced Malachy was dead and had been more concerned someone was stealing her car. They hadn't.

All she had to do was wait and if he was alive, he would walk down the roadway past her car. She had found a small parking space off the road, which was in complete darkness. It must have been where the other car had been hence why they hadn't seen it.

Malachy suddenly felt the air pressure from the car and instinctively dived out of the way. A loud thud was heard then the car engine started followed by the screech of tires and a car racing off into the night.

He had flown through the air, not sure if Rosa's car had hit him or not, his body was racked with pain. When he landed in a bush like tree it engulfed him.

He had thought of the bushes eating him slowly. After a few minutes of lying entangled in the branches he checked to see if anything was broken. To his relief everything seemed in working order.

He lay in the bushes a little longer his eyes closed. As he opened them, he saw the orange glow of the hillside golf course driving range. It instantly gave him his bearing. The city had built a dam to catch the water from the hillside. He was sitting in a bush on the edge of the basin of the dam. He was grateful it hadn't rained lately, and the basin was dry.

He climbed out of the bush and then could see where he had dived from, a concrete ramp from the roadway and he must have been at the top of the ramp when the car came for him. He assumed it was Rosa driving the car and she must have hit him, since she drove away. He forced himself up the ramp and onto the roadway. The smell, which hit him as he emerged, made his stomach want to vomit. Rosa had hit a skunk, it in turn had sprayed the area with its pungent aroma.

He walked quickly around the dead animal and down the road, increasing his pace as he did. If the lights of the golf course driving range could be seen, then he wasn't far from civilization. He prayed Rosa had given up on him.

Janice sat on the sofa, the first time in her life she was glad to be home. Her hair was wrapped in a large pink towel, wet from the shower she had just taken. She hadn't felt scared, when she arrived inside the house. It was just the thought that someone maybe hiding when she arrived which had made her apprehensive. Once inside and she had checked every room, she felt secure.

She had taken the money from the bag and put it in her hiding place. She had used the hiding place since she was a just a teenager. Her mother or one of her many boyfriends went through her room. She had felt violated for years until she had found the hiding place beneath the floor in the bathroom. It was like a metal box. She had crawled under the house to see what it was. Someone had fixed a metal box beneath the bathroom floor and it had become her secret box.

When the bathroom door was enhanced with a lock it made it easier for Janice to hide her secret things. The lock appeared after she had caught her mother having sex in the bathroom with one of her paramours. The next day a lock was fitted to Janice delight.

She sat back on the sofa and rested her head on the back. Her thoughts wandered. Trying to understand why Malachy had driven away with the woman Sandra had called Rosa. He had never mentioned Rosa in the office before and suddenly he was driving away with her.

"Sounds suspicious to me," she said to herself.

The light on her answering machine flashed, she hadn't noticed it before but now it caught her attention. She had a message, maybe two. What if Henry had called, Henry she moaned as she pressed the playback button.

"Janice this is Misses Jordan from the department store, we have been talking, the management and myself, and we may have been a little hasty in laying you off. Could you call me, I'm sure you would like to return to work with your friends here at the store."

"What a cheek, if they think I'm going back they are mistaken," shouted Janice to the answering machine. She deleted the message.

"Next message," said the machine's internal electronic voice.

"Hello my name is Estefania Soriano, I'm Anthony's mother could you call me back. Anthony wants to know if you're safe. He is still at the police station his father is there with him."

She gave a number. Janice wrote it down on a piece of paper. She pressed the saved message button and the machine told her it would be saved for thirty days.

"Next Message."

"If you know what's good for you, you'll disappear bitch. End of message"

Janice sat on the arm of the sofa and stared at the machine, she felt frightened and quickly pressed the play button.

"Next message." The same voice, "Get out of town; we don't want your sort around here." The noise of children in the background became louder. "Will you shut the fuck up, Kevin, oh shit she knows it's me… err just Joking."

The phone went dead Janice pressed the saved button. The next message started. It began with silence then the same man's voice began to speak. "err sorry about the message just a little bit of fun. I didn't mean anything by it err please no need to go to the police. Okay. End of message." She again pushed the saved button.

She sat quietly on the edge of the sofa wondering why Henry hadn't called. Then she remembered he didn't have her home number. She had given him Malachy's cell phone number.

The doorbell followed by a knocking on the door made her jump. She put the safety chain on the door before opening a little.

The man from across the road who had left the messages stood nervously at the door. He had one of his little girls standing by his side. He tried the screen door but Janice had instinctively locked it.

"Can I talk to you, I really need to apologize, and it was a stupid thing to do."

Janice closed the door and removed the chain, before opening the door wide. She didn't unlock the screen door. The man looked pathetic as he stood in his dirty grey shorts and white tee shirt. The light from the forty-watt bulb, which hung precariously by the side of the door, didn't help his appearance.

"You scared me I should really go to the police."

"Yes, and I am sorry, I don't know why I did it."

"What did you mean my sort?"

"Terrorists."

"Terrorists? I'm no terrorist, whatever gave you that idea?"

"The police said you were involved with some terrorist group who planned to take over the world. Or was it your boyfriend."

"I don't have a boyfriend, not at this moment and I have never belonged to a terrorist group."

"Well you don't look the sort, my wife said they must be wrong, she said you were a little crazy but not a terrorist."

"So, you thought you would scare me, maybe I should go to the police."

"Please don't, I'm on parole and they would put me away if you do."

"I just want to be left alone, so please leave me alone."

"You won't go to the police then?"

"Not as long as you leave me alone."

"Right and if you ever need any help just ask."

"Thanks."

The man took the little girl's hand and they began to walk down the path.

"She's a nice lady daddy."

"Yes, I think she is, and daddy was told too many lies."

"Who told you daddy?"

"The police sweetheart."

"I don't like the police for telling my daddy lies."

Janice stood and watched them cross the road she was glad she had locked the screen door.

"I need to call Henry," she said out loud. "Now where did I put his number?"

She searched her bag and finally emptied everything out before she found the number.

Dialing the number immediately she waited in anticipation for it to ring. The timer on her telephone told her she had been on the phone for forty-three second and the phone on his end hadn't rung yet. When it did it continued for some time before the answering machine clicked in. "You have reached the answering machine of Henry please leave a message."

After the beep Janice rapidly said. "Henry this is Janice my home phone number is…"

The crash and then banging on the screen door made Janice give a scream. She put down the phone on its cradle, and then remembered she hadn't given Henry her number.

The black shape at the screen door banged again. Janice went over and tried to see whom it was. She closed the front door quickly; she wasn't going to open the door to someone she didn't recognize.

The banging continued followed by a weak cry of "help me Janice."

Janice opened the door slowly, no one was standing outside. She opened the screen door and couldn't see anyone standing on the porch. She let the screen door go and a hand shot out and grabbed it. This was followed by a man falling into the living room and sprawling onto the floor. Janice screamed.

The man's face arms and hands were boated with red bumps. He looked like million bees had stung his body.

"Janice."

She looked closer at the man she wasn't sure, but it could be...

"Malachy?"

"Yes."

"What happened?"

Malachy fell unconscious.

Janice dialed nine one, one.

CHAPTER FIFTEEN

Hostage

Malachy lay in the hospital bed. He had been sedated so he could rest and relax from the pain. The door of the private room opened, and Henry stood looking into the room.

"Henry?"

"Janice?"

They hugged. He kissed her gentle on the lips, and then step back to look at her.

"I went to your home after I heard your message. I thought something had happened to you. Your neighbor told me you had gone in an ambulance to the hospital."

"It not me, its Malachy fell into a poison oak tree. They are watching his breathing, but the doctor thinks he will pull through."

"Thank God, it wasn't you."

"How did you know where I lived?"

"I have caller ID and then reverse the number look up on the internet."

"Clever."

"I've been calling but I just kept getting a voice message."

"It was Malachy's cell number I gave you."

"I see. Your neighbors seem a little worried."

"So, he should be, he left me some horrible messages. I kept them maybe you could listen to them sometime and let me know what I should do."

A nurse entered the room she looked at the two of them and then at Malachy.

"I think you both should leave now. Mr. Moss needs rest. You can come back in the morning."

"Yes of course, may we have a few minutes more please?"

"Are you family."

"He is the only family I've got."

"Five minutes and not a minute more then you must go."

"We will nurse," said Henry.

The nurse swept out of the room taking the smell of disinfectant with her.

"I didn't know you are related."

"We're not really, but he is sort of the brother I would like to have had. Along with Anthony."

"So, what happened?"

"I'm not really sure. He drove away from the police station. I think with some woman called Rosa, that's her name."

"Did he know her?"

"She worked with him, then the next thing I know he is falling into my living room looking like the monster from mars."

Henry moved closer to the bed to get a proper look at Malachy. The wheals on his face had distorted the shape of it. This was not helped by the breathing tubes sticking out of the corner of his cracked lips.

"His breathing is what they are worried about."

"Why?"

"Because…"

"How did he get like this?" interrupted Henry.

"The doctor said he had fallen into either a poison ivy or poison oak tree. His whole body is covered with lumps."

"How do you know that?"

"The nurse told me silly, I didn't look."

Henry blushed and gave an embarrassed smile.

"From what the nurse told me he will be okay in a day or two. That is if his breathing doesn't have a problem."

"Let's hope he gets better, your adopted brother.'

Janice gave a deep sigh, blew Malachy a kiss.

"Let's go, I'm getting hungry."

"Me too, I haven't eaten anything since lunch time and that was a stew I made."

Janice took a slip of paper out of her bag and slipped into a book on the bedside table.

"Malachy if you can hear me that is the list Ant found."

The nurse opened the door, she looked at them, and from her expression she wanted them to go as quickly as possible.

"Thank you for allowing us to stay a little longer with my brother, we will come back in the morning."

Janice picked up Malachy's cell phone, which had been placed on top of his bedside table and slipped it into her bag.

"Let me give you my number, just in case something happens."

The nurse took down the number, and held the door open for them to leave.

Henry led the way to his car and opened the passenger side door. Janice stood awkwardly by it not knowing what she was supposed to do. In the many films she had watched the lady carefully sat down and swung her legs into the car. For Janice this felt false. Henry misinterpreted the hesitation and reluctantly said, "Let me take you home."

Janice sat, swung her legs into the car and was surprised how gentle Henry closed the door. She fiddled with the seat belt, once buckled she sat stiffly looking straight ahead.

Henry drove carefully and defensively and as each mile passed Janice began to relax. Turning into the road Janice lived on two thoughts came into her mind. How did he know where she lived? Oh yes, he told her in the yellow pages and the second thought was more perplexing. Why is there a fire in her front garden?

Henry pulled into the curb and jumped out of the car. Several of the neighbors were attempting to throw buckets of water on the flames. The manager from the nearby apartment complex was trying to make his water hose reach her garden. The sound of the Burbank Fire Department could be heard as it screeched towards her house.

Janice stood next to Henry, her hand slipped into his. He squeezed it, then held it gently but firmly. Her car sat on the driveway engulfed in flames on the sidewall of the house someone had sprayed 'Your next.'

The man who had made the threatening phone calls appeared next to them.

"I didn't do it honestly but I did see who did."

"Who?" snapped Henry.

"A crazy woman."

Before he could continue the fire, brigade arrived and made Henry, Janice and the other bystanders move across the street. It took only a few minutes of high-pressure water to extinguish the flames.

One of the firemen spoke to an elderly man in the crowd who pointed to Janice. The fireman dressed in his uniform of yellow trousers and tunic approached her. She smiled to herself she could see him on a calendar of hunky fireman. He would be July or August all sweaty looking with black soot on his face. It was with this thought in her mind when he asked her "Was that your car miss?"

"Yes." was all she could reply.

Henry looked at her in bewilderment.

"Sorry, yes it was her car."

Janice looked at the fireman and as though she was a machine, said, "I think it may have been set on fire on purpose."

"According to one of the neighbors it was a crazy woman."

"Which neighbor sir?"

Henry pointed to the phone message man who was standing on the opposite side of the street looking very anxious.

"I think it was a woman called Rosa."

"Sorry," said the fireman looking at Janice with an expression of suspicion.

"I think it was a woman called Rosa, she tried to kill a friend of mine tonight and I think she was trying to warn me."

"I see hence the message on your house. I think the police will need to speak to you."

"They already have fat lot of good they were too."

"I can't comment on that miss, but I don't think you should stay by yourself tonight."

"I will be with her," said Henry taking Janice's hand and squeezing it again.

The fireman left and joined his colleagues who were wrapping up their equipment.

"Let's go inside and I will make you a hot drink." Henry guided Janice to her front door and held out his hand for the keys. She stood looking at him, unable to understand what he wanted.

A car parked in the alleyway exploded into a ball of flames, this was followed by another car and then another. The fire chief rushed to the alley, while the other firemen unwrapped their hoses and reconnected them to the street fire hydrants.

Janice stood staring at the flames, the shock had washed over her body and she began to shake. Henry took her bag and searched for the keys. He opened the door and led her into the living room. The flames from the fire lit the room and he sat her carefully down on the sofa.

"It's not going to stop is it?"

"Nothing going to happen while I'm here."

"What about when you're gone?"

"Who said I was going?"

A knock at the door made then both jumped. Henry collected himself and opened the door as he switched on the main lights. A tall police officer stood on the porch. He had a large clipboard in one hand and several pens in the other. Henry opened the screen door.

"Good evening sir. I believe you may have some information regarding the cars which have been set on fire."

"My girlfriend, does, it was her car which was set on fire first."

"Does she have any idea who may have done it, the fire chief indicated she might."

"You'd better come in and please officer she has had a shocking tonight, so please be gentle with her."

"Yes of course sir."

The officer entered the house and immediately began to fire a one question after the other at Janice.

"So, you know who did it?"

"What?" replied Janice still in a state of shock.

"Do you know who set your car on fire?"

"I don't know for sure. I think it was a woman called Rosa."

"And why did you think it was a woman called Rosa?"

"Because." Janice stared at the flames she could see through the window.

"Because what?" snapped the police officer.

"Because she tried to kill Malachy."

"Malachy who is Malachy?"

"A friend."

"Why would this woman called Rosa try to kill your friend?"

"Because."

"Officer, Janice has been through a lot the last few days, I don't think she is making much sense at the moment."

"That's true."

"Maybe you could come back tomorrow morning."

Before the officer could answer the door opened and another officer entered the room.

"Six more cars on fire. Whoever is doing this is moving towards Glendale."

"I'm getting nothing here I'll call back in the morning. Let's go."

Both officers left the house; Henry closed the door and locked it. He checked it several time to makes sure it was closed.

Janice lay down on the sofa. "I'm tired," she said before curling up into a ball.

Henry turned on a table lamp and switched off the main overhead light. The room looked cozy in this light. The big awkward furniture no longer dominated the room, it dissolved into the shadows. It was just like his mother's solid old-fashioned wooden furniture acquired from some old relative.

"You rest I'm going to make some tea."

The kitchen was clean, spotless. It looks like no one ever cooked in the kitchen. The white tiled counter tops looked new and the grouting hadn't even been marked. The stainless-steel stove gleamed pristine new.

He opened a cupboard and found it full of tin cans. The refrigerator was the same it was as though Janice was expecting an army to arrive and she was going to have to feed them all.

On the window ledge above the sink was a small wooden sign, which read 'use filter water only.' He filled the kettle with filtered water from the faucet and placed it on the stove. After a search he found mugs and tea bags.

Janice was curled up on the sofa, and Henry looked around the room, although he had turned off the main light, he could see most of the room. The house had two bedrooms and from the neatness and young woman's clothing this was Janice room. The other was like his mothers and looked as if it had been left untouched. He ran his fingers long the surface of a chest of drawers. A habit he had acquired from his mother who would go into departments stores and check for dirt and dust. The room was dust free. The whistle on the kettle blew and he ran back to the kitchen.

A young Hispanic woman stood at the counter pouring hot water into the mugs.

"You are?" she snapped as he appeared in the doorway.

"Henry."

"Why are you here?"

"I'm Janice's boyfriend."

"I see."

"Who are you?"

"I'm Rosa Peronine."

"Oh!"

"Oh, is that all you have to say, you obviously know who I am by that expression."

"It was you who set the cars on fire."

"Maybe, maybe not."

"You did or you didn't?"

"Where's your girlfriend?"

"She is sleeping."

"Good let's hope she never wakes up."

"Why?"

"She knows too much for her own good."

"About what in particular?"

"If I told you then you would know too much."

"True."

"Janice doesn't know anything, she a little different to other women."

"Brainless is what you mean."

"That's a little harsh and not absolutely true but she doesn't know anything."

"What did she tell the police officer?"

"Nothing, she said she didn't know who did it. I think she may think it was the man across the street."

"The nutter you mean."

"You know him?"

"No, I just saw him trying to explain why he was making a threatening phone calls to little missy sleepy head."

"What do you want Rosa?"

"Nothing."

"Then why did you break into Janice's house?"

"Because."

"What?"

"Because, that's what little miss sleepy head said to the police."

"You were here?"

"Yes."

"I thought you were out setting cars on fire."

"Not me. That was a local kids gang, doing it just for fun."

"Then if you were here you know what Janice said to the police which was nothing because she doesn't know anything."

"I didn't hear every word said." Rosa dunked the tea bag in the cup removed it and gave it a squeeze to release all the liquid. She looked around to place the tea bag and not seeing a trash bag threw it into the sink.

"Not having your tea?"

"In a moment, I'm trying to work out why you broke into Janice's house."

"She hasn't told you, has she?"

"She hasn't told me because she doesn't know anything."

"Oh, Henry I think she does, but maybe she doesn't talk."

"I think you should go."

"Not until I'm sure."

"Of what?"

"That she doesn't know anything or can't tell anyone."

"I'm sure if she was here, she would tell you she doesn't know anything and what little she does know she not telling anyone."

"Well there's only one way to stop her." Rosa dragged her index finger across her throat in a cutting motion.

"I won't let you do that."

"You, you couldn't stop a fly."

"I'm a security guard and we are trained…"

"To look tough, but that's all. You know the building I work in they have three little and I mean little women as security guards, a real joke that. Cheap labor that's what they are."

"I think you should leave."

"Not until I've done what I came to do."

"You're not going to harm Janice."

"I'm not going to harm her just make sure she can't talk."

"What about me?"

"You too."

Rosa produced the gun from her coat pocket and pointed it at Henry. At first, he wasn't sure if it was real, but from what he could see it looked real enough.

"Move it."

Henry slowly walked towards the living room. His heart was pounding, he had never found himself in this position before. He had confronted several belligerent customers at the mall but not one who threatened him with a gun. The living room looked darker than it had before.

"Where is she?"

"On the sofa."

"Wake her up."

"No."

"Do as I say, or you will be first."

Rosa pointed the gun at Henry, turned and then fired at the sofa. Janice screamed 'Henry' then silence. Henry ran around the front of the sofa expecting to see Janice lying dead. Rosa backed up towards a door, which suddenly and forcible opened. The door hit Rosa in the back and caused her to lose balance. She dropped the gun and fell to the floor.

Henry jumped over the sofa and put his foot on the gun, which lay a few feet from Rosa. He wasn't sure who was behind the door as he thought he saw Janice lying on the sofa. He realized the table lamp had been switched off before they had entered the living room. This made it difficult for him to recall seeing if Janice was on the sofa or it was just cushions, with her sweater draped over them.

Rosa had hit the floor with some force and lay stunned for a few moments. The door which had hit Rosa closed and a muffled voice said 'sorry'.

Rosa still a little dazed dragged herself back into the kitchen. Henry followed and watched as she put her head under the faucet and let the water run over her head. She lifted her head and shook it letting the water spray across the room. Henry raised his hand to shield himself from the water, Rosa without looking back at him ran from the kitchen and into the back yard.

Henry bolted the back door and checked all the windows. He suddenly remembered the gun lying on the floor and Janice was she okay or did she get shot. He returned to the living room to find the gun still on the floor where Rosa had dropped it. He carefully picked it up and placed it in a drawer in the sideboard. Checking the sofa to see if Janice was lying there, he was relieved to find she wasn't, it was her sweater with bullet holes in it draped over a cushion.

He knocked on the door, which had hit Rosa, no one replied so he knocked again. Still no reply he knocked harder and no one answered. He tried the doorknob and as it turned, he opened the door, it was a bathroom.

And no one was inside, he switched on the light to check but it was empty. He closed the door and leaning against it, if Janice wasn't on the sofa or in the bathroom, then where was she. He went to her bedroom and checked the bed, hoping to see Janice lying on it asleep. She wasn't nor was she in the other bedroom.

He returned to the sofa and sank into a chair had this just been a bad dream. The door to the bathroom opened and Janice quietly entered the living room she could see Henry sitting in the chair, his masculine frame sat erect. She crossed the room and sat on the sofa picking up her sweater.

"She ruined my sweater."

Henry had fallen asleep.

Janice checked the windows and door to see if they were all locked and curled up on the sofa. She fell into a deep sleep. In her dream she woke to find herself sitting on the living room floor counting money which had been washed and dried earlier. A knock at the door made her make a mad scramble to hide the money. A second knock on the door, and she cautiously opened it to reveal Henry standing smiling at her.

He pushed past her, turns, and grabs her in his arms and kisses her passionately on the lips. His hands stroke her body, she had never had anyone do this before and it was for her a very nice feeling. He blew into her ear.

"It tickles."

"Good, I want to make love with you."

"But."

"No buts. I've plenty of condoms."

"What," said Janice pulling away from Henry.

He was pulling a hand full of condoms out of his pocket and throwing them into the air.

Janice awoke suddenly to a loud knocking at her door. The room was dark, and she was alone. In her semi sleepy state, she opened the door. A tall woman in her mid-twenties stood holding a crying baby in her left arm. The woman had aged before her time and her dress was stained with food and baby vomit.

She looked at Janice, and then shifted the baby to the other arm.

"Listen you little bitch, leave my husband alone."

"I don't know your husband."

"Oh yes you do, I smelt you on his clothes. Find one of your own."

"But I don't know your husband."

"He says you do."

The woman looked out into the street at a line of parked cars. Henry was sitting in a white Cadillac; he gave an acknowledging wave.

"Sorry I didn't know he was married."

"Oh, they all say that, married and five children and another one on the way." Said the wife patting herself on the stomach.

"What are they?"

"What do you care what my children are, you just want to steal their daddy."

"I don't."

"Liar," said the wife then she spat at Janice. From somewhere in the babies clothing she produced a gun and pointed it at Janice.

"Well you're the last, bitch."

"No." screamed Janice as the gun went off.

She awoke to find herself lying on the sofa, the room was lit by the table lamp. Henry sat in the armchairs her mother always used and was talking to someone on the phone.

"Mother, listen I am staying with Janice tonight, she had a shock and needs me here."

Janice lay back on the sofa she wasn't sure if she was still dreaming or if this was for real.

Henry raised his voice slightly a firmness entered the tone. "I'm staying here, look Janice is my girlfriend and if she will have me, I will marry her. So, mother stop your drama and accept, I'm going to get married."

A thrill spread through Janice's body, someone wanted her as his wife. She must be dreaming.

"I know you haven't met her and maybe I won't let you until we get married. Because you will do your best to hate her and Janice is different, she is nothing like you. So, go to bed mother and we may see you at lunch time tomorrow."

He put the phone down. Janice stirred and sat up on the sofa and looked at him.

"Yes, I will."

Henry looked at her, "You will what."

"Marry you."

Henry smiled, not just an ordinary smile but also his whole body smiled. He rose from the chair and knelt before Janice.

He kissed her on the lips.

"You heard."

"Yes, my mother was like that."

"No, no one can have a mother like mine she is so manipulating."

"She doesn't want to lose you."

"Well my sweet she is going to have to."

"Do you really mean it?"

"Yes."

She leaned forward and kissed him. "Thank you."

"I will propose properly later when we have sorted out this mess. But understand Janice Smart you are going to be my bride."

Janice gave a girlish giggle.

"I had a series of dreams, no nightmares before I woke up."

"What were they?"

"Well first you arrived and said you were going to make mad passionate love to me and then threw condoms into the air."

"Are you serious?"

"Then your wife arrived with one of your five children and spat at me before shooting me."

"Oh."

"Oh, is all that you can say?"

"You don't know what happened do you?"

"What do you mean?"

"Well my sweet we had a visitor."

"Really who? I don't remember."

"I think you may have been asleep the whole time and saved your own life by being so."

"Who was it?"

"Rosa."

"Rosa, what happened, why didn't you wake me up?"

"Because she had a gun."

"Really and what happened?"

"She came into the kitchen and threatened to kill you. Then came in here and fired at the sofa. I thought she had killed you."

"Where was I?"

"Then you open the bathroom door and knocked Rosa over and she dropped the gun. You must have really hit her because she left the gun and after putting her head under the faucet in the kitchen she left by the back door."

"Where is the gun now."

"In the drawer over there."

"We'd better give the gun to the police."

"I locked all the doors and windows, then called mother to tell her I wasn't coming home tonight."

"Is she really that bad?"

"My father ran away he couldn't take it anymore. I don't know where he is."

"Sorry."

"No, it's okay at one point I had three jobs not because of the money just to stay out of the house and away from mother."

"This is not going to be easy, is it?"

"It will be fine if we stick together and never believe a word she says."

"Just like my mother."

"Mothers who'd have them."

"I hope to be a mother one day."

The squawk of the police communicator could be heard before the knock on the front door. Henry opened the door, the Police officer looked apprehensive, his right hand on his gun in its holster.

"Sorry to bother you sir but we have had reports about gunfire."

"Oh yes you had better come in."

The officer entered the house his hand still on his gun.

"Someone fired at the house I ran outside they ran off and dropped the gun."

"A foolish thing to do."

"True officer, I wasn't thinking."

"If it should ever happen again sir, stay indoors and call the police."

"Right I didn't think any way we have the gun in the drawer and my girlfriend, and I were just about to call you guys to report it."

"It was my fault we didn't call straight away I was a little upset."

"I can understand miss."

"I didn't touch it because there might be fingerprints on it."

"Very responsible sir."

Henry opened the drawer the officer took a zip lock bag out of his breast pocket and picked the gun by the nozzle dropping it into the bag.

The front door violently swung open Rosa stepped inside a shotgun in her hands.

"That's mine," she said pointing the shotgun at the gun in the zip lock bag.

The officer gripped his gun in its holster, looked at Rosa and calmly said, "Put the gun down."

"Fuck off," retorted Rosa and fired a shot at the officer.

It missed him she continued to point the gun at him and caught sight of his gun in its holster.

"Put the gun in the bag and your own gun on the sideboard."

The officer didn't react but stood his ground.

"Do it or you will be first."

The officer reluctantly placed the guns on the sideboard. Rosa indicated with the gun for him to sit on the sofa. He sat down squeezing next to Henry. He had years of training and when it came to a situation like this nothing, he had learnt could help him. If he survived this ordeal, he was going talk to his superiors about the inadequate training in a hostage situation.

"So little missy perfect girlfriend is awake now, good then she can watch me kill them first before I kill her."

"Calm down miss, I'm sure we can talk this out."

"Shut it I don't talk or listen to pigs."

The officer's communicator squawked.

"Turn that off."

"If I do that, they will come looking for me."

"Good then we can have a pig slaughter party."

"She's a little upset I think it may be worthwhile to switch it off," said Henry grasping the consequences if he does.

"You maybe be right." The officer understanding the nod of Henry's head, he switched off his communicator.

"Okay who wants to die first? Don't be shy isn't it an American thing always wanting to be first at everything."

"No one wants to die," said the officer.

"Oh yes they do, don't you missy. You know too much."

"I don't know anything miss."

"Senorita."

"Okay enough just tell me what this is all about at least I have the right to know before I die," said the officer, remembering the training, keep a hostage taker talking.

"You have no right pig," spat Rosa.

"Rosa," screamed Janice.

"What?"

"Stop this now. I don't know anything Malachy didn't tell me anything."

"Malachy, where is the squealer."

"He's in hospital."

"So, I did hit him, will he die?"

"I'm not sure."

"Let's hope so."

The telephone next to Rosa rang, all four looked at it. It rang several times before Rosa picked it up.

"Yes, oh yes your little boy is here fucking the brains out of missy bimbo." She hung the phone up.

"Your name is Henry right."

"Yes."

"That was your mother."

"Great, thanks, how am I going to explain this?"

"You won't have to you will be dead remember."

"Not yet," said Janice.

"So, Malachy Rolling Moss didn't tell you shit."

"No."

"What about the kid?"

"Anthony doesn't know anything he is just a kid."

"So, no one knows anything, bullshit missy."

The phone rang again. Rosa threw the phone at Henry.

"Answer it."

"Hello, yes, no, I will call you later." He hung up.
The front of the house suddenly became illuminated.
Rosa became agitated.

"What's happening?"

"The place is surrounded, I told you if I switched off
my communicator, they would come looking for
me."

"Shut the fuck up. I got to think, where is Bob when
I need him."

Janice moved to the edge of the sofa, she leaned forward.

"Rosa none of us knows what's really happening.
We can say it was a lovers' tiff they'll give you probation. That's right isn't it officer."

"Yes, just probation."

"Maybe, what about Malachy?"

"Oh, he'll die. When I left the hospital, they said he
wouldn't last the night out and he was in a coma, so
he wasn't able to talk to anyone."

"No one else needs to die," said the officer.

"No one else, you know. Who told you this bitch? I
knew it bullshit."

"Thanks a lot," said Janice to the officer and sat back
into the sofa.

She wished she was next to Henry, but the officer had
sat down between them.

"What I meant…"

"Cut it pig you've said enough."

The phone rang and Henry answered it automatically.

"Yes." He listened then holding the phone receiver
out towards Rosa.

"It's the police outside they want to talk to you."

"You talk to them I don't talk to pigs."

"She says she doesn't want to talk to you."

'Stop," yelled Rosa. "Tell them I want a car to the airport, LAX then a plane to Chile and ten million dollars."

"She wants a car to LAX, a plane to Chile and ten million dollars."

"And no bullshit from you pigs."

"And no bullshit."

"Tell them they have twelve hours."

"You have twelve hours only. Anything else Rosa?"

"No. Put the phone down."

Silently they waited, Rosa becoming increasingly agitated. It seemed like hours to Janice and she picked up a cushion and hugged it. Her right hand stroked it and while her fingers smoothed over the cushion, she found a hole. She looked carefully at it.

"There's a hole in my cushion."

"What," screamed Rosa coming out of a daze.

"There is a hole in my cushion."

"So, get over it, it's only a hole."

"But how did it get there?"

"Tell you later," said Henry.

"I'd tell her now, there won't be a later not for you anyway."

"So," snapped Janice the tension rising inside her.

"Rosa shot at you earlier."

"So I did hear gunfire, it wasn't in my dream."

"Yes, she tried to kill you earlier when you were sleeping on the sofa, only you had gone to the toilet."

"Shut the fuck up," shouted Rosa.

"Don't tell my fiancée to shut up."

Janice in anger threw the cushion at Rosa hitting her in the face. The shotgun discharged into the ceiling. The

police officer was out of his seat and had disarmed
Rosa before she realized what had happened. Henry
grabbed the shot gun and placed it on the floor away
from Rosa.

The front door bust open and armed squat team members entered the house.

Henry and Janice sat on the sofa holding each other
while the officers stood around talking to each other.

The phone rang, Henry answered it.

"Mother, listen Mother will you listen and turn on
the television, any news channel. That's right the
hostage siege in Burbank. Well mother I was one of
the hostages. It's over now and I'm okay so is
Janice. Okay mother I'll see you sometime tomorrow." He closed the phone.

"Is your mother okay?"

"She is now, she's gone to tell the neighbors, this is
the best thing that could have happened as far as my
mother is concerned. I'm sure I will be the hero of it
all in her eyes."

"You are to me."

The police left. Henry locked all the doors. Janice
was looking at the ceiling when he returned to the living room.

"We will need to fix that hole."

"I will and give the whole place a fresh coat of paint
and I will change all the locks and put better ones on.
So, we can make it our home."

He took Janice in his arms and kissed her.

CHAPTER SIXTEEN

A Little Insurance

Ant lay on his bed the anticipation of an argument with his father had made him very tense. The drive from the police station had been in silence even his mother hadn't spoken to him. He knew he was about to have big problems. There had been no mention of his sister, even though he had asked many times what happened to her. He could tell from his mother's eyes that something very bad had happen to his sister and it was his fault.

He had seen her shot but hadn't stayed around to find out if she had lived or not. He felt bad and wanted to cry. Nor had he heard from Malachy or Janice, but he had seen the news item about the siege in Burbank at Janice's house. The police station waiting room television was turned on when the siege was over and he saw Janice and Henry with the police.

He looked at his sister's bed it looked like it hadn't been slept in. He wished his own bed would just swallow him and he wouldn't have to face the inevitable. His father had dropped his mother and him off at the apartment. He was told to go to his room until his father's returned. His mother had gone into the kitchen to prepare a meal. When he asked again about his sister his mother put her hands up to her mouth. He felt alone, everything that had happened no longer seemed important. Even though he and his friends had won the battle he felt like they were defeated.

He sat up and rearranged the pillow on his bed and taking his sketch pad he turned to a blank page and began to draw a picture of Janice, when he had completed it, he drew Malachy. It wasn't until he tried to draw himself, he found he had a problem. He looked in the mirror above his sister's bed and drew what he saw.

Doorbell rang and his mother called for him to answer it. He slowly dragged himself off the bed and opened the front door. Two men dressed in black and wearing ski masks stood facing him. Both had guns. They indicated for him to move inside, and as they passed each room one of then checked to see if anyone was inside. Once in the living room, one of the men went into the kitchen and pushed Estefania into the living room.

She came and stood next to Anthony who for the first time became really scared of what was going to happen.

"Nasaán ang iyong asawa?"

"I don't understand Tagalog," said Estefania obviously lying.

"Where is your husband?"

"Out. I don't know where."

"At the police station," said Anthony

The two men looked at each other then one of them indicating with his lips which he pushed forward through the hole in the ski mask to leave.

"Tell your husband he is a dead man."

The two men left the apartment slamming the door behind them.

"Mama what's happening, who were those men?"

"Philippine Free Army, they murdered your sister."

"What?"

"She's dead."

"Yes, that is why your father is so sad."

"It was nothing to do with the problems I had?"

"No, your father had been fighting the PFA for many years. They kill many of his family and friends. He killed one of their leaders several years ago and they vowed they would find your father and kill him."

"I didn't know."

"We shall have to move again."

"Maybe if we went somewhere there were no Filipino's we would be okay."

"We tried that when you were young, and they found us."

"Mama I have helped to stop one murderer now I shall save my father."

She smiled at him and kissed him on his forehead, then returned to the kitchen. He went back to his bedroom, he thought of his sister never coming back and sleeping in her bed hit him. They may not always be loving siblings, but he loved her all the same.

He heard the front door open and his father's voice calling to his mother. He hoped, as his father walked down the passageway, he would look in on Anthony, but he didn't.

How long did he have to wait for his father, he just wanted to get it over with? Would his father tell him about the PFA? He heard the phone ring and his mother answer it this was followed by his father running out of the apartment.

"Anthony stay, in your room," said his mother closing his bedroom door.

He looked at the sketch again of Janice, Malachy, and himself. Janice looked young and vibrant. Malachy could do with a little work on the face. He didn't think he had captured himself very well and needed to work harder on self-imagery.

He heard the phone ring again his mother went onto Tagalog. She was obviously talking with his father. He heard the telephone being replaced on the cradle. His mother knocked on his door.

"You okay Anthony?"

"Yes Mama, can I take a shower."

"Of course, but don't take too long."

The water ran over his body, it was as though he was washing away his past. It felt refreshing, so much so he didn't want to get out of the shower. His mother knocked on the door.

He took his time drying himself, the shower had helped him relax and now he was ready for his father. Too many questions unanswered.

He heard the doorbell ring. But no one spoke and he wondered if at any minute the PFA would bust in on him and drag him out into the street naked. The doorbell rang again, it sounded like one of his mother's friends come to stare at the criminal element in the Soriano family.

He returned to his room and put his dirty clothes in the laundry basket he and his sister had shared. His sketchpad was no longer on the bed and he distinctively remembered leaving it there.

The door open and his mother stood looking at her son in just his underwear. The Soriano family had never been modest about their bodies, so he didn't react as his mother watched him dress.

"I need to talk to you when you're dressed."

Anthony nodded he was now ready for his father.

His mother stopped him leaving the room and rearranged his blond dyed hair.

"It'll grow out."

"I know but it does make you look innocent, like a choir boy."

Estefania led her son into the living room. And they sat opposite each other at the dining table.

"Where's dad?"

"Gone for now. He won't be home for some time"

"Mama what's happening to our family is all my fault."

"No."

"But Susan's dead and dad's runaway."

"Your father hasn't run away he has gone into hiding."

"Why?"

"When your father was a young man like you, he took revenge on the NPA for killing members of his family

"Dad's a rebel."

"They vowed to find and kill him. That happened twenty years ago and was the reason we were able to obtain our green cards."

"Your father had pictures of our house after they had burnt it down, with a lodger inside."

"I see, and that's why dad was always wanting to move apartments?"

"Yes. Anthony do you really prefer to be called Ant."

"Anthony from you, and maybe everyone else I think it's time to change."
"Going forward it is just you, and I, things may be very difficult. We will have very little money your father will only send what he can."
"I will leave school and get a job, then go to art school at night."
"We will see."
"Mama I am sorry."
"For what?"
"For all the problems I have caused. I did meet some really nice people, friends Malachy and Janice."
"Oh yes Janice what a very nice girl she is and getting married too."
"To Henry?"
"I think that is who she said, she came around and left something for you."
His mother gave him a package. On it was written 'first installment ten more to go'. He opened the package removing the newspaper wrapping. He sat for a few minutes looking at the pile of money. Estefania's mouth dropped open.
"Anthony there is a note."
He opened the pink paper note and read aloud.
"Anthony formerly known as Ant the greatest graffiti artist in the world. You may remember when we left Bob's condo, I was carrying a different bag. I found a big and I mean big jar full of money in a kitchen cupboard. It's our reward for solving the murders no ifs or buts. Malachy, you and I will share it equally. There is forty thousand dollars in this package and ten more of the same to be sent. I think so as not to arouse anyone interest about the

money we should receive the installments every six months I hope you agree.
I am really sorry about your sister.
Love Janice Smart soon to be Mrs. Janice Kal-waski. "

"Mama dad should be told. I can look after our needs and he can use his money to find a way for him to be safe."
"I think we should move."
"Not out of Burbank."
"No but start a fresh, too much has happened here."
"That's true."
"And the landlord said he wanted us out, because we bring trouble."
"The racist."
She put her hand on top of his and gave them a little squeeze.
Malachy Rolling Moss lay looking at the ceiling of his hospital room. After so many visitors he was glad to some time to himself. The police, FBI and others had been questioning him for hours despite the protest from the nurses. After they had left the nurse had turned the light down low so he could rest.
When the door opened at first, he thought the woman standing in the doorway was Rosa. As she moved into the room, he realized that Sandra Cartwright had for some reason decide to visit him.
"Hello Malachy, how are you; you look terrible."
"Sandra, I didn't expect to see you."
"Well I felt as your coworker I should come and see how you are."
"I'm okay except for the lumps."

"I can see, Malachy when you were in our condo you or one of your friends took a list and my husband Bob would like it back."

"So, he is still your husband?"

"Yes, until death do us part."

"And if I don't know what you're talking about?"

"I think that would be very unwise my friend."

"So, the police haven't caught Bob yet?"

"No he is as they say a fugitive, he will be on America's most wanted. His mother will just love that she always said he would be famous."

"Here is your list and I hope this will be the end of the matter." He took a piece of paper from a book on his bedside table and handed it to Sandra.

"Oh yes, you won't be hearing from us again. This is the only evidence that Bob and I were ever involved with Mark's money laundering. He will now take the blame for it all and he's dead."

"Poor Mark."

"Not really, so bye Malachy and I think you should look for another job the company is closing the Los Angeles office."

"I will."

Sandra left the same way she had entered the light making her look just like Rosa. He understood now why Bob had liked them both.

It was over and he could now stop worrying, famous last words he thought. It will never be over he would always have to check his safety. People like Bob and Sandra could change their minds whenever they wanted to. It was the reason he had made a copy of the piece of paper. An insurance policy.

He lay back on the bed and closed his eyes, for now it was a time to rest.

The ten most played CD while writing
Its Murder in Downtown Burbank.
Music is an inspiration to create pictures in your head.

OMD	Liberator
Westlife	Various + If I let you go
LFO	LFO
Mantovani	Incomparable Film Hits
Madness	Madness
Edith Piaf	The Very Best of Edith Piaf
PunJabi MC	Beware
Blur	Parklife
Erik Satie on piano	Various with Michel Legrand
Flying Pickets (Original Group)	The Best of the Flying Pickets

ABOUT THE AUTHOR

Edward Arno was born in a field in Frankley Beech, Birmingham, England. His father was a milkman and his mother was a house parlor maid. They met during a bombing raid at the end of the Second World War. Growing up on a council estate, he attended the local public schools. The Issigonis Mini auto plant at Longbridge was the symphonic sound of his childhood. He moved to America to pursue a screenwriting and directing career.

He resides in Burbank, California and is also an active member of the Mystery Writers of America.

Website: www.edwardarno.com
Facebook: Edward Arno Author
YouTube: Edward Arno

www.ingramcontent.com/pod-product-compliance
Lightning Source LLC
Chambersburg PA
CBHW070619260626
47161CB00007B/2503